CEIVED

SEP 21 2022

MADRONA

NO LONGER PROPERTY OF
SEATTLE PUBLIC LIBRARY

FOUR
TREASURES
of the
SKY

FOUR TREASURES

of the

SKY

Jenny Tinghui Zhang

FLATIRON
BOOKS
NEW YORK

This is a work of fiction. All of the characters, organizations, and events portrayed in this novel are either products of the author's imagination or are used fictitiously.

FOUR TREASURES OF THE SKY. Copyright © 2022 by Jenny Tinghui Zhang. All rights reserved. Printed in the United States of America. For information, address Flatiron Books, 120 Broadway, New York, NY 10271.

www.flatironbooks.com

Designed by Donna Sinisgalli Noetzel

Library of Congress Cataloging-in-Publication Data

Names: Zhang, Jenny, author.
Title: Four treasures of the sky / Jenny Tinghui Zhang.
Description: First Edition. | New York : Flatiron Books, 2022.
Identifiers: LCCN 2021041625 | ISBN 9781250811783
   (hardcover) | ISBN 9781250811790 (ebook)
Classification: LCC PS3626.H36 F68 2022 | DDC 813/.6—dc23
LC record available at https://lccn.loc.gov/2021041625

Our books may be purchased in bulk for promotional, educational, or business use. Please contact your local bookseller or the Macmillan Corporate and Premium Sales Department at 1-800-221-7945, extension 5442, or by email at MacmillanSpecialMarkets@macmillan.com.

First Edition: 2022

10 9 8 7 6 5 4 3 2 1

For my parents

PART I

Zhifu, China

1882

1

When I am kidnapped, it does not happen in an alleyway. It does not happen in the middle of the night. It does not happen when I am alone.

When I am kidnapped, I am thirteen and standing in the middle of the Zhifu fish market on Beach Road, watching a fleshy woman assemble whitefish the shape of spades into a pile. The woman squats, her knees in her armpits, rearranging the fish so the best ones rise to the top. Around us, a dozen fishmongers do the same, their own piles of fish suspended in nets, squirming. Below the nets are pails to catch the water sliding off fish bodies. The ground is glossy with water from the ones that are not yet dead. When they flail in the air, they gleam like silver firecrackers.

The whole place smells wet and raw.

Someone yells about red snapper. Fresh, they say. Straight from the Gulf of Pechili. Another voice tumbles over that one, louder, brighter. Real shark fin! Boost sexual potency, make skin better, increase energy for your little emperor!

This is poetry to the house servants who came to the fish market for their masters. Bodies surge in the direction of the shark fin voice, knocking and grinding for the promise of a promotion, of rank advancement, of favorability. It could all rest on the quality of shark fin.

While the others clamor, I remain staring at the fish woman, who continues to rearrange her pile. Her fish are not in a net like the others, but laid out on a tarp. At her shuffling, loose fish slide down from the top of the heap to the tarp's edge, where they remain vulnerable and unattended.

Hunger presses against the walls of my stomach. It would be so easy to snatch one. In the time it takes for me to approach, grab the fish farthest from her, and sprint away, the woman would barely be able to rise to her feet. I finger the silver pieces in my pants before letting them fall back into the lining. This money should be saved, not wasted on some limp fish. I would just take one or two, nothing she could not make up the next day. The ocean holds plenty.

But by the time I decide, the fish woman has noticed me. She knows immediately who I am, sees the gnawing in my belly, an insistence that hollows all the things it touches. My body betrays me; it is as thin as a reed. She recognizes what she sees in all the urchins who dare slide into the fish market, and before I can look away, she is in front of me, body heaving.

What do you want?

Her eyes are narrowed. She flaps at me, hands the size of pans.

I duck one, then two blows. Away, away! she yells. Behind her, the whitefish wait in their pile, glistening. There is still time to grab a few and run away.

But the rest of the market has noticed us by now.

I saw that scamp here yesterday, someone shouts. Grab him and we will give him a good whipping!

The fishmongers nearby roar in agreement. They emerge from behind their fish and form a barricade around me and the woman. I have stayed too long, I think, as their shoulders lock against each other. There will be a lot to explain to Master Wang if I ever get home. If I am still allowed to stay at home.

Get him, someone else yells gleefully. The woman lunges forward, hands outstretched. Her gums are the color of rot. Behind her, the fishmongers' faces fatten with anticipation. I close my eyes and brace.

But what I am expecting does not come. Instead, a pressure descends on my shoulder, warm and sure. I open my eyes. The woman is frozen, her arms outstretched. The fishmongers inhale together.

Where have you been, a voice says. It comes from above, the color of honey. I have been looking all over for you.

I raise my head. A slender man with a large forehead and a pointed chin smiles down at me. He is young, but he carries himself with the weight of someone older. I have heard tales of immortals who descend from the sky, of dragons that turn into wardens who turn into human forms. Of those who protect people like me.

The man winks at me.

You know this scoundrel? the fish woman pants. Her arms now hang at her sides, red and splotched.

Scoundrel? The man laughs. This is no scoundrel. This is my nephew.

The fishmongers around us groan and begin to disperse, returning to their unmanned fish. There would be no excitement today. Red snapper, red snapper, the first voice offers again.

But the fish woman does not believe the man. I can tell. She glares at him, then at me, daring me to look away. Something about the man's hand on my shoulder, the calm heat of it, tells me that if I do, we will never leave this place. I continue to stare back at the fish woman, unblinking.

If you have a problem, the man continues, you can speak with my father, Master Eng.

And just like that, as if the man has spoken magic into the air, the fish woman looks away first. I blink one, two, three times, the backs of my eyelids raw.

I am so sorry, Brother Eng, she says, bowing. So dark in here, and the fish are making me light-headed. I will send Master Eng my best fish to make up for this terrible mistake.

We leave the market together, me and this tall winking stranger. He keeps his hand on my shoulder until we are both back on the street. It is midday, and the light from the sun casts everything into greens and gold. A merchant walks past us with a sow in tow, her teats swinging.

We are in the foreign business center of Zhifu's Beach Road. Over the tile roofs and the British consulate, a rush of green fields swells toward faraway hills. The cotton roar of the beach is at our backs, the sea breeze one long exhale around us. The air here is rich with salt. Everything clings to me, and I to everything.

I have come because there is always something to be found here. In places where foreigners roam, I find silver pieces, embroidered handkerchiefs, dropped gloves. The frivolous things with which Westerners garnish their bodies. Today brought two pieces of silver. They jingle in my pocket next to the four pieces I earned from Master Wang. Today, I could call myself wealthy.

In the daylight, I inspect my strange winking man. He feels rich, but he is not dressed like the other rich men I have seen. Instead of a silk chang shan, he wears a white shirt with a shiny fabric dangling from his neck. His black jacket is heavy and open, instead of buttoned to the neck, and his pants are tight. Most odd of all is his hair—not braided into a queue but shorn and cropped close to his head.

What do you think, little nephew? my savior says, still smiling.

I am a girl, I blurt out. I cannot help myself.

He laughs. The sunlight reflects two yellow teeth. I think of tales where men have yellow teeth, how those teeth grew from pieces of gold. That I knew, he says, but being a boy worked out better for us both, in this case.

He scans me, eyes bright with intent. Are you hungry? Are you here alone? Where is your family?

I tell him, Yes, I am starving. I am eager for him to show me his mercy. There are things I want to ask him, too, like, Who are you? Where did you come from? Who is Master Eng, and why did the fish woman back away so suddenly when you said his name?

Let me tell you all about it, he says, placing his hand back on my shoulder. He suggests noodles—there is a good shop just down the street.

Something tells me that this invitation is not one to be taken lightly. I nod and offer him a shy smile. This is answer enough. He steers me farther away from the fish market and we stroll down the street together, passing the post office, three more foreign consulates, and a church. Passersby stare at us before returning to themselves, momentarily stunned by this odd father-and-son duo, one dressed like a character from the theater, the other wan and skittish. Behind us, the ocean froths.

With every noodle shop we pass I ask my savior, Is it this one? With every noodle shop we pass he says, No, little nephew, not quite yet. We keep walking until I do not know where we are anymore, and by the time we are done walking, I understand that we will never arrive at the noodle shop.

It is the first day of spring.

2

This is a story of a magical stone. It is a story told to me by my grand-mother. It is also the story of how I got my name.

—

In the story, the goddess Nuwa is attempting to repair the heavens. She melts rock and molds it into 36,501 building blocks of stone, but only uses 36,500, leaving one stone block behind.

This one stone block can move as it pleases. It can grow into the size of a temple or shrink to a garlic bulb. It has undergone the ministration of a goddess, after all. But having been left behind, it drifts from one day to the next, thinking itself unworthy and ashamed of its own disuse.

One day, the stone comes across a Daoist priest and a Buddhist monk. They are so impressed with its magical powers that they decide to bring it along on their travels. Thus, the stone enters the world of mortals.

Much later, a boy is born with a piece of magical jade in his mouth. They say this boy is the reincarnation of the stone.

What else? The boy falls in love with his younger cousin, Lin Daiyu, a sickly girl with a dead mother. But the boy's family rebukes their love, insisting that he marry a wealthier, healthier cousin named Xue Baochai. On the boy's wedding day, the family disguises Xue Baochai under layers of heavy veils. They lie to the boy, who believes that she is Lin Daiyu.

When Lin Daiyu learns of this plan, she falls ill in her bed, spitting up blood. She dies. The boy, having no idea, goes through with the marriage, believing himself and his new bride happy and inseparable. When he finds out the truth, he goes mad.

Almost a century later, under a mulberry tree in a small fishing village, a young woman finishes reading this story and puts a hand to her belly, thinking, *Daiyu*.

At least this is the story I have been told.

I have always hated my name. Lin Daiyu was weak. I would be nothing like her, I promised myself. I did not want to be melancholic or jealous or spiteful. And I would never let myself die of a broken heart.

They named me after a tragedy, I would complain to my grandmother.

No, dear Daiyu, they named you after a poet.

My parents were born in Zhifu, near the ocean. This is how I like to imagine that they met—the tides gently pushing them toward each other until the day they stood face-to-face. An imperative, from the water. After they married, they opened a tapestry shop and ran it together, my mother weaving the tapestries while my father sold them to the wives of government officials and other wealthy merchants. My mother saw to it that every design, be it phoenix, crane, or chrysanthemum, leapt off the fabric. The phoenix surged, the crane bent, the chrysanthemums flowered. Under her, the tapestries came to life. It was no surprise that theirs became the most popular tapestry shop in all of Zhifu.

Then, for reasons they did not tell me and I did not think to ask, my parents moved to a small fishing village just outside the city. My mother had not wanted to move, that much I knew. Zhifu was filling with foreigners, transforming from a seaside town to a crowded port, and she wanted the child sleeping in her belly to attend the Western schools that had begun opening up across the city. Pregnant, her hands swollen and no longer able to thread silk in the ke si loom, she waited for me to come into the world. Movers loaded her loom and threads into a buggy, and she turned to look upon her beloved store one last time.

It was late summer when my father, mother, and grandmother arrived in the little fishing village six days outside of Zhifu. Inside my mother's stomach, I had grown from a bean into a small fist. That autumn, I came into the world, a child of the country. When I finally slipped out, my mother told me, she imagined drinking salt water, the liquid sliding all the way down her body and pooling in my own mouth, so that I would always know how to find my way to the sea.

It must have worked. Our village sat next to a river that fed the ocean, and in those early years I walked along the riverbank often, following the black-tailed gulls until I reached the ocean's mouth. I hugged the water's edge, counting the riches that it held: life, memory, even doom. My mother spoke of the sea with romance, my father with reverence, my grandmother with caution. I felt none of those things. Standing beneath the gulls and swifts and terns, I only felt myself, one who held nothing, carried nothing, and offered nothing. I was simply beginning.

We lived in a three-bay house facing the north. We were not rich, but we were not poor, either. My father continued the tapestry business, despite living in a village where no one had enough money to afford my mother's designs. But business, it seemed, was better than ever. Our house became a frequent stop for bureaucrats passing through on their way to and from Zhifu on government affairs, sometimes to rest from their journey, other times to buy a gift for their wives and concubines back home. One look at my mother's pink peonies, silver pheasants, or golden dragons—reserved for only the highest-ranking officials—and they were entranced. I still remember the regulars: a burly man with many chins, the big brother who had one leg shorter than the other, the uncle who always wanted to show me his sword.

There were others, too, men and sometimes women who came by our house and spoke to my parents in hushed voices. These visitors were not dressed in official court clothing but simple black shan ku, looking more like brothers and sisters from the church than officials.

Often they left with tapestries, and I wondered if my parents were giving out donations for charity. There was one guest who always brought sweets and candies for me. I looked forward to his visits the most, and was delighted when I found him in our dining room one morning, hunched over porridge and pickled radish.

The journey to my home is far, little one, he told me, seeing the surprise on my face. Your parents are very generous.

There is no need to speak to her, my grandmother snapped from the kitchen.

He apologized, but when my grandmother was not looking, he passed me another candy across the table, a secret between us.

Perhaps it was because of this encounter that my grandmother began taking me into her garden when visitors were present. In Zhifu, there had been no room for all the vegetables and herbs she wanted to grow, but here, the land could be hers. In the empty lot behind our house, she tossed the soil and packed the earth tight with seeds. By the time I was tall enough to see out the window, I had already eaten a lifetime of green peppers and crushed mint, although I did not know what they were called back then.

In that garden, I learned to care for living things. I thought it perplexing that a thing could be called living, yet be so slow to show its capacity for life. I wanted immediacy, for a bud to turn into a ripe fruit in the span of a day. But there were many things my grandmother wanted to teach me about gardening that did not have to do with gardening, and patience was one of them. We grew hairy ginseng, turnips that looked like white slippers, and cucumbers with wrinkled skin. We planted green peppers in the sun and dried string green beans on wooden poles, their long fingerlike bodies reaching limply for the earth. The tomatoes were sensitive and needy, so we tended to them often, caressing their yellow-green skins that strained with a mysterious energy.

The herbs were more interesting to me for their healing uses: We had ma huang shrubs with rigid branches and seeds that looked like small red lanterns, and huang lian, which we used for dye and digestion.

We grew chai hu, a peculiar plant with a stem threading through the leaf like the tail of a kite, to ward off liver disease. The most fickle was huang qi, a plant with hairy stems and small yellow flowers. These were the hardest for my grandmother to grow, as the huang qi did not like our wet soil, and the seeds had to be rubbed with a rough stone and soaked overnight. Huang qi was always popular with the merchants and neighbors who bought from my grandmother. They ground the dried root into powder, took it with ginseng to strengthen the body. An infinite herb, they called it.

You are learning to be a real master, my mother would tell me. She was short and slender with skin the color of milk, except for her hands, which were spotted with delicate red marks. When I was much younger, she allowed me to sit on her lap to watch as she threaded the silk through, brushing it down with the shuttle the way you would a horse. When I turned ten, I was finally old enough to help her with more important tasks, like boiling the silk to make it soft.

It was my mother who taught me how to be good with my hands. My mother who showed me how to slice potatoes into ribbons and fold paper into fans. My work in the garden left calluses on my palms, but my mother would sand them down with a stone until they were ready again for delicate work. No matter how rough the hands, she would tell me, it is your good-heartedness that makes you soft.

While my mother taught me to work my hands, my father taught me to work my mind, surprising me in quiet moments with questions that frustrated and occupied me. What is the difference between a child and an adult? he asked on my eleventh birthday. Once, when I did not finish my dinner, he asked without looking at me, How many grains of rice does it take to keep a village full? Another time, when I ran through the grass barefoot and came back crying, a thorn in my left heel, he asked, When does a father feel the most pain? He followed me with curious, knowing eyes, as if he could see a small root within me that was ready to burst out and bloom.

These were my favorite memories of my time at home—being cared for and loved by all of them, every sign of that love passed on through the things they taught me. The village could disappear and our house could blow away, but if I had my mother, my father, and my grandmother, I knew that I would be able to do anything—the four of us, capable and strong and bound by love.

In the quieter moments, my mother would invite me to return to her lap, braiding ribbons into my hair. They began simply, only one or two twists and braids, but as I grew older, she added in golds, beads, tassels, flowers. I came to think of my head as a reflection of my mother's affection. The more elaborate the hair, the vaster her love.

If we were living in Zhifu, she would say, adjusting the ribbon on my crown, your many talents would bring you more suitors than you would know what to do with. She was always speaking like this, dreaming of what our lives would be like if we had stayed. I heard her talk about Zhifu often with fondness, but in my mind, it remained a blurred dream I could not access.

If we were living in Zhifu, I had thought, my feet would be broken and reshaped by now. I knew what they did to a girl's feet in the city. To be a lady of the house was to have your feet forever broken, to marry a man with money, to have his children, and then to grow old, feet coalescing into lumps of dried, cracking dough. This was not the future I wanted. In our village, the most ambitious families broke their daughters' feet by five, the best age for breaking. At five, the bones have not hardened too much and the girl would be old enough to withstand the pain. She would grow into a woman with tiny feet, a perfect wife or concubine for a rich city man. If a friend had her feet freshly broken, I would not see her for many days, and even if I stopped by, I could not stay, the rot of skin and bone overwhelming. Eventually, this rot turned into a potato that turned into a hoof, so that when we played outside, my friends could not run and jump and fly, but instead sat, their bound feet lifeless in the dirt, waiting for the day their parents sold them off.

My parents did not bind my feet, perhaps because they feared that I could not survive it, perhaps because they did not plan on us ever leaving the fishing village. I was happy with that. I had no desire to be a city man's toy. I dreamed of becoming a fisherman and living out the rest of my days on a boat, feet big and proud, my only way of balancing against the thrust of the waves.

—

Then, when I turned twelve, my parents disappeared. An empty kitchen, their dark bedroom, a bed untouched, my father's office unlocked and open, papers scattered everywhere. My mother's lonely loom. That morning was like any other morning, except that my parents were gone and did not return that night, nor the next night, nor the night after that.

I waited, sitting on our front steps, then inside my mother's weaving room, then walking in circles in the kitchen until my feet throbbed, then folding and unfolding the blanket in their bedroom. My grandmother followed me, pleading with me to eat something, drink this, lie down to sleep, take a rest, anything. You must tell me where they went, I wailed. All she could do was push a cup of tea into my hands and rub my neck.

I waited with my head down. I did not sleep for three nights.

On the morning of the fourth day, two men arrived at our door with dragons embroidered on their robes. They stomped through our little house, the dragons writhing and twirling as the men overturned pots and slashed our pillows. They tore apart my mother's loom, even though they could see that there was nothing hidden within it. I could feel the neighbors peeking out their windows, eyes wide and fearful.

We know they live here, one of the men said. Do you know the punishment for hiding criminals?

No one here but us, my grandmother protested again and again. My son and his wife died years ago. Everything lost in the fire!

Then they turned to me, teeth bared. The man who questioned us approached me. I could not stop staring at the dragon on his sleeve, red and gold with a black eye, tongue like a whip in mid-flight.

Listen to me, he said. I know your father. You must tell us where he is.

He did not sound menacing, but calm and steady. I thought then of everyone who had been through our house. They knew my father, too. They could tell us where he was. I remembered the man I found in our dining room who gave me candy. We could begin with him.

I opened my mouth to tell them what I knew. But whether it was by my own design or the will of an immortal, no sound came out. Something that felt like a hand clamped around my neck and squeezed when I tried to take a breath. I shook my head, trying to dislodge the words.

No good, the other man said to his companion. A crazy woman and a mute runt. Are you certain this is the right house?

The first man did not say anything. He stared at me, then beckoned to the other man. They both turned and walked out the front door. As their robes gleamed in the sunlight, I watched the dragons fly away.

⸺

You must never speak about your parents to anyone, my grandmother told me after they left. From now on, we must behave as if we will never see them again. It is better for everyone this way.

But I did not want to listen. I believed that my parents would return. I made their bed and smoothed out their clothes. I put the most intricate ribbon in my hair, one I knew my mother would find pretty. I even tried to put her loom back together with paste I found in my father's study. I would be here for their return, and they would be glad to see me. And so it was for that day, and every day after that.

When autumn came and my parents had been gone for three months, I thought about the woman with whom I shared my name. In the story, Lin Daiyu's mother dies when she is very young, her father following not long after. I wondered if my parents had disappeared because of my name. If they disappeared because this was always meant to be.

If you let yourself think that way, my grandmother told me, you will likely make it come true.

As if it were not true already, I said. I never hated Lin Daiyu more.

———

A letter came that spring, sender unknown: My parents had been arrested.

Any day, my grandmother said, setting fire to the letter. Any day, the people who captured your parents will come for you, too.

I could not understand, and my grandmother gave me no answers. She dressed me in boys' clothes and gave me a quilted jacket. She shaved my head. I watched my hair fall to the floor in black crescents, trying not to cry, thinking of my mother and how I would no longer have any hair for her to adorn if she ever came back. Go to Zhifu, my grandmother told me, stuffing cotton into black men's shoes and fitting them on my feet. Disappear in the city. You are good with your hands—you will find honest work.

What will Grandmother do? I asked her.

Grandmother will do the same thing she has always done, she said. Grandmother will grow good herbs to make people heal. There is not much they can do with a crazy old lady like me. It is you they have to worry about.

Neighbor Hu brought his wagon in the middle of the night. I climbed into the back with a sack of clothes, man tou, and a few coins from my parents' stores. My grandmother tried to give me more, but I closed my fingers into fists and flattened my pockets. She would need that money when those men in the dragon robes returned.

Do not write me letters, she said, putting a cap over my bald head. I missed my long hair already, missed the warmth it kept around my neck. We were still on the heel of a hard winter, and in the night breeze, I shivered. Letters will be intercepted. Instead, let us speak to each other when it rains.

What if it does not rain where I go? I asked her. We will only be able to speak once in a while.

That is how it should be, she said. My heart would break over and over again, otherwise.

I asked if I would ever see her again. I was crying. I knew older friends who had been sent away when they were young, families desperate to lessen the burden of an extra mouth. I had never imagined I would be sent away, too. But my parents were gone now, and as I lay in the back of neighbor Hu's wagon, wrapped in my quilted jacket, I knew that my life was veering toward something new and much more difficult. Gone were the days of playing in the ditch behind our village. No more would I help my grandmother pour tea to an orange sun. I would never see my friends again. I would never sleep in my bed again. Our house was a shell without its creatures. I would not be here for the first pepper to grow in the garden this year, nor would I be here for its first taste—bittersweet, cool, untrained. Somehow, the thought of the pepper was what turned my sobs into wails.

My grandmother put her hands to my eyes, as if she could brush the entire well of my tears away. Then she adjusted the tarp to cover me.

When it is safe to come back, she said, you will know.

I could not tell, in the dark, if she was crying, too, but her voice was clotted.

I clutched the sack of clothes and man tou, still warm, to my chest as neighbor Hu's wagon took me away, trying to hold the faces of my parents, my grandmother, my home tight in my memory. The pinch of skin at the corner of my father's eyes when he smiled. The warm spot between my mother's hair and the nape of her neck. The reassuring light from my parents' room when I woke from a nightmare. The images rotated in front of me, prayer beads to cling to. I will never forget, I repeated to myself.

Neighbor Hu's wagon stumbled over a rock, and the tarp covering me slid down, revealing the starless night sky. I lifted my head to gaze back at the house one more time. In the dark, my grandmother's figure looked hunched and soft. It occurred to me that I had never seen her from this far away before.

She would need help with the garden. The quilted jacket I wore belonged to her. Did she have enough warm clothes for next winter? I should have made sure that someone could come check on her every day. Tears soaked my face again. I watched my grandmother shrink until darkness took her, until I could only imagine that it was still her out there in front of our house, waiting, watching, not moving from her post until she was sure we were gone. I prayed that it would rain soon.

3

This is the story of a girl who arrived in Zhifu on the back of a wagon.

The journey took six days. I lay in the back of neighbor Hu's wagon, coming in and out of sleep, eating man tou from my sack, thinking, thinking.

I would have to become a new person. I could no longer be Daiyu, but someone else, someone impossible to trace back to me. I would become Feng, a boy—it was safer that way. No home, no parents, no past. No grandmother.

On the fifth day, rain came. One of the axles broke, flipping the wagon over and me with it. Neighbor Hu knelt by the wagon, cursing, and repaired the broken axle. Back under the tarp, muddied clothes sinking into my skin, I listened to the rain, like fingers drumming on wood, and smiled, thinking of my grandmother. Your Daiyu misses you, I whispered. I closed my eyes and imagined what she would say back.

On the sixth day, I woke to bright sun on my forehead and the smell of the ocean. Smelling it made me feel as if we had never left the fishing village, but this familiarity did not last long. Neighbor Hu removed the tarp and helped me out of his wagon. We were in some sort of alleyway. Around us, the clatter of voices in dialects I had never heard before. Good luck, he said, giving me a halfhearted pat on the back. I will tell your grandmother you made it. He gazed at me with hopelessness, as if this was the last time he expected to see me alive. I tried not to let him see that I saw, instead bowing and thanking him for his trouble. Neighbor Hu returned to his wagon and maneuvered it out of the alley.

Feng, a boy born from the wind, I said to myself.

Good. Begin.

———

Hello, I called into the dumpling house. I am Feng and I would like to work for you.

Why would I hire you? the chef laughed. So you can slit my throat while I sleep and steal all my money?

Hello, I called into the tapestry shop. I am Feng and I know a thing or two about working the loom.

Be gone, the shop owner spat. There is no room for scum like you.

It was the same when I stopped into cafés or teahouses or spice shops. I needed a good wash, new clothes, shoes that did not stink with mud. In my dishevelment, I looked no different from the urchins who roamed the streets, the ones who looked like hunger was the only thing keeping them alive. I watched as they skirted in and out of the shops, pockets slowly filling with stolen goods. They could pick the city clean, if not for the vigilant store owners who chased them out with brooms. The same store owners who turned me away without waiting to hear what I had to say.

I tried to remember all the things my parents had told me about Zhifu. I knew that it had slowly become filled with foreigners as it grew into one of the biggest ports in all of China. It sat against the ocean, where ships came bearing cotton and iron and left with soybean oil and vermicelli noodles. Along the narrow streets, shop fronts for every whim and need stood loud and bright. There was a place for buying wine, another where you could browse fine hats in all colors and textures. Squeezed next door was a medicinal herb store that smelled of ginger and dirt. I breathed into it for a moment, remembering my grandmother's garden, before the girl behind the counter took out her broom. Above these shops sat another level of what looked like apartments and offices, some with a small deck that opened over the street. I had never seen so many buildings before, and so little sky.

I saw foreigners, too, for the first time in my life. Wai guo ren, my parents had called them. They crowded into the shops, their bodies large and confident, with skin that looked like it had been rubbed raw. I did not know that hair could be anything but black, but on these foreigners' heads there was mud, sandalwood, faded leather, straw. I even saw a man with hair the color of carrots. I could not stop staring, only looking away when he caught my eye.

Through these curious streets I wandered, the sounds of the city carrying me; merchants called, music played, unfamiliar words slipped from mouths that did not look like mine. I wandered in and out of buildings with the same hopeful face, but everywhere was as before: There is no work for the likes of *you* here.

When night came, I crawled under an abandoned fruit cart, belly full of bruised apples and pears—all I could buy with the money my grandmother had given me. It was not as chilly as it had been the nights before. I hugged the quilted jacket around me and dreamed that the two men came back to our home and took my grandmother away.

The next day brought more of the same. I found myself in the business district, where the streets were lined with buildings in odd shapes and textures, their windows sometimes square, sometimes curved, sometimes like flowers encased in warped metal bars. I walked past a foreign post office made out of gray bricks, its windows like round-toe shoes. As I puzzled over these windows, a flaxen-haired man emerged. He was talking to himself, his mustache a muscular thing flexing with his lips. For a moment, I wondered if the foreigners would take pity on me. Would they offer shelter, food, work? But as the thought crossed my mind, the flaxen-haired man noticed me and began walking in my direction. I raced away before he could get any closer, alarmed by the desire in his eyes.

What to do? I wished my grandmother had given me more information before I left. I wished my parents had told me more about Zhifu, or that I could remember more of it. Most of all, I wished none of this had ever happened, that we could go back to being the family we were, when Zhifu was only a story and keeping the garden alive my only worry.

Was I angry? I was. At my parents, for leaving. At my grandmother, for sending me away and not coming with me. At those men, who entered our precious home and tore it apart. This new life of wandering aimlessly through the streets was not the one I had promised myself. I once dreamed of taking over my parents' tapestry business, perhaps even creating beautiful designs of my own. I would catch fish from the ocean, trade them for flour and sugar and seaweed from my friends' families. We would always be full, and we would become a family that could outlast seasons, empires, even death.

When evening came on the fifth day, I had walked so much that my heels felt as if they had been beaten with stones. I was light-headed, my body weightless, and in my head was a glimmering fog that prevented me from remembering which roads I had already stumbled down. Before I even find work I shall die of hunger, I told myself. I was a floating body, a strand of thread that the wind found, and no one around me cared or noticed. Perhaps I had already disappeared, I thought wildly. If the body eats itself from the inside out, what will be the last thing to go?

I dreamed of the dumplings my grandmother made, those plump, heavy pockets filled with pork and chive or shrimp and zucchini. I liked to eat her dumplings fresh from the pot, so that the steaming juice that leaked out from one bite was enough to scald. If I closed my eyes, I could smell them again—that savory heat, the smooth laminate of the dumpling skin, and the promise of what lay inside.

It was not just my imagination. I could really smell them. My eyes opened, and everything became vivid again. There, just a few steps ahead and to my left, was a dumpling house. I stumbled forward, but quickly stopped—the shopkeeper was sweeping and the lanterns had all been extinguished inside. The shop was closed.

If hunger had pushed me into a fog, then hunger was now pulling me out of it. I scurried down the alleyway next to the shop, until it spat me out onto a dirt corridor smelling of overripe oranges. I could feel my stomach pulsing in time with my heart.

There, I waited.

The store owner came, as I knew he would. He had finished his sweeping and was now walking outside through the back door carrying a tray of discarded dumplings. He cast its contents into the trash pile and returned inside, locking the door behind him. I looked around. Night was beginning to fall, and no one else was in the corridor.

I darted forward, my mouth wet. The dumplings lay on top of a dirty rag, but they were still pearly, close to bulging. Even through the smell of rank fruit and dirty water, I was ravenous. I took all the dumplings and stuffed them into my pants. That night, I slept on the steps of a church, the dumplings swelling happily in my stomach.

4

My grandmother was right—I was good with my hands. This was the gift my mother had given me. When I woke in the morning, head cleared by the new fullness in my belly, I counted on my hands all the things I could do with them.

I could fold dumplings and press petals into the tips of bao zi. Peel apple skin with a small knife, break the ends off green beans without losing too much of the flesh. These fingers would keep me alive. All I needed was for someone to take a chance on me.

From shop to shop I ran, and always the caterwauling of the shop-keepers followed me: Go away, no one wants you here, do not come back again.

I am good with my hands, I pleaded to the seventh or eighth or was it the ninth shopkeeper, a place with hand-pulled noodles. I used to weave with my mother—my fingers will be good for the noodles.

You are very skinny and small, even for an urchin boy, the shop-keeper told me, her eyes passing up and down my frame like a shadow. You know no one will take a hungry pup like you in—you need to learn discipline before anyone can trust you.

She was kinder than the others. She did not bring out a broom and threaten to flay me.

This is the most I can do for you, she said, and she pointed at the door.

She was telling me to go. I bowed at her and turned to leave.

Not so fast, she called as I stepped out onto the street. Do you see what I am telling you? There, on the door. Do you see?

I did see. I had thought it was a painting of a tree at first, the strokes long and sure, like roots overtaking the page. But as I got closer, I realized that it was not a tree, but a Chinese character, one I did not recognize. It was not written like any character I had seen before—the ink was black and bold, each line and hook and dot thick where it needed to be, thin where it needed to be, perfect in weight, perfect in balance. Somehow, even though I did not know anything about the character or the person who created it, I felt at peace. The drawing poured into me, filling me with harmony.

That was a gift to me, the shopkeeper said. I have heard the artist could use some help.

I asked where I could find this artist, hoping her goodwill would not run out.

She tugged at her apron, looking to see if any customers had entered the store. None had. I have a daughter your age, she told me. That is why I do not kick you out into the street. Look for a red building with a peanut-colored roof. That is all I will tell you. Fate will decide if you are meant to find it.

It was the first touch of hope I allowed myself to feel since arriving in Zhifu. I flew out of the hand-pulled noodle shop, nearly colliding with a man carrying a crate of chickens.

A red building with a peanut-colored roof? I asked desperately.

Get away before I beat you, he snarled.

If the person I was looking for was truly an artist, then I knew exactly where to go to find someone who could help. I dodged the man's foot and took off for the tapestry shop I had solicited on my first day.

The owner stood as if he had been expecting me. He raised a hand, ready to slap out of my arms whatever precious treasure I would steal.

I told you no beggars, he warned. The sleeves of his chang shan fluttered, making him look like a large bird.

Please, I said, panting, can you tell me where to find a red building with a peanut-colored roof? One where a calligraphy artist might live?

The owner regarded me, suspicious and confused.

What do you want to know that for? Looking to rob a good man of his art?

No, I said. I thought of my mother. Being surrounded by tapestries again brought her back to me with a sharp, painful tug. I was in her room once more, sitting on her lap and watching as her hands danced back and forth across the loom, her nails like pearls, her chest warm against my back, the sumptuous vibrations of her hums a lullaby.

Hey, what are you doing? the owner asked, bewildered, jolting me out of my memory. Why are you crying?

He was right. I had not realized it, but my face was wet and my mouth was slack. The weight of the past few days pressed down on me, sinking me into the earth's center. I did not want any of this.

I am sorry, sir, I said, wiping my tears with my palm. I knew someone who wove tapestries just like yours, only they made flowers, birds, even dragons.

At this, the owner seemed to soften. You knew someone who wove tapestries, he repeated. Here, in Zhifu? What is their name? Do I know them?

No, I said, shaking my head. And you probably never will. They disappeared not long ago. But they taught me much about how to use my hands. And that is why I am here, sir. I am looking for work, but I need to learn discipline first. I am searching for a place where I can be good with my hands. Do you know where the red building with the peanut-colored roof is? Tell me and I will leave you alone, and if I ever come back, I will be more disciplined and trustworthy, I promise, sir.

Night would come soon. I watched the owner take in my words, waiting for the strike that would banish me from his shop. The seconds swelled between us.

But the blow I expected did not come. Instead, the owner opened his mouth.

5

When I woke the next morning, a man was looking down at me, his foot in my side.

I jerked up. The man peered at me over his glasses, his hands clasped behind his back. He wore a gray chang shan with peach blossoms embroidered on the sleeves. He looked, I thought, like my father.

Why are you sleeping on the steps of my school?

He did not sound disgusted or upset, only curious.

I am sorry, sir, I told him, scrambling away. Please do not call your guards.

Wait, he said, holding out one hand. The fingers were stained with black. You did not answer my question.

I told him that I was Feng and in need of work. The lie was easy by now, slid out of me as if it were the real thing. I have come to your school to be your apprentice.

But I am not looking for an apprentice, he said. Why would you think that I was?

A woman at a hand-pulled noodle shop, I told him. She said you could use some help.

I see. I wonder why she would think that. Well, Feng who is in need of work, I am sorry to disappoint you. I am not hiring.

I glanced down at my clothes. The legs of my pants were dusty from the steps where I had slept. An idea bloomed.

Wait, I told him. If you are not looking for an apprentice, then perhaps you are looking for someone who can keep your school tidy. I came because I saw how beautiful your art was in the noodle shop. I have never seen that way of writing before. Surely a place that produces such beauty should also look the part?

I had never been so bold with an adult before. I bit my lip, waiting for the retaliation for my cleverness.

But his hands did not move. Instead, his eyes flickered down to the dirt on my pants, then to his steps. What makes you the right person for this task?

I thought of my mother and my grandmother. I am very good with my hands, I told him.

Then hold out your hands, he said.

I did so reluctantly; they were a girl's hands, knuckles soft and pillowed, any calluses from the garden already long gone. Not a day of hard work under these hands. The man bent down and turned them over, inspecting my palms, squeezing the flesh below my thumbs. He stared for what felt like a long time, so long that I began to wonder if he had fallen asleep. But when he straightened again, he was very much awake, with a satisfied look on his face.

You did not lie, he said. Would you like a job, Feng with the good hands?

The sun was rising, spraying his gray hair with ocher. I gazed into his spectacles, not asking what he saw in my hands but instead saying yes.

Then stand, he told me. I did, knowing that I was standing properly for the first time in my life. Your name means wind, he said. And I expect you to move like the wind—no laziness, no uncertainty. When you work for me, you work for real.

His name was Master Wang, and the red building with the peanut-colored roof was his calligraphy school.

We walked in together. Light seeped into the classroom from the shaded windows, leaving slits of white on the wooden floors. The class-room was divided into twelve stations, each with a brush, what I assumed was an ink pot, long sheaves of rice paper, and other materials I did not recognize. On the walls, tapestries filled with black characters fell from the ceiling to the floor. The characters were heroic and elaborate, suspended in dance. They looked as if they had been arranged into shape by forces greater than themselves.

Master Wang's private chambers lay across from this room, shuttered off by a screen. We walked past without stopping. The last room was small and filled with supplies, unused ink pots, scrolls of rice paper. This was where I would sleep.

Class begins when the sun finishes rising and ends at the first sign of dark, Master Wang told me, searching the supply room for a broom. You will sweep the steps outside and the courtyard before and after class every day. Anything else you do with your time is up to you, but be warned; your actions will reflect on my school wherever you go.

He found the broom and gave it to me. The handle was thick—I could barely wrap my fingers around it. I tried to hide this from Master Wang, afraid that this would mean I could no longer have the job. But he turned and led me through the back of the school, to a courtyard laid in stone. Each tile had a Chinese character etched in the center. In the middle of the courtyard was a fountain where two dragons wrapped themselves around four pots. A small garden circled the fountain. I thought of my grandmother with a deep longing, then bid the memory to leave. This was the time to concentrate.

No stone untouched, Master Wang was saying. As you so astutely observed, a calligraphy school must reflect the beauty it creates indoors by keeping a presentable outdoors as well.

I nodded, not thinking to ask why, then, he had let it get so dirty outside, nor why the peanut-colored roof looked like it was sagging. He spoke as if every word was final, and that was enough for me.

The sun was high in the sky by now, overturning the courtyard in light. Class is about to begin, Feng, he said. You have someplace to be, you who are good with your hands.

I bowed because it felt right, and headed for the front steps, broom in both hands. Overhead, the sun followed. The day was beautiful, the flowers beautiful, the calligraphy beautiful, the stone tiles beautiful. Even so, I would not have minded if it rained.

—

That next morning, I did as I was told. I woke before the sun and dragged the broom out of the closet, to the front of the school. I swept each step three times and watched as the dust from my broom clouded the morning, reminding me of my mother clapping flour from her hands. When I returned inside, I found a bowl of porridge and mustard greens waiting for me outside my sleeping quarters.

Master Wang's students were all men. They filed into the building in a straight line and moved with precision, as if they modeled themselves after the very characters they painted. Erect, stern-faced, obedient, they knelt down at their stations and shifted back their sleeves, awaiting their instructor.

Good morning, class, he would say when he entered.

Good morning, Master, they replied as one.

Who watched the sun rise today? he asked, voice steady.

Not I, Master, they rang out in unison.

I ask that you watch it tomorrow, and the next day, and every day after that, Master Wang said, and one day you will understand how the characters you paint can fill a whole world.

The students were silent, but I was entranced. It was not just the way he spoke, as balanced as a lily pad floating on a pond, but what he said. I did not understand what he meant by his phrase, but I knew that if there was ever a person to give me the answers to life, it would be him.

From then on, I vowed that I would find my place in Master Wang's school. It was always the same: The mornings were for sweeping, and then when the sun rose and I had wolfed down my bowl of porridge and the small saucer of vegetables that accompanied it, I would linger in the hallway to watch the students enter, envious of how secure they were, how they came from a home and would be returning to it.

During the day, I walked to the city center. Meals with Master Wang were meager in their simplicity—the food always seemed to disappear just before I could reach fullness. I craved meat, missed most the steamed fish that had been such a constant in my childhood. I longed for luminescent prawns and sauces of ginger and garlic and haw berries. The act of eating had always been a celebration with my parents and grandmother, but with Master Wang it was a mere task to accomplish before turning to more important things. Hunger is good, he told me the first time I ever asked for a second helping of rice. It allows an artist's spirit to focus. I never asked again after that.

It was this same hunger that brought me back to the city center day after day. I wanted to consume everything—the buns and sesame cakes and hand-pulled noodles, the unrecognizable words of foreigners, the fleshy, stinging smell of the ocean. So this was the city my parents loved, I thought. I could eat all the food from the stalls, gorge on every wooden beam that held up each building, and still I would want more. This was newness. This was possibility. It was greater than a hunger in my belly—it existed in my heart, too, and I knew that one day, this hunger would overtake me. But not yet. Not yet.

In the afternoon, I returned to the school and swayed in the court-yard, memorizing the characters on the stone tiles below me. Sometimes the students threw half-eaten apples into the courtyard. If the weather was nice and Master Wang opened the windows, I could listen in on class, letting myself be seized by his unwavering tenor.

From these sessions, I learned that the ink brush, ink stick, paper, and inkstone were called the Four Treasures of the Study. I learned that, in addition to painting the right strokes in the right order, the artist was also responsible for maintaining a balance of self in order to create good calligraphy.

Calligraphy, Master Wang would call out, is not only about the methods of writing but also about cultivating one's character. He believed in it as a philosophy, not only as a practice. It was something to be carried for the rest of the calligrapher's life, the ink replacing blood, the brush replacing arms. To be a calligrapher was to apply the principles of calligraphy to every action, reaction, and decision, whether on or off the page. This is the kind of person you can become, Master Wang told his students, the kind who approaches the world as a blank sheet of paper every time.

For him, there was no such thing as anxiety, danger, worry, or loss. There was always an answer if the principles of calligraphy were applied—see the character, let what you know guide you. In life, he was the same: See the desired outcome, let what you know guide you to it. And above all, you must practice.

What makes good handwriting? he would ask the students.

A steady hand, someone answered.

Patience and a keen eye, said another.

A good basic foundation, tried a third.

All true, Master Wang said. But you are forgetting the most important of them all: to be a good human. In calligraphy, you must have respect for what you are writing and who you are writing for. But above all, you must have respect for yourself. It is the monumental task of creating unity between the person you are and the person you could be. Think: What kind of person could you become, both as yourself and as an artist?

An awed silence followed. The students had heard enough to fill their dreams for years. And I? I finally had an answer and a path to follow, one that would help me overcome the burden of my name and the fate that came with it. If calligraphy was the key to separating myself from Lin Daiyu, then I would practice it as Master Wang instructed. I would become someone who did not bend to the will of fate and the stories she was named after, but instead a person all her own, with a legacy that was hers.

And perhaps by then, my parents would come back to me.

I began at once. In the courtyard, with a long birch branch in hand, I traced over the characters in the stone tiles, waving and flicking the branch as if I could conjure something from the earth. It felt silly, and I knew what it must have looked like to an outsider: a girlish-looking boy, a boyish-looking girl, play-writing and thinking he or she could be brave. The branch was foreign in my hand, the movements awkward. When class finished for the day and the students exited, I did not have enough time to hide what I had been doing. They found me scratching at the tiles with my branch and began laughing, pointing to the stick dangling from my untrained hand. I dropped the branch and ran back inside, searching for the broom, biting my lip and furious with myself.

The Daiyu of a few months ago, the one who still had a grandmother at her side and a warm bed that was all hers, would have let the dream of mastering calligraphy rest. Trying hard at something—and being scoffed at for it—had never been part of that Daiyu's understanding. But something was happening to me, had been happening from the moment my grandmother sent me away on the cart to Zhifu. I was ravenous for what calligraphy might bring me, and just as I knew I would never be a city man's wife, I also knew that calligraphy must be in my future. It would not be easy. It was just as Master Wang said—I had to practice.

My first few days in Zhifu had prepared me for this moment—

every store owner who had turned me away, every disgusted eye I defiantly faced, was a stone given to me, until eventually, I had enough stones to build a fortress around myself. Let their scoffs come, I thought that night. At least I have my fortress. And it is impenetrable.

The next afternoon, after my chores were complete, I was back in the courtyard, birch branch in hand. The day was cooler than usual and the windows were open. Master Wang's voice floated through, and I let it envelop me, guiding my hand through the air.

Look closer, it said. Your calligraphy will reveal much about you. From one glance at what you have written, I can determine your emotions and your spirit. I can gauge your discipline and identify your style. There are many more secrets your writing will uncover, and you will meet them when the time is right.

I pocketed every word. This knowledge was precious to me, my way forward into the world.

I never had a formal education, but under Master Wang's tutelage, I could feel myself becoming the person I thought I wanted to be. That person was someone strong and noble like my father, someone good-hearted and skilled like my mother, someone who could care for things with a gentle judiciousness like my grandmother. If I could become that person, I thought, then I would at least remain close to them, even if they were no longer near. And, I thought, none of those things involved Lin Daiyu or her story.

The day came when I no longer needed to trace the stone tiles in order to write. Instead, I turned my gaze upward, letting the characters appear before me, thick and muscular and straight, just like the ones inside Master Wang's school. I carved and whipped my hand through the air, until the characters could fill up the sky. They were inviting me to take hold of them, to mold them out of nothing. Or perhaps, to mold them out of myself.

⸺

In addition to sweeping the steps outside, my daily work expanded to cleaning the classroom after the students went home. I moved silently around the space, always afraid of disturbing the wet ink still hanging in the air. Through the twelve stations I wove, broom in hand, transfixed on the characters the students left behind. By then, I knew the names and purposes of all the materials: brush, paper, paperweight, desk pad, ink, ink stick, inkstone, seal, seal paste.

A good brush is flexible, Master Wang would say. With one stroke, it should produce multitudes, whether that be an ear, a claw, or a mountain. The softer the brush, the more possibilities it can create and the greater the variations in the strokes.

In Master Wang's classroom, there were brushes of all sizes. Some were as large as mops, their heads thick and blunt and sopping when dipped into inkwells, which could be as big as buckets. Other brushes measured less than a knuckle, the hairs needling together into a fine point. I liked that there was never one correct answer for which brush to use. The question is not about the brush, Master Wang told his students. The question is about what the paper demands.

Paper, the third Treasure of the Study, came in many varieties as well. Some were made of straw or grass, others bamboo or even hemp. Master Wang favored single-layer Xuan paper, on which ink bled quickly. But this was why—in order to be a master, a calligrapher had to be able to control even the most sensitive of natures.

———

One evening, I noticed that a student had written the character for eternal 永 incorrectly—instead of beginning the stroke at the top and brushing down, he had written it from the bottom up. Everything was backward, bottom-heavy. Before I could stop myself, I knelt down on the cushion in front of the station and picked up the brush the student left behind. The body was made out of bamboo, the head some kind of hair. Master Wang once told the students that when they were older, they could make a brush using the hair of their newborn child. This would be the greatest honor.

Could I be so bold? I dipped the tip of the brush in the inkstone, where a small well of ink remained from the day's lessons. On the student's paper, I crossed out the character and rewrote it, dragging my arm across, the weight of the brush surprising. Writing with a real brush, not a birch branch, was different—there was so much more to consider here, like the movement of the brush hair and the mercurial nature of the ink. Every mark, every mistake, would leave a trail. I had become so accustomed to simply moving my wrist and imagining that the outcome was perfect. Now, with a live, beating brush in hand, I could see that there was still much for me to learn. Even so, I felt different pieces of my being sliding into place, as if I had just unlocked an extraordinary secret about myself.

When I finished, I sat back and stared at the character. It was far from pleasing, but it was still a formidable thing, the fresh ink inhaling and exhaling the paper around it. Once used on paper, Master Wang told his students, Chinese ink will last for centuries without fading. When you find yourself arrested by a particularly breathtaking scroll, when the strokes look like they could bleed you dry, remember that each character carries multiple histories and that what you are looking at is entire centuries past.

Ecstatic, I began practicing the characters I had learned from the courtyard tiles, until the entire page was filled. Only when the crickets began their orchestral vibrations did I remember I had not yet finished my chores.

The next day, Master Wang's voice floated out from the window. Who wrote these? he asked the student whose paper I had written on. The student insisted that the characters were his own, but Master Wang called him a liar. You are proud and selfish, Jia Zhen, Master Wang said. And your calligraphy will always reflect that. Thus, I can no longer call you my student.

I continued sweeping outside, forgetting to breathe.

The disgraced student named Jia Zhen found me in the courtyard later. He was not the first student to be sent away—Master Wang had little tolerance for those who violated the rules of his school, and as a result, the pool of students had dwindled down to just six. Without Jia Zhen, now five. I know it was you, he said, throwing me to the ground and kicking me. No one will come to save you. No one will miss you because you have no one. He would not stop kicking. I curled into myself, not knowing if my face was wet from tears or blood.

This was the way Master Wang found me later as night set in and the classroom remained unswept. Your writing is not bad, he told me as he helped me sit up, but you should write like you are following your heart. Watch the arc of cormorants in the sky, trace the path a leaf takes when it falls, remember the lines a woman's loose hair makes in the wind. That is calligraphy.

I was no longer simply sweeping when I entered the classroom at night. I was also learning. After the day's classes ended, Master Wang remained in his lecture position at the front of the room, and I listened, spellbound by the lingering smell of ink and wet paper, my hand following his as he conducted his fingers through the air.

I learned that a calligrapher's power begins when she wields the brush, that the choices from there, like how wet the ink is or how hard she presses the brush into the paper or how quickly her arm turns, are what imbue the strokes with the spirit for their final form.

This is called the intention, Master Wang said. This is called the idea. When he lectured, he did not look at me, but instead at something above me, as if he were talking to the self I would one day become. Around us, the tapestries of characters waved in the night breeze. They were pieces he had collected throughout the years, written by the hands of his teachers and more renowned calligraphers.

Every calligrapher, every artist, starts the same way, he said. They set out to create art. But this intentionality is what makes the art become work rather than art. What you must practice is creating art without a destination or plan in mind, relying only on your discipline and training and good spirit. This is a stage few calligraphers will ever reach. This is what following your heart looks like.

He had no children. I did not know anything about his family. In this way, we were perfect for each other. At night, while he read and prepared for the next day's lesson, I would sit on my cot and practice writing the characters into my palm.

When your calligraphy becomes very good, he told me, you may have a chance of writing for important officials. Your work will get you noticed, Feng the boy with good hands.

I grew bolder with each lesson. I would no longer be just Feng, a boy with no past and no future. How many characters had I learned by now—one thousand, two? My grandmother had sent me to Zhifu to simply survive, but now my dreams were growing bigger. I wanted to be a teacher like Master Wang. I wanted the world to see what I could create. These are your fingers and eyes, Mother, I thought as I brushed ink across the page. This is your patience and fortitude, Father. And this is the opportunity to live that you have given me, Grandmother.

Your final aim, Master Wang's lecture concluded, is to reach a state of freedom where you and the artist you could be are one. This is what we call unified, when you will finally be *with yourself*.

Yes, Master Wang, I would say, before dipping the brush into the ink and starting anew. I never questioned him, only drank in his words and let them carry me through the days. He did not pay me for my work, beyond the lessons, and I never asked. But sometimes, if I wrote a character very well, he would slip me a piece of silver. I saved as much as I could, envisioning a future when I could be the master of my own calligraphy school, buying only the best supplies for my students. The reward for following my heart, it seemed, was character by character.

But I should have known that this would not last.

7

What I know now: I have been poisoned.

⬩

When I wake, I do so quietly. Sleep swills at my ears, my mind still struggling to reach the waking world. I do not recall ever falling asleep, nor do I recall dreaming.

My body is heavy, a weight I have never felt before. When I lived in the fishing village, I was only ever light and buoyant, bouncing from the ocean to the fields, to the steps outside our home. Along the streets of Zhifu, I was quick to learn, quick to survive. Now the glue coating my throat is the same one that seals me to the spot where I lie. I drag my eyes from corner to corner beneath my lids, urging them to focus. There is a pulsing in my skull, one that replicates in my palms and the soles of my feet.

I try to sit up.

The first thing I notice: I am lying on a mat on the floor. I am in some sort of room.

The second thing: It is dark in this room. I can make out the shadows of solid things and the pallet beneath me, but not much else. In the dark, this room seems like it could go on for years and years. I pat down my body for the other things I cannot see: shirt, pants, socks, shoes. Nothing hurts, except my head. Nothing feels out of place, except that everything is out of place.

What do I remember? Completing my chores and taking my daily walk from Master Wang's to Beach Road. The fish market, the fish woman. Her swinging arms. The circle of fishmongers, greedy for a fight. The surprising weight on my shoulder. A man in strange clothes looking down at me. Short hair. Sunlight. Two yellow teeth. The promise of food. Walking. Walking. Walking.

I press my fingers to my temples. There is no swelling, no tenderness. What else do I remember? The buildings we passed: a church, a few restaurants, an apothecary, a meat market. The coarse smell of the ocean. There was some conversation, too, but I cannot remember what was said. In front of every memory, smoke and shadow. The only thing I am certain of is the man's face, his large forehead and pointed chin. The godlike pull of him.

Before I can remember any more, the poison returns in a swell of foamy pink. I fall back to the floor, my eyes blurring.

———

Something hovers over me when I wake the second time. I gasp, my chest cinched. It is the winking man and he is here to kill me.

Without a word, he reaches down to grab me by my shirt and drag me upright. For a terrible moment, I imagine him throwing me into a bottomless pit that must exist in this room, but then my back touches something cold and hard. Propped up against the wall, I am nothing more than a limp creature.

Breathe, the winking man says.

I try. Two in, one out. I close my eyes and think of my grandmother counting the beats, her hands on my knees. Two in, one out, Daiyu. Repeat.

Where am I? I demand. My voice is hoarse.

He does not answer. I hear rustling, then a flick. The room finally comes into light. It is not the dungeon I had imagined, but a room very much like the one I had back home. I see a table, a chair, my legs out underneath me, the door. Above me, there is a square window near the ceiling that has been painted over with newspapers and glue. The room is not small, but it seems to be steadily shrinking in on me and the winking man, adjusting its size just for us. We are the only things that matter.

The winking man kneels down, lantern in hand. He is not an immortal turned dragon turned warden turned human who has come to save me. In the lantern light, his face could be fire.

I want to go home, I tell him.

What is your name? he asks, ignoring me. His voice, which I had remembered as supple and kind, now rings with danger.

What is your name? he asks again.

I am silent.

He slaps me with the back of his hand. When the knuckles meet my cheek, they make a noise that sounds like a spark.

Feng, I whisper. I will myself not to cry.

Good. He smiles. How old are you, Feng?

I am afraid of what he will do with me if I tell him.

We will call you fourteen, he says to my silence. The light in the lantern flickers. Feng the orphan, you are fourteen. And you will always be fourteen.

Now he stands, looking down at me.

Let me go home, I say. If I beg enough, I think, he could turn back into the kind man who saved me in the fish market.

But he does not. Instead, he puts a finger to his lips and begins to walk away. With each step, the light from the lantern shrinks, the room slowly disappearing around me. When he is at the door, all I can see is a faint orb of yellow.

Please, I call out, not knowing what comes after, but knowing that it will be worse. I tell him again, I want to go home.

The yellow orb shudders. Feng the orphan, he says, there is a long way to go before we get home.

8

The character for black 黑 is made up of mouth, fire, and earth. Mouth sits on top of earth. Earth's tip bisects mouth. Underneath both, fire.

But a mouth is pink. The earth is brown. Fire is light. When I first learned the character, I could not understand why these three things created black.

If you do not know, Master Wang told me, you will never be able to write the word the way it was meant to be written.

When the winking man left, he took the light with him, too. And I think I finally know why those three things came together to create black. Sitting in this black now, I see myself inside a gaping mouth, one breath from falling into the hellfire of the earth. I trace black with my finger, and even though I cannot see it, I know that this time, I have finally written it the way it was meant to be written.

Black, or the way time disappears and something else suspends in its place. The way of being alone.

—

I try to remember: How much time has passed since I was kidnapped? It was midday, now it must be night. I am not even sure it is the same day, the same night.

In the dark, I hug my knees to my chest and clutch my elbows. If

I let the fear take me, I will never find my way back. Search for something real, I tell myself. Hold on and do not let go.

A red building with a peanut-colored roof. The water fountain in the courtyard, the dill weed growing in the garden. The eager voices of the students as they call out answers. Master Wang, lecturing about leaving emptiness in the palm. Master Wang, my real savior.

I squeeze my eyes shut and plead for him to come into this room with me. I plead for him to take me out of it.

What would he think when I did not show up the next morning? Would he be worried, or would he have known it was coming all along—that this mysterious boy who appeared off the street must have moved on in life, maybe to be a scoundrel somewhere else, maybe to be dead. Would it matter? Life at the school would move on. In calligraphy, as in life, we do not retouch strokes, Master Wang often said. We must accept that what is done is done.

The older girls in my fishing village always told the same story: Years before my parents arrived, a young girl named Bai He lived there. She was the daughter of a welder and her skin looked like glass.

If you saw Bai He in the daylight, it looked like her skin was drinking up the sun. At night, she outshone the moon. When she smiled, the light came to needlepoints at the top of her cheekbones. The daughter of a welder should not have had such good skin, but Bai He was the exception. She had been blessed with something pure. There is starlight on that girl's face, the neighbors said.

When Bai He turned twelve, high-ranking men from the city began to frequent her parents' house. News had spread far about this special girl with glass skin, and they hoped to see with their own eyes. The girls in the village would crowd outside the windows, shoes digging into the dirt, yearning to catch a glimpse of the visitors. They knew the farmer boys with dirt-smeared mouths, knew their own fathers and their hard palms. But they had never seen men as powerful as these.

One by one, the city men entered Bai He's home, moving with a square assurance. Every step was certain, every movement a declaration: I am not afraid of anything. This was the confidence of having comfort and money and a good life.

During these visits, Bai He would enter the front room with a veil over her face. The city men's bodies would stiffen in anticipation, knuckles white over their knees. Our daughter's skin is one of a kind, her parents said, addressing the room. You have never seen anything like it. Skin like this is surely a gift from the immortals above.

They slid sentence after sentence between the city men and Bai He, until it felt like the veil would never come off. Outside, the neighborhood girls whined with impatience, their hands clutching the windowsill. Who would Bai He choose? What did true love look like?

Then the talking finally stopped. Bai He would lift her veil, revealing the glass face underneath. Outside, the girls stared with envy. Inside, the room stilled as the men drank her in. Pearls from the ocean could be called beautiful, but none as beautiful as her face.

All the girls in the village knew she was going places that none of them would ever experience. Next to her, their skin was dull and mottled. They would have to beg of the world. But Bai He would always have it at her fingers. After seeing what they saw that day, some girls promised to eat only white rice. Others decided they would pluck a hair from Bai He's head. They all believed that there had to be a way to steal the magic that lived in her body.

The next morning, the village woke to the sound of wails. Bai He's parents ran from door to door, frenzied and hysterical. Our Bai He has been stolen, they cried. Someone took her in the night.

The rest of the village did not answer. A girl with glass skin disappears, what can you do? Let that many men into your house, you will be bound for trouble, they said.

Perhaps that was the price to pay for her glass skin, others said. They closed their doors and put blankets against the windows to block the sound of her parents' grief. Do not be like Bai He, they warned their children. Do not try to be beautiful. You see what that will get you?

The story of Bai He was meant to scare the girls in our village. I knew that. But even so, I was glad for how little like her I was. I had a head shaped like an egg and eyes that made me look like I was always tired or crying. My face settled often into solemnity. There is a seriousness to you, my grandmother used to say, that underlines your every move.

It was better to look like a sullen boy than a girl with glass skin. Bai He was taken because she stood out too much. That would never be me.

Until it was.

Again, that old anguish surges at the memory of the fishing village, the three-bay house, and then, finally, of my parents. The eerie stillness of their empty bedroom. The hushed loom. The moment a loss so great tunneled through me and nothing, not even 36,501 stones, could repair the chasm it left behind. Why did you go? Why did you not take me with you? Was it so easy to leave me? The characters hurl past as if on fire: deception, betrayal, rejection. And, finally, shame. For this anger, for this blame. For needing to forgive at all. Whatever caused them to leave was not their fault. I have to believe that. I have to hold on to that, or else I will never resurface from this despair.

I press my back against the cold wall as the echoes of the poison return. Black, or the way longing can burn a hole through your lungs.

⁓

When I wake again, I know that something is in the dark with me. I am sure of it. Something shuffles around the room, sliding up and down the walls, oozing its way across the dirt floor. I need to sit up and look, but my body is a plank, rigid and heavy.

Blink, I tell myself.

Now lift your hand.

My hand does not move.

Whatever it is comes closer. I feel its breath running up my body, and a prickling starts at my toes and travels up to my navel. It is above me now, peering down, gloating at my inability to fight. I stare back up at it, my eyes swimming through the darkness that gives this thing its power.

Move, I want to scream. But the scream is trapped within me, just like the rest of my body.

I tell myself that I am making things up. The dark has turned me crazy. The poison is playing its part. But I also know that whatever it is, it has been following me for a very long time.

Lin Daiyu? I ask into the dark.

Even though she does not answer, I know I am right.

9

Light enters the room early through the papered window. For one warm moment, I am certain I am in my old room and my parents and grandmother are already awake, waiting for me to join them at breakfast. Happiness, real happiness. My arms lift and extend, so close to grabbing this elation. It was all a nightmare. I am safe. I am home.

I open my eyes. The room slides back into focus. The table and chair are still there, my pallet still here, the dirt floor as cold and unforgiving as before. My elation evaporates. I, along with everything else, am still here.

The door opens, and a hand slides in a tray. Wait, I cry. The door slams shut before I can get my next words out. I crawl to the tray and gaze into a bowl of porridge. It goes down in one quick gulp. I crawl back to my pallet, my stomach somehow emptier.

The door opens, and the same hand removes the tray. I open my mouth to shout again, but before I can, a woman enters the room.

She carries a cane and a sack. Her hair is the color of white hay. The yell dies in my throat. Wherever I am cannot be that bad if there is a granny here, too, I reason.

I am expecting kindness and warmth from her, none of which she will give me. Instead, her milky eyes pass over me, and I know I am no more significant than a dog. She is here, she tells me coldly, to teach me

English. Then she points to the chair with her cane, and I understand that I am to sit on it.

From her sack, she withdraws a book and sets it on the table. Printed inside are characters unfamiliar to me—some are angular, others rounded and fat. The woman sounds out the characters, which I later learn are called letters, each one needle-thin.

Now you, she says, her cane hovering over my head.

Ay, I try. *Bee. Si. Dee. Eee.* My voice wavers.

The woman tells me to do it again. I make the noises, watching her cane dip with each letter. *Ayf. Jee. A-ch. Ay.* We are a tempo, the cane and I.

When she leaves many hours later, as night turns the room purple and gray, I draw myself into a ball, the sounds clinking against each other in my head.

Waiting there, in what I cannot see, is Lin Daiyu, watching me.

———

What do you know of the English language? the old woman asks.

It is spoken half a world away, I tell her. I imagine ships, smoke, sharp white faces with hair the colors of autumn leaves.

The English alphabet, she says, is limited. Twenty-six letters, each calcified in their ways, each with their particular set of rules. Think of them as adults. Think of them as grown. Put them together in a specific sequence to create a specific word.

It should be simple, I think.

But the first hurdle: sound. The letters do not sound like the words they form, and there are many combinations to consider. Each combination gives birth to a different sound, a different meaning. The English alphabet is limited, but the possibilities are infinite and irrational.

V: Put the two front teeth on the bottom lip and blow.

Th: Stick the tongue in between the teeth and hum around it.

Tr: Clamp down the teeth and breathe.

Dr: Do the same, but groan.

St: Hiss and stop, hard.

Pl: Like you are imitating a horse's snort.

In Chinese, every syllable is vital, to be given the same amount of stress and weight as the ones around it. But in English, there are hierarchies to every word and all the sounds within that word. The most important sounds are spoken with vigor, while the unimportant ones are tucked in between, reduced and hidden. It is its own kind of music—every sentence has a certain rhythm to it, every word its own metronome. English, it seems, is a matter of timing and chaos.

I imagine each word as a seesaw, unsure of which way it will fall. One side will always be heavier than the other. The question is how to decide.

We stop once during the day for lunch, the same meal of steamed man tou and dried anchovies, both dishes so hard they tear the roof of my mouth. The woman does not exist to me outside of the lessons — she becomes English and English becomes her.

It is like this every day.

Do you know if I can go home? I ask her. Do you know what he wants with me? Why do I have to learn English?

The he, of course, is the winking man, who I have not seen since the day I was taken. I begin to wonder if he was even real, or if I had dreamed it, somehow leading myself to this place. Perhaps, I tell myself in moments of desperation, this was the way it was always meant to be.

Every day, the old woman pretends she cannot hear my questions. Instead, she makes noises, then tells me what they mean. I memorize words, conjure their images in the dark. CAT: orange and solitary. WAGON: neighbor Hu. WIND: Feng, a boy born from the wind.

At my most alone, I trace English letters in the dirt floor. Next to them, I write the Chinese characters that match their sounds. The one that puzzles me most is the English letter *I*. Companion sound in Chinese: love. I, in English, to represent the self. Love 愛, in Chinese, a heart to be given away. I, in English, an independence, an identity.

Love, in Chinese, a giving up of self for another. How funny, I think, that these two sound-twins should represent such different things. It is another truth I am learning about English and the people who created it.

To mark each day that passes, deciphered from the old woman's coming and going, I scratch lines into the wall. I run my fingers over them, press my face against the wood until I know the marks have embedded themselves into my cheek flesh. Once, as I did this, I thought I heard the sound of something scratching back at me against the wall, as if there was someone on the other side making marks just like me.

———

There are fifty marks when we begin reading and composing sentences.

In English, plurality and time matter. You cannot talk about an action without also talking about when it happened. Past, present, or future can define an entire experience. This is the hardest part.

It is not enough to say that someone gives you something, the old woman tells me. You have to express when. Everything is rooted in time. Say *give*. Say *gives*. Say *given*. Say *gave*.

Give. Gives. Given. Gave. I want to ask her why. Why is it so important in English and not in Chinese? What difference does the question of time make?

The Chinese character for time 時 is made with the character for sun, to represent the four seasons. Master Wang told me that in ancient China, time was kept according to the position of the sun in the sky. Inherent in this character is the understanding that time is circular—that no matter how much the sun moves, it will always come back around again.

In English, time is spelled with four letters. A finite thing made of finite letters. Maybe this is the difference, I think. For those who speak English, there is a limit to time. That is why it is so important to differentiate among past, present, and future.

When I know this, I also know that I will be able to write time perfectly for the rest of my life—in both languages.

This is how I begin to understand English.

⸻

You are ready, the old woman tells me one day.

I ask her, For what? She does not answer.

When she leaves that night, I feel for my marks against the wall. Time is important here. As in, how much time has passed?

Three hundred and eighty marks beneath my fingers. Three hundred and eighty days since I first started counting, since I went to the fish market looking for the taste of the ocean and the bowl of noodles that never came. The trees must be full again, the grass back to green. Outside, the sea must be swelling. Master Wang's school will have all the windows open to air out the smell of stale ink. How many half-eaten apples litter the courtyard from the new wave of students? The dragon fountain, merry and bubbling.

I let out a sob, then cover it, the sound loathsome and hopeless. An entire year has passed. Time is important, this I know now. As in, how much time has to pass for a forgetting to occur?

10

The next night, the winking man comes to my room.

How are you, little nephew? he asks. He lights a lantern and orange floods his face. We both know that three hundred and eighty-one days stand between us.

I taught myself to believe that the winking man had always been a repulsive figure with many heads and a tongue made out of flames. But he is the same tall, graceful stranger who found me at the fish market. The only thing that has changed is a small scar under his right eye. If I saw him on the street, I think, would I follow him all over again? It is this that frightens me most. Even now, I will never know what he is capable of becoming.

He comes closer, kneeling down before me and holding the lantern to my face. The light is so strong that it forces me to turn away. He rakes the lantern up and down, reading the length of my body.

You are small for your age, he says, not entirely to me. Good for tight spaces.

He sits back on his heels. Do you know why we have been teaching you English, Feng the orphan?

I think I do know; I think I have begun to guess it. But I do not speak. I do not want to open myself to him again.

From now on, the winking man says, switching to English, you will only speak in English.

The air between us tightens. I nod.

How long have you been in America? he asks.

I have never been to America, I say in my new language. The words snake around us, bringing us closer.

You have, he says softly. You have been in America for five years. Tell me again.

I have been in America for five years.

He hands me a paper and an object that is not a calligraphy brush, but a thin cylinder with a sharp point at the end. I hold it the way I would a brush, my hand large and awkward around its shortness.

Write this down, he says. My name is Feng. I am fourteen years old. I have been living in America for five years. My parents owned a noodle shop in New York City. They are dead. I came to San Francisco to work in a noodle shop.

I do as I am told. I do not know how to write *San Francisco*. The winking man takes the paper and pen, and writes it for me. On the page, the letters look like a long, scaled dragon.

Memorize this, he says. Practice this. Burn it into your brain. That is what you will say if our plans go awry.

Can I go home? I ask.

He stands up, knees cracking one after the other. Oh yes, he says. You will be home very soon.

I know you have others like me in here, I say. It is not a question, but a demand. The scratching sounds against my wall were real, the yelps I heard when my door opened and closed, all real. The world that exists outside my room is one in which I am not so alone.

He turns to me, his face unreadable. For a moment, I wonder if I have finally stumped him. But then his mouth curls and he waggles a finger at me, its long shadow dancing eerily across the walls.

Perhaps there *are* others, he says. Or perhaps you are entirely alone.

He leaves. I blink into the dark, trying to climb my way toward what any of this means.

———

In the night, I dream. Or is it a memory? Lin Daiyu comes to me, and I finally see her in the light. She is small, slight, birdlike. I reach for her. For the first time, I am happy to see her. Tell me what to do, sister, I beg. This time, I will follow you.

She turns and walks away from me, her hair twisting in the wind. I run after her, calling. But what I am yelling is in English, and I know she cannot understand me. I try to switch back to Chinese, but the words morph in my mouth before I can stop them. I want to ask her how to escape this prison, how to leave the winking man behind. I want her to lead me to the same freedom she has found, the one that exists only in death.

For every step I take, she takes two, as if she is sped up and I am slowed down. Lin Daiyu, I call out to her, my legs churning. You would turn away from your sister?

At this, she stops. She turns to face me. The Lin Daiyu I see looks like me but does not look like me. Not my brown eyes but blue ones. Her nose is farther down her face. Her lips, as smooth and pink as a fish. My Lin Daiyu opens her mouth, but nothing comes out. Instead, blood seeps out of her nostrils, out of the corners of her eyes, out of her ears.

Someone is screaming. I realize that someone is me.

When I wake, my shirt is stuck to my chest like a wet film. My breaths are hard, chopping up the dark.

Are you there? I whisper. Why will you not help me?

The room is empty. Lin Daiyu cannot help me now, just as she has never helped me before. She has never been real, I tell myself, but I am. For once, I wish our places were switched.

11

The next evening, the door opens again, but this time, it does not close.

Three men enter. They are hunched and burly, their bodies shaped like small boulders. The winking man follows them in, holding his lantern.

He tells me to stand. I do, my hips grinding in their sockets. I spend most of the day sitting now, and standing hurts my legs. He hands me a parcel of something bunched and soft.

Put these on, he says.

The light in his lantern reminds me of a full moon, the kind that looks so big and heavy that it might fall out of the sky. For a wild moment, I wonder what would happen if I knocked this lantern to the ground and broke the light inside—if I could set this entire place on fire and take myself with it.

Now, the winking man says. The three men behind him rub their fists.

I do as I am told, lifting the sodden shirt off my torso. The pants come next. I slip out of them easily, watching as they flutter to the ground.

Naked before them, I look down at my body. It has been a long time since I have seen myself in the light. Two small ponds of flesh on my chest, each end dipped in rust. The netting of my rib cage pokes through the skin on my torso. My belly, small and soft, droops, framed by sharp hip bones. I can barely see the tops of my thighs. My feet are the only part of me that look big, like they should belong to someone much larger than me. But they are the same size. It is the rest of me that has shrunk around them.

On instinct, my hands move to cover the parts of me that are most private. A new fear strikes, something I have wondered about since the day of the kidnapping.

The winking man's eyes rove. There is time to fatten you up later, he says. He points at the parcel of clothes. Now those, he says.

The clothes inside are all black and too large for me. Wearing them, I feel even less of my body than before. Now the winking man instructs me to kneel down before them. I do, my knees sharpening against the dirt.

One of the three men steps forward with a pair of scissors. I shrink. Do not move, he warns. He stands behind me and picks up a piece of my hair, limp with oil, now long enough to reach my chin. He slides the scissors through. I hear a slice. When I look down, there is a blade of black on the floor. My mother's face flashes before me. I urge her to look away.

Snip snip snip goes the man with the scissors. More black falls to the floor. Each time it does, my mother's face fades a little more, until I can no longer see her.

When he is done, the man with the scissors returns to stand by the winking man.

What is your name? the winking man asks me.

Feng, I say automatically.

Where are you from?

New York City.

Where are your parents?

Dead.

Why are you here?

To work in a noodle shop.

Good, good, the winking man says, a smile on his lips. Now, Feng, you are truly ready.

He nods to his three men, who exit the room. He scratches his neck. Then he addresses me.

Have you ever been with a man, nephew?

This, I think, is what I have been waiting for. From the moment the winking man took me, this was always the destination. I have seen the way dogs wrestle in the night, heard cats yowl like they are being skinned alive. The smoky-eyed apple farmer's boy who once followed me behind a water wheel and put his hand on my belly. The blood that stirred from his touch.

Now I imagine the winking man rocking above me, his oily eyes boring into mine, the whiskers on top of his lip rubbing my skin raw. The unwelcome weight of him. No, I tell him, praying that is all.

As if he has seen my mind, he smirks. I am not talking about me, nephew. I am talking about white men. Do you know about white men, what they like?

The winking man disappears from above me, replaced by the flaxen-haired man I saw outside the foreign post office in Zhifu. He heaves and grunts. His belly envelops my abdomen, and I am engulfed by him, my body no longer mine but a part of his. I shake my head, No, no, no.

This is something you will learn, the winking man says. He fingers the lapel on his suit. They will teach you. The white men will love to spend money on you. They love the small ones like yourself. Will you be my best? I think so. Now come here and let me look at you.

I rise and walk to him slowly. I cannot stop thinking about what he has just said. They, he said. Small, he said. Money, he said. It all falls before me like ash.

Up close, he resembles a fox. The scar under his eye could be a blade of grass. Without warning, he pinches my face with one hand. His touch suspends everything in my body. I feel my heart protest, the blood straining.

You will behave?

I nod, trying not to bite my cheeks where they are pressed into my teeth. He lets go of me and takes something from his pocket. Close your eyes, he commands.

I feel him rubbing something over my face and neck. It smells like tar. He turns me around and continues rubbing it on my shoulders.

Hands, he says.

I turn and offer my hands up to him. He rubs this substance, which I can now see is black, over my palms, runs it across my nails, paints it in the webbing between my fingers. The act reminds me of winter, when my grandmother would rub my hands after I had been outside too long. She would spin my hand in hers, like she was trying to start a fire, until each hand returned to me red and burning.

But this is not my home, and this man is not my grandmother. Nor is he Master Wang, who told me that one day, my palms would make me famous.

My hands fall back to my sides.

The three men return, carrying a big bucket that reaches their hips. It is ready for us, Jasper, one of them says to the winking man. I stare at the bucket, a cave deepening in my chest.

I think you know what to do, the winking man named Jasper says.

I do know. I know that there is nothing else I can do. Between staying in this prison forever, or the bucket, which must lead to anything else, I will choose the bucket.

I walk to it. It is much larger up close and I barely come up to the lip. One of the men kneels before me, binding my wrists and ankles with rope. When he is finished, he stands and hooks his palms under my armpits, lifting me up. In his hands, I dangle like a cloth doll. He deposits me in the bucket. I am able to fit if I sit with my knees to my chest. Inside, it smells burnt, smoky.

Jasper's head appears from above, gazing down at me. Do not move, do not make a sound, he says.

Another noise of dragging and clinking. Head down, he says. A million pieces of something begin to fill the bucket. I dare to look—

small clumps of coal, sharp and shaped like sugar candy. They wedge in the empty spaces between my limbs, first pooling around my feet, then slowly eating up my legs, my waist, then my arms and my chest, until I can feel them pressed against my throat. When the pouring stops, I cannot move. If someone were to look down into the bucket, they would not see me, but a blur of black against the coal.

It is too hard to breathe, I tell Jasper. The coal clinks as I speak.

He says nothing but reaches down and loops a rope with a small burlap pouch around my neck. The pouch is heavy, but it smells fresh and cool, like mint grass. My chest opens, as if someone has reached into my mouth and breathed air in.

Inside is a special stone, Jasper says. Something to help you breathe. And to help you think of me.

I inhale the mint grass scent of the burlap pouch, hating him.

If you hear a tap, he tells me, that means the lid will be opened. Keep your head down. If, when you arrive, you are somehow caught by the authorities, you will recite what I have told you. If you try to escape, you will die. If you make a sound, you will die.

As if this is not already death.

The last thing is a wad of cloth, which Jasper shoves in my mouth and ties into place with rope. He pulls back to inspect his work, fingers still on my cheek. Before I understand what is happening, he slams my head against the side of the bucket. I cry out, but it is drowned by the new cloth in my mouth. Jasper straightens, looking satisfied.

They are ready for you, one of the men says from above. I hear a loud thud and see the round of a lid against the bucket lip. The men grunt. The lid grows larger and larger above me, eclipsing the light.

Jasper's head appears again, in what sliver of space is left. He regards me, my body buried and small, my face blackened, the whites of my eyes the only thing to distinguish me from the coal.

This is the story, rewritten: One day, a tall man spots a girl pretending to be a boy in the middle of a fish market. He can read her hunger from the way her body caves into itself. He has a hunger, too, one that he is skilled at hiding. Except in the eyes. This time, the girl pretending to be a boy sees it. When she turns to face him in the sunlight, she sees the truth and she runs. The man leaves empty-handed. The girl goes home.

From the bottom of the bucket, I gaze up at those eyes now. Art is evidence of the mind that created it, Master Wang once told me. Whoever created Jasper's eyes knew to leave a hint behind, something you had to squint to see. But it was there. It had always been there. That day in the fish market, I just did not know that I had to look. His name is Jasper, and he kidnapped me. I want to say his name, I want to sound it out so he knows what I know: that in the middle of his English name is the Chinese sound for death and dying.

But the coal squeezes me, holds my voice in place.

See you in America, nephew, Jasper says, winking one last time.

The lid slides shut.

PART II

San Francisco, California

1883

1

The man outside the window has done this before. His hat sits low on his face, shading his nose, but the tight line of his mouth is still visible, and it is wet. It says he is no stranger to what he is about to do. It says he knows exactly what he wants and how to obtain it.

The man raises a crooked finger. We straighten to attention. The finger stirs the air, then lists and trails, as if searching for a forgotten memory. When it passes over us, we shudder, somehow able to feel the heat of his touch through the glass.

Then it stops.

A pause, then the confirmation. Inside the window, we inhale as one. We each believe he is pointing at us.

What he wants is not us, though. What he wants is Swallow, the girl to the left of me. When we realize this, we soften in relief. But not Swallow. She smiles at the man and bows her head, but I feel her body sharpen, an awareness that begins in her shoulders and pulls down through the rest of her.

Out, a guard commands from behind.

We file out of the viewing room one by one, our silk dresses whispering with each step. In the main room we stand, and now the man from outside has entered as well. He stares at Swallow as if he knows everything about her, everything about us.

I should keep my head down, but I cannot stop myself from watching. Swallow gives the man a coy, closemouthed smile, her body already shifting into something to be given over, something that is not hers. A shadow shaped like a bell descends from somewhere, as it always does. It is Madam Lee, and she is here to lead Swallow over to the man, whose eyes now rove all over her body. Hungry dog, I think.

A good choice, Madam Lee is saying. Her voice is low, velvety. Would you like a closer look?

The man grunts, then nods.

Turn around for our customer, she tells Swallow. Before us all, Swallow spins, her hips careening first, then her shoulders, then the slender line of her neck, exposed and ripe. Her pinned hair gleams against her head like a river at night. She has done her makeup with soft plums and gold, her lips as red as wine. Dressed in periwinkle silk pants and a silk shirt embroidered with flowers, she could be a princess ready for court.

So, Madam Lee says to the man, her tone hard now, pressing. You will take her?

The man licks his lips, his tongue sharp and pale. He reaches into his jacket and pulls out a wad of money, which Madam Lee receives with both hands. Then the man takes Swallow's hand. Amid all their hands, hers look particularly small.

We keep our heads down as they walk upstairs, to the bedrooms.

Madam Lee turns to the rest of us then, nostrils rapidly expanding. The rest of you, she says, and her voice is slow again, melodic but deadly, should return to your places.

And so we reenter the little viewing room with the window that faces the street.

One by one, girls around me are chosen. One by one, they spin in front of the men, and the men nod, hand over the money to Madam Lee, and lead their girls upstairs. The guards stand by and watch as they do every night. I do not know their names.

Slowly, girl by girl and man by man, the ceiling grows heavy with their thumps and moans.

By the end of the night, it is just me and two other girls. One of them is Jade, an older girl with creases around her mouth from how often she bites her lips. She has been here awhile, maybe the longest. Today is the fourteenth day she has not had a customer, although once she was the top girl at the brothel. The others think it has something to do with the growing bloat of her belly, how she has stopped bleeding every month.

I need some work now, she whines. Where have all the men gone? They do not know what they are missing.

The other girl, named Pearl, simply cries into her forearms. Her only customer did not come tonight like he promised.

Above us, the girls' noises form a symphony. Some are low and guttural. Others yelp like dogs. A few could be singing. Underneath them, the rumble of the men, sometimes their rage and their shouts, and then the knocking, the violent knocking that seems to go on and on.

I hated the noise when I first arrived. Now I have to remember to hear it at all.

Ta ma de, Jade spits, I will be kicked out if I do not get a customer soon. She turns to Pearl, whose weeping only grows louder. What are you crying for, girl? At least you have someone who comes with a fat wallet.

One by one, the men reappear down the stairs, readjusting their clothes, brushing down their hair, putting on their hats. I cannot stand to look at them, the gluttony on their faces, the way they carry themselves as if they have been in battle and won. Returning to the daylight, where they can hide in the sun.

It is good to come often, Madam Lee says to each one of them, her lips contorted into a simper. I sit in the corner of the room with my sullen face, and when one of the men glances at me for too long, I turn my head away.

Later, as the sun crests over the bay, Madam Lee asks me to join her in her office, where she sits behind a large desk carved out of dark wood. The office is small, made smaller by the two men guarding the door, and by Madam Lee's presence. She is bigger than the women I saw in Zhifu, but there is no roundness to her, only menace.

What do you think of last night's business? she asks, rolling a cigarette between two jeweled fingers.

Good, Madam Lee, I say. A girl was once whipped for not calling her Madam. The next day, we could see blood and pus through her shirt.

Sit, she tells me. Sit and talk to me.

There is danger here, danger if I sit and danger if I walk away. I sit.

Madame Lee takes a long suck from the cigarette. It makes a thin, wispy sound, the end flaring orange before withering to black. I imagine the air around her toxic, her presence deadly enough to decay plants and poison flowers.

When you came to me, she says, you were so thin. I could pick you up with two fingers. Now look at you. A healthy girl with a good flush and a pink tongue.

I eat and sleep well thanks to Madam Lee's kindness, I say without feeling.

Yes, she says. Yes, you do.

A pause as she takes another suck. I watch the smoke curl in the space between us.

It is not cheap to rent a room in this city, she tells me. To have an entire building to ourselves—well, I doubt you could even imagine how much that costs. But thanks to the great generosity of the Hip Yee tong, we are able to live here in comfort and peace. What do you think, Peony? Do you enjoy living here?

I do, I lie.

The tong feeds us. They clothe us. They protect us. Yes, they protect you, Peony. I protect you.

Thank you, Madam Lee, I say, bowing my head.

What a polite girl, she says. Without warning, she slams the cigarette down on the table, the stem crumpling into a pile of ash underneath her fingers. Up close, her hands reveal skin thinning with age, wrinkling like the filmy layer on top of hot milk. The hands betray her; no matter how much powder she doused herself with, we would always know that she was capable of dying, just like anyone else.

If a girl is not making any money, she says, is that fair? If she is not doing anything in return for the tong's kindness, then she is simply taking advantage, is she not? What do you think, Peony? You who have lived here so well for a month already.

I know what she wants me to say. I am afraid to say it.

Today, you are done learning, she says, dragging her nails across the top of the table. Tomorrow, you will take your first customers. My sweet small girl who speaks English so well. You will make us a fortune with those sad eyes alone.

Another pause. I hate her for saying these things—my eyes, so unremarkable, so completely mine, now vulgar and corrupted by her. But all I can say is Yes, Madam Lee.

She knows this. Relishes it, even. Because we both know what will happen if I do not comply: There are shacks called cribs, where girls are holed up like cattle, where the only customers they get are sailors, teenage boys, and drunkards. I know that these girls' bodies are spent and broken and diseased, and most of them are taken to a hospital that is no hospital at all, but a dismal, windowless room in the back alleys of Chinatown. The door locks. Inside: a lamp, a cup of water, a cup of boiled rice. Death never waited long for those girls.

A girl like you would not last one day in the cribs, Madam Lee says, as if she can hear my thoughts. In here, I feed you. I give you nice clean clothes. I make you up to look pretty. I give you a bed. How many Chinese girls can say the same? We are not like those miserable holes on Bartlett Alley. We are the finest brothel in this entire city. In here, you have it the best of all. Look around you. It will not get better than this.

You are right, Madam Lee, I tell her. I will work hard to make up for your kindness.

I knew you would be a good girl, she says, reaching out to pet me. Her eyes flare with pleasure. I feel her open palm on my scalp, like an octopus dripping down my head and tightening its body to suffocate me.

Tomorrow, she breathes, we break you in.

She releases me. I stand and feel that my green satin pants are wet. She watches me walk to the door, watches me struggle to open it.

Before I am out, she calls to me, One more thing. You will have Jade's room beginning tonight.

But where will Jade sleep? I ask. The brothel is split into three floors, with most of us on the second floor, where we share one room for sleeping and another two for entertaining customers. The third floor, with its private rooms, is reserved for the top girls, like Swallow and Iris and Jade before her belly started to grow. Only girls who bring in the most expensive customers are allowed their own rooms. I have not yet brought in a single one.

Madam Lee does not answer. The guards know that this is a sign she is done with me, and push me out the door. I make my way back upstairs to our sleeping quarters and gather my things, which are not many—my work clothes, my makeup, ribbons and pins for my hair. Jade's room is at the end of the hallway on the third floor, one of the larger ones. When I reach it, I knock on the door, expecting her to be in there.

Madam Lee did not tell you? Iris says, her round face peeking out from the room next door. They took Jade away in the night.

Oh, I say. No, she did not.

She cannot work here with that thing growing inside her anyway, Iris says. What man wants a used-up whore?

She smirks and disappears into her room. I do the same. But this is not my room. It is Jade's room. Jade, who I just saw a few hours ago, now on her way to the cribs, where she will take customers for twenty-five cents, fifty if she is lucky. I wonder what will happen to the baby. Women in the cribs do not last longer than two years, someone told me when I first arrived at the barracoon. Either you die of disease or you die because of a man. To which I asked, What is the difference?

I light the lantern. Jade's room is neat, painted in a dark scarlet from wall to wall. A barred window looks down onto the gray street below. It still smells like her, the whistle of citrus layering the air. She was here for such a long time, before any of us.

She could not be more than twenty, twenty-one. Did she say something about having family back in China? I cannot remember. I am beginning to forget which information belongs to which girl. We are an anonymous clan of bodies and histories, and maybe we are all headed to the same place. Does it matter? It is only a question of time before we are all taken in the middle of the night and replaced with another younger, prettier girl.

One whole month I have managed to stay safe, unhandled. When I first arrived, I promised to make myself as small as possible. If a man looked at me, I would turn my face into something ugly. It was not so hard to match the things I felt on the inside. But I was foolish to think that I had any power of choice. I was bought for a reason, and now I have to make good on that promise.

In this moment, I think of Bai He, the girl with glass skin from the stories in my village. I once believed that her skin was her burden to bear. But now, sitting here with the knowledge that by this time tomorrow, I will no longer have my girlhood, I am realizing a truth: Bai He's skin was not the burden. Her burden was being a girl. And if there is such a burden, then none of us are free from it, not even me.

2

This is the story of a coal bucket that floated across an ocean.

—

The journey to San Francisco took three weeks, or so I am told. From that room in Zhifu, packed tight inside the coal bucket, I was placed in the back of a cart, and when we finally stopped moving, I could hear the crescendo of the ocean.

Voices everywhere, not unlike the clamor at the fish market. They were merchants, but this time, most of these voices were foreign.

Set that one over there, someone said close to me. These two on that ship. What is your name?

Jasper's voice now. Shipment to San Francisco, it said. Property of Master Eng and his estate, for delivery to the Hip Yee tong.

Yes, sir, the other voice said, suddenly cowed. We are well aware of your special delivery.

I was lifted, the coal cascading down my neck. They were carrying me off again, but something about the bray of the ocean, the harried voices and all the languages that came with them, told me that this next leg of the journey would be difficult to come back from.

If I had known all the things I do now, I would have cried for it. But all I could see was the wall of the bucket. It was all Jasper allowed me to see. The last thing I thought I could hear was the voice of someone—perhaps him—singing goodbye.

—

Later, when the lid slid off, I imagined myself leaping out. But even as I tried to tug myself up, the coal pressed my thighs down. I was not far, I thought, from being turned into a piece of coal myself.

One of Jasper's men was looking down at me. Do not even think about calling for help, he said, lowering his hand to undo the rope at my mouth. If you do, you die.

I nodded. Anything to get the cloth out of my mouth.

Eat, he said. In his other hand was a man tou the size of a bunched-up sock, the skin gray and loose. I stared at the thing, and then lunged for it.

When I was finished—it did not take very long—the man reached down again, this time with a canteen in hand. I lunged again, but he pushed my head back.

I will do it, he said.

I nodded and tilted my head back even more, desperate for something to cool my insides. He touched the lip to my open mouth. I wanted for all the water in the world to enter my body at that moment. But it was over before I could even wash the man tou away. The man lifted the canteen back up and screwed the cap on. Then he stuffed the cloth back in my mouth and secured it with the rope.

I will be back every two days, he said. Maybe three. Stay quiet.

And then he closed the lid.

What can I say about being in such a small space in the dark? I was contorted, my knees to my chin, my back curled like a monkey tail. After some time, the ache of my bent limbs became so unbearable that I wondered if I could kick myself through the bucket with all the might that was building up in my legs. But this was just a wish. The pain numbed after the first day, and then it dulled to a murmur. When I slept, which was all the time, I rested my head on my knees, the sway of the ocean rocking me to a distant shore that was not exactly sleep, but a fevered state between dreaming and waking.

I saw things then. The memories came to me easily, but I could no longer tell the difference between what was real and what was not. Everything swam before me, a distant song of memory and wishing.

I saw my parents before they were taken, my father's bare smile and the graying hair on his chin. I saw my mother's hands flashing like birds as she worked the loom. And I saw my grandmother, her arms full of her garden, face browned by the sun. I wondered if it had rained since I left Zhifu. If I was in the ocean, I reasoned, I was floating on rain. And so I spoke to my grandmother, telling her how much I missed her and also telling her everything that had happened to me since I last saw her—but not the most horrible parts, as I did not want her to worry. The tears came hot and fast, and I caught them in my mouth, imagining them to be salted pork or cured fish.

I saw Master Wang and the calligraphy school, too, smelled the pungent ink fresh on long columns of paper. The classroom's windows were open, and beyond the windows, more scrolls drying in the courtyard. I tried to read all the characters, but they were nothing more than spiders on top of snow.

The one I did not see, though, was Lin Daiyu. I knew why. In the story, Lin Daiyu never leaves China—instead, she dies there. As the ship carried me farther and farther away from my home, I wondered if she and I had finally been separated. The younger Daiyu would have been delighted and victorious—we were finally rid of each other, our stories split. But now that Lin Daiyu was no longer here, the older Daiyu was afraid.

This was what I wanted all along, was it not? This was what it meant to be alone for the first time in my life.

———

On the third day, the lid of the bucket slid off again, and the man reappeared as promised with another man tou and the water canteen.

Do you want to stand? he asked when I finished.

I nodded. He reached into the bucket and grabbed my arm, pulling. I felt myself being lifted, and a sharp stabbing pain shot through the crooks of my knees, nearly buckling me. My legs had not been straight for so long, and now they were being pried apart against their will, each increment a violation of bone and unused muscle and dormant tendon. I bit my lip to stop myself from crying out, letting the tears speak instead. Until I was standing again. Until I could see.

The man released me. I gripped the sides of the bucket, putting all of my weight on my hands.

I could tell from the groaning walls and the darkness that we were on a lower level, a storage room by the looks of it. With my limited vision, I could see the tops of other crates, containers, and buckets like mine. Some were stacked on top of each other, while others stood solitary and lonely. I wondered how many of them housed actual supplies, actual food, actual spices, and how many held other girls like me. Were they all Jasper's girls? Did they belong to other bad men?

That is enough, the man said. Get back down and stop looking around.

Please come again tomorrow, I pleaded before he stuffed the cloth in my mouth. I could not imagine another three days without food or water or standing. My pants were soiled and sour from the few times I had relieved myself when there was nothing left to do.

He did not say anything. I felt myself crumpling back into the bucket, the putrid stench of what little excrement I had reaching for me.

Stay quiet, the man said. He slid the lid shut.

It continued on like this. The man came mostly at night when the ship was quiet, feeding me, letting me stand for a few minutes at a time. Once, he even lifted me out of the bucket and commanded me to hop in place. I did so, feeling as if I had acquired a set of legs that were not mine, the way my hips rocked around my bones, awkward and painful. I went long periods without passing anything, my body feeble with only man tou and water. Nothing to digest, nothing to excrete. Around my neck, the burlap pouch dug a small hole into my chest bone, its mint grass coolness the only thing left between me and suffocation.

Delirium then. At first it was frenzied, as if my mind were pulling away from itself. There was heat inside my ears, a storm behind my eyes. Everything felt hot to the touch. This was dying, I remember thinking.

Then bliss. I was lifted from myself, floating over everything. I could see the ocean, could see the ship, could even see me, crouching and exhausted and thin, slumped over my knees. But it was good. It was even beautiful. The person inside that bucket was someone else. I was protected, I was wild, I was within everything. I forgot the hunger and the pain. I only knew effervescence.

I remembered then, with more clarity than any other moment in my life, a day before any of this ever happened, when my father brought home cherries because he knew my mother liked to eat them. I did not care for cherries—they were either too sweet or too sour, and the pits only made the fruit more cumbersome. I did not like the way their red flesh stained my fingers and the corners of my mouth.

But my mother loved them. Would do anything to eat them. When my father brought those cherries home that day, it was the most excited I had ever seen her. She all but burst from her loom, clapping her hands together and bouncing on her feet. The smile on her face was wide, the way the moon can be.

And my father poured the cherries into a bowl and we gathered around the bowl, each plucking out a cherry with the stem still on. I watched my mother roll hers, plump and shiny, in her palms, like she was praying with it. Then she dropped it into her mouth while still holding the stem, and after a moment, that was all there was—a stem.

You swallowed the seed, I said, bewildered. I always had nightmares about things getting stuck in my throat.

She smiled at my horror. Sometimes, she said, I think if I swallow things I love, they will grow inside of me.

Do not be like her, my father warned me, but he was smiling, too.

I did not ever grow to like cherries, but I did like that memory of my mother and my father and my grandmother, who liked cherries more than white peaches but less than apples. And me. We were together, gathering to take part in something that only made one of us exquisitely happy, but, by doing so, made all of us happy. Watching you eat fills my stomach, my mother used to tell me. I knew what she meant. When I finally pulled myself out of that memory, I felt full from it.

Other times, I thought about Lin Daiyu, willing her to come. She could take me out of here and we would float above the world, our bodies as thin as paper, as light as the last day of winter. I wanted to pour myself into her mouth, to sleep inside her body for years and years. For her to grow me inside her. At the height of my confusion, I think I wanted to love her.

But Lin Daiyu did not come.

The character for joy 樂 is silk threads over a tree. Like music in a forest, the melody that skims treetops. The character looks the way joy feels, Master Wang had told me. Like you are above everything, like you cannot keep yourself from igniting.

I smiled to think of this. And when the man slid the lid off the bucket for the last time, he must have seen me—eyes closed, tears streaking down my face, my body dressed in coal, and a ladle where my mouth should have been.

He must have feared me then.

One day, the ship stopped moving.

By then, I did not know that I had a body anymore. But I did know that it was important to keep whatever I had still. I reentered myself and waited.

Banging, then laughter. A clamor of men entered the storage room, the loudness of them knocking fear back into me for the first time in weeks. I heard the sound of heavy crates and boxes being shifted and carried away. I heard a man tell another man to not worry about this one, to let him carry it.

This one is special, he said.

It stinks in here, the other man said.

I was being lifted and carried away again—but this time not just in my dreams. And that must have been when I came crashing back down. I was not flying. I was inside a bucket filled with coal and my own urine, and in my stomach, there was nothing, in my head, there was nothing, in my heart, there was nothing. It was not the glorious beginning I felt when I stood by the ocean, but an emptiness that had no promise of being filled. They took me out of the ship, and when the sun hit the bucket, it was as if the entire thing had burst into flames.

For a moment, I believed I was back in Zhifu. It was the sound of gulls that fooled me, their cries dipping in and out. Then the foamy shush of the ocean and the groaning of the dock as it rocked. The air was cool.

Over here, over here, someone yelled in English. I felt myself being carried toward this new voice.

This is the one? it asked.

Whoever was carrying me grunted in affirmation.

Good, the voice said. Set it there.

An exchange of words. The sound of a horse whinnying. I felt myself being lowered, and then finally, everything stopped. After weeks of being moved by the ocean, I was still.

Jasper hopes the honorable members of the Hip Yee tong will be pleased with this delivery, a voice said. And then, once more, I thought I could hear it: someone singing goodbye.

A whip cracked. We were moving again, but the smell of the ocean was growing fainter with each second. Inside the bucket, the coal resettled around me.

I was in America.

———

What else can I say? Shall I speak of how I was taken to a holding pen, what they called a barracoon, on St. Louis Alley in Chinatown? It smelled like urine and feces and also sour melon peels. Shall I speak of how they threw off the lid of the bucket, how the sun sank into my eyes, how they dragged me out by my arms? My legs did not respond, so they tied me to a pole, the rope around my waist digging into the hollow between my ribs and hip bones.

Shall I speak of how they stripped me of my clothes, my soiled, putrid clothes, and cut off the burlap pouch necklace? Shall I speak of how they doused me with cold water, and how a part of me was glad to be able to feel anything at all? Or shall I speak of the barracoon itself, how they threw me in there with other girls like me, all naked, all trembling, all wet?

Instead, I shall speak of the woman I saw enter the building. We were all there on the floor, corralled in the middle. It was dank and un-furnished. Fifty or so girls. Our whimpers bounced off the bare walls, all of us stripped to the bone and bracing for death. There was us in the middle, and then there was them: the men who surrounded us, staring. I thought about the fish market in Zhifu and the way those fish lay in piles, how I and many others walked around each vendor, gazing hungrily at the fish, minds already racing forward to what it would taste like, how long it would take to scale, whether or not the meat was good, whether the eyeballs would pop in our mouths, how buttery the brain would taste, how soft the bones would be, soft enough to break between our teeth and leave in a wet pile on the table. That was what it reminded me of. Being a fish.

I noticed the woman because she was the only woman in the group of men who entered the building. Her face was beautiful, her mouth big and imperious, her eyes narrowed and lined with black. I noticed the woman because of what she wore, a white dress embroidered with a silver phoenix, and I thought, this must be a ruthless woman indeed if she chooses to wear the color of death. And I noticed her because the men parted for her, the sheer existence of her, the way she stepped through them like wind cutting through hanging sheets.

Some of the men would point to a girl here and there, and then one of the handlers would rush forward, dragging the girl to whoever had singled her out. She would be passed over to her new owner, shrinking and crying, and in exchange the handler would receive a wad of paper, which I later discovered was money. We were being sold one by one, some in groups, and yet all I could think about was what would happen to the ones who would be left over at the end of this day. Where would we go?

The woman had not once pointed at a girl. She stood at the front, eyes tracking over every girl's body. Her face was blank, her arms crossed. There was something different about this woman, not just in the way she stood, which was like an empress, but in the way she did not seem to notice any of the men around her who continued to stare at her out of the sides of their eyes. They hated her, but only because they feared her, I realized.

And then she raised her hand and nodded.

You, one of the handlers said, walking up to the girl next to me. She jerked away from him, crying. He grabbed her wrist—she fell to the floor—and dragged her to the woman, who then snapped her fingers. Two men appeared from behind. They took the girl, who was wailing now, and disappeared back into the crowd.

I felt something hot. I looked up. The woman's eyes were on me, unblinking. There was a cruelty to her, I decided. The handler, who had not left her side, stood on his toes to whisper to her. She did not take her eyes off me. And then she raised her hand and nodded.

Almost immediately, the handler was in front of me, hands on my wrist. You, he said, already pulling me toward the woman. I felt myself complying. If I tried to run, my legs would dissolve beneath me.

I stood in front of the woman as straight as I could. I would not cry.

Her eyes assessed me, starting at my feet, then up my legs, my torso, my breasts, and finally my face. You are the one who knows English? she said. Her voice was deep and booming, a disarming power behind it.

Well, the handler said, shaking my wrist. Answer her!

Yes.

Very advanced, the handler said proudly. More than any girl here. Studied with the best in China. She will be sure to please your white guests.

That might be, the woman said, but she is very skinny. My girls need to have meat on their bones. Am I to run my stores dry feeding her until she fattens up? That does not seem like a fair trade for the price you are asking.

Ah, madam, the handler whined, her price is final.

Then I will just take the one, the woman said, turning away.

No, he said. Wait. I can offer you a deal.

The woman stopped.

Two thousand instead of two thousand four hundred, the handler said. I cannot go any lower. Any lower and my boss will be displeased.

The woman smiled. What do you think? she asked, addressing me. Is that a fair price for you?

I gaped at her. We both knew I did not know what that amount meant.

Two thousand then, she said, snapping her fingers. The two men I saw earlier emerged suddenly, grabbing my shoulders.

Wait, I called to no one.

The two men dragged me to a carriage with a buggy, which stood waiting just outside. They clothed me and loaded me onto the buggy, where the first girl sat, her limbs folded tight into her body. We did not speak to each other. To do so would be to confirm that this was real.

The carriage creaked with the weight of the woman, who was giving instructions to the driver. We were moving now, getting farther away from the building.

Down the street we drove. The roads were lopsided, shoving us back and forth as we went up and down hill after hill. An unsettling fog hung over us, gobbling up the carriage as it charged forward. If only we went a little farther up each hill, I thought, we could reach the clouds somehow. And then I could fly away.

The carriage turned down another street and I gasped before reminding myself again that I was no longer in Zhifu. The buildings here looked like the ones I had seen in China—the same red lanterns hanging off storefronts, the same red banners painted with gold characters plastering the buildings. Around me, a mixture of Chinese and English, their speakers dipping in and out of each language as effortlessly as a stone skipping over water. I saw a man sitting on a stool, cracking sunflower seeds with his teeth. Someone else was playing a flute, but I did not see where it came from. I could even smell the papery richness of su bing. We were in America, but how could this America look so much like China?

We finally stopped outside a brown-gold building in the middle of a busy street. The carriage doors opened, and the woman walked out to stand in front of us. The other girl sniffled, looking down. I stared at the woman defiantly, daring her to do something.

Well, she said, I have done you both a favor. Are you not grateful?

Neither of us said anything. The madam asked you a question, one of her men barked. Answer her!

I looked at her hard, the madam. In another world, she could capture emperors. In this world, in the daylight that had begun to spread, her smile took over her entire face, pushing all her other features together. It was grotesque to me.

They will learn, she said.

The men reached inside and pulled us from the buggy. I stumbled down the steps and scuttled forward to catch myself from falling, my legs still soft from disuse. It was then that I looked up at the building where we had stopped. There were no lights on inside—to a passerby, it would appear abandoned. A sign outside said WASH'ING AND IRON'ING, and indeed, the smell of something soapy and earthen surrounded the place. On either side, what looked like lodging.

Inside, the woman said. She turned to the building and walked in.

Come on, I said to the girl, grabbing her hand. It was sticky with snot and tears. I breathed in, feeling my chest lighten without the burlap pouch necklace. This gave me a kind of courage. The girl pulled back, whimpering, but I dragged her with me through the front door.

This was our new home. Someone would show us to our rooms.

3

None of us know how Madam Lee became Madam Lee, but there are rumors, like the one where once, she was no madam at all. She was just one of us.

She was deathly beautiful, Jade would say—

The mistress of a powerful captain, Iris would follow—

She charged an ounce of gold for men to have a look at her! Swan would finish.

Somewhere in that rumor, Madam Lee became one of the highest-paid prostitutes in San Francisco. With that money, she opened her own brothel, working with the Hip Yee tong to import girls. And as terrified as we are of Madam Lee, we fear the tongs even more. We know they control Chinatown, running the restaurants, the opium dens, the gambling houses, the brothels and laundries and brothels-as-laundries. I do not see the tong, but I feel them the same way I feel Jasper's presence over me—an unseen hand around my neck, a cold palm against the small of my back. Sometimes we hear their voices in the street below and the loud pops that follow, splitting open the sky. Just last week, one of the tongs ambushed a restaurant with gunfire, killing the patrons of a rival tong inside.

During the day, Madam Lee's brothel transforms. We transform, too, from women with painted faces to girls who wash clothes. Some of the girls have done the job before, while others like me are learning for the first time.

I discovered early on that Madam Lee's brothel does not exist, at least not legally. It is only a laundry and we are only ever allowed to speak about it as such. Many years before I arrived, the city of San Francisco had tried to be stricter on brothels, although, Swan told me, that had only been for show. In reality, many within the government and law enforcement were working with the tongs to make sure business kept running smoothly. Some even pocketed ten dollars for every girl sold.

It is not just us who hide so well in plain sight. It is everyone in this city. The men who come visit us at night turn into demons, their shadows the size of caves. By day, they are merchants, scholars, businessmen. I am beginning to realize that everyone has two faces to them: the face they show to the world and the one on the inside, that keeps all its secrets.

I still do not know who my faces are, or which one is which.

If the police stop by, which is very infrequently, all they will see is a cramped laundry filled with sixteen girls running around, hair in knots, sweat crowning our flushed faces. Madam Lee owns all three floors of the building, which makes it easy for her to maintain the lie. On the ground floor is the foyer and waiting room, which holds the façade as the front of the laundry during the day. It takes three girls to overturn the room, first rolling away the lush tapestries and rugs, then hiding the vases and jades in cupboards. They crowd the room with clothes and linens. The final touch: pushing a large shelf in front of the stairs that lead to our bedrooms. All anyone sees when they enter is a drab but neat operation, propelled by necessity and efficiency. We must make a convincing show of it, because once, when an inspector stopped by and took a tour of the shop, he left exclaiming that not many places still did laundry manually anymore. Maybe he would start bringing his laundry to our shop from now on, he said. And he did.

Madam Lee believes in doing the laundry by hand instead of relying on the steam machines that other launderers have begun investing in. We wash and iron in the back room, working next to kettles of boiling water. The hand irons are heavy and must be heated repeatedly over hot coals anytime the temperature drops—but not so hot as not to damage the clothes. In many ways, I find laundry more exhausting and demanding than the work we are meant to do at night. Perhaps this is because I have not yet had to do any real work at night, I remind myself.

You are sha, Swan tells me when I express this. She is the eldest and has no trouble taking advantage of the title, treating us like we are her foolish little sisters. None of us are allowed to speak our native tongues in the brothel, but Swan likes to flirt with this rule, switching between Chinese and English when Madam Lee is not listening. She does this, I believe, to show that she still has something that belongs to her. You feel this way now, she continues. It will be different once you start getting customers.

When we do laundry, we wear no makeup, scrubbed clean instead, our foreheads luminous. Look as plain as possible, Madam Lee warns us. In daylight, we are still only children. Many of the girls shave their eyebrows so they can draw their own penciled arches at night. Some have bound feet.

Swallow is barefaced and fresh, and without her makeup, I can see three freckles running down her cheek. Pearl, the crying girl I arrived in the buggy with, looks even younger than she is, her nose a shiny peach knob. Swan, who can be so sharp and cutting at night, looks as if she has just woken from a nap, her skin puffy and smooth without the rice powder. She is good at folding, so she works with the folding girls. Pearl works with the washing girls. Swallow and I are with the girls who iron clothes. You can tell who the ironing girls are by their red hands and forearms. Always raw, bones bruised. At night, we sand down our calluses and put white powder on our fingers. My hands are bigger now, can carry more than before. They have changed since the days of helping my mother or working in the garden or holding a calligraphy brush. These are still good hands, I remind myself. These are still my hands.

In the laundry room, the girls let themselves forget what awaits them at night. They swap gossip and jokes, let out exasperated, theatrical sighs when the work feels hard. I am reminded of older sisters I will never have. And even in the face of the scalding wash water and the strain that comes with being bent over all day, I could say that I enjoy the work. Because this is where I get to know the girls.

Swan has been in America for three years already, kidnapped from Beijing when she was seventeen. *Wo yi wei* I was joining a theater troupe, she tells us. I was born to be famous. And she is famous, in the brothel at least. The customers like her sharp tongue, which she uses to make them feel like naughty schoolboys. Out of all the girls here, Swan knows the most about the goings-on of the brothel—who comes, who leaves, who stays. She lords her knowledge over us, as if this somehow makes her special, but we have all heard her screaming in her sleep. She is afraid, the same as the rest of us.

Iris, my new neighbor, is an orphan. She does not remember how she got to the brothel, only that one day she was on the streets in Kaiping and the next, a woman—was it Madam Lee?—was holding her hand and guiding her to a big building that smelled like honey. She is giggly and shrill. She likes to gossip, and I think she actually likes it here. Not long ago, she told us about how fifty men from two rival tongs fought over a Chinese slave girl in an alley off Waverly Place. She told us as if to say, I want to be that slave girl.

Pearl is the youngest, another kidnapped by a henchman for the tong. She misses her brothers and sisters in Guangzhou very much. Sometimes I hear her crying when she thinks the rest of us cannot hear. Pearl wants to be a dancer and believes she can. Her only customer keeps promising that his connection with a dance company will cash in. So Pearl waits, taking him into her bedroom week after week.

All of us, led by a person we deemed a savior, only to find out that we were wrong and how much that wrong cost. When I hear their stories, I realize that the tong has hundreds of Jaspers out there waiting to snatch little girls. All of us were special. None of us were special.

Swallow is the mystery. Bone-white and silent—not quiet, but silent—she has no history and no future that she speaks of. She has the most customers of us all, and perhaps her silence is why. There is something about her that can be rewritten over and over again.

In my first few days at the brothel, I wanted to know her. She was a character I could neither read nor write, her face shifting between day and night—sometimes just a girl, other times a willow of a woman. Younger or older than me, here by choice or by circumstance, I did not know. If I held out my finger and tried to trace her, all that came out was a closed fist.

I heard she came here herself, some of the girls whispered. Walked right in and asked to see the madam of the brothel. What kind of girl would do that?

The other girls said that Swallow was selfish, that she wanted all the customers for herself. Always itching to have more, they cawed. She was always placing herself closest to Madam Lee, accepting the best clothes and jewelry to attract the higher-paying customers.

I thought this, too, until I saw what she did for Pearl. On our fourth day there, Pearl was chosen by a man built like a door. She should have simpered and smiled the way she had been taught. Instead, she fell to the ground, wailing. He would be her first, and he looked like he could break her. I felt the other girls step away from her, as if being near her would somehow affect their desirability, too.

Only Swallow had stepped forward. I will take care of you, she told him through the glass. As long as you say nothing of this to our madam.

To the guard waiting for us outside the viewing room, she promised something similar.

The customer was not too upset about the exchange. He came in and acted as if he had wanted Swallow all along. Madam Lee knew nothing, and Pearl stayed silent—red-faced, but silent.

Swallow was not at work the next day. The other girls did their washing and folding and ironing with their tongues between their teeth. The customer had been a rich one, they could tell based on the shine on his shoes. Selfish bitch, Jade had trilled when she saw

Swallow's empty station. Spent all night on her back and is now sleeping in, getting fat. She took your customer from you, Pearly girl, do you realize that?

I finished my work early. Instead of returning to our sleeping quarters, I continued to the third floor and stopped at Swallow's door. I wanted to see if it was true what they said, that she was lying on her bed while the rest of us burned our hands in hot water. Her door was ajar. I slowed my steps, let time expand and stretch before me.

She was not on her bed. Instead, I found her at her vanity, the various powders and pencils and rouges laid out before her in preparation for our evening work. Her reflection looked very tired, dark circles under each eye.

It was difficult to watch her, more difficult to pull away. Hunched at her door, so close to entering the space she occupied, I realized then why she was the favorite among the guests. Even with an exhausted, half-done face, she was intoxicating. It was not simply the small chin or the tender lips, not her pliant frame, not the entrancing, well-placed smiles. It was her entire way of being—that careful mystery, that undecipherability, even when she was alone. Every movement brought with it a new question that must be answered. I saw a girl who was a woman, who had the most extreme knowledge of herself. That was her power. That was the reason for her silence—not a silence at all, but a contentment with simply existing as she was.

And the customers? The men? They wanted to consume that power. That was why they kept choosing her again and again. Could I blame them? Swallow had in her something that could feed a hungry village forever, if only she would share. If only they could get her to share.

She lowered her hand and dipped it into the white powder, revealing the other side of her face. I held back a gasp. One side of her face was immaculately drawn, white and pristine, but the naked side was bruised in browns, violets, and blues.

That was when I knew: She had not taken Pearl's customer because she was greedy for his patronage. She had taken him because she saw, better than any of us, what he was: a brute and a drunk.

After that, the mystery of Swallow became no mystery to me. All I had to do was look hard enough. The girls would say that she was always standing close to Madam Lee to crowd out the rest of them. I knew better. She placed herself closest to Madam Lee because then she could block the rest of us from the madam's wrath, like when she threw boiling water on a girl for speaking too quietly. The girls would say that Swallow was vain, always starving herself to make her face lovelier. I knew better. The food she did not eat went into our bowls. And when the girls said that Swallow was arrogant and snobbish, that she hated all of us, I knew best. To care about others was to let yourself become soft, and you could not be soft in a place like this. And so Swallow had to remain hard and distant—for all of us, but most of all, for herself.

Silent, solemn, sensual Swallow. When I finally understood her motivations, I also knew how to write her name 燕. A dark-red bird with a mouth that looks like pincers. Widespread wings. A flared tail. Some would say the character was simply a drawing of a bird, but I knew that there was another truth: To write the character for Swallow's name, one must also include fire beneath it all. She would never let herself be burned. Instead, she would be the fire.

I saw her for who she was, and I thought: This is the kind of person I want to be.

—

I am at the same ironing station as Swallow, but my mind is not on laundry. It is on my conversation with Madam Lee from the night before. I have heard enough from the other girls of what happens when a man is alone with a woman, the pain she is said to endure, the blood that leaves a trail. I have never even kissed anyone before.

Are you thinking about tonight?

Looking up, I see that it is Swallow who has spoken to me. I want to shout to someone, anyone—Swallow has spoken, Swallow has spoken! But I stop myself. This moment feels like it should be between us, like she is giving me a gift that only I am meant to receive.

How did you know? I ask. I am afraid that if I use too many words, or the wrong words, she will fly away.

I had a feeling when she asked to see you, she says. I imagine her lying awake in bed after all the men have left her room and it is just her, body pressed against the mat, still alive and remembering. How can a body survive? Swallow lowers the iron down onto a shirt. It sighs with satisfaction, steam rushing up from the table surface and clouding her hands.

This will be your first one?

I nod. I have never done this before, I say. Then I wish I had not spoken. My grandmother taught me that the truth of my past, of my real identity, is the only thing I have to protect myself. Every piece I give away chips at that protection.

She lifts the iron again and sets it down next to the shirt. I watch her hands as they wield the iron, admiring their capability, their smoothness. They remind me of my mother's.

Are you afraid? she asks, looking up at me. The bruises on her face, finally healing after the assault, have turned pink. They could almost be pretty in the daylight.

Yes, I say. I do not know what to do.

She peels the shirt off the table and inspects it for wrinkles. It looks perfect to me, a sheet of pure white. Then she passes it over to the next table, where some of the girls are folding, their gossip crackling over our conversation.

Hand me another shirt, she says, pointing. I reach for one from the pile and spread it out on the table.

All you have to do, she says, smoothing the shirt out, is whatever they want you to do. It is the simplest task of all, actually.

But I do not know what that means, I say.

All it is, is make-believe, she says. It is not real. To them it is real, but to you, it is nothing. That is how you have to think of it. As nothing. It is not you and you are not it. You are still you outside of it.

I do not understand, I say.

When they do it, she says, and she raises her hands and cups one over the other, it will hurt, especially if it is your first time. You will feel like you are exploding down there, and you will want to gasp and cry. But do not. Sometimes that makes them angry, other times it makes them want to do it more. You have to forget that it hurts. You have to go somewhere else. Do you have somewhere else you can go?

Yes, I say, thinking of the courtyard of Master Wang's school, thinking of my grandmother's garden, thinking of my mother's warm embrace and the loom rushing back and forth.

Good, she says, hands returning to the iron. Go there and wait. Your body will know what to do. Your mind is what is important, though. You have not yet begun your bleeding, have you?

I shake my head. Good, she says. At least that is one less thing to worry about.

Where do you go? I ask. I may be overstepping, but I do not want to stop.

She removes the iron. I watch her fingers pass over the newly crisp shirt, easing out the creases. I go to sleep, she says, her eyes meeting mine.

———

We have one hour between the laundry and the brothel. During this time, each girl scrubs her body down from the cooked-steam smell of the day. Each girl who is lucky, who is not considered too fat, gets a bowl of rice. She wears the outfit laid out on her bed—sometimes a silk blouse and pants, other times a satin dress. Whatever Madam Lee feels is appropriate for the customers who will come that day. Each girl sits at her mirror and takes out the arsenal of makeup given to her—pots of rouge for the cheeks and lips, rice powder for the face, black paint for the eyebrows and eyes. Some of the girls apply rouge to the whole upper lip, and a cherry-like dot in the middle of the lower lip. The white men like that, they say, like that we look even more Chinese this way.

The older girls do their own hair. Younger, inexperienced ones like me wait our turn as the hairdresser moves between us. Sometimes, when her hands spread through my hair, I close my eyes and imagine the hands of someone who loves me very much massaging my scalp into dough.

Tonight, I am to wear a peach long-sleeve blouse with white buttons and a lined collar, and a matching skirt. I hate the clothes Madam Lee makes us wear, designed to her taste and sewn by an old woman down the street. In China, the clothes we wear would be laughed at, easily identified as gaudy imitations. Here, they make the white men go crazy.

When I look in the mirror with my clothes and makeup on, I see a girl with eyes wrapped in black and lids the color of wine. Her brows are a canopy above her eyes. She is as white as porcelain and her lips shine with blood. After two years of pretending to be Feng, a boy born from the wind, it is shocking to see myself this way. When I move, I wonder if I am really the one moving at all.

My grandmother once told me, when I complained about my name, that everyone revered Lin Daiyu as a beauty. I think it has something to do with how morbid her story was. Would she have been as beautiful if she did not die for the man she loved?

Now I am beginning to understand that tragedy makes things beautiful. Maybe that is why, night after night, we paint our eyebrows into long arcs that make our eyes look sad.

I trace the character for man 男 in my palm. Man: a field and a plow, the plow a symbol of power.

Once, I thought love was simple—an embrace, a gentle kiss on the forehead. I never even knew that there could be something that was so *not* love, something like this. A violation of the body, a burst of crimson. Whoever this man is will be the one entering me, and he will also be the one who takes everything away. I could mourn the loss of my girlhood now, but I do not let myself. Mourning it would be giving power to whoever takes it.

Man: Without power, he is just a piece of arable land.

To choose between this and the crib is no choice at all. Instead, I must believe that one day, there will be an out. Lin Daiyu found hers: She let herself die. Me? I am not quite ready yet.

Tonight, I am not Daiyu. Tonight, you can call me Peony.

———

When I descend and enter the main room, the other girls are already waiting. We are, all of us, transformed, as if the difference between day and night could be a whole person. Pearl is small in her silk dress, a flower stitched to her chest. Iris bounces on her feet, her wrists clanging with bracelets. Swan has on the most makeup of all of us, the dot on her bottom lip moving as she brushes her tongue over her teeth. Swallow is looking away, her chin angled to the side. We do not speak of Jade, who is missing, although none of us move to take the place where she usually stands.

I give Pearl a small smile. She looks at me, her eyes round and already filling with tears. She is wondering if her customer will come tonight and save her from Madam Lee's wrath. At some point, I think, she will have to be brave.

Madam Lee enters. She speaks to us every night before opening to remind us of what we are really here for. During this time, she also inspects us, making sure our wrists are as white as our faces, that we have not gained too much weight where it matters, that we look fresh, pleasing to the eye, delicious. She is proud of us, she tells us often.

Some of you girls may notice, she begins, that we are missing someone tonight. I want you to look at the spot where Jade usually stands. Jade was sent away last night because she was stealing from me.

At this, some of the girls shift their weight. One coughs into her hand.

Madam Lee does not notice, or she pretends not to. Jade slept here, she ate here, she used my resources, but she was not making me any money. She came back empty-handed for almost three weeks in a row. Imagine that. Imagine giving someone everything and having them give you nothing in return. It is no different from stealing.

None of us say a word. What Madam Lee says is always true.

As you know, Madam Lee continues, this is not the first time this has happened. There have been many girls who have stolen from me, and I gave them the punishment they deserved: I got rid of them. I am telling you about Jade because she was here before any of you, yet she still suffered the consequences for her actions. I do not want you to get complacent, thinking you are safe here just because you have been here longer than anyone else. I expect you all to work hard, and bring me the money you owe me to live here and benefit from my kindness.

She inhales.

We look at our feet and the carpet, where red and bronze vines wrap around each other. Against my leg, I practice writing the character for jade 玉, an emperor with a lopsided dash in one of the corners, meant to look like three pieces of jade strung together. It is the same jade that lives in my real name.

Understood? Madam Lee asks. Each one of us can feel her gaze on the top of our head. We nod as a group.

Good, she says. Now go be sweet girls to our guests.

We fall into the official order before entering the room with the window—the youngest girls at the front, the more experienced ones in the middle, the tallest ones at the back. I go to stand at the front of the line, but Madam Lee stops me. Peony, she calls.

The girls chitter, glancing at me as they file into the room. Even Swallow, who has done this one hundred times, gives me a look before disappearing. When they are gone and it is just the two of us, Madam Lee walks toward me, her fingers choked by rings.

I have an interesting offer for you, she says. Sit.

I do, careful not to wrinkle my skirt. Madam Lee remains standing, her eyes glinting as they rake over my body.

We have a special customer coming in tonight, she tells me. He is the son of someone who has been very generous to the Hip Yee tong. The tong has ordered that I give him a girl free of charge, as a show of their gratitude.

This customer, she continues, requested something very specific, something only you can provide. Are you not curious what that is?

I hear Swan's voice forcing its way into my ear. Yi ci, it sings, a customer asked me to sit on his chest and tu my breakfast. Can you believe it? When I finally did it, he da ku out of pleasure!

Everyone already knows I have the best girls, Madam Lee says to my silence, her hand on my thigh. But our new customer is very peculiar. He will only take a girl who has not been with a white man before.

She presses harder, her rings digging into my flesh.

You see why you are perfect? Madam Lee says. All of my girls have slept with many, many men. Except you, Peony. You who have never been broken in. Tonight, you will be the perfect gift for our special customer.

Her hand leaves my thigh then. She strokes my cheek, then rubs her fingers together, rolling the rice powder between them. You should consider yourself lucky, she tells me. The tong will be very pleased.

I do what I am expected to do. I nod, keep my elbows close to my body, smile. I will treat him well, I say, thinking of where Jade must be by now. I will never let myself end up in a place like that.

Good girl, Madam Lee says, reaching out to stroke my cheek again. I squeeze my hands together until my nails are close to piercing the flesh to stop myself from turning away. Our customer is already on his way, she says. You will be his for the entire evening.

Before she leaves, she turns back to me. I am trying to look strong and brave, the way I have seen Swallow look. And, Peony, she says, my name dripping from her mouth, you will do whatever he asks.

She leaves me to wait. I imagine the kind of man who would make this type of request, whether or not he will be gentle with me. Or if he will hit me the way that man hit Swallow. I think of the bruise that made one side of her face look like murky water, wondering how my own face would wear it.

The lamps in here are shaded with red and black, so that everything looks like a secret. Ta men do it to hide the imperfections in our faces, Swan would say. Even bruised apples look good in the dark.

Every sound of a carriage passing by outside, every laugh or yell, makes my body tighten, my limbs press closer. How can I do this? I ask myself. Can it kill a person? When the customer finally walks in, I do not know if I will even have the strength to rise from the sofa.

A flicker on the heavy wooden armchair facing me. My eyes snap to it, each nerve awake for changes in the atmosphere, trying to memorize every detail about this room, about me, before it all changes. Tomorrow, this room will not look the same. Tomorrow, I will not be the same in it.

The flicker grows, stretching out over the armchair. Then it is no longer a flicker, but a shape and a hue. White, growing whiter. It could be smoke from the burning incense sticks or the shadows passing by out on the street. It could be a girl from a story, a girl who could now be called a woman. I close my eyes, searching for calm. When I open them, I see Lin Daiyu before me.

Hello, she says. Her voice is somewhat hoarse, as if she has been crying or has not used it for a while.

My shoulders collapse against the sofa. I had convinced myself that the journey across the ocean had finally separated us, but here she is now, her face as white as a swan's breast, her silver-black hair inexplicably wet. She does not look like the Lin Daiyu from the story but like the Lin Daiyu who appeared in my dream: blue eyes, a longer nose, those pinkish lips. Her satin jacket and skirt gleam bright in the dim dread of the room. She wears a fishing net as a shawl.

Have you been swimming? I ask, dumb. Then, remembering where I am and what is about to happen, I stand and wave my arms at her. You should go, I say, wishing anything but. She is here, somehow, and I am not so alone after all. We both crossed an ocean, only to end up here.

Do not be so dramatic, she says. I am only here because you asked for my help, whether you like it or not.

My eyes flit to the clock on the wall. Nearly nine. The customer would not be long now. But Lin Daiyu cannot be here when he arrives. I do not yet know if she exists only for me, or if others would be able to see her, too. Where could she hide?

As if she knows the answer, Lin Daiyu rises from her place on the armchair and walks toward me. A younger me, perhaps the me who existed before any of this, wants to run. But something else—is it her?—is holding me down.

She stands before me now, her blue eyes drooping. When you are remembered for being the face of tragedy, your face must always be reaching for the center of the earth, I think. Then she puts her damp hands on my face and guides my mouth open. We stare at each other, her the story who looks like me, me the girl with a vacant body. There was a time when I hated her, then another when I was terrified of her, then another where I was so delirious, I could have been in love with her. Now I do not know how I feel. But Lin Daiyu does not wait for me to find out. She climbs inside my mouth before I can do anything and disappears.

Madam Lee erupts from her office, her cheeks ablaze. He is here, she cries. She flies to the brothel door, one hand on the pin in her hair, the other beckoning me to stand. Are you ready?

I stand, feeling Lin Daiyu spread herself out inside me. What do you think? she asks against my neck. Are we ready?

4

The man is not a man but a boy.

I can tell from the way he holds himself in, as if his body grew faster than the rest of him and he does not yet feel at home in it. His plum chang shan drapes over his shoulders, a sheet over wire. The boy stands and stares, at once defiant and fearful, waiting for someone to doubt him.

It is a shock to see him here. His eyes are the shape of tiny fish, his hair brownish-black, reminding me of wood ear mushrooms. Looking at him makes my heart pull for my family, for my home. He might not be much older than I am.

The boy is not alone. On either side of him stand two men, faces white and identical. I think of the character for twins 雙, the pair of birds that sit on top. Birds follow and mimic each other in flight, and that is how these white men move, too, two pairs of arms crossing left on top of right, two chests rising and falling with the same hot breath. The boy looks like he wants to get as far away from them as he can.

Welcome, Madam Lee says to all three. She bows.

The two white men do not return her bow. This is her? one of them asks. Inside me, Lin Daiyu tilts my head down, eyes fluttering to the floor.

This is Peony, Madam Lee says, her voice as laden as summer. A gift from the Hip Yee tong. She will do perfectly.

You hear that? the other one says to the boy. She is yours to do whatever with, Mule. Can she come here? Pee-oh-nee, come here.

Madam Lee turns to me, nodding. I shuffle in the direction of their voices, my cloth shoes noiseless against the massive rugs on the floor.

She comes on command, the first one says gleefully. Can you do a twirl? Do a twirl for us, pretty girl.

I imagine Swallow, the way her hips guide her in an oval, how her back morphs into a serpent dancing in midair. I move to my right and turn, jutting out my hips.

That is good, I hear them say. Oh, that is good.

When I am facing them again, I look up, searching for the eyes of my customer. He has a weak face, the kind where the chin disappears into the neck. I count three black bristles on his upper lip, all sprouting in different directions. He does not look at me, instead staring at the space next to me, lips trembling. He is, I realize, just as afraid as I am.

We will come back in the morning, Mule, one of the white men says, pushing the boy forward. He stumbles and falls into me. On instinct, I grab him.

The two white men laugh. Looks like she *will* be taking care of you tonight.

I take the boy's hand—soft as a belly—and lead him to the stairs.

—

He sits on my bed. I stand by the door. In the room next to us, Iris has already begun entertaining her first customer of the night. Her giggles ripple through the wall. The boy and I do not look at each other.

Inside me, Lin Daiyu breathes again. I watch as my feet move forward, walking toward where he sits on the bed. Lin Daiyu blows on my neck. I am raising my hand. I am setting it on his shoulder.

He jerks at the touch. What—what are you doing? he asks.

Is this not what you wanted? I say. Sir, Lin Daiyu adds.

He puffs out his chest now, straightens up. Tries to look tough. How can I be sure you are what I want? he retorts. I want a girl who has never slept with a white man before. I know all you whores do, how you let them defile you. I will not have a girl who has let herself be tainted like that.

I have not, I swear to him. I have not been with anyone before.

He stares at me, the tough man of him cracking. The little boy peeks through again. I am your first?

Yes, I say. Something sinks within me. You have much to teach me, I tell him.

He deflates. I have never been with anyone either, he says.

We face each other, both curious, wondering what the other will do. If I keep talking to him, I think, I can delay the act, push it farther away with my words.

Why are you here? I ask. Who were those men with you?

He looks glad for the delay, too. They are my brothers, he tells me. My half brothers.

Are your parents Chinese?

My mother is, he says. My father is white.

How? I say. I search for traces of whiteness on him. Downstairs, I had only seen the things that made him familiar to me—dark hair, wide cheekbones, the color of home in his eyes. Now I begin to find that which makes him strange—the high nose bridge, the jutting brow. He could be a blur of two faces.

My father met my mother in China, he says. I can see the story is precious to him, painful, too. It is enough to distract him from the matter at hand. He took me back to America with him when I was just a child. I have a little sister, too, but she is still in China. He left them both behind.

But who, I ask, are your half brothers?

The boy grimaces, the corners of his lips darkening. My father already had a family here. They did not appreciate him bringing home a little half-Chinese boy. Now they say they do not believe I am a man. They say my man parts are defective and spoiled.

I cannot help but glance down.

Sorry, he says. I see that he has tears in his eyes. I am talking too much. I always talk too much.

Is that why you are here? I ask. To prove them wrong?

He turns and wipes a sleeve across his eyes. Yes, he says. They tell me I will not become a man unless I sleep with a girl.

I feel sympathy for him. I have suffered, yes, but at least I know that I was once loved.

The boy turns back to me now, his eyes dry and red. What do you care? he says, voice in a growl. Take off your clothes!

The growl is forced, fake. I am not afraid of him.

But I follow his order. I unbutton my shirt, casting it off quietly, then drop my skirt. He closes his eyes, unable to watch. From the moment I stepped into the brothel, Madam Lee fed me four meals a day, letting me have extra porridge at breakfast and two servings of meat at dinner. You need to ripen up here and here, she would say, pointing and pinching. No man wants to lie with a little boy. As the days passed, I saw my legs swell, my arms fatten. My breasts were growing, too, inflating to little mounds that sat awkward and new on my chest.

When I am naked before him, he can only look at my feet. Next to us, the sounds of Iris's moans.

The boy stands and motions to the bed. His face is steely now, the tears hard against his cheeks.

Where should I go? I ask myself, thinking of Swallow's words. I lie down. Which place sounds nice?

The boy climbs on top of me, his legs prying mine apart, arms walling me in. His mouth smells like pears. I will myself to find a place to go.

His face plummets down, nose smashing into mine. His cheek-bones grind around my face. A kiss, I think. His hands are all over me, but they do not want to be. Against his palms, I feel like something scalding hot.

Damn it, he curses, and then his hands are moving toward his pants. I do not want to watch. Instead, I listen for the sound of button through hole, then the rustle as he slides them off.

I remember seeing my parents embrace when I was younger, the way my mother simply folded herself into my father's arms. My father would raise her head up and put one kiss on her forehead, then another on her lips. I liked the way they looked together, both bodies leaning against each other, seeking the other like a surrendering, the way trees slowly grow toward their source of water. This, I always thought, was how you loved.

Now, as the boy's thighs stick against mine, I know that this is not what I saw all those years ago.

Where can I go? Not to that moment of watching my parents embrace. That memory is too sacred. Nothing with my grandmother in it. The boy's face is coming closer again, panting now, and I still have nowhere to go. Think, think. I do not want to be here when it happens. The only thing left to do is squeeze my eyes shut and hope it is enough to make myself disappear.

This is what she has been waiting for. From inside of me, Lin Daiyu blows again, and I feel her sliding down my body, limbs inflating against my own. Let me try, she says.

And I think, I am happy to let you stay here for a while.

Something stings against my cheek. I open my eyes. The boy's face is hovering above mine, his eyes wide. Another drop on my forehead. I realize that he is crying.

I cannot do it, he says. He slides off me, the bed groaning with him. I cannot do it. I am less of a man, just like they said.

I sit up, too. You are not less of a man, I tell him. Inside, Lin Daiyu scoffs but retreats.

I will never become a man if I cannot do it, he says, turning away from me.

You do not have to do anything, I say. You can tell them you did it. If they ask, I will say the same.

He faces me. How old are you, little sister?

Fourteen, I say. This is the truth.

The same age as my sister, he says. Every so often I get her letters, asking me when I can come home or when she can come visit me. I do not think I want her to come visit me, do you? I am afraid she will end up in a place like this.

He laughs, then quickly looks down. Sorry, he says. You can put your clothes back on.

Do not be sorry, I tell him. I stand, slipping back into my skirt and buttoning my shirt back up to my neck. I think of Jasper, how I should have known to recoil at his touch and let those fishmongers catch me instead.

Maybe your sister would be smarter than me, I say to this memory.

—

Madam Lee is pleased the next day. At breakfast, she shows off my stained sheets to the rest of the girls. I pray no one will notice that the shade of my lost blood is the same as the rouge I use for my lips.

Said you were everything he hoped for, she purrs to me. I knew you would not let me down. Peony, my pride. The tong will be very happy indeed.

Yes, Madam, I say, thinking of the boy's tears on my face, the pliancy of his thighs, his little sister. Thank you, Madam.

The girls are jealous of me that day. During my laundry shift, I look up to find their eyes watching me, mouths cursing behind pink-white hands. I look down and feign concentration on the shirt I am ironing.

How did you do? Swallow asks.

It was easier than I thought, I tell her.

Swallow laughs at my simple answer, then tries to hide it. I see some of the girls look up and throw us hateful glances. Swan is one of them.

Madam Lee called me her pride. What did that make the girls who had been taking customers all this time? I give Swan an apologetic smile, but she looks away, pretending as if she did not see it.

But it feels good to have made Swallow laugh. It feels good that we are sharing this sliver of sameness. For the first time, it feels like I might have a friend here.

That night, Madam Lee holds me back again as the girls line up one by one. The customer from last night is coming back, she says, her smile tighter this time. The tong would like me to gift you to him again, free of charge.

I wish she would not do this in front of the other girls. One of them whistles through her teeth. Swallow puts out a hand to shush her.

When the boy comes, he is straddled by his two half brothers again. It was that good, they tell Madam Lee. Our boy wants another go!

Now that I think about it, one of them says, leering at me, I might want a go with this one, too. If she is as good as Mule says she is.

If you take me, I say, not looking into his face, who will your brother have? He will not be with a girl who has been with a white man, have you forgotten?

The half brother is livid. He steps forward and grabs my arm, fingers screwing into my bone.

What did you say to me, Chinese whore?

A snap, then a yelp. One of our guards has hit him in the face. The half brother is on the floor, holding a palm to the side of his head.

Apologies, sir, Madam Lee says, but she is not sorry at all. Only paying customers can touch the merchandise.

The half brother spits on the floor. The other half brother helps him up. They push the boy forward, cursing.

You will get yours, they tell me. Do not think we will forget.

⬤

I told them I did it, the boy says when we are in my room. And they told me I should come back if it was as good as I said it was. I said I would. But really, I think I just want to talk to you.

His name is Samuel, which is where Mule comes from. He is eighteen, already a man by years. His father is a powerful banker, one who helps the tong divert and hide profits from their illegal activities, including this one. He does not know if he will be able to see his mother and sister again.

Can I ask, he says, tentative, who you were before this? Where are you from? Where is your family?

I want to trust him, but I also remember how the trust of a stranger led me here. Instead, I tell him about the ocean, the way the water thrummed and roared, and about the lilt of the seagulls as they floated overhead. His mouth waters with my stories. He has never eaten fish from that side of the world before. I tell him they taste like the ocean's heart, if it has one.

What does it feel like to have a white father and Chinese mother? I ask him in return. After what I have seen in this brothel, I cannot imagine a white man being kind to a Chinese woman.

I do not really know, he says, looking at his hands. I was so young when my father brought me here. I do not even remember what my mother looks like.

And your stepmother?

She hates me, he says. Calls me a stain, the filth of the Orient. I call her a yellow-haired demon, one with ice in her eyes. I just wish I could say it to her face.

You must hate it very much, I offer.

He nods. I want to leave, he says, a boyishness lighting up his eyes. You ever heard of Idaho? That is where a bunch of Chinese men are going. They need men to work the mines there. I think I could do that. I could work in a mine, show everyone how much of a man I can be.

Idaho? I repeat.

It is to the east. Well, just a little east. Ever heard of Boise? It is supposed to be a hub of Chinese. They call it the Wild West. A place where you can be anybody.

I-da-ho. If I sound it out as Chinese, it means "to love a big monkey." The thought makes me laugh.

Sounds good, right? Samuel says, watching me. There are groups leaving all the time. I think I am going to join one of them soon. Anywhere must be better than here.

But you have money, food, a home here, I say. Why would you give that all up to go work in mines?

You have the same, he says, gesturing to the room. But are you telling me you want to stay here?

———

After Samuel leaves, I lie in my bed, listening to Iris hum as she takes the combs out of her hair. She has had a string of good nights and Madam Lee will be sure to praise her the next day.

I cannot stop thinking about what Samuel said. Once he leaves for Idaho, what will become of me? Will I have to start taking more customers to make up for the money Madam Lee could have received if I were not a gift? It does not matter. My time here is limited. One day, I will no longer be desirable to anyone, and when that day comes, I will be out on the streets, begging, and then I will be dying.

Lin Daiyu sleeps inside me. Every so often, a small cough escapes from her, which I feel against my lowest rib bones. The same sickness that followed her through childhood seems to exist here with her now. Rest, I tell her. I do not need for her to wake to know that neither of us can stay here.

5

Samuel visits nightly. It is the only way he can get his half brothers to leave him alone. Even his father is somewhat proud, he tells me. It costs nothing for him to have his son become a man.

The Hip Yee tong is very grateful to your father for his generosity, Madam Lee tells him every night before handing me over. Still, I watch her smile thin with each exchange.

Samuel's visits mean that Madam Lee cannot sell me to any other customer. I am the only girl in the brothel who does not make money, yet as the tong's gift, I am also the most protected. The other girls, with the exception of Pearl and Swallow, have stopped talking to me. Even Swan, who was not unkind to me—but did she like anybody?—will not look at me. To them, I have managed to somehow become the tong's favorite girl without doing any real work.

It must not be very good, one of the girls announces during laundry. Iris says you can barely hear anything when he is in there. What does she do, put him to sleep?

Do not listen to them, Swallow tells me. We have become closer in our isolation from the others. In many ways, I think she is the only one who can understand. I begin looking forward to the mornings when we can hover over the laundry, our whispers like netting holding us together.

How can you stand it? I catch the narrowed eyes of a few girls ringing water out of pants.

I have been here since I was six, she says. Her head is bent down, brow pinched as she focuses on the hot iron in her hands. You learn early on how to stand things.

This is the first piece of information Swallow has offered about her life before the brothel. It surprises me, but I do not let her know. Six. It makes sense, then, why she does not seem to be afraid of Madam Lee and why Madam Lee, in turn, treats her differently from the rest of us. Swallow is not just good at her job—she was raised for it.

That evening, when the girls line up for Madam Lee's check, I think I see it: There is a delicate understanding between Swallow and the madam, one none of us would ever know to pay attention to. It is something I have seen before from my own mother: how she always knew, even before I did, what I was going to do. There was fondness, yes, but also a supreme knowledge in the thing you created. To Madam Lee, Swallow was as good as a daughter.

�----

Pearl is in Swan's usual spot as we work on laundry. I look around— Swan is nowhere to be seen.

She has not had a customer for almost ten days now, Swallow says when she notices me searching. Did you think Madam Lee would let her stay, at her age?

I hang my head. Swan is gone, and in the brothel, it will be as if she was never here. In the morning, a new girl will be moved to her bed. First Jade, now Swan. Who was next? Would it be me, once Samuel's guaranteed patronage was gone?

It is quiet in the laundry room that day. The girls speak softly; they do not gossip. No one has the heart for it. Swan's absence is another reminder to us all: You are not safe here.

�----

You could come with me to Idaho, Samuel says when I tell him of Swan and the cribs. Leave this place behind. They cannot hurt you if they do not have you.

It had crossed my mind. But a greater desire overshadowed the promise of Idaho: the three-bay house facing the sea, my grandmother, and me. Finding my parents. I have to get back home.

Can I get to China from there? I ask him. Is there a port like there is here?

Why? he asks, laughing. Are you trying to go?

I cannot stay here, I tell him.

He regards me, an unfamiliar expression on his face. Sure, he says finally. Sure, you can get to China from there.

All right, I say, a fragile happiness arising. I will have to disguise myself as a man. I will need new papers.

I can take care of all of that, he says. Give me two weeks and we will go. It will be nice to be together. I can protect you.

—

In San Francisco, it rains all the time. Never big storms, but light mists that hang in the air long after the rain has stopped. Tonight, after Samuel leaves, it rains again, but this time the rain is hard and fast, flaying my window in an urgent staccato.

It rains well into the morning and afternoon. The girls do not like it, say it makes their heads hurt and their hair wild. They are glad to be inside on days like these. I keep my head down and do my work, but my heart is full of the rain and my grandmother.

—

In the late afternoon, Madam Lee pulls me out of laundry work and leads me to her office.

Your boy's father is happy, she says, which means the tong is very happy. So I want to thank you, Peony.

I should be the one thanking you, I return.

She finds this funny and laughs, but her eyes remain hard. Such a good girl, she says in the same sweet tone she used when we last spoke. I know that whatever is coming next will not be good.

You must have noticed that Swan is no longer with us, she continues.

I did, I say.

I sent her away, she says. She mimes a pout. Such a shame, really. If only she could control her big mouth.

Had it been her big mouth? Or had it been her maturing face? I look down at my shoes. The reason does not matter, only what Madam Lee says.

The thing is, she says, bending down, her nose close to my face, Swan left behind some very wealthy customers. And here I think to myself, is it fair that one of my ripest girls should be wasted on one half-Chinese runt? All those men with deep pockets—would you like to know what they taste like, too?

But I am a gift from the tong to one man only, I say. If I sleep with other men, I am no longer his. Madam, I add.

She did not expect to hear this from me. The visage slips, and I see for the first time Madam Lee's real face, not the one she puts on to talk to customers, not even the one she uses to talk to us. This face is one that is expressionless, that cares only for business and capital and power. These are the things that make her face cruel.

You are dumber than I thought, she says. Understand what I am saying: I have men lining up for one night with you. They ask me every time they visit, and every time, I have to say, No, sir, that one is not for sale. Do you know how much money they are offering me? You do not, because you do not know what it means to be in my position. Here is what you will do: When you are not with that boy, you will begin taking other customers. You will say nothing to him.

And if the tong finds out? I ask.

She slaps me then, snapping my head to one side. I do not think that will be a problem, she says. Then, just as quickly as it left, her mask returns. Look at you, dear girl. Ever since you took your first, you have been looking lovelier. Your cheeks are redder, your hair has more shine. Can you blame the men for wanting you?

There is nothing more for me to say. There was never anything for me to say. This had been Madam Lee's plan all along—to appease the tong while also pocketing extra money for herself at my expense. I rise to leave, my cheek stinging from the force of her hand.

Peony, Madam Lee calls before I close the door, her voice no longer feigning sweetness, tonight will be your last with only that boy. Tomorrow, you will open yourself to the world.

—

The yellow-haired woman, Samuel's stepmother, fed him sour mutton for breakfast. He tells me he spent the entire afternoon vomiting as the two half brothers laughed, throwing punches at his stomach. Now he sits on my bed, neck red and eyes glazed over, breath reeking of rawhide.

It has to be tomorrow, I tell him. I have hardly listened to what he has been saying, thinking instead of my conversation with Madam Lee. We must depart for Idaho tomorrow.

Samuel stops, gazing at me with astonishment. I tell him what Madam Lee told me, how tomorrow, if I am still here, my body will be torn apart by the worst kinds of men. I can see his eyes grow red at the thought. He is thinking of his little sister.

Is there a group we can leave with? I ask.

There always is, he says. I can find one for us and we can join them. That is not the hard part. The hard part is getting identification papers in such a short time.

I tell him that is not the only hard part. Security at Madam Lee's is tight. Guards wait at the front door surveying each customer who walks in and out. A man cannot enter the brothel as one and leave as two.

All right, Samuel says, sitting down. What about during the day?

During the day is even harder. I explain to him that the laundry is a tight operation—one girl missing will offset the entire thing. If I do not show up to work, Madam Lee will immediately know.

We sit, thinking in silence. Iris has a new customer tonight, a drunk one by the sound of it. All we need is a moment when the guards are not looking, a moment when I can squeeze through the open door. I am small enough. I can run. I will run as fast as I need to in order to never return to this life.

Suddenly, Samuel springs off the bed. I got it, he says, dancing around. I got it.

He explains it to me then, his plan. I am not sure if it is a good plan, but I agree to do it. If we pull it off, I will owe you my life, I tell him.

Peony, he says.

No, I think. *Daiyu.*

Good.

Begin.

6

I have something to tell you, I say to Swallow.

The next morning, we are back in the laundry room, Swallow and me and the other girls. The brothel had a busy night. Many of the girls rock where they stand, having only sipped a few hours of sleep before the morning's work began. They cannot hide their widemouthed yawns. Pearl rubs her eyes with the insides of her wrists. It is not playing around today but staring ahead, her eyes unfocused. Even Swallow has violet wells under her eyes.

Something to tell me, she repeats slowly, her eyes fixed on the shirt in her hands. What could it be? You are not thinking of running away, are you?

I did not expect for her to guess it. But if she has guessed it, I think, then surely it means that she wants to do the same?

I am, I tell her.

For a moment, I think she does not hear me. She bends over the shirt, smoothing it out on the table. A column of black hair falls in front of her face. She tucks it behind her left ear.

How?

I want to tell you, I say. But I can only tell you if you promise to come with me.

She looks up at me then, smiling. It is sad and knowing, like she has been waiting to hear me ask since the day I arrived.

You know I cannot do that, Peony.

No, I say. I do not know that. No one deserves to stay here like this.

I do, she says.

Swallow is my friend or perhaps something closer. In the early hours of morning as I lay in bed listening to vendors rolling out their tarps and ladles scraping hot woks, I imagined what it would be like if we could go away together. We would take care of each other, find a new way to survive. I could teach her calligraphy and we would make a living doing that. Or we could start our own laundry business. Everyone needed laundry, no matter where they lived.

But now, the dream is cracking. Swallow's calm *no* is making me angry. I feel something ugly rise up from a dark place and hurtle toward my mouth.

You think you will be young and beautiful forever, I hiss. Below, my iron exhales with steam. I glance around and meet Pearl's eyes. I do not know how long she has been watching us. But that does not matter to me now. With each day that passes, I tell Swallow, you are fading. One day, men will not even look at you. What then? You will be in the cribs or out on the street, and then you will die!

I do not mean to say such things. Or perhaps I do. All I know is that I need her to come with me.

Do you think Madam Lee will be the one running this place forever? she asks. The shirt in her hands is smooth now, but she keeps pressing and gliding her palm across.

I pause. Truthfully, I had not given any thought to Madam Lee or the future of the brothel. In my mind, it would always exist, just as Madam Lee would always exist. But at Swallow's question, I realize how shortsighted I have been. Madam Lee will expire one day, just like the girls she tosses out onto the street. And then what? The brothel would have to go on—there were the tong and benefactors and other crooked people who would see to that. This was the way the world worked.

I know what the girls say about me, Swallow says. That I came here willingly. That I walked right up to Madam Lee and asked to be a whore. Is that what you think, too?

She looks at me then, her eyes like wet stones.

I did once, I say.

Do you want to know the truth? she says. My father brought me here. I had three older brothers and we did not have enough food to eat. He dragged me from our home, all the way to Madam Lee's front steps. He threw me at her feet, telling her he would take whatever she could spare. She gave him two hundred dollars. I watched him leave with the money in his hand. He did not even look back at me.

I say nothing, remembering Bai He and the girls in my village who went to the city with their parents and never returned.

Three brothers, Swallow says bitterly. Three brothers, and putting food in their mouths was more important than me.

It is the anger still holding me. It is the anger that will not let me meet her gaze.

The tong wants me to start training to become madam in a few months, she says finally. They want Madam Lee to head up a new brothel across the city.

And what did you say? I ask, knowing the answer.

I said I would.

A shriek. Both of us start. One of the girls has burned her hand. She rushes to the sink and runs it under the faucet. I am looking at the girl's hand, shiny and red. I am looking, but I am not seeing.

So you would keep this place of torture alive, I say.

These places will always be alive, she says. But at least here, as the madam, I can do so much more. I can do more for these girls in here than out there.

Liar!

I am trying to keep my voice low, but I do a poor job of it. I once thought that Swallow was better than the rest of us. Better than Madam Lee, better than the girls who clawed and bit each other for customers. She was above it all. Only now I see how foolish I had been to trust her. She is nothing but another Madam Lee, and one day she will have a whole harem of girls working for her, dying for her. I revisit the character for her name 燕. There is the fire, yes, but I have been looking at it all wrong. There is a reason the fire lies below the other characters, below mouth and north and twenty. The fire is there because it is greedy and seeks to burn everything above it. It is what Swallow is: consumptive and destructive.

I pity you, I tell her.

Yes, pity me, she says, and she returns to the shirt, rubbing it between her fingers. I accepted long ago that this would be my fate. If I were to run away with you, what could I do? How do I contribute? This life is all I have ever known, Peony. I know that is not your real name. Swallow is not my real name, either. Except that it is. It is the name that was given to me when I came. For you, there was a you before this and there will be a you after this. For you, leaving is easy. Leaving is an escape. For me, it is the opposite. Can you understand?

I cannot, not now. She is nothing more than a coward, too trapped by her circumstance to see outside of it. I want to tell her that she is so much more than this brothel, that she should be a Swallow who is safe and happy and free. But the girl in front of me is not that kind of woman. She does not believe she is that kind of woman.

I understand, I tell her instead. The anger is fading now, replaced by mourning. You will not say anything to Madam Lee or the others?

That I can promise you, she says. This is not your home. You do not belong here. You have to keep going, Peony. I know you can keep going.

I want, in that moment, to cry. It bubbles in me the way hot water does in the kettle before it shrieks. But I bury it. If I do manage to escape tonight, if I am far away from this place, never to return again, if I can begin to forget who Madam Lee and her girls and the men are, then, only then, will I allow myself to cry.

7

After the laundry is finished, I find myself in my room, sitting on the bed, hardly able to breathe.

The plan. I have to remember the plan.

So many things could go wrong. And the consequences are real, deadly. Madam Lee would throw me out onto the streets. Or she would even kill me herself. Perhaps she would feed me to the feral dogs in the alleyway behind the brothel, the ones who yipped and moaned long into the night, their cries no different from the ones that snaked out from the closed doors around mine.

I run it over and over again in my head. The scenarios that could occur. If this happened, then what? If that happened, what would I do next? There can be no room for mistakes.

You know, Samuel had said the night before, that what happens also depends on our luck, right?

There is no such thing as luck, I told him. Luck is just readiness that meets opportunity.

It was something I learned from Master Wang. Stop focusing on luck, he had said. Start focusing on how to create it for yourself. You think a calligraphy master relies on luck? What happens on the paper is practice meeting the open invitation of the page.

Practice, he said. Practice will make you calm, and through the calmness, make your energy full and your spirit complete.

Practice, I think to myself now. I sit down at my vanity. The plan, the plan, the plan. There is no other option. It has to work. I walk my-self through every second of the plan, open every closed door, clear out all the shelves. Again. Again. Against the browned wood, I trace a boar under a roof. Roof: a quick dot at the top, then the strong horizontal cap. Boar: the hooked vertical line, the many shorter lines that feather off from it. This is what we call home 家.

I trace this character and all its strokes into the wood over and over again, until this turns into practice, too, until I am back in the calligraphy school in Zhifu and not in a brothel in San Francisco. The wood hums against my finger. My arm whips and sweeps, a wing in mid-flight.

If it could have been like this, always like this, I would have been happy.

Master Wang was right: Practice does make me calm. In my trac-ing, I find my mind wandering further away from those visions of fail-ure and despair, and instead remembering, with each stroke, with each ridge of wood that passes under my finger, the sensation of knowing. Of being certain. It has been so long since I have been certain. What security and peace could certainty bring? This, I realize, is what I long for most—the safety in knowing. And right now, I know very little, if anything at all.

Practice. Yes, Master Wang, I think as my arm moves independent of my body. I have not had much opportunity so far, but I am at least practicing.

———

I do my makeup simple tonight. If we escape, I do not want too many people looking at me. Instead, it needs to be something I can quickly wipe off my face. A swipe of rouge on my lips, light powder on my face. Instead of blotting out my eyebrows and painting new ones on, I use a charcoal pencil to outline them—something I can scrub off with tissue.

Tonight, I tell the hairdresser that Madam Lee wants me to do my own hair. I pull it back and secure it with a fake jade comb. Something to stay out of my face when I run.

When I look at myself in the mirror, I see for the first time how much I have changed from what I remember. No longer a little girl, and not a woman, but something in between. There is a newness in me, a fight in my eyes. I could outwit a tiger if I needed to. I could ride on the back of an eagle and make him lose the way home. I wonder if that is Lin Daiyu looking out at me from within, or if it really is me after all.

Outside my door, one of the girls laughs. It startles me, and the fight in my eyes vanishes. I blink once, twice, and when I look at my reflection again, I am a demure lamb, a pure kitten. I am whatever they want me to be, just as Swallow said, and perhaps that will be my greatest weapon.

⸺

The girls are already lined up when I come down. Madam Lee is walking along the line, inspecting each one of them. Swallow is somewhere in the middle, but she is not looking at me.

Pearl, Madam Lee says, using her fan to tap the girl's thigh. Are we feeding you too much pork?

No, Madam, Pearl squeaks, terrified. She tries to rearrange her dress.

Madam Lee pokes the mound of Pearl's belly, the tip of her fingernail disappearing. I think we might be, she says. You will stop eating lunch and dinner, only breakfast. What man wants to sleep with a slovenly pig, do you agree?

Pearl's chest rises and falls so fast it looks like she is trying to get rid of the air in her body. Do not cry, do not cry, I will her in my head. Madam Lee moves on to the next girl, her eyes scanning. The girl trembles, but Madam Lee is satisfied. Next is Cloud, a tall girl with one gray-blue eye, the other black-brown.

Cloud, Madam Lee says, and already the girl shrinks. The customer yesterday told me a funny story. He said that you refused one of his requests. Do you know what I am speaking of?

The girl stares at the floor, trembling.

Cloud, Madam Lee says again. And then she slaps her. The sound echoes around the room, a crack that splits us all in half. No one dares to move. No one except Cloud, who lets out a painful wail, the tears flowing freely now.

Pathetic girl, Madam Lee sneers. You do not deserve to work here. Do you think you run the show? When you disobey a customer, you disobey me.

She waves. The guards emerge. Cloud starts howling when she sees them.

Please, Madam, I will do better, I will do anything they want, please just let me stay.

But the guards are already dragging her away through the laundry room to the back door. We hear her cries growing more distant, until something slams and all is quiet.

Madam Lee moves down the line again. Let that be a lesson to all you girls, she says. You disobey a customer, you disobey me.

The next few girls get off easy—one of them has painted her eyes wrong, another is wearing a hairstyle that makes her look like a peasant's daughter. These are easy fixes, and Madam Lee makes them promise to never do it again before moving on. The last girl she stops at is Swallow.

We all hold our breaths. Swallow is near-impeccable—Madam Lee has never before stopped to critique her. It seems this is a surprise to Swallow as well, because she glances up before quickly looking back down.

Swallow, my dear, Madam Lee croons. My honest and obedient and hardworking Swallow. Is there anything you would like to tell me?

Swallow says nothing. She shakes her head.

Nothing about anything you may have heard, Madam Lee asks again, about someone who may be trying to leave our home?

I do not know anything, Madam, Swallow says. Her voice is quiet but firm. Who would want to leave this lovely home?

Madam Lee does not move on. She stays with Swallow, looking at her, smiling. I recognize the smile—it is Jasper's. The same smile he gave me before sliding the lid shut.

But before she can say anything, the door of the brothel bursts open. Three bodies crash inside. The girls break the line and dart in all directions, their silk dresses slipping through the air like colorful eels. The two guards disperse—one rushing toward the girls, the other leaping forward to protect Madam Lee.

I catch a flash of black hair mixed with yellow. It is Samuel and his two half brothers, the three of them entangled like a knot of snakes.

Stop them, Madam Lee screeches.

The guards rush forward to pull the three men apart. Samuel is panting. Dark liquid trails out of his nose. I wonder if he is hurt, but then he glances at me and nods. This is my signal. I move from my spot near the stairs, closer to the middle of the room. No one looks at me.

How dare you, Madam Lee pants. How dare you behave this way at my place of business?

We came here for the girl, says one of the half brothers.

Girl, Madam Lee repeats. What girl?

That girl, the other half brother says, jabbing his finger in my direction.

The room falls silent then, a whisk of heads as everyone turns to stare at me. I can feel Swallow's eyes against my skin.

Her? Madam Lee says, incredulous. I have special instructions from my bosses that she is to go to your brother, you know this. Why not choose any other girl, gentlemen? I can give you four, five, whatever satisfies your appetites!

Is that so, the first half brother says, jerking away from the guard holding him. Then why did Mule tell us you are loaning her out to other men starting tonight?

Madam Lee gapes at them. Now there is no turning back, I think. The plan really has to work. Anything less will result in her wrath, and my death.

All day he has been boasting about how good she is in bed, the other half brother says. His voice is different from that of his brother—lower, more gravelly. Something like a wolf.

We want to see for ourselves, the first half brother says. We want to see if she is really as good as he says she is. If it is true: that she can turn a man inside out.

The girls, their mouths open in horror, turn to stare at Madam Lee. In the past, the policy was clear: If a customer destroyed property or disrespected the madam in any way, they would be banned for life. These two men were not far from doing both.

Madam Lee says nothing for a long time. Then she waves her hand and the guards stand back.

You have broken into my home and disturbed the peace, she says. You have scared my girls. And now you want to do business with me. Can you see how this does not look good for you, gentlemen?

Maybe, the second half brother says. But I wonder how happy your bosses would be to learn that you are running your own little business on the side and disobeying their orders. What is stopping us from walking there right now and telling them? I imagine they will throw you out into the street, or slit your throat, or cut those jewels off your fingers. He spits on the ground at her feet. Madam, he says, smirking. You should be so lucky.

Madam Lee does not speak. I can see that she is turning his words over in her head. I wonder if she will do it—if her reason will best her pride.

Very well, she says finally. The heat in the room dissipates. From now on, she is yours whenever you like. I thank you for your discretion, gentlemen. Our little secret.

Hold on, hold on, the first half brother says. We should inspect the merchandise before we purchase.

That is right, the second half brother says, rubbing his hands. All these whores look the same. We want to see her up close.

Madam Lee turns to me. She does not have to say anything, because I already know what to do. I walk toward the two half brothers and Samuel, every eye in the room emblazoned on my back. With each step, I will myself to keep going. Remember how my feet work, remember how to breathe. The plan. I have to stick to the plan.

And then I am standing in front of them.

I can see how slick their lips are. If I look, really look, I can see some hint of Samuel in there, too. They stare at me, both of them starving.

So, the first half brother says.

Ah, the second half brother says.

I begin. The spin that I have practiced, the secretive smile and downcast eyes (shaded with copper and root), the neck exposed. All as I have practiced. I spin, and I can hear the two half brothers panting now. I spin and catch Madam Lee's eye—she is bigger than ever, her cheeks rosy from the agitation, but she is pleased—I spin again and catch Pearl's eye—she is full of awe, her mouth hanging open—I spin again and try to catch Swallow's eye—she is not looking at me but at the floor, and then at the guards, and then at the floor again—and finally I spin one last time, catching Samuel's eye, and this is the eye I have been waiting for all along.

I nod.

You—cannot—have—her!

Samuel bursts to life, shoving the first half brother with everything in his small, taut body. Years of frustration and rage and sadness and isolation, and it is all here now as he winds up his body and shoots forward. The force sends the first half brother flying into the group of girls huddled at the far end of the room. He lands on top of them, pinning two to the ground. The guards rush to free them.

But Samuel is not finished. He shoves the second half brother, perhaps stronger this time, filled with even more rage and desperation. This time, the second half brother lands on one of the guards.

Now!

This is my cue. Samuel grabs my hand and I feel myself being jerked backward. Madam Lee snaps her head and lunges for us, her mouth a horrible O. The half brothers are scrambling up, disentangling themselves from the girls, and the guards, dumb with surprise and without a proper command from Madam Lee, are too late.

What no one, not Madam Lee, not the guards, not any of the girls, realized is that the door was opened when the three men crashed through, but it was never closed. Except me and Samuel. This is the way we have planned it. This is the way we will win.

Samuel's hand on mine is the only thing I know, the only thing I can follow. He pulls me out the door—I do not know if my feet even touch the ground—and then we are out, out from the brothel, out from the horror, the girls' shrieks trailing behind me, Madam Lee's livid roar splintering every bone in the city.

The guards explode from the brothel to the sound of Madam Lee's orders (Get them! Get them!) and chase after us. Something has taken over that is not me, something allows my feet to match the pace of Samuel's, lets my arms pump as hard as his. We are running—flying—down the street, through the red and yellow lights of the businesses around us, through the sound of music and laughter and the clanging of pots and pans, the incessant drumming, and somewhere I think I hear mahjong tiles being shuffled, the pieces gliding over one another. Our bodies are guided by a force beyond just ourselves. I turn my head to see the guards trying to match our speed, but they are slowing and we are speeding up. We have magic on our side.

Around us, people dart out of the way in too-late surprise. Samuel knows the route, knows where he is taking me. We take sharp turns into alleyways, emerge on unfamiliar streets, double back, turn, turn, turn. I have never been on the streets of San Francisco before, and what I did not account for is just how steep the hills are. My legs burn, thighs soft, nothing more than pulverized meat, and the flesh where my shoulder meets my chest protests as my arms pull back and forward, back and forward. But we do not stop. We keep running. We run until we are a desert, until our lungs are hot sand and a snake writhes in my throat.

And then it is just us, and we are alone with our breaths, which are no more than rasps. Samuel presses a finger to his mouth, eyes wide.

We listen. For footsteps, yells, the sound of bodies slamming against the earth. But there is nothing. Still, we do not move. We have to make sure. One minute, then five, then ten. Nothing. Another minute, another five, another ten.

Again, nothing.

Samuel looks at me then, and he has a grin on his face, the happiest he has ever looked in front of me. I see relief settle into his body, all the wretched parts of him releasing.

We are free.

I grin back. And then I do as I have promised. I allow myself to cry.

8

Samuel pulls out a loose stone from the wall behind me. I watch as his hand disappears and returns with a parcel. He places it in my arms.

Put these on, he says.

This part of the plan was my idea. They would never take a Chinese girl to Idaho. But what was another Chinese boy? Another body in the mines.

I begin to unbutton my dress. How eager I am to rid myself of this wretched uniform. But something stops me. Looking up, I realize there are two glints in the night, the whites of Samuel's eyes as they follow me.

Turn around, I say. I do not think I am being mean.

The whites slide away. Too slowly, I notice. But now is not the time. I can deal with that later.

I finish with the buttons of my dress and inch it down my body, the fabric catching on the parts where sweat has pooled and hardened into a sticky brine. The cool night breeze of the city stings against my skin. I check to see that the white glints have not returned—they have not.

In place of my brothel garments, I put on what Samuel brought: black pants, black chang shan, black cloth shoes. It feels good to be in clothes that hide my body again, like I am swimming into the ocean and no one, not Madam Lee, not Jasper, can ever reach me.

You can turn around, I tell Samuel.

I take out the last thing in the parcel, a pair of scissors, and I hand them to him.

I know it is dark, I say, kneeling down and removing the comb from my hair. Just do the best you can.

A deep breath from him. Then, for the third time in my life, I hear the sharp slice as the scissors make their first cut somewhere around my cheek. A piece of softness falls down my body; I can hear it as it passes by. Another slice. My head already feels lighter. Everything feels lighter without the weight of the brothel on me. The slices keep going and I stop counting, instead imagining which girl Madam Lee will have given my room to. My bet is on Pearl.

She knew, I say to Samuel as he cuts. Madam Lee—she knew someone was trying to escape. She asked Swallow about it. How do you think she knew?

The walls are not thick, Samuel replies. He is making sure the cut is even.

Still, I murmur. What will happen to them? I am thinking of Swallow, whether she will tell Madam Lee the truth. Maybe she would. She was more ambitious than I knew.

The tong that owns your brothel will be angry, Samuel says. If they find out that Madam Lee was going behind their back, they will likely punish her.

She said they paid a hefty price for me, I tell him.

Then they may send someone to get you back.

I say nothing. This is one part of the plan I did not think about. For me, the brothel began and ended with that building. But as the words leave Samuel's mouth, I know that being followed is a certainty. Would it be Jasper?

When will it end? I murmur.

Samuel says nothing. He does not have the heart to tell me that this is the way it must be.

When he is finished, Samuel clears his throat. I reach behind and rub my neck, feeling very much as I did when my grandmother cut my hair for that first time before sending me off to Zhifu. The exposed skin is taut and full of life. I grasp at the spiky edges of my hair. He cut it shorter than I wanted.

Thank you, I tell him. Now what?

Not far from here, there is an inn where three Chinese men wait for him, ready to leave for Boise in the morning. They do not know you are coming, he tells me, looking down. They think it is only me. It is the best I could do with such short notice. But we will figure something out.

It was the best you could do, I reassure him, trying not to sound worried.

I almost forgot, he says, reaching in his pocket. From it, he draws out my new identification paper. Madam Lee had forged papers made for all her girls, but without her protection, I would never be Peony again.

How did you get it so quickly? I ask.

I went to a rival tong, he says proudly. I told them I would give them information about the Hip Yee tong and who was helping them funnel their money, in exchange for two identification papers. It was not a hard decision for them.

Samuel, I say, imagining this thin stick of a boy. They could have kidnapped or killed you.

But they did not, he says. And now we have a way to leave. Light a match, will you?

I do as he asks, holding the flame over the paper. Across the top reads UNITED STATES OF AMERICA—certificate of residence. Underneath, the details of the person I am to become, Jacob Li, along with a picture of my new identity. In the bottom left corner is a photo of a young boy. We look nothing alike, I think.

I feel a sudden sharpening then, as if everything before was told through the same fog that lurked over the city. It is clearer than ever that I am no longer in a room in Zhifu, no longer held in a coal bucket, no longer captive in the brothel. Here, I am finally free, but with that freedom comes a new decree: to stay free, you must stay hidden. How quickly I must slip into this new identity, I think. No time to air Daiyu out.

I blow out the match, then reach my hand out to take the paper, but

Samuel folds it and puts it in his pocket. I will hold on to the papers for now, he says. For us both.

———

I do not know where in the city we are, but I do know that we are far away from the brothel, getting farther away from the ocean. We arrive at an inn, where the innkeeper asks to see our papers before we say a word. Samuel makes a great show of taking them out, handing them over with pompous assurance, but I am nervous. The boy in the picture does not look like me, but he is young enough to have been me at one point. The innkeeper cannot tell the difference. He nods and motions us upstairs. I can tell he does not enjoy our company.

We climb to the fourth floor, then walk to the second door on the left. Samuel opens it and beckons me inside.

Three men, like he promised. All Chinese, like he promised. They are sitting on the floor, and when I enter, they start, confused. There is a stripped cot in the corner and next to it, a table with a jug of water. On the floor, the men have laid out the blankets and sheets from the bed. Three packs sit by the window.

You are late, one of the men says. He looks older, with graying hair. And you brought someone?

Everyone, Samuel says, this is—

Jacob, I say quickly, remembering my identification paper. The name is Jacob Li.

Hm, the gray-haired man says. I understand that he is in charge here. Who are you, Jacob?

Jacob, Samuel says lightly, is my friend. He heard about our journey to Boise and he wants to come with us.

Oh, the gray-haired man says, coming closer. We do not have any more room for a fifth person.

Look at him, Samuel says, he is small.

I can help, I say, keeping my voice low and gruff, just the way I practiced it. I can do whatever you need me to do.

The gray-haired man snorts. He is getting closer to me now. I want to back away, but the door is behind me. You have some dirt on your eye Jacob, did you know that?

I pray that my face does not move, that my lips do not open in a dumb moment of panic. I rub the remnants of my eyeshadow off with the sleeve of my chang shan, hoping they have not connected it by now. The gray-haired man laughs again, then returns to where he sat when we entered.

It does not matter, he says. What is one more body? You two can sleep on the floor. There are not enough blankets for all of us, so you will just have to stay warm in the clothes you are wearing. Or, he says, and his eyes flash, maybe you can keep each other warm. You would like that, boy? I bet you would.

The other two men laugh at this. I realize that the gray-haired man is addressing Samuel. I expect him to retaliate in some way, but his cheeks are pink and all he does is nod. He motions to me, and I edge toward the corner of the room as far away from the three men as possible, very aware that all three are watching me, even when they are not.

In the night, I cannot sleep. My head is too filled with fear for what is to come. The snores from the three men rumble around the room. The hard, wooden floor insists against my hip bone. Samuel cannot sleep, either. I know, because I do not hear him move.

I think about the brothel. About Madam Lee's face as she saw what was happening, her rage and fear, yes fear, as Samuel pulled me out the door. The girls' panic as the half brothers landed on them, and the half brothers' curses. The one person who I did not see: Swallow. What was she doing in those last few moments before I disappeared?

If I ever return to San Francisco, perhaps Swallow will be in charge of the brothel, and perhaps she will no longer be called Swallow, but Madam. At least by then, I know that Peony will be a distant memory. The thought pleases me, and I allow myself to smile into the darkness. Somewhere within me, I think I can feel Lin Daiyu smiling, too.

⸺

We are up before the sun rises. The room is distorted with darkness, the three men fuzzed shapes as they slowly rise, moan, and stretch. Samuel is sitting with his elbows on his knees, watching me.

Did you sleep? he asks.

A little, I lie.

We funnel down the stairs. The inn is quiet, the innkeeper nowhere to be seen. Each man has a small bundle, but I have nothing, only the clothes Samuel gave me.

I have to remember to hunch when I walk, to make my steps heavier and spread my body out. My shoulders are spades, my arms, hammers. Every movement an assertion, every moment of stillness a punctuation.

All calligraphy, Master Wang once told me, leads back to the Dao, the heavenly nature in humans. We communicate the Dao by making good lines. As such, a perfect line will be the utmost achievement.

To make a good line: Move the tip of the brush at the middle of each stroke. This will prevent any wayward brush hairs from creating spikes along the line. A good line, whether thick or thin, communicates inner strength. It belongs fully to itself, leaving no room for weakness or disarray of spirit.

This is the kind of man I can pretend to be, I decide as I move with the other men. Someone strong and continuous and whole, not a nowhere girl like Daiyu.

I think it is working. Because the three other men do not look at me as we stand outside the inn. We are waiting for something. Samuel glances at me, shivering. In San Francisco, the mornings are cold no matter the season and the water in the air could be ice.

You will never survive in Idaho if you think this is cold, the gray-haired man tells Samuel. Toughen up, boy! Be a man.

I nudge Samuel, my way of telling him to ignore the gray-haired man. He pulls away from me. I see him clench his jaw to stop from shivering.

A cart arrives. The man driving it is white. He jumps off the front and stands beside the cart, inspecting us.

I thought you said four, he says to the gray-haired man. He is talking about me.

He is small, the gray-haired man says. He points to Samuel. He has money.

The driver walks over to Samuel, eyeing us both. One hundred, he says. Each.

Samuel laughs nervously. Sir, he says, that is double what the others are paying.

I said one hundred, the driver repeats. Or do you have problems with your ears, coolie?

Samuel sighs. He reaches into his pockets and pulls out a pouch. The driver eyes him intently. Next to him, I feel very small.

Good, that is good, boy, the driver says when Samuel hands him the money. All right, get on.

We climb onto the cart. I sit with my knees up to my chin, my bottom pressed into the wood. The driver climbs into the front seat and shouts Yah! at his horses. The cart moves forward, groaning with the weight of us.

That money was supposed to be for food and lodging for when we get to Boise, Samuel whispers to me.

I shrug even though his words bring panic, knowing that the gray-haired man is staring at us with narrowed eyes. He is calculating something. I jut out my chin, hoping it makes me look more manly. He does not look away.

Is he taking us all the way to Boise? I ask Samuel. I have no idea how far away it is.

Samuel laughs into his shirtsleeve. No, he is taking us to the train station.

———

Once, my grandmother told me, long before you were in this world, a British merchant built a long railroad outside the Xuanwu Gate in Beijing. He wanted to show the technology to the imperial court. But the government feared the train. They found it exceedingly special and strange in the utmost. And then they had it dismantled.

Before now, I have always imagined something between a snake and a dragon, a creature that could make itself fly across the world. As we come up to the railroad station, I can hear the rumbling, feel the earth vibrating in my bones. I know I am right—a train must be a beast, moving and alive.

The cart stops outside the ticketing station. The man ties his horses to a post and comes around to the back to give us our tickets.

When you get to Boise, he says, tell 'em Jordy sent you. They will take you to the right place.

We jump down from the cart one by one. It feels odd to be around people again and be so free. I am not beholden to anyone, I realize, for the first time in a long time. Here, white and Chinese faces mill about carrying parcels and luggage, darting and dodging as they make their way to the train. It reminds me of my first few days in Zhifu, stunned by the commotion and the sounds of so many voices. I feel like a child again.

We follow the gray-haired man to the ticket box, where someone inspects our papers, then our tickets, and ushers us through. And then I see it. The train. Not a snake, not a dragon, not something in between, but a large towering machine of black. It is shiny with the sun and breathing smoke. Beneath its massive wheels, I see the rails my grandmother told me about. I wonder how in the world someone could build such a thing.

Train in Chinese is "fire chariot." I think this is the largest fire I have ever seen.

———

Our compartment is at the very end of the train. Because I am the extra man, I have to share a bed. The three men do not ask but put their sacks on each of the bunks. Samuel and I look at each other.

Like I said, the gray-haired man says, you can keep each other warm. He and the two other men snicker, climbing into their bunks.

Well, Samuel says, watching me.

Well, I say, avoiding his gaze.

We sit on the bunk and we wait. The train vibrates at a frenetic frequency, its shudders itching the skin on my feet. *Chuh-chuh-chuh-chuh*, it breathes. Like it is panting and asking everyone on board to pant with it.

When the train starts, I grab Samuel before remembering that this is not what a man does. My entire world is moving again, just like it did when I was in the coal bucket on the ship, but this time, this time, I promise myself, I will not be trapped. This time, I am going to something better. I have to be.

Daiyu to Feng to Peony to Jacob Li. When will I be me again? And if I become me again, will I know who she is?

⟨⟩

That night, Samuel and I squeeze into our bunk. He tells me to take the inside because I am smaller. The gray-haired man takes the bunk above us, groaning as he lies down. The mattress sinks a little under his weight, and I want to prod it, make sure he is still there. We have all come a long way. I never even asked them where they were from.

You are lucky you are both small, boys, he says to us from above. If you were men, you could not fit.

I keep quiet.

Something warm on my waist. Samuel's hand. I feel him asking me, with that hand, if it is okay for him to be so close to me. We have not touched like this since the day he came to my room and climbed on top of me. He is asking, with his hand on the small of my back, whether or not I remember.

I reach behind and give his hand a squeeze. Then I set it back on his side and hope that is enough. Get some sleep now, I am telling him. Get some sleep now, I tell myself.

The first thing I do in Boise is look for the ocean.

For as long as I can remember, there has always been an ocean at my back, always the smell of salt in my hair. Whether in China or America, at least there would always be the same body of water. In that way, I like to think, I can never be too far from where I was.

But Boise does not have an ocean. There are no ports, no gulls floating in the sky, no wetness in the air. Most of the faces are white. Very few, I realize as we walk out of the station, look like mine. We are an anomaly here, shuffling together through the streets in our chang shan, one of the men's queues drawing the stare of a young boy with green eyes. He tugs at his mother's skirt and points. She looks at us and ushers him along, but not before drawing her lips into a tight pinch and wrinkling her nose.

I thought you said it would be easy to get to China from here, I whisper to Samuel.

It will be, he says.

Where are all the Chinese? I demand. You said there are a lot here.

There are, he says. Or, there were.

In Boise, there are many trees. In the August afternoon, the breeze feels delicious and cool. Autumn announces itself across the city, reds, oranges, and royal yellows coating the tops of the cottonwoods and maples. Everything feels more spread out, like we have all been given room to simply be. I can make it here, I think.

We arrive at an inn downtown, where groups of Chinese gather outside. Some are dressed in jackets and trousers, while others wear long chang shan like us. Many have kept their whip-like queues. I am struck by them—different from the men of my home, yet the same; flesh, bone, blood, all familiar, all so close to me. A great urge rises in me, to ask them to take me home, to speak to them in a language that is not English, to simply stand next to them and feel, for a moment, relief.

Inside, the innkeeper, who is also Chinese, welcomes us. The inn is attached to a Chinese temple, but where the temples in Zhifu were majestic with their curled-leaf roofs and precious tiles, this temple is just another unremarkable two-story log building.

Not what you were expecting? Samuel jokes, seeing my confusion. Then, more seriously, he explains that these kinds of temples can be found throughout Idaho and the greater west. Stories he heard from the Chinese who had returned from the region. You could call them temples, he says, or you could call them meeting places. You could even call them gambling houses. Out here, this is all we have. At least in these temples, no white man is allowed to step inside.

Where are the others? I ask.

The innkeeper pulls out a map for me, circling the towns and regions known to have temples. I take the map and put it in my breast pocket. Samuel says *all we have* and I remember that now, I am part of the *we*. I like knowing that these temples are peppered across the state, that even in a place so unfamiliar as this, there are small reminders of what home might feel like.

Samuel pays for our room with the money he has left. I make sure he asks for two beds. It is small, shabby, but it is the first time we have been alone in a while. The three other men pile into the room next to us, the floorboards creaking as their bodies disperse and settle. In the morning, we will meet with the man who will help us find work.

Well, Samuel says, sitting down on what I take will be his bed.

Well, I say, in my normal voice, not the low-pitched one I have created for myself.

I am safe. Finally, finally, after running and darting and hiding and dodging, I am safe. There is no Jasper here, no Madam Lee, no half brothers. I think about the character for flying 飛, its body a nest of wings, and stroke it into my thigh, brushing my finger back and forth, back and forth, each stroke growing bolder, happier, freer, until I imagine the character must be bigger than my thigh, bigger than the cot, bigger than even this room.

I still cannot be myself here, but that is all right. At least I can imagine being made of wings.

———

I dream of a forest. High trees, their branches an awning. The grass is just a little wet. I am barefoot.

I am not alone. My first thought is that Lin Daiyu is with me, but I feel heavy, and so she must still be inside me. Whoever it is, I cannot see them. But I feel them next to me and I hear them. I turn, but where they are is shrouded in a dense fog.

We are walking somewhere, me and this unseen stranger. Around us, the trills of birds, their songs not comforting, but eerie and taunting.

My companion stops. I keep going. They are saying something to me, shouting, but the shouting is muffled and all I hear is a roar in my ears like the ocean in Zhifu, like a blanket moving over my head, suffocating me.

———

In the night, I feel a pressure against my back. I jerk up, but something slides across my throat, a blade that is sharp and cold.

Stay quiet, says a whisper in my ear. Or I will tell everyone who you really are.

I know this voice. It belongs to the gray-haired man.

Thought I would not find out? he pants, breath sour. I knew something was different about you.

A shadow glides across the room. Samuel is here, too, I remember. Samuel, my kind savior, Samuel, the weeping boy who has helped me get this far.

Help, I call to him.

But he does not move. Instead, he sinks to the floor. My heart with him.

And then the gray-haired man is tearing down my pants. And then he is fumbling with his own. And then I feel something press against my buttocks, something soft and limp and lukewarm. Again and again, I feel his organ thrumming against me, pulpy and desperate. He cannot, I realize, do it.

The gray-haired man curses. Something else slides down my back then: a hand, the fingers cold. It drags down my skin until finally it shoves itself between my legs and I feel that same coldness enter me in the place where no one has ever touched, until now.

He is ragged against my shorn hair, dampening the back of my ear with his breath. Inside me, his dry fingers scrape at my walls, like he is trying to empty me of something that he wants to put inside himself. I think of his dirty nails, mud caked underneath, the square knuckles on each finger, and I feel everything. His nails will leave scars. Stop, I think. Stop, stop, stop.

Across from us, Samuel begins to cry.

This must be the thing that wakes her. The gray-haired man's fingers continue slamming into me, the pain now white. I could be scrubbed inside out. With each stab of his hand, I feel Lin Daiyu jostle inside me, until she is bigger than both of us, until she sits up and out of me, and is looking down at the bodies beneath her.

I wait for her to turn the knife on him and slit his throat. Or rip the fingers from his hands. Or do anything other than what she is doing, which is screaming Stop, stop, stop, just like me. Here the two of us are, both motherless, fatherless girls, one a ghost and the other not far from it, both believing so much of themselves but amounting to nothing in the end. Look at us, Lin Daiyu, I want to tell her between our cries. Perhaps we are no different after all.

When he finishes, and I do not know what *finishes* means because I am only watching the candlelight stretch across Samuel's frame, the gray-haired man rolls away, leaving a milky sludge on the mattress. I scramble out from his slack arms, pulling my pants back up over my waist. It feels strange to be standing. I am leaking out of my body.

Thanks, boy, he says to Samuel. He buttons his pants. Maybe now I will call you a man.

All I can see is Jasper, all I can feel is his silvery smile, how he would laugh if he could see me now, how the gray-haired man was no different from Madam Lee, who was no different from Jasper himself. How evil like this was all connected. The space between my legs feels emptied, useless. The gray-haired man leers as if to say, We should do this again. And then he leaves.

The figure crumpled against the wall lets out another sob.

You let him do this to me, I say. You did nothing to stop it. What would your sister say?

Samuel curls into himself and moans. I am crying, too.

You are no better than your demon half brothers, I say.

Floating above us is Lin Daiyu. Her tears explode when they touch Samuel's skin. Shame on you! she screams. May death find you quickly!

He already knew, Samuel says. He said he just wanted to come in here and speak with you. He said a real man would understand.

He was right, I spit. Before, you were good. Now you are nothing more than a man.

He recoils at this, and I am glad for it. The pain in my belly flares. The gray-haired man took the most precious part of me, something I did not want to give. That I was not ready to give. It was mine to begin with. Why could it not be mine forever, or for as long as I wanted?

You said you would owe your life to me if we escaped, Samuel whimpers.

Not like this, I say.

He does not raise his head to look. Just leave, he sobs. Leave if you hate me so.

The elation from my new freedom is long gone. I can no longer trust him, just as I should never have trusted anybody. I should have known better. I do know better.

Lin Daiyu descends from the ceiling and trickles back down my throat, both our tears disappearing with her. I slip into my shoes and square my shoulders, become Jacob Li again. I try not to think about the stinging in between my legs, how much I want to cry and never stop. Instead, I try to feel the certainty of Lin Daiyu's weight inside me. Before stepping outside, I shove my hand into Samuel's jacket pocket and take my identification paper. He does not move.

Outside, the hallway is quiet and black, but it does not suffocate me. For once, I am glad to see it. I step out into the darkness.

You are not alone, I repeat to myself.

You are not alone, Lin Daiyu confirms. Behind us, Samuel lets out a wretched wail.

I shut the door.

PART III

Pierce, Idaho

Spring 1885

1

The lady lies still in bed. She wants to sit up, but her maid urges her not to, telling her that doing so will strain her greatly. She knows it is better to listen, so she remains supine, gazing at the tapestry that tents over her bed. Above, cotton-white clouds, a field of reeds. The wind pulling everything sideways. In this tapestry sky, black cranes hang, their thin bodies reminding her of an aunt's painted eyebrows. She stares up, wondering when the dirt in her throat will fall away.

What began as whispers—that the man she loves is to marry someone else—grows into a strangling decree. Too loud, too loud, she thinks. Gone are the days when she believed she and the man could be together. There was always some prophecy, always one fate standing in the way. She knows better now. It was not to be.

With her back against the silken pillows, she feels the thing inside her called blood drumming against the back of her skin. It wants out.

My lady should lie down, her maid urges. The lady does not hear her. She knows that this feeling must be what they call heartbreak. It is the same thing she felt when her mother died, but somehow, this time, it is much worse. All she knows now is that she must get it out of her.

The lady feels a great swelling, like an entire world is balling itself up inside her. It is in her stomach now, a mass of mourning. It is in her chest now, pressing against her rib cage. It is in her throat now, a sack full of pulp bursting open.

The lady does not know where this is leading, but she knows that meeting it will make her feel better. So she opens her mouth, and out it comes, crimson splattering against her white nightgown and the honey-silk quilt, and even across the toes of her socked feet. Her maids leap back.

The lady thinks it is the most beautiful thing she has ever seen. And she feels much better. Why are you looking at me like that, she wants to say to her maids. But when she opens her mouth, no words come out. Only the thing called blood, and it is ferocious now.

The lady feels herself sinking into the bed, her body enveloped by the pillows, which are now also painted red. She tilts her head down and watches as the red soaks the front of her nightgown. It is warm against her sternum, and then it is very cold.

Her maids are moving quickly now, shouting to each other, asking what they should do. One of them asks if they should go get *him*, another says it may not be a good idea, this being his wedding day. Some of them are crying. The lady wants to tell them to be quiet, to let her enjoy this moment, but they do not understand. They cannot help but be afraid.

The lady is not afraid. She allows herself to look back up at the ceiling. If she lets her eyes slide and blur, she can make the cranes' wings move up and down. The reeds sway from side to side.

She thinks about the man, once a boy. Newly married. She had planned to wait for him, always. And he had promised to wait for her. The thought crosses her mind that he was lying to her all along, but she chooses to leave it behind. And, she thinks, it does not matter anymore. It is over, thank goodness it is over.

Her maids are quiet now, afraid to move. They watch her with teary eyes. Many are still sobbing. She remembers the day she arrived here, when she was just a motherless, sickly child. She is still a motherless, sickly child, but at least now she knows that that is not all she is.

The cranes above her are folding and expanding, their wings luring her forward. She reaches out to them and feels herself slipping away, feels her body being carried into the sky. She did not know before that she could fly.

Later, when they tell her beloved the news (but not in front of his new wife), they tell him that she died peacefully. They do not tell him that she began coughing up blood, that she could not stop. They do not tell him it drowned her from the inside out.

2

The blizzard comes sometime in the night. When I wake, my breaths escape in clouds of gray. Morning. Outside, the world has frozen over. I stay in bed just a little longer and close my eyes. My toes are hard with cold.

On mornings like this, I unwrap the heat-filled memories of my childhood, hoping they will warm me. Here is one: heat radiating off the suan cai my grandmother pickled in her large brown jars. Later, for dinner, the crimped strands lay pungent and delicious next to slices of pork and potato. Another: heat in the folds of the scarves around my mother's neck. The most important one: seeing snow while sitting on top of my father's shoulders. My head turned to the sky as his shoulders warmed the crooks of my knees. If you could only raise me a little higher, I urged him, then I can see what snow looks like before it turns into snow.

When winter came to our little fishing village, the cold did not move. Instead, it hung in the air. My father said the cold was attaching itself to all the drops of water that had not yet found their home in the ocean, and that was what made it stick to our clothes, our hair, even our bones. I loved the cold, loved that it gathered us together inside our house. The colder it became outside, the warmer we grew inside, the four of us circling each other like cats licking up heat.

When I open my eyes, I am back in the closet of the store. I can see the red blanket on top of me, my clothes hanging on the wall, the brown wood of the sliding door. The sun is out, which means I should not be far behind it.

I press my hands into the crooks of my knees, hoping to catch the heat for one moment longer. Beneath them, I imagine my father's shoulders.

Nam tells me there will be no shipments today. Too much snow, he says, no one can get in. Sweep the front, Jacob, please?

I put on fur boots, disappear inside my overcoat.

Pierce is a mining town that became popular a few years ago. Now it enjoys the excesses of that popularity. Nam and Lum tell me that its mining days are over, much of the land exhausted from a boom that already happened. Many of those who came here during the boom have left, but the traces of money and hope they brought with them remain.

Once, there were many Chinese here, Nam told me early on. They worked in the mines and they earned good money for their work. They all came to our store! Now, no one left. There is just Cheng's barbershop and the laundry. And us.

Is that what you and Lum did before the store? I asked. Mining?

He did not answer, instead gazing to a far-off place, replaying a memory I knew I would never get to see. I did not blame him for this—it was how I must look, I thought, whenever I saw home.

The store, called Pierce Big Store, sits in a building downtown that once belonged to a failed perfumery, squeezed between a leather goods store and a tailor. Just by looking at it, you would not imagine that there is much space inside, but the store is surprising in its own way; step in and you will see that the shop room is narrow, yes, but also long. So long that Nam and Lum are able to fit in shelves and bins for the food, the household items, even some hardware that they sell. In the back is a small nook where they have arranged baskets for various herbs and medicinal ingredients—lotus seeds, dried dates, wolfberries—so that the store always gives off a bitter smell, but one that makes me think of my grandmother's garden. From there, a beaded curtain separates the shop room from the rest of the space. To the right, a smaller room once used as a closet. To the left, a larger room where Nam and Lum sleep. Down the hall, an inventory room for storing all the new shipments and, not much farther down, a tiny kitchenette and washroom. I sleep in the small room once used as a closet. It is no different from my room at Master Wang's school, and so I come to love it. The hallway leads out to the back alleyway. Nam and Lum hang their laundry there, creating our own version of a fence through which the neighboring stores cannot see.

Out front, I shovel until the sun hangs overhead. One by one, heads emerge from their doors, bemoaning the blizzard's damage. The post office will remain shuttered. Next door, the tailor tells his wife that they will be lucky to get even one customer today. Cheng the barber waves to me from his empty shop. Down the street, the curtains of Foster's Goods slide away, the man inside gazing out the window and mouthing curses. He will not receive any shipments today, either. The snow has halted everything.

Nam is organizing money in the till by the time I come back inside. He watches as I shrug off my overcoat. The snow falls to the floor in clumps.

Is it cold outside? he asks. He likes to do this, ask me questions he already knows the answers to. It is his way of offering me kindness.

I nod, the tips of my ears burning from the cold. I can clean this up, I say, gesturing to the water on the floor.

He tells me to go help Lum with the remaining inventory from yesterday first. And make sure you drink some hot water, he says. It is not good for the body to be so cold.

⚊

To anyone tracking the course of my life, it would seem that a portion has been lifted and redrawn to here, to now. Only the redrawing is not exact; in place of Master Wang, I have two men from the south of

China, both speaking an unfamiliar kind of Chinese filled with lilting vowels and imperceptible tones. In place of calligraphy and calligraphers, there are canned goods, dried fruits, odds and ends, and the people who buy them. And instead of Zhifu, I find myself in a place called Pierce, in a place called Idaho, in a place called America.

But the work is the same. The sweeping, the cleaning and tidying— all of it mimics my days with Master Wang and the school, and in that way, I find myself feeling something that could be called glad. Before the first customer steps into the store, I will have swept and mopped the floor twice, dusted the shelves, restocked the beans (our best-selling product), cleaned the windows. Immaculate, Nam often calls my work. When he says this, I feel a quiet sense of pride. See? I want to say to Master Wang, who I dream will walk in one day. The things you have taught me, they have not gone to waste.

It is an improbable dream, I know. Master Wang would never leave the school. But more and more, I find myself wishing someone could see all that I can do with the things I know.

By the time the cleaning is done and the doors have opened, I will have moved to the back room, where I receive new shipments and take inventory. If Lum is not meeting with a vendor or sending letters to out-of-state liaisons, he will join me for this part. He loves, above all else, the beauty in organization.

This is their silent understanding: Nam deals with customers, Lum deals with numbers. In the back, I count inventory while Lum makes notes in his ledger. It is easy work, quiet. At lunch, we sit on top of unpacked boxes eating steamed rice and salted duck eggs. Sometimes, a slice of ham from the butcher down the street. Nam will join us, but he always eats very quickly; he loves to greet the customers.

Short and round, somewhere in his fifties, Nam has a face as plump as a bun with all the features placed at the exact center, so that there always seems to be more flesh than face. When he laughs, which is often, he reminds me of a newborn, the cheeks opalescent, the eyes tiny beetles, the mouth open in unabashed glee. His queue matches the rest of him, robust, generous, buoyant. When I see it whip behind him, I understand why he is the one who deals with people. It seems he could sell anyone anything with his earnest nature and endless cheer. Always amenable, always looking to please.

Lum is different. He is a full head taller than Nam, which makes him a giant to me, with sharp features and round spectacles. His queue touches the floor. Master Wang once told me that men with long queues respect their bodies and their ancestors' bodies, and so this is how I know that Lum must be a decent man. He moves swiftly, speaks little, and smiles even less. He reminds me of a wooden flute, straight and upright, and so thin that the wind could blow straight through him.

Together, they make an odd pair. But they work well, having been business partners for years, and they give me the thing I value most: the ability to be anonymous, to work in silence and exist without being questioned. In return, I give them the same, letting their story remain a mystery to me. The more I know, I reason, the easier it will be to get attached. I learned this well from Swallow.

Ever since most of the Chinese left, Pierce Big Store has not been doing well. Nam and Lum are optimistic. Especially Nam, who is always thinking of a better day. Whether by bad fortune or their own doing, the store sits down the street from the only other general store in Pierce. Foster's Goods has been around for almost as long as the town, and its customers are loyal. The entire town of Pierce is loyal. But Nam and Lum are confident that we can bring in more customers, so they lower prices, order in bulk. Hard work will never betray you, Lum tells us often. It is one of his sayings.

The customers who still come are mostly Chinese. They were not born here, but traveled from Guangdong with hopes of gold and work, searching for money that they would one day bring back to their families. You remind me of my son, one of them tells me, tears filling his brown eyes. You remind me of everything, I want to reply. It is a childish truth. What he reminds me of is something I did not know could go missing—the feeling of being where you should be. There is a difference between being a newcomer to a city and being in a world that does not resemble you, that reminds you every moment of your strangeness. This is what Idaho is to me. And so, when our Chinese customers come asking for millet and green onions, buying licorice and cinnamon, I watch them with tenderness, following their movements. I miss you, and I do not even know you, I want to say to the miner, the launderer, the servant. But I always stop myself from getting any closer, remembering that night at the inn in Boise, the pain between my legs and the wailing.

The few white customers who do come into our store are furtive, quiet. They act as if they have done something wrong by being here. They never stay for long. Because they are so few, I give them their own names and stories. There is a woman who wears black and only buys ginger root. I call her a widow. There is a group of young schoolboys who stand outside the store shoving and laughing, each daring the other to come inside. The one who finally does, I call him a soldier.

These customers are not enough to keep the store running forever, but Nam and Lum are not worried yet—they have a plan to bring in more white customers by matching the inventory at Foster's Goods. I am not worried, either. What happens with the store, with the customers, with Nam and Lum, is not important to me. The days pass by without touching me, as if I have been plucked out and removed and placed to watch from the side. I am the character for lost 迷, a grain of rice walking nowhere. When I speak, my mouth moves but I am far away. When I sweep, my hands feel ocean water, not the handle of a broom. My body may be here in Pierce, but my heart is searching for Zhifu.

Samuel lied. Idaho is not closer to China, because Idaho does not touch the ocean. Here, there are no ships that can carry me back home. There is only land, mountain, valley. Repeat. So much dirt and so much green. When, fresh from the violence with the gray-haired man, I asked the first person I saw if he could point me to the docks, he laughed in my face. And I realized then what I must have known this whole time.

When Nam and Lum bicker about the store and bemoan the

weather, I nod and murmur in agreement, letting that be speech enough. I am thinking of my mother, my father, my grandmother, of Master Wang and the calligraphy school. Up until the moment I arrived in Pierce and found the store, my life had been split in two: before the kidnapping and after. Now there is a third split, a new possibility: the return. This is where my happiness lies, and when the snow and the cold and the nightmares of my past threaten to crush me, I think of my future, the one where I get to see my family again, the one where I return to Master Wang's tutelage and grow into my own calligraphy master. In this future, I am whole and content and well. In this future, I am unified.

3

This is the story of how a boy became a man.

━━━

I changed when I left Samuel in Boise that night. When I emerged back onto the street, the black yawn of the inn's stairs behind me, a new reality gripped me. I was in a city I did not recognize, and I had just been violated in the most unspeakable way. There was no stopping other men from doing what the gray-haired man did. I was too small. A shadow passed before me—a patrolman or some drunkard stumbling home—and when he turned to look at me, I realized that I would never be truly safe again—not like this.

I had escaped the brothel, but I would never escape the bad men. They were the same, whether it was in China, or San Francisco, or Idaho. It was easy to spot a wounded animal if you were hungry enough—and these men were always hungry enough.

That night, I did not sleep. I walked through the city until I found a church whose arched doors were big and tall, and cast me in their shadow when I huddled underneath. It was only August, but it was already much windier than San Francisco. I put my fingers in my mouth, sucking on them to keep them warm. Inside me, Lin Daiyu slept fitfully, jerking and thrashing against my rib cage. She could not stop seeing the gray-haired man in the shadows. She could not stop remembering.

I wanted to fight the memory of the gray-haired man's hand inside me. It was never his to take. And then I became filled with rage. I could not be Daiyu anymore, I decided then. Not until I could be certain that I would not be vulnerable to these bad men again. Not until I returned to my home.

What does it mean to be a man? Being a boy was not so difficult. Whether I was a street urchin inside a fish market or Feng the calligraphy student, I could simply call myself a boy and become one. But being a man demands more. For the ruse to work, the transformation must take place under the skin, in all the corners of myself that I have not yet even come to understand.

What does it mean to be a man? My experiences then told me everything: It was a matter of believing oneself invincible and strong, and owed everything.

For the rest of my journey, I, Daiyu, would have to stay hidden. In her place, Jacob Li would emerge.

I left Boise the next day, in search of towns with Chinese temples like the one attached to our inn. I had the map of Idaho from the innkeeper and no plan, but I believed that towns with Chinese temples would at least mean that I would not stand out too much. I wandered through mining camps and small towns, places called Meridian and Middleton and Emmett. If the town did indeed have a temple, I never stepped inside, reminded of the gray-haired man and his furious, clawing fingers. If I could just keep moving, I thought, I could outlast and overcome the violence. So I moved, and when I began to feel that unbearable sensation, of being unsafe and unclean and raw, then I moved again, and again, and again, until winter came and I was in a place called Idaho City with snow up to my knees, where I could move no more.

In Idaho City, I let Jacob Li take over completely. This was what I learned: In America, being a boy was easy, but being a man was essential. As a man, I could look at other men without fear of being seen.

But as a man, I could see, too. I saw the way they looked at women when they thought no one else was watching, the way their eyes tried to see inside her skin. In these men, I also saw Jasper, the gray-haired man, Samuel, every customer from the brothel, the two half brothers. I even saw Madam Lee. They were everywhere, these bad men. The only way to escape them was to be the most believable version of a man myself.

I kept my eye on the men around me, tracing their movements and mannerisms. It always began with the body. The feet, two roots firmly planted into the earth. The legs, demanding, capable, built for walking, and kicking, and running, and striding, and leaving whenever you wanted and going anywhere you wanted without being stopped. The part just below the navel, the place where all the power could be found. A place I do not talk about. The midsection, made for loud laughter, ripe with the knowledge that death was less fearsome for a man. In that knowledge, the belly was free to expand and shrink as it pleased. The chest, closer to a shield of armor than skin and bones. The arms, there to take, to swing, to pilfer, to enact. The hands, at once palms and closed fists. The neck, never vulnerable. The head, certain.

I practiced what I saw—swinging my weight, narrowing my brows, keeping my chest and shoulders wide and powerful. This way of moving was not easy; it belonged to someone who knew complete freedom. I had not known this, and so I moved like less of a man. But I moved nonetheless. I learned to hide my natural reactions, my propensity to laugh at small things that enchanted me, to instead handle things with terseness and deliberation, not tenderness.

That winter, I worked at a butcher shop where I was not even permitted to look at the meat. Lin Daiyu continued to sleep inside me, the ceaseless Idaho wind blowing her into a stupor. By then, my cheeks were grooves, my teeth mean. During the day, I was a raw nerve, always with one eye in front and one eye in back, every movement, gesture, and word a question of whether or not I had revealed myself. At night, I stayed in once-abandoned log cabins converted into lodgings with all the other Chinese laborers, most of them miners chasing gold in places already picked over by the white men. Others would go on to work in the laundries, where they sprayed water from their mouths to iron clothes. I barely slept, remembering how the last time I let myself fall asleep, I woke to find a man's fist inside me. Instead, I lay there, listening for any changes in sound, my body clenched, every fiber of every muscle wound tight. Sometimes, I half dreamed that Jasper or the tong would burst through the door and drag me into the dark. On nights like these, I kept myself awake by pinching the inside of my arm.

The winter took, but it also gave. It forced me to stay put for a while, the first time I stopped moving since leaving Samuel in Boise. Out of that stasis, a plan emerged: I needed to find a way to return to China. I knew I was far from the ocean, with little money to pay for the fare. I could not go back to California—I was fearful of the tong and its spies but more fearful of Jasper. It had to be a different way.

In a large courthouse in downtown Idaho City, I gave a young page five dollars in exchange for a map of Idaho and the surrounding region. From this map, I learned that there were other routes to the ocean, ports with ships in a place called Washington Territory. I could travel north and eventually make my way west, until all I could see was ocean and sky. From there, find a ship heading back to China. In China, find my grandmother. With my grandmother, find my parents. One day, Master Wang. One day, open my own calligraphy school. The dream was difficult but not impossible. All I needed, it turned out, was to stop moving, to make enough money for the journey to the west, and back to China.

But when spring came, the butcher told me he had no more work, even though the shop was busier than ever. I was not the only one—the laborers I lodged with found themselves jobless, too, their former employers suddenly doing just fine without any extra help. I had to move again, spending what little wages I had on a ride to the next town, and the next, taking whatever job I could find. I only ever earned as much as fifty cents for a day's work. I carried very little.

I worked as a shoeshine, a launderer, even an interpreter for a white family. I sold flowers, carrying them in two baskets that I balanced with a pole on one shoulder. But the jobs were hard to find and harder to keep—it was as if every town dried up at my touch. I reminded myself how to feel satiated on nearly nothing, saving what little food I could afford until the end of the day, when I could eat it all as one big meal. At least then I could pretend that I was full, even if only for a moment.

Throughout it all, Lin Daiyu continued to sleep.

When my last job, another laundry job, ended in Elk City, I climbed on the back of a wagon heading northwest. I was not the only one—there was always a group of us moving from place to place, looking to make it. Most of the men were from Guangzhou, and so we could not speak to one another, instead understanding through the common language of silence. One by one, the men hopped off when the wagon stopped. Some were looking for their own piece of land. Others, running away. Some, like me, were trying to find their way back home.

When the wagon stopped for the last time, I was the only one left. I found myself standing in front of a store, watching two men who looked like me repainting the words PIERCE BIG STORE on the sign outside.

Unlike Master Wang, Nam and Lum did not ask me to prove myself. They hired me on the spot, offering food, shelter, and a small stipend for my work. And so I altered the plan: If I could save just two hundred dollars, I could finally start my journey west, to Washington Territory, and make my way back to China. The money would pay for travel, lodging, food, ship fare. Most importantly, it would offer me protection. I pledged to wait out the winter, work through the spring, saving as much as I could, and leave at the end of summer. Pierce would be the last of Idaho for me.

By then, it was easy to call myself Jacob Li. I kept my hair short, above the ears, afraid that growing it out for a queue would reveal too much softness in my face. But there were other things I did not account for. One day, Nam wondered out loud how my throat could still be so flat at my age. From then on, I wore a kerchief wrapped around my neck, hiding its smoothness.

Then there were the more difficult things. The two small mounds on my chest belonged to a woman, the kind of woman that men wanted. I was no such thing, and I did not want men to want me, so I bound my chest with cream-colored cloth, and with each wrapping, I felt myself straightening up, holding my power in my chest, becoming tighter, less vulnerable.

When I woke one morning shortly after arriving in Pierce and felt the cold glue between my legs, I knew, without even having to check, that it had arrived. When it happened at the brothel, Madam Lee forced the girls to stuff cotton deep within themselves and serve the next customer. But even so, the girls held secret celebrations when one of us bled for the first time. A sign that you are finally a woman, they said. That morning, as I washed my rust-stained undergarments with cold water, rubbing the fabric against itself, I let myself open a small sob. Once upon a time, becoming a woman, an adult, was something I looked forward to. Now that I finally was one, it made everything so much harder.

The bleeding lasted four days. My stomach was a ship in a storm at sea, lurching and thrashing against itself. I cut up spare rags from around the store and stuffed them into my pants, dashing out to change them every other hour. I woke up early to wash the rags, then repeated the process. When the bleeding finally stopped on the fourth day, I breathed again.

It was lonely being Jacob Li.

As my final act of transformation, I forced myself to stop writing calligraphy when I was Jacob Li. Jacob Li did not know calligraphy. His hands were uncouth, rough, somewhat clumsy. His hands could not hold a brush. Sometimes, when the store was not busy and I stared at the floor, trying to remember what the ocean felt like in my hair, I found myself moving my finger to write a character against my thigh. Jacob Li would squeeze his hands into a fist, pushing this urge back down.

Only at night, when there is no one to see, can I rest and let my hands roam free. I touch my thighs to feel that they are still there and that they are whole. I massage my breasts, which itch from the fabric of the binding, and feel how they grow or shrink from day to day. Most of all, I let my hands do all the calligraphy they want, writing and rewriting the characters that have been with me all this time, my friends and teachers in times of need. The feeling of my finger tracing the strokes, the dots, and the lines is enough to make me want to cry. It is a reminder that I have not lost myself yet, that I am still alive.

Before I fall asleep, I repeat the plan, as I do every night. Leave Pierce at the end of summer. Head west to Washington Territory. Find my way back to the ocean.

4

He walks in on a day when the snow has hardened into one white shell and every step sounds like a grinding of bones. It is a slow day, so Nam asks me to manage the front of the store while he does inventory in the back. Lum is away on business.

He walks in, and he is as tall as Lum, with a back as straight as a board. Black hair, strong black brows, bare neck. The skin there is autumnal.

He asks for the owner of the store. His voice is smooth, from the chest. The sound wraps around me, urging the hair on my arms and legs and even behind my ears to attention. I tell him Nam is in the back, and would he like me to go get him?

No rush, he says, I can wait. I try to busy myself, but my eyes keep darting up. He is a young Chinese man, one of the youngest I have seen in Pierce. Something about him, the smooth tan-peach of his skin, reminds me of home in a way I have not felt in a long time.

Nam has heard the door, and so he emerges from the back. Why did you not tell me we have a customer? he says to me. He rushes up to greet the young man, brushing his hands on his pants.

Hello, the young man says. Do you sell rosin here?

Nam says no, but he can place an order and get a shipment in, if that is what the young man needs. Neither of us understand the request, but the promise of a new customer makes him jolly. The young man joins Nam at the counter and lists off brand names for the kind of rosin he is looking for.

Jacob, Nam calls to me, I need you in the back. A new shipment of rice just arrived, and you need to check it all.

The young man turns to regard me then, letting my name fit the mold of the person standing before him. His face is calm, eyes wistful. To him, I am just a boy.

I think about him for the rest of the day.

—

Three weeks pass. Dirty snow crusts the roads, pushed aside to make way for the resumption of life after the blizzard. The streets are muddy, the well-worn earth frothing up in peaks of brown waves. In place of the blizzard, a squalling wind enters, cutting the naked trees and lashing at our faces. I watch as the wooden sign for Foster's Goods blows back and forth. People pass by, walking as fast as they can—no one dares stay outside for too long.

Inside the store, though, it is warm. The furnace in the corner glows happily, and when there are no customers, I stand in front of it, turning my hands over and over until they are orange. It is another slow day. Lum is meeting with a vendor across town. Nam tells me to stay in the front and help customers.

I hear the door open behind me and the howl of wind that follows. Hello, he says.

Today, the young man is wearing a black overcoat. He has on a cap that makes him look boyish, a disarming effect against the broad confidence of his jaw.

I am glad to see you again, he says. I was told my shipment has arrived?

He walks to me without hesitation. His legs move, but the rest of him does not, as if his torso is being held up by a string. I jut out my jaw and straighten, hoping to mimic his own posture.

Yes, I hear myself saying. I walk back behind the counter. He follows, bringing with him the smell of tea and very old wood. Inside my head, there is a faint roaring, as if the wind now lives within me.

The rosin is there in a drawer under the counter, neatly packed in brown paper and wrap-tied with a hemp string. I bring it out and place it on the counter.

How much do I owe you? the young man asks, taking out a small pouch.

I tell him fifty cents. My voice does not want to come out. He nods, begins placing the coins on the counter one by one.

I should be counting the coins, but instead I am looking at his hands. They are good hands. The fingers there are long, with knuckles that sit low, sturdy and sure. The nails are wide and flat, the thumb muscular, the palms smooth. These hands look more like fans than hands, like they could open and cover the whole world.

Are you all right? I hear him ask.

Sorry, I say, looking away. I usher the coins into my palm and deposit them in the till. Thank you, come again soon.

Would it be possible to make this a recurring monthly order? he asks at the door. I see him there, one hand on the knob, and I think about how the only thing separating him from the warmth of this store and the violent wind is this door. And how I wish he would stay in here, share in this heat. He turns the knob. I wince, expecting the wind to drag him away. Do not go, I want to say to him. Instead, I just nod.

He opens the door. The wind moans, blowing his coat back a little. Keep warm, he tells me, eyebrows raising in concern.

I watch him walk away, a blur of black against the gray of the day. He keeps his head down to avoid the wind, one hand on his cap and the other deep in his pocket, holding the rosin. I watch him until I can no longer see him, running my fingers over the place where his coins once were.

I go tell Nam about the rosin. And then I return to the furnace, turning my hands over. It is after five turns that I realize that my hands do not need reheating. Nor does my face, nor any of my limbs. My body already burns.

—

After he leaves, I tell myself to stay away. Because by now, I know what danger feels like: the skin flares, the legs swell with blood. The stomach feels starved even though it has just been filled. I do not know why the young man makes me feel the way I do, but I know what my body is trying to tell me: He is a threat. This time, I promise to listen. I will not be caught again. There will be no more Jaspers, no more Madam Lees, no more Samuels or gray-haired men. There will only be me.

Again and again, Master Wang would say, practice the strokes again and again, until you can close your eyes and the character materializes out of the air. Until you know something so well that all your body has to do is follow.

I have been practicing for this moment, putting myself through danger again and again, waiting for the one day when I could recognize it. Since the beginning, being myself has led only to darkness. Instead, practice erasing and overturning and re-creating the self, until all I have to do is disappear.

—

In the weeks that follow, I find ways to disappear when I see the young man at the store. It is easy to duck into the back and stay there until I hear the door open and close again. Lum does not question me, only gives me commands over his ledger. Nam always seems to notice that I am gone after the fact, not before. I do not care. To them, I am just the odd little Jacob Li.

But at least I am alive. At least I have enough breath to last another night. I tell myself to forget about him, whoever he is. I give a name to the feeling that settles within me when I hear his voice spreading through the store. And I tell myself that nothing good ever comes from being burned alive.

5

In March, the snow still comes, sometimes in a dusting, other times like a blanket falling on top of us, until everything, corners, edges, valleys, peaks, *everything* is covered. I like seeing how the world changes when it is touched by snow—branches now doubled with a white shadow, sharp rocks made round and soft, and me, reveling in the fact that there is a great equalizer for man and beast after all, the one that asks us to bow in the face of what we cannot control. On days when work is slow, I walk through town, imagining what the trees look like in the summer, whether or not they have flowers. They could be lavender, coral, white. They could be berries instead.

But business is finally getting better. Nam and Lum are happy. The owner of Foster's Goods, however, is not. We see him lingering outside our store, silent and immovable. The cold does not bother him. He is a heavy man, a fight of a man. The pride of Pierce, according to Lum, who found a profile about Foster in the *Pierce City Miner*. Foster was a wrestling champion in his youth, and he still bears the signs with broad, bullish shoulders and deformed ears. The sight of him makes me uncomfortable—he is a different kind of menacing from those I have encountered before. Perhaps it is because he does not have to do anything. He knows that his presence is a disturbance on its own.

When Foster takes his place in front of the store for the fourth time in a week, I ask Nam and Lum if I should tell him to leave.

Do not speak to that man, Lum barks. He is suspicious of Foster's motives, as he is with everyone, and on these days, he holds his ledger closer to his chest, as if doing so will make the store impenetrable.

Nam wrings his hands, but he defers to Lum on matters like these. I have no doubt Foster means well, he tells me later, when Lum leaves. He is just worried about his business, the same as us.

Because our white customers are starting to multiply. Before my eyes, they swim into one big white being. Hello, how do you do, may I help you find anything, I say to them. I am to be their concierge, as Nam puts it, someone who can give them exactly what they need at a moment's notice. This is another way we can elevate ourselves above Foster's Goods.

Your English is not bad, a woman with ice hair says to me, as if she has gifted me something precious.

I tell her thank you, even though I do not know where the compliment is. Inside, I want to tell her how I came to learn it. I want to tell her about the room with one small window, up so high that not even a good ladder would reach it. About the old woman and her cane. About crouching over those books and letting alien sounds fall out of my mouth. I want to tell her about being stuffed into a bucket full of coal and floating across the ocean, all to arrive here, in front of a woman who tells me that my English is not bad and expects that to be a good thing.

Instead, I nod, bow my body into a sickle, so that she can see how grateful I am.

Others do not have such nice things to say. One elderly man tells me to stop staring at him, calling me a yellow heathen. A little girl points at me and asks her father why I look the way I do. A boy not much younger than me snickers and makes a gesture with his fingers. Another woman backs away and calls for her husband, who rushes over, threatening to have me arrested for speaking to his wife. It reminds me of the way men would look at us at Madam Lee's—like we were something entirely different, and thus terrifying. In the brothel, they would overcome this fear by overcoming us. I am not so sure what they will do here, but I am beginning to realize that in this place called Idaho, which they call the West, being Chinese can be something like a disease. Almost every other day, it seems, one of the sheriff's men will come in and ask to see our papers. I hand over the yellowing page I took from Samuel, now the most precious thing I own. Like the innkeeper in San Francisco the night of my escape, the sheriff's men do not see a difference between me and the boy whose picture is on my identification paper. All they can see is Chinese.

More than ever before, I am very much aware of what I am. The space between my eyes and my nose, my nose and my lips, my lips and my chin, can be something that makes me different, inferior even. If my parents could see me, they would be laughing—What makes you think you are so special? they would ask. But here, I *am* special. The white people make me that way. Why else would they step aside when I walk by, or avoid my eyes, or whisper things that I cannot hear under their breath? My body is covered in the syllables of another language, the scroll of a kingdom that has existed long before they did and will continue existing long after they are gone. I am something they cannot fathom. I am something they fear. We all are.

Still, despite our disease of Chineseness, the customers increase. The prices are too good for them to deny. They are alert as they shop, flitting about the shelves, one eye on the goods and the other looking for someone who might recognize them, who will ask them why they are here buying soap from a coolie store when a fine American one exists down the street. When they pay, they do not speak, but jam the coins on the counter before speeding out with their heads bowed.

On a day late in March when the temperature lifts and the sun throws its light against our windows, I watch a group gather outside the store.

It is early morning, and we are not yet open, so I wave and point to the CLOSED sign on the door.

My waves go unanswered.

Instead, they pack together in front of the store. I recognize some of them, I think: a white man who walks past the store every day but never enters, who stares inside as if he can start a fire with just his eyes; a white woman who I sometimes see at the deli; a blond man who came inside once just to tell us that he would not be buying anything, ever. There are many more that I do not recognize, but the look in their eyes tells me that I need only to know one to know them all.

In their hands are signs bearing letters painted in big black print. OBNOXIOUS RACE, reads one of them. SMALL BOYS, reads another. HEATHEN. COOLIE. CHINEES.

I am still trying to understand what these signs mean when the group starts shouting. It starts with one voice, brittle and cold. Then another joins, this time sharp and nasal, then another, booming and furious, then another and another, until they are no longer separate voices but one whole. In front of my eyes, they transform from human beings into shapes with necks and arms and legs, and one singular voice, a terrible voice that sounds the way a train does when it comes to a stop.

The Chinese must go, the voice chants. Must go, must go, the Chinese must go!

One of the white men at the front of the crowd steps forward and presses his face up against the window, baring his teeth. I see two canines the color of pig intestines. He stretches his lips so that they pull across the glass, and a glint of spittle flashes in between each tooth. His eyelids peel back, revealing thin crimson patterns against the whites of his eyes. When he sees me looking at him, he steps back and spits at my face. It lands against the glass and slides down, but I flinch all the same. The crowd cheers.

This is when everything falls into place. The signs are about us. The shouts are directed at us. This crowd is here for us.

Nam rushes forward from the back, hearing the chants breaking against our large glass windows. We are closed, he says to me first. Then his eyes skate to the crowd outside, to the letters on their signs, and his voice is lost.

They just came, I tell him. I realize that I am shouting.

Still, Nam does not move. I do not know what he has come from, what he has endured, but I know that this must be something he has never encountered before. Something thuds against the glass and we both recoil—someone has thrown a rotten apple.

I decide to act; before the next object can land against the window, I reach up to release the blinds. They fall down with a slapping noise, and in an instant, the angry faces disappear. But their voices are still thunderous. If the rotten apples do not break the window, I think, then their voices might just do it.

What do we do? I ask Nam, backing away from the window to stand beside him. We cannot open the store with this going on outside.

Nam rubs his temples, squeezes his eyes shut. He is muttering something. Nam, I say loudly, and this time I place my hands on his arms, give him a shake. What do we do?

Let me think, Nam says, voice feeble. He sounds, for the first time, like an old man.

We know you are in there, the crowd shouts. Cowards! Sneaky bastards! Come out, come out, dusky throats!

Even with the blinds drawn, we are too vulnerable, too exposed. Hiding the faces outside gave them more power to grow, mutate into something giant and deadly. No longer humans but beasts.

They do not know us, Nam says, sounding hurt. I must speak to them. This is all a misunderstanding. Yes. They must listen.

I imagine the man with the bared teeth, his face stretching across the window. I tell Nam that I do not think they will listen.

But it is too late. Nam moves with surprising speed for a man his age, darting out from beside me and to the door before I can stop him. I open my mouth to shout NO, my hand outstretched, but the commotion of the crowd has already swelled. And then he disappears and the door clicks behind him.

Again, as I have felt it so many times before—the quick, instant drop of fear. I run to the window and slide a finger between the blinds.

Outside, Nam stands, his round body firmly planted into the ground. The crowd backs away at the sight of him, recoiling as one. He is saying something to them, and his voice is calm and strong. The crowd quiets. It seems to be listening.

But something is happening the longer Nam speaks. The crowd is making noises again, rumblings at first, then louder and louder, until their bodies could groan under the weight of their anger. I can no longer hear Nam's voice. I do not think he can, either. The man who bared his teeth is back at the front now, staring down Nam and shouting, his ears as red as plums.

It happens then—quickly, almost too quickly for my eyes to catch. An object flies past the man's ear and lands just beside Nam's right foot. Nam bends to look down at it. I can tell by the way he stills that he is confused, then terrified. I press the blinds down with my fingers to get a better look, and then I see the rock at his side.

Before Nam or I can react, another one hurtles through the air, this time hitting the window just above my head. I gasp, snatching my hands back from the blinds.

And then I know without even having to see it that the world has broken outside. Voices that are no longer voices but feral snarls. When I look through the blinds again, the crowd has scattered, but not to return to their homes—no, they are surging forward. I cannot see Nam anymore—the crowd has closed in on him, their signs pounding the sky, and more and more rocks are hitting the windows, peppering the glass like hail.

I have to get him inside, I think. They could kill him.

The door is just there. I can see it. I have opened and closed it hundreds of times. All I have to do is walk a few steps, cross the threshold, and step outside.

But the thing that has kept me alive so far also holds me in place. That reliable instinct—to protect myself, to run away—returns, and my body is all too quick to welcome it. My body remembers well.

Move, I scream. I stand there, trying to break out of myself, while the voices outside reach something close to killing. I scream at my hands, my arms, my legs, these things I do not recognize anymore, just as I cannot even recognize the heart that beats within me.

Once again, she hears me. Once again, she has come to save me. I feel my mouth opening, feel something long and elbowed and slippery fall onto the floor. Lin Daiyu crawls out of me, and now she will save me. Save us.

I see her rushing to the door, but I am the one doing it. I see her hand clamp down on the knob. I see her turning it. I hear the voices outside, let them carry me forward. Their fury shocks me like cold water. Lin Daiyu tells me to put my arms over my face, and I do. Lin Daiyu tells me that she will look for Nam, tells me to watch out for the rocks.

He is there, lying on the ground, curled into a ball. The crowd dances around him, kicking and spitting on him. Stop, I cry, and I hate that I am crying because I do not think that many men cry. Lin Daiyu pushes me toward him.

I will kill anyone who hurts you, she promises.

Nam is not moving. I kneel beside him. I cannot stop crying. Please, I tell the crowd. They are so loud and their teeth so sharp. I tell them, He did nothing wrong. I tell them, Leave us alone.

Someone waves the OBNOXIOUS RACE sign in my face. I look up and see the white man who bared his teeth at me. Up close, his face is full of pockmarks, and he looks delighted, as if he has found gold on the ground. His hand is raised in a fist. If this mob discovers that I am a girl, what will stop them from violating me the way the gray-haired man did? I lunge and cover Nam with my body, praying that Lin Daiyu will do what she promised.

But whatever I am waiting for does not come. Instead, I feel someone lifting me up by my chang shan and dragging me away from the crowd. No, I shout, thinking of Nam, who is still on the ground.

Stop fighting, the voice who drags me shouts. Stop! We must get back inside.

The last thing I see before the door closes is the white man with the bared teeth. The crowd continues to jostle around him, but he is standing still. He lifts his hand and points at me, mouth in a grotesque grin. Then he turns to the crowd and waves them away like flies. The voices die down. One by one, they return to being men, women. One by one, they spit on the door of Pierce Big Store before turning to leave.

6

It is over, a voice says from a place years away from me. You are safe now.

But Nam, I say. I am crying into my arm. All I can see is his body out there, nothing more than a bag of dirt, and the brutes who kicked him over and over again.

He is here, the voice answers. It is closer to me than before. We are safe. You can look now.

I wait for Lin Daiyu to tell me otherwise. Hearing nothing, I raise my head.

Nam is lying with his back on the floor, legs in the shape of a number four, arms limp over his belly, but he is groaning, not dead. I scramble over to him.

I am not hurt, he says when he sees me. Are you, Jacob?

I shake my head, tell him no, I am fine. He sees my tears and laughs.

You are crying for me, he says. You are sweet.

Someone moves behind us. I remember that we are not alone. There was someone who saved us both, who emerged from the crowd and pulled us away, to safety. I swivel around to face our savior and thank him, but my voice falters.

Him. The young man who comes in to buy his rosin. After all the work I have done to avoid him, he still found his way in.

Are you all right? the young man asks. Would you like to get up?

He reaches out with a gloved hand.

I do not take it. Jasper had been a savior, but he saved me from one threat only to throw me into something worse. Samuel, too. The word *savior* means nothing.

You, I say. Why are you here?

Nam hits me on the arm. What is wrong with you? he says. This young man saved our lives.

But Nam is old and gullible. I know better. The crowd was small at first, but it grew. It would have been difficult for someone to push their way through it, especially if they were Chinese. That meant only one thing—this man was a part of the crowd to begin with.

You are one of them, I shout. I look around wildly for Lin Daiyu. Now is the time for her to make good on her promise. But I am shocked to find her sitting on top of the counter, combing her fingers through her hair. She ignores me.

I promise, the young man says, I am not.

Liar! I jump to my feet, trying to pull Nam away from the young man. He protests, swats my hands away. You came from the crowd and now you are in here with us. What do you want? Why did they send you? Is it because you look like us? Did they think we would trust you?

Jacob, Nam murmurs. A string of blood dribbles down his chin.

The sight of his blood, coupled with the horror of what just took place, overcomes me. I let go of Nam—he falls to the floor in a soft thump—and fling myself away as bile shoots from my mouth.

Let me, the young man says. My body convulses again before he can finish his sentence, the vomit as thin as water. In the black of my head, the faces of the crowd spin, their mouths opening and closing, mouths as red as the thing spilling down Nam's chin. I am certain that if I vomit enough, everything will go back to the way it was. The protest will never have happened, this young man would not be in front of us now, Nam and I would not be on the floor. I would return to being just Jacob Li, silent and reliable.

But when I am finished and all I can do is make empty sounds at the floor, I realize that vomiting everything up has only left me with nothing.

I wipe my mouth with the back of my hand and try to stand.

He needs help, the young man says, gesturing to Nam. He may have broken a rib or two. And you are not well. Will you please let me help? At least let me wait until the doctor arrives. I sent for him when I saw the mob.

His words are kind, yet I do not trust any of it. I turn to say something to Nam, but he is already nodding, beckoning the young man closer with a hand. The young man does not hesitate. He walks forward and bends down, threading one hand under Nam's head, the other to support Nam's back. Then they both look at me.

Jacob, Nam says. Come help.

———

Just a bruise, says the doctor. The rib is only bruised.

Nam is not to exert himself, which means no carrying heavy things, no lifting his arms above chest height, no standing for too long. He recites this to Lum, who has just returned from a four-day trip to the neighboring county of Murray, and then tells us that we were lucky.

The doctor leaves. The street is quiet and empty when he steps outside. Lum watches him go, furious. He does not understand how this could have happened. Nam and I try to explain, but even we cannot fully comprehend.

Is there anything that can be done? Lum asks finally, and we know that he does not expect us to have an answer.

The young man, who has waited in the shadows, reenters with a pot of hot tea.

But you, Lum says. You saved them.

Nelson, the young man says. My name is Nelson Wong.

I am Lee Kee Nam, Nam says. This is Leslie Lum and Jacob Li.

Nelson dips his head at each of us before pouring the tea. He does it simply, without the flourishes or gestures that I have seen from the men who took tea with my parents. The liquid is a warm amber. I want nothing more than to curl around it, but a voice from within stops me.

Poison, it warns.

It is too late—the tea has been delivered to its owners who can only anticipate the relief it will bring. Before I can act, Lum moves first, taking a hungry gulp. I wait for him to let go of his cup, for his cup to hit the floor and break. I wait for his eyes to bulge, his hands to clutch his neck, for his breathing to turn into choking. My wooden stool topples behind me. I am ready to throw the hot tea in Nelson's face.

Lum swallows, inhales, then takes another sip. He sets the tea cup down and rubs his hands together. He looks the same as he ever did.

What is wrong with you? Lum says, seeing me. Drink your tea—it is hot.

I right my stool and sit, my cheeks burning. I do not look at Nelson.

How did you know what was happening? Lum asks Nelson.

Nelson says, I was walking into town when I saw people running. I started running, too, I do not know why. I just knew something was wrong. When I got to where all the people had stopped, I saw what was happening. I saw the two of you.

As he speaks, I reach down for my teacup, searching for something to hold. It is scalding, but I leave my fingers against the cup, willing the liquid to burn through the ceramic and wash away all the pain I am holding in my body.

Nelson turns to me suddenly, his eyes meeting mine for the first time since that morning. I tighten my grip on the cup.

You should have stayed inside, he says. That was very dangerous. You could have both been killed.

What fear I have of him disappears, replaced by fury. I do not need him to tell me the difference between right and wrong.

You want me to have stayed inside? Nam could have been killed.

I wait for Nelson to throw something back at me, but he does not. Instead, he holds my gaze. My retort hangs in the air, the anger enveloping all of us.

I am sorry, he says. You were just trying to help your friend.

I wonder if he is making fun of me now. I did what anyone would do, I say, and let that be it.

It was Foster, Lum says. We have all seen him standing outside the store like some specter. He is angry at us for taking his customers.

Foster was not out there, Nam says, startling us all. He has not spoken for a long time, gaze fixed on the front door, but now he looks at Nelson, searching. Who were they? Do you know them?

Nelson sits back and sighs. I notice a welt under his jaw.

I do know them, he says. They have been growing. That crowd today, they were not simply protesting you or your store. They were protesting against all Chinese.

The three of us sit with this. *Protesting against all Chinese.* I remember the small mining towns I passed through the year before, how the jobs seemed to disappear so suddenly, and without explanation. It starts to make sense.

Lum is the first to break the silence. Does this have to do, he says, with the law passed by the president?

Law, I repeat. What law is this?

The law that says if you are Chinese, you can no longer enter America, Lum says, his eyes flashing behind his glasses. We should consider ourselves lucky to be here at all, ha!

But no one else is laughing, especially not Nelson. It does, he says. Ever since it passed, the people in this town have been growing louder about how they do not want us living here. Not just here, either. It is all over the place. My friend in Boise says there are protests almost every week, and the crowd grows each time.

Silence again, but this time, it could be sadness, too. I look at my hands, still so small and girl-like. These hands would have done nothing to protect me from those fiends outside.

We need a plan, Lum says. If they come back.

No, Nam says. We should not engage. Maybe they will go away.

Lum shakes his head, face reddening. You heard what this young man said. They come every week in Boise. They will grow. If this happens here, how will we survive? What customers will want to shop here?

We cannot fight them, Nam says, slumping, as if his body has a leak somewhere. If we ignore, maybe they will go away. Maybe they will see we are good, honest people. We do not want trouble.

Lum snorts. You think they will go away? They will not go away. You will see. Tomorrow or the day after tomorrow or the day after that, they will be back. And that Foster man, he will be back, too.

Nam slams his good hand down on the table. I have never seen him like this, not the jolly man I have lived alongside for the past few months. But the morning's events seem to have changed something in him. For the first time, he looks bigger than Lum.

You do not get to lecture me, he says. You did not get attacked. It was me. And I say we ignore.

Lum looks down. I can tell that he does not agree, but he also does not want to fight. Not now. Fine, he says, then turns away. But if they come back and put a gun to your head, do not come to me for help. Just remember what you said: Ignore them. Let us see how that works.

———

I could not help but notice, Nelson says to me later, your hands.

It is nearly evening, and the slow retreat of the sun gives me that somber feeling of things coming to an end before one is ready. When the tea went cold and Nam drooped in his seat, I took him to bed, laying him down as gently as I could, and applied a hot towel to his stomach. Nelson offered to stay and help Lum make dinner.

I am standing at the front windows, replaying the scene from earlier, when I hear him speak behind me. This is it, I think. He has seen my hands, and he knows that I am not who I say I am. He was not sent by the mob from earlier, but by the tong and Jasper to find me. I wonder if this is the moment when he puts a sack over my head, drags me off into the night. I turn to face him.

Just do it already, I tell him. I am tired of it all.

What? Nelson says. I only meant—I only noticed your hands because they look like the hands of an artist.

For the third time today, Nelson Wong surprises me. I teeter in place without anything to say.

I play violin, he says, gesturing with his hands. I know an artist when I see one.

Violin, I say. I do not remember learning this word in my English studies.

Siu tai kam? he says. Xiao ti qin? His Chinese is round and distant, something he has to search for. He was not born with our language in his mouth, I realize.

Even so, I recognize the word. Along with it, a memory comes to me, something mournful and guttural floating through an open window. The way loss might sound if it were turned into music. My mother, closing her eyes and putting her hands to her heart. This song, she said, makes me think of my mother.

I am sorry if I made you upset today, Nelson says.

I never played violin, I tell him. I do not know why I am telling him things that are true. But my mother always admired musicians and so do I.

His face lights up at this, even though it is dark by now. You should come by and hear me play sometime.

Another surprise. The idea is ridiculous, the last thing I would ever expect to hear. Is this how he chooses to lure me into whatever evil he has planned? I wait for my body to burn again, for the warning within my belly. Instead, there is only an insistent humming.

This feeling is new to me, but I cannot tell if it is bad this time. Even so, I do not know its name, and so I am afraid.

Maybe, I tell Nelson.

7

After the protest, things are quiet for a while. The only remnants from that day are the small crack on the window, not so different from a stain or water smudge, and Nam's bruised rib. I sweep the store, dust in between each can and jar and sack, and fill the shelves until they burst with new merchandise. We are a bountiful, plentiful store, Lum says when he sees my work. Who would not want to come here?

Nam and Lum cannot stop talking about Nelson, how he must be a guardian sent to watch over us. I know a thing or two about guardians, I want to tell them when they are praising his height and his kind countenance. How quick he is. That is a good young man, Lum keeps saying. You could learn a thing or two from him, Jacob, if you are to be in this world.

It is not bad to have friends, Nam says. You do not want to grow old like me, with only Lum to die with. You want family. Are you listening, Jacob?

Something is happening to me. I should be thinking about staying away from Nelson Wong, but instead, I am remembering his hands and the nails on his fingers, wide and flat, white half-moons at the nail beds. I am remembering that moment when, as we carried Nam to the bed and waited for the doctor to arrive, his fingers danced across my back and how quickly he apologized for it.

At night, I trace his name on my thigh. Nelson. In Chinese, Ni Er Sen.

I pull the characters apart. If I can understand his name, I can know what his intentions are. His name does not yield easily. Ni and Er are just sounds meant to mimic their English counterparts. The last one, Sen 森, is a forest. Two trees on bottom and one on top.

Three trees, one forest. Nelson, like a forest, must contain plenty. He must be a man of many things—but what those things are, I still do not know.

Time will tell, Lin Daiyu promises me. *The musician's hands will never lie. They hold the answer to a river's cry.*

A year of sleep has been good for her. Since the mob woke her, she grows stronger with each day, until she no longer needs to sleep inside me. Instead, she appears when she wants and walks around without my asking. She reminds me more and more of the Lin Daiyu in the story, the one who plays tricks and composes poems and sings about her flower grave. Her cough dwindles, until all she has to do is clear her throat.

He cannot be all that bad if he plays the qin, she tells me. I play, too, and I am not all that bad. Or have you forgotten?

I tell her no, I have not forgotten. Lin Daiyu swells with satisfaction and I wonder if she must have a point about Nelson.

The burning returns, but this time it is gentle, like the afternoon sun settling itself into my skin. When I sleep, it is there with me, and when I wake, it bounces off me, rosy and purple from the glow of my dreams. I search for the threat I once feared, but it is slipping away, replaced by this new feeling that still has no name.

Can you tell me what this is? I ask Lin Daiyu. Today, she sits on top of the counter in the store, filling her mouth with flowers that have frozen over. They are dead, but they are still beautiful, crusted in ice. When she bites down, they splinter and crack against her teeth.

I am hardly one to know anything about men, she says. Water leaks out of her mouth, falling into a wet spot on the floor.

I am not talking about what happened to *you*, I say, running over to wipe the puddle up with my shirt sleeve.

Then what *are* you talking about?

I want to know if Nelson Wong is a bad man, I say. I want to know if this feeling I am feeling is good or bad.

Peach blossoms, pink silk bursting into spring. Fair is the maiden who is asked to sing.

Be serious, I say. I am asking you a real question.

How should I know, she protests. It was not long ago that you wanted nothing to do with me. Now look at you! Asking me for advice. Do you really trust in me that much?

If Nam and Lum or a customer were to come in now, they would throw me on a cart and ship me off to the place where lunatics go. But there are things I want to say to the girl I was named after.

Can you blame me, I say, for hating you when I was younger?

Lin Daiyu finishes the last of her flowers and licks her fingertips. You hurt my feelings, she says. But now you see that I am not something to be hated. Now you need me. You have always needed me.

I say nothing. She already knows everything I have to say anyway.

Lin Daiyu regards me. Nelson Wong is not a bad man, she says finally. In fact, I rather like him. But your question about whether or not this feeling is good or bad? I do not know the answer to that. All I can say is that it is both good and bad.

She stops, then laughs. She says, Or is it neither?

I want to push her off the counter where she is sitting. This is no help to me at all, I say. I am a foolish girl talking to ghosts.

Fine, she says, rising to find more flowers. But I told you the truth as I know it. It is not my fault that you are too stubborn to believe me. You have always been this way, have I told you that?

—

Lum was right—the mob does come back. Seven days after the incident, we hear the same voices-as-one, feel the same march toward our door as their boots kick up dirt and wet snow and dead things. Celestial beings! Locusts of Egypt! Go back to your Flowery Kingdom! We stick to the plan: lock the doors, let loose the blinds, keep quiet. Do not try to reason, do not show your face. This time, the mob stays for an hour before leaving. I sit with my back against the door, as if my body is enough to prevent them from breaking in. But Lum sits there with me, too, and he tells me to sit up straight and tall.

This is how you become a man, Jacob, he says.

8

In West Idaho, three Chinese miners are accused of looting. They are taken into the woods, where they are each tied to a tree by their queues. Then their throats are slit.

In South Idaho, a Chinese man is dropped from a gate by a rope.

In East Idaho, a fourteen-year-old Chinese boy is dragged from his family's apartment and hanged with clothesline.

In North Idaho, an ax flies through the night and splits a lantern. A Chinese temple burns, bodies glowing inside.

In Pierce, just outside our door, the mob comes every week.

—

In the middle of May, snow turns into water, soaking the earth. I like the way the sun feels on my head, a quiet heat holding my scalp.

Today, the doctor pronounces Nam's rib healed. In celebration of his recovery, Nam and Lum give me the day off. Go do something other than be here, they tell me. We will be fine without you.

I have not ventured out since the day Nam got hurt. After that, the store felt like the only place in the world where I could be safe. At least inside the store, I was with my own people, and I was protected. There was no danger of my true identity being revealed. But today, there is no mob and the street is clear. The sky is the kind of blue that hurts my eyes. The businesses around us have opened their windows. Even Foster's Goods looks friendly.

I cannot remember the last time I had a free day to myself. I could go to the bakery, take the path to the church, look at the courthouse. I could walk to the snowcapped mountains that border town, continue walking until Pierce ends and something else begins.

Or, Lin Daiyu whispers, her breath itching up my neck, you could go see *him*.

She finds my confusion toward Nelson amusing, no different from a frivolous game. Stop, I tell her. I step out into the street, adjusting the kerchief over my throat.

He wants you to go, she continues. He *invited* you.

That was a month ago, I say. The young man named Nelson Wong had been by only a few times since, once to pick up his rosin, the other times to check on Nam. I stayed hidden in the back during his visits, palms pressed against my face to calm its hot flush. I tell Lin Daiyu, He has probably forgotten his invitation by now.

A month is nothing when you have lived as long as me, Lin Daiyu retorts.

———

The trail leading to the mountains is still too damp with snow, the courthouse is full, and the church looks morose for such a bright day. A breeze tugs at my kerchief. I know that it is trying to pull me in one final direction. I turn and begin walking north, back through downtown to the Twinflower Inn.

If I get hurt, I tell Lin Daiyu, it is your fault.

She says nothing, just laughs in a way that sounds like there is a bird trapped in her throat.

———

Nelson Wong has not forgotten about his invitation. When he opens the door and sees me there, one foot already behind me and ready to run away, he jumps back and ushers me inside.

Lin Daiyu's hands push me forward.

Nelson rents one of the larger rooms at the Twinflower Inn. When I ask how he can afford such a place, he tells me he has a generous friend.

The first thing I see is an instrument lying on a squat table in front of the fireplace. This must be his violin. It does not look like the stringed instruments I have seen before, whose bodies resembled fish with flesh picked clean off their bones. Instead, it is a woman's body, curved and spacious and full. In front of the fire, the xiao ti qin turns a deep apricot.

Nelson asks if I would like anything to drink, then disappears to pour me some tea. I revolve around the room. At my childhood home in the fishing village, my mother's tapestries adorned the walls. At Master Wang's, calligraphy pieces expanded before us. At Madam Lee's, shiny red-gold wallpaper watched our every movement.

But in Nelson's room, the walls are empty. The only thing I can trace back to the man now walking toward me is a photograph on the mantel above the fireplace. There is someone who looks like a father, someone who looks like a mother, and then a tinier version of Nelson. An acorn nose, oval eyes, the eyelids that almost taper. He stares at me, holding something in his mouth. His parents are smiling.

I pine for my own.

Nelson invites me to sit, apologizing for how hot it is in the room. My fingers move better when it is warm, he explains. He pedals his fingers up and down an invisible neck to show me. I tell him that I do not mind.

It could be the heat of the room, but there is a serenity about him, a certain gentleness that I have learned not to expect from a man. He, like the bare walls of his room, is exactly as he appears. I have not met a man like this before.

I am glad you came to visit, he says. I was afraid I did something to offend you. When I asked you about your hands, for example.

Tell him you thought he was trying to kill you, Lin Daiyu teases, pinching my arm.

I ignore her. Nam's rib is finally healed, I offer instead.

That is wonderful news, Nelson says.

I realize I am sitting the way Daiyu would, with her legs closed, her knees pressed against each other, hands pleated in her lap. Across from me, Nelson has his legs spread so that the space between them makes a diamond. His body is more relaxed, open. I shift my feet, trying to mimic him.

Is the fire too hot? he asks, seeing me.

I tell him no. I tell him this is a nice room at a nice inn. I tell him that he did nothing to offend me and that I am sorry if I made it seem that way.

He smiles at the last part. I just hoped we could be friends, he says. There are not many of us left in Pierce.

Nam told me there were many Chinese here before, I say.

He nods. Drinks his tea. There were, he says, especially when the mines were open. Tons of Chinese worked there. My father was one of them.

There—a mention of his past before he became who he is now. His words are like a lightning bug flitting around in the dark. I snatch at it with both hands and hold on to it, knowing that there is very little time before that light goes out.

Where are your parents now? I ask.

My father died a few years ago, he says. The mines destroyed his lungs. My mother died not too long afterward. I think because of a broken heart.

Oh, I say. I am sorry.

You are very kind, Nelson tells me. Sometimes I think I could lose myself in the sadness. But then I remind myself of how fortunate I am. I had my parents for as long as I could. There are many who lose their parents much younger.

His words are brave, but his eyes tell a different story, one of loneliness and perhaps even fear. He looks away quickly, but not before I see it—the same story that lives in me.

Before I can stop myself, I blurt out, I do not have my parents, either.

The words leave my mouth and float away, finally exposed in the world. Next to me, Lin Daiyu sucks in air through her teeth, her playfulness gone. Why would you tell him that? she hisses. You should not tell anyone about your true self.

I mean, I stutter, I do not know where they are. They are missing.

Nelson's eyes meet mine and this time he does not hide the pain in his eyes. Oh, Jacob, he says. Is that why you look very sad all the time?

So he saw it after all. I could try as hard as I could to erase my true self from my appearance, but it would always find a way—the same sullenness that underlined my childhood had followed me to adulthood. Now amplified by real tragedy, it would always be obvious on my face. Yes, I want to say to Nelson. I want to cry. After so many years of lying and hiding, this is the closest I have come to telling the truth. Lin Daiyu is shaking her head, but I ignore her.

I do not mean to look sad, I say instead. It is another truth.

Nelson says, It was the first thing I noticed about you.

My grandmother would say I always looked like I was crying, I tell him. The third truth escapes easily now.

He laughs. I drink my tea. Jasmine. Something more than tea settles into me, comfortable and covetous. In front of Nelson, I feel like a great heaviness has been set aside. I remember a special kind of paper Master Wang once showed me, a mature paper that was dyed orange, so that its pattern resembled a tiger's stripes. You could only achieve this effect by heavily treating the paper, which in turn made it dense and rigid but produced an eye-catching quality that made the surface of the paper glitter like snow. A reminder that what is hardened can also be beautiful.

You will come again? Nelson asks before I leave. I tell him yes, even though Lin Daiyu tries to cover my mouth.

Good, he says. We will be great friends.

9

Sheriff Bates is a man of shoulders. His face, now mottled and pock-marked, hints at past handsomeness, a patina gradually stripped away by time. Now all that remains is a stiff yellow mustache and egg-white eyebrows. Preceding his every movement is a hard, insistent stomach.

The idea was Lum's. The protests outside the store had finally stopped, but in their place, new terrors rose. The signs the mob once carried now plaster our windows. As part of my daily chores, I take a rag and a bucket of warm water outside to rub off posters declaring EXPEL THE COOLIES and calling us CHINEE BEASTS and JOHN CHINAMAN. The next morning, they reappear.

The posters are a small annoyance compared to the other things. Packages arrive at our doorstep wrapped in brown paper, revealed to be feces and bile and some animal's organ. After the third time, I throw the packages away without opening them. But still they come.

Someone, I do not know who, comes into the store one day, and by the time they leave, there are dead rats dropped along corners, propped up in between cans of tomatoes, draped on top of bags of rice. It takes a whole afternoon to clean the store and get rid of the smell. Even then, we have to leave the windows open at night and sleep with our blankets over our mouths.

One morning we wake to find that someone has broken in and urinated all over the tea. This, somehow, is the final straw.

You have to do something, Lum tells the sheriff.

We did everything right, Nam says, his hands open. We have a license, we have paperwork. We have every right to be here.

Still, the sheriff does not walk inside the store. You do not know who did any of this?

That is why we asked you, Lum says. We have some idea, but we are not sure.

I am sorry, gents, Sheriff Bates says. I cannot arrest if I do not even have a suspect.

But you do, Lum says, his voice strained. That mob. Round them up and ask every single one! Ask Foster why he comes and stands outside our store like a specter!

The sheriff wavers. I could do that, he says. But it would take a lot of work and noise. And if I were you, I would ease up on accusing Mister Foster of anything. I am not sure you want that sort of attention on yourself.

When I was a child, I thought there was nothing more right or true than a guardian of the law. In front of this aging sheriff, I think I am beginning to see the truth about those who hold power.

So you will do nothing? Nam asks. This is another question he already knows the answer to.

Get me a suspect or credible witness, the sheriff says, turning to leave. Until then, chin up, gents. Not a bad time to think about leaving town. That Chinee laundry just shut down, did you know? People are packing out.

Lum curses at the spot where the sheriff stood. Nam's hands are still outstretched, but they are empty, holding nothing. We have to consider, Lum says finally, the possibility of leaving. Nam lets out a strangled noise, then walks away to the back of the store.

We have to consider, Lum says again, this time to me.

Summer has just begun, and soon, summer's end will come. If I am to begin my journey to Washington Territory, I cannot afford to move again and hunt for work. This store has to work. This town has to work. And, even though I do not want to say it, I am thinking of another reason to be here.

Witness, Lum mutters. Where can we find a witness?

There is one, I say.

※

You want me to come forward?

We are in Nelson's room again, and this time, we are drinking. For me, it is the first time. My mother always told me that alcohol was something reserved for men and deities. I am pretending to be one of those things. The first taste makes my tongue curl, the corners of my mouth watering. A fire follows the drink's path down into my belly. I contort my face without meaning to, which makes Nelson laugh.

It is the only way Sheriff Bates will do something, I say.

I can only tell him what I saw, Nelson says. One or two faces. I do not remember everyone who was there.

At least it is something, I say.

Nelson touches my arm then. Something inside me relents.

You should know, Jacob. Sheriff Bates and men like him are . . . biased.

I ask him what that means.

Let me put it this way, he says. I do not think Sheriff Bates would go out of his way to throw one of his own in jail.

He does not explain what he means by *his own*.

But let us talk about something else, Nelson says. Let me play for you.

Oh good, Lin Daiyu says, emerging from the fireplace, her nose red. Let me assess his skill.

He sets his drink down and rises, body aglow. With his left hand, he sweeps the violin under his chin, in the space where shoulder and chest and neck converge. I imagine him doing this many times over the course of his life, the violin pressing against his collarbone and the music vibrating from that bone through the rest of his body, until his entire skeleton echoes with song.

When he places his bow on the strings and begins to play, everything falls away. I know the peeling sorrow of the er hu, the hollow whistle of the flute, the raindrops of the gu qin. But until this moment, I did not know the violin.

The first note is a wail, but then Nelson's fingers dance and skip, his bow slicing at the strings. The music is an infantry, and then it is an army, close to becoming so large that not this room, not this town, not even this world could hold it. The melody flexes and Nelson flexes with it, it dips and soars and so does he, his body no longer a body, but an instrument, too, the muscle that the song uses to carry out its demand. The rich vibrato pours into me. His fingers are down the violin's neck now, the thumb hooked, his other four tapping and striking the thinnest string. A cloud of rosin rises with each stroke of the bow like a flower releasing pollen. It is an operatic, beautiful release.

And looking at him, my heart is full. I did not know men could create something like this.

I am a little drunk, he says when the music ends. Red blossoms on his neck, the place where the violin dug into his flesh.

It was splendid, I tell him. I do not know if this is the way a man compliments another man, but the drink has made me bold. You play like you *are* the music. You make it sound like it is alive.

It was just fine, Lin Daiyu mutters, crawling back into the fireplace.

My mother once told me that I needed to play with more emotion, Nelson says. I wonder what she would think of the way I play now.

I imagine the woman from the picture on the mantel, now completely in this room with us, leaning over a younger Nelson and correcting his fingers.

Is she the one who taught you?

Nelson nods. She played ever since she was a child, he says. My first violin belonged to her.

We fall into a natural silence. My eyes are on the floor, but my pulse is racing, in danger of running away from me. There was no hesitation with Nelson, no question. Not even a thought. He simply lifted the violin into the air and let music command him. This must be what Master Wang meant by a calligrapher reaching his ultimate form. I envy him.

10

Somewhere in Pierce, a white man wakes to find an apologetic sheriff at his door. He is brought in for questioning regarding the vandalization of the Chinese store. He is told that a witness remembers seeing him at the protests, and maybe other witnesses have seen him lingering around the store. The man denies it, and the sheriff is inclined to believe him, but alas, something must be done. For his alleged crimes, the man is held for two days.

It appears to have worked. After the arrest, things are better at the store. Posters no longer paper our window every morning. The packages stop. No more dead rats. Business is resuming as normal. Perhaps, Nam says, we have finally walked out from under the shadow of the mountain.

But even if the harassment stops for us, it seems to be getting worse in other places. Not long after the Chinese laundry closes, Cheng's barbershop follows. Getting too dangerous here, he tells Nam. Going back to Guangzhou. I read in the paper—the fourth page, a tiny corner mention—about a mob ransacking a Chinatown and lynching its inhabitants. The bodies are poked and jeered at, castrated and decapitated. The journalist justifies it as Americans' *right of revolution*.

11

Sometimes, in between his lessons, Nelson will drop by the store. He tells me that he is simply there to pass the time, but I can tell by the way he stiffens when white customers enter that he is here in case anything happens. Nelson is taller than most of the Chinese in Pierce, and with his purposeful step and serious nose, it is easy to see that he will not be easily shaken.

We linger between the shelves, a box of canned prunes at my feet still waiting to be organized. Nelson points to apricots, plums, peaches, asking me what the word for each would be in my version of Chinese. He only learned a few words when he was little. His parents, who came from the same region as Nam and Lum, wanted him to speak good English.

Xing, I tell him patiently. Li zi. Tao.

Tao, he tries, lips wrapping themselves around the sound. His earnest expression makes me laugh.

And Nam, who cannot bear to be strict like Lum, calls my name from the counter, asking if my work is done yet. Nelson and I duck our heads, hands to our mouths, laughing even harder, and move over to the medicines and herbs. Nelson picks up a dried yellow root, and I tell him that it is called huang qi.

Hm, he says, feeling its flatness with his thumb. But I do not know what we would call this in English.

Perhaps we should not try, I tell him. Some things are better left as they were intended to be.

I do not tell him of mornings in the garden with my grandmother, who loved huang qi most.

We share a name, this root and I, Nelson says. Do you think this means I will lead an immortal life?

I think it means you are both somewhat yellow, I tell him. It is a good thing.

It is Nelson's turn to laugh. Again, Nam asks mildly if my work is done for the day. On afternoons like these, we return to being giddy children. It is a way we are glad to feel, because it means that the worst thing that could happen to us is getting scolded by Nam. The real world can wait for a while, I think.

Other times, Nelson brings me small gifts, although he never calls them that, like a piece of candy or a slice of meat from the deli. I worry you are not getting enough to eat, he tells me sincerely, pushing the food into my hands. You are too thin for a man your age.

Other times, he will look at me for a long moment before saying, I wish I had a brother growing up. Maybe I just wish I had a brother like you.

I tell him that it is not too late. We can be brothers now.

———

It was easy to craft a narrative for Nam and Lum. All they needed to hear was that I would be a good worker. They did not care about where I came from, or how I got there, or who I was.

But Nelson is not Nam and Lum. Nelson pauses, asks questions, waits for things to make sense and come to completion. He is thoughtful, contemplative. He is, after all, a musician. He was born in Pierce to a former violinist at a traveling theater company and a miner father. He teaches violin to ten students who will never become master violinists.

I am fine with that, he tells me. It is not about how good they get at it but helping them create their own music. Even if it does not sound perfect, I think it is beautiful because they are the ones playing it.

He is different from Master Wang, who only believed in spreading art if it was the right kind, if it had been done according to the proper rules. Nelson wants to spread all the art he can, because to him, everything is art.

He tells me I look too serious, that I should not be afraid to lead with my chest. Then he will place his hands on my shoulders and guide them back. In his hands, I arch, a bow pulled taut.

Be careful with him, Lin Daiyu warns.

I do not know what you are talking about, I tell her.

Before long, Nelson asks. I already know his question. I am ready to answer.

First: Where did you come from? Then: Who are you? And: Where do you want to be? With Nelson, I learn that Jacob Li cannot just be Jacob Li. He must also be Jacob Li, a son, a resident, someone who desires. He must be a complete person.

What I tell Nelson is a cobbled-together version of many lies and half-truths: that I worked at a noodle shop in San Francisco and came to Idaho looking for better work and higher wages. I am trying to make enough money to go back to China to find my parents.

It must be his calm demeanor, the way he looks at anyone with a steady gaze, that makes it so easy to tell him shades of the truth. Because even though I will be gone by the time summer ends, I like knowing that I am leaving behind pieces of myself that are real. To Nelson, at least, they matter.

Lin Daiyu no longer finds amusement in any of this. She warns that I am becoming careless and willful. She urges me to stop.

I know you are trying to protect me, I tell her, but perhaps it is too much.

She bristles at this. I do not mind—I am getting better at telling her no.

12

On a bright day in late May, Nelson shows up at the store, his face radiant. Today, the sun is out after a week of clouds, and it makes everything feel more inviting.

What have you been doing? he asks when he sees my flushed cheeks.

I tell him I was lifting heavy boxes in the back, which is not true. What I had been doing was counting the money I saved for my journey back to China. Nearly two years in Idaho, and one hundred and forty dollars to show for it. With just three more months before my journey west, I am nearly at my goal of two hundred.

Two hundred to travel to Washington Territory and pay for my passage across. Would it be enough? It has to be, I tell myself. I could wait a little longer, yes, I could wait. But that would mean crossing the ocean in the wintertime, and I do not know if I can survive.

Can you spare an hour or two? Nelson asks. Something hums off him, a frenetic energy that I have never seen before.

No, you cannot, Lin Daiyu says crossly.

I do not think Nam and Lum would mind, I say. We are closing soon anyway.

It would be a shame to waste a day like this, Nelson agrees.

We head south toward the schoolhouse. Lin Daiyu does not follow.

Nelson walks quickly, and I have to jog to keep up. When we reach the school, we skirt around the left side of the building. Nelson looks behind us, checking that we are alone.

Nelson, I say, where are we going?

He does not answer, just beckons me to follow.

Behind the school, a path leads into the trees. To a passerby, the path would look like any other matted patch of field, but as I get closer, I see that the grass is bent in a purposeful way, marking the hint of a trail.

Come on, Nelson urges, and he ducks into the trees.

I can tell that not many people have walked this path before. The hemlocks push against us, their needles catching on my shirt. We pass a small turtle pond, a cluster of fallen Douglas firs, patches of wildflowers. All things that I think Nelson wants to show me, but he keeps walking, moving forward with a singular purpose. When we reach a thicket of brambles, he finally stops. I think that this is the end—surely there is nothing beyond this massive wall of thorns and tangled branches, but Nelson is already bending down to thread his body through.

You have to squeeze a little, I hear him call.

I am small enough, I know. I slip through, a branch dragging across the back of my neck. I check to make sure my kerchief is still there. When I straighten again, I see the path before us and Nelson already rushing ahead.

This, he says breathlessly, is what I wanted to show you.

He stands at the center of a clearing encircled by hemlock trees, arms outstretched and grinning. Above him, the trees bend to form a green ceiling. The sun breaks open, dappling the grass in glassy light. I remember, even through Jacob Li's carefully crafted barrier, the character for joy 樂, how it cannot exist without a tree.

I join him in the center and look up.

I found it a few days ago, Nelson says. I do not think anyone knows that it is here.

What were you looking for? I ask.

Perhaps I will tell you later, he says.

Nelson has packed corn bread, boiled eggs, iced tea in a can. I can see why he likes it here. Out here, the world stops. Or, at least, the world becomes very small—it is just us and the grass and the hemlocks, encased beneath the sapphire sky. The wind slows, fenced out by the trees.

I take many breaths. In Idaho, it is more difficult to breathe, like my lungs cannot fully expand to take in all the air they should. Sometimes, I think of my time in the coal bucket, wonder if breathing all that coal damaged me. Next to me, Nelson lies down in the grass, a few patches of snow still glistening on the ground. His eyes are closed, hands interlaced on his stomach.

Once, I wanted a fish from the fish market. I wanted it so badly that I could not see anything else, could only feel the satisfaction of it slipping down my throat. I craved nothing more than the fullness that would come, the heat from being fed.

Looking at Nelson now, I realize that I want him the way I wanted the fish: badly, and with abandon. He is perfect inside this clearing, we are perfect, one of us sleeping, the other one wanting. I want to wrap him around me, to wear him as my armor—him so sure, the one with the music and the bow and the endless light. And I wonder, what do we call this feeling, the one where you want something so badly that you would feed them to yourself?

What are you thinking about? he says. Not asleep after all.

I tell him the weather, how nice the sun feels. And I ask him the same question.

I am thinking, he says, opening his eyes, about how you know so much about me, but I know almost nothing about you. You have told me some things, yes. But I think there is more to know.

Lin Daiyu appears from behind a tree. Between these massive oaks and pines, she looks like a husk of corn. Be careful, she says, pulling up her dress as she walks to us.

For once, my instinct is not to lie. I could keep telling Nelson the same half-truths I had already begun telling him. Or I could unspool the tangle of lies, the fibers that decide what is Daiyu and what is Jacob Li, until I become wholly, completely myself again. It would be so easy, in this place where everything seems good and true.

But then I remember Samuel, his pale, nervous face and eager smile, and I remember the gray-haired man's body thrumming against me, how the softness of him was not a softness at all, but something disgusting and cruel. Nelson would not be like Samuel or the gray-haired man, this I know. But Nelson is still a man.

Instead, I tell him a truth so outlandish that it sounds like a lie. I tell him that I was kidnapped in China, and arrived in San Francisco inside a coal bucket.

His brows press together. I am sorry, Jacob, he says. There is pain in his voice, and I realize that it is for me. I want to reach out then and touch him, but I do not.

Everyone has their tragic story, I say, hoping I sound like a man.

That does not mean they should have to suffer, he says softly, sitting up. There must be a way for us to undo some of this pain. I have been thinking. Perhaps we can begin by finding your parents?

Lin Daiyu lets out a shriek of laughter. For a moment, I think Nelson is joking, and I almost join Lin Daiyu in her laughs. But then Nelson stands, his eyes like embers, and I realize that he is serious.

I know you miss them very much, he says.

I do not expect him to say this. His words dissolve a gate within me, through which pour memories. My mother leading a client—a general's wife—around her newest tapestry piece, where a phoenix breathes white smoke into the sky. My father taking tea with a general, their laughs rolling through the entire house like someone had let the thunder in. And me with the never-ending pull in my heart, for them, for us, for whatever magic exists in this world to take me back and let me stay there forever. Nelson's words invite something new—a permission, perhaps, to mourn.

Yes, I say to him.

Then let me help, Nelson says. I have an old friend in Boise. Met him when I was younger, when my mother sent me to study with a violinist there. His family is very well connected in China. He can use those connections, figure out what happened to your parents.

The entire plan sounds dangerous, already leaking water. I begin to regret telling Nelson a semblance of the truth. Could his friend even be trusted? If they manage to find my parents, they would surely discover that I was not Jacob Li after all, but Daiyu, the daughter that went missing. What came after, I did not know, nor did I want to find out.

Nelson, I say finally, choosing my words carefully. I have not told you the complete truth. You see, my parents are not missing. My parents are dead.

What?

Jacob Li takes over, lying as I have never lied before. I did not lie, I say to Nelson. They *are* missing, in a way. Forgive me, it was too painful to say it out loud to you the first time.

Oh, Nelson says, sitting back down. I see, in the way his face changes, that he chooses to believe Jacob Li. He says, I was hoping I could help you. My friend would not mind. He is very kind. How wonderful would it be if you could find out what happened to your home?

The child in me that is Daiyu will not go away without a fight. She imagines what it would be like to know exactly where her parents are, to receive a slip of paper with their address on it. To show up at their home, wherever it is now, and to let them know that she is still their daughter after all this time. They are out there waiting for her.

Perhaps there is a way you and your friend could help, I say. With this sentence, I know that I am opening a world I cannot step back from. There is now a hole in the fabric of the sky and it will continue spreading until I have my answer, until I am able to repair it the way Nuwa did. I look Nelson in the eye and feel myself growing sturdy and true.

I tell him, My parents are gone, but there are two people who I would like to find. They took care of me after my parents left. They were kind to me as I was growing up. I would like to know what happened to them, perhaps even thank them.

I am talking, of course, about my own parents, but Nelson does not know. Nelson thinks that my parents are dead and that I was raised by two strangers. This is the way it should be. If my parents are not my parents, then Jacob Li and Daiyu can stay separate.

When Nelson and I part that day, we have a plan: We will go to Boise together to meet his friend. I do not have to make any decisions now. We will have a nice dinner and then see a concert with a violinist he likes. We will sit in a theater hall and listen to beautiful music and our shoulders will touch without meaning to, and we will look at each other and smile.

—

Back at the store, Lin Daiyu sits facing me on my bed. Have you forgotten, she demands, how my story ended?

But this is not the same, I tell her. We are not the same.

You say that, she retorts, throwing her luminous head back. But look at us. No family, alone in a place that is not our home. Loving those who will only cause us pain in the end. Just you wait for the ending. You will see.

This is not the same, I repeat.

13

The friend is tall like Nelson. He arrives in a maroon chang shan and black pants. I can tell by the soft sheen of the fabric that he has money to spare. Like Nam and Lum, and unlike Nelson, he wears a queue, one that falls past his hips, the hair as robust as rolled-up dough. It is the afternoon, and the sun bounces off his forehead with a gleam that reminds me of fresh-cut melons.

His name is William. In Chinese, he would be called Weilian, denoting strength and honesty. I can trust a name like that, I convince myself.

We meet in a restaurant in downtown Boise called The Larch. William leads, then Nelson, then me, then Lin Daiyu trailing behind us all, her feet barely touching the floorboards. Inside, it is musty, the smell of cork, and the windows are closed, throwing the restaurant into forced darkness. I notice the whites of the restaurant patrons' eyes, even whiter than their faces, as they follow us through the dining room. But William, our leader, does not seem to notice. His head is up, shoulders back and straight, held together by an invisible pin. He walks proudly, confidently, as if daring those who stare to stop him.

I shove my hands in my pockets to stop them from shaking. Boise is too full of memories of what happened the last time I was here. The inn attached to the Chinese temple. Samuel's long shadow against the wall. Nelson turns back to make sure that I am still there, and I remind myself to straighten. Behind me, Lin Daiyu rubs a hand up and down my back.

We sit at a table in the back corner. It is my first time in a restaurant where I am the patron, and the newness of being so exposed makes me uneasy. But William and Nelson, who have no reason to hide, sit freely, their bodies comfortable with belonging. I mimic William and drape myself on my chair. I am glad our backs are against a wall.

One by one, the eyes of the patrons dim and flicker away, returning to their own tables. I am reminded of the hungry foxes outside the calligraphy school, eyes looking at everything but us. They thought that if we did not see them looking, we would not know they were there. But we always saw. We saw and we knew they were playing a game with us, those hungry foxes who pretended to read the walls. Really, they were waiting for a moment when our guards lowered, when we would truly look away and they could take everything.

It has been a long time since William and Nelson have seen each other, but they speak comfortably all the same. Watching them, I think of the girls at the brothel. Once, they were the closest things to friends that I had. I wonder what they would say if they could see me now, a short man with even shorter hair. And I wonder if they are getting enough to eat, if their bodies are healthy, how they will leave the brothel. I know that they will never leave of their own accord, but it is nice to imagine for a moment.

William is asking Nelson about Pierce—*that dull old town*—about his students—*those ungrateful puppies*—about when Nelson is finally going to do as he once promised and travel around the world with his friend—*I am still waiting, N, I am still waiting!* When William talks, his entire body moves. When he laughs, he balloons, then crumples against whatever is nearest him—Nelson, the table's edge, the back of the chair. More than once, Nelson has to reach out to steady the water glasses in the wake of William's laughter.

So, William says finally, turning to me. The famous Jacob Li. Nelson has had much to say about you.

Is that so? I say, making my voice gruffer than usual. William looks like he is the same age as Nelson, which might as well be the same age as me. Being around men my age makes me feel even more vulnerable, as if they can see by simple self-knowledge that I am not like them.

I told William what you told me, Nelson says gently. About the couple you are searching for.

The couple. My parents. The lie, so inextricably linked to my real life, handed to a complete stranger. I hope it is worth it, Lin Daiyu mutters.

William leans into the center of the table. I have very good connections in China, he says to us, but to me most of all, the one who needs to hear it. I can help you find almost anyone you are looking for.

I press my lips together, thinking of what my grandmother would say. From the beginning, she had taught me to keep my mouth shut, to never tell the truth about who I was. She would want me to stay quiet now. But since my initial conversation with Nelson, I could not help thinking: Had not the worst things already happened to me? Even by protecting my identity and shielding myself with other identities, I was still kidnapped, shipped across the ocean, sold to a brothel, betrayed by a man I thought I could call a friend.

And. And I want to know where my parents are. There are things that can be blurred, facts that can be so close to the truth that they might become the truth. Practice makes truth. Now it is just a matter of telling the story.

My parents died when I was born, I tell the table, the well-rehearsed words falling out easily. I feel Nelson leaning in, having never heard the complete story of my life until now. Even Lin Daiyu stills, her eyes narrowed and curious.

In my head, I see the truth, my real-life past, and a knife sliding underneath—a delicate maneuver, performed by only the most skilled of hands—to remove it. What remains is something that looks like my past, but obfuscated.

I was an orphan in my village, I say, but I survived by the good grace of the people who lived there. A couple. They took care of me, made sure I had enough to eat, even when they did not. Their names were Lu Yijian and Liu Yunxiang.

I have not said their names in so long. In fact, I do not think I ever have out loud. There was never a reason to call them anything but Die and Niang.

This couple, I continue, treated me as if I were their own. Despite what was happening in their lives, they made me feel like a true son.

In many ways, telling this lie is easier. Telling the lie means that it is all happening to someone who is not me.

When I was twelve or so, I continue, they disappeared. Later, I found out that they were arrested. I do not know what happened to them from there, but they were never heard from again. Not too long after that, I was kidnapped and brought to America.

William shakes his head and whistles. Nelson is looking at me as if he has never seen me before.

Now is the moment to perform my final act. I want to find them, I say to their entranced faces. I want to tell them thank you, to let them know that I am alive and well, and that their hard work did not go unnoticed or unthanked.

The lie is complete, the story perfected. Master Wang would be proud, I think. My practice really did turn into my own kind of art. William sits back now, a look of astonishment on his face. This selfless couple deserves to know that you are alive. You were right to come to me!

William promises us that he will do what we need him to do. He is flush with sentimentality. Forget the stories we have been taught, he says, slapping his hand down on the table. Your story is true, but it did not just happen to you. It has happened to many people like you.

Our lunch arrives. It takes four waiters to carry it all: hot cakes, fennel sausages, fried potatoes, boiled ham and vegetables, oyster pie, cutlets. Roast mutton and currant jelly, a dish called beef alamode. William sees my wide eyes and laughs, telling me he has already paid for it. The entire restaurant stares at us, offended by our boldness, and then I understand why William has chosen a white restaurant instead of one in Chinatown. Nelson shakes his head in a way that tells me William has a habit of doing this. I know, now, who is paying for his suite at the Twinflower Inn.

In the seat next to me, Lin Daiyu moans, her eyes on the oyster pie.

Eat as much as you want, William says. He is still watching me.

I hesitate at first, spooning a few potatoes onto my plate. The outside is fragrant, dusted with rosemary, and the inside hot, lush, a little sweet. One bite turns into ten, and then I cannot stop. I cannot remember the last time I was allowed to eat like this, without a goal in mind or a deed to pay back. This is what simply being alive must be like, I think as I slide my knife into a cutlet. This is the joy of not having to worry about anything.

You were saying, Nelson says, turning to William, how America has become hugely disappointing for you.

William's mouth is already full with ham, but he answers anyway. Be honest, Nelson, he says. Things have been worse since that awful law was passed. And now you say there are mobs in your town? Are you really surprised?

I was there, I say, eager to be a part of the conversation. I work at the store where this has been happening.

Then surely you can tell us better than our idealistic Nelson, William says, now waving a forkful of mutton around. Jacob, how would you say the new law has affected you?

We are talking of the law banning Chinese? I ask, wary of saying the wrong thing.

The Exclusion Act, yes, William says, studying me closely. In my mind, I write out exclusion 排: a hand next to wrong.

Awful, I say, knowing this is what William wants to hear. I would have expected them to treat our kind better.

William stops chewing.

You must be joking, he says. *Treat our kind better?* Have you forgotten? He turns to Nelson, indignant. Nelson, tell me he is joking.

The old panic returns—the one where I am close to being found out. I open my mouth to give them an answer, any excuse, but Nelson speaks before I can.

Perhaps we are being too presumptuous, he says gently. We forget that Jacob's journey to America has not been the easiest. Perhaps you did not know because you were not allowed to know.

I say nothing, hoping this makes his words true.

Nearly a decade ago, Nelson explains, there was a law called the Page Act that banned Chinese women from entering.

And now, William interjects, with this new Exclusion Act, it is just the final touch on their grand painting of what America is supposed to look like. Despicable!

I see, I say.

I always wondered why I was chosen that day in the fish market. Why they made me so skinny, so dirty, cut my hair, stuffed me in coal. Why I had to be Feng the orphan instead of Daiyu. Jasper picked me out because I was a girl who looked like a boy. My sullen face and tired eyes, once the things that protected me, had turned out to be my greatest weakness. I was easy to pass as a boy, even easier to pass as a bucket of coal. When Jasper saw me in the fish market that day, he saw someone who could be rewritten.

Nelson is speaking now. I pull myself out from that room in Zhifu and try to put his words together. Ever since then, he is saying, things have been bad for the Chinese here. Things were bad before, I mean. But the law just gave people a reason to be open with their hatred.

But I do not understand, I say. What did we do to them? Why do they hate us?

William laughs. Why? A nearby table's eyes flicker to us, full of distaste. William stares back, his lip curled. They hate us because they think we are a threat to them. They think we will take their jobs. They are afraid we will seduce their women. They hate us because they believe, even if they will not admit it, that we are better than them. And it is not just here—it is happening everywhere.

My father was a miner, Nelson reminds us quietly. He got the worst of it, because they were afraid of the Chinese stealing mining jobs.

It is especially bad in the West, William agrees. Here, people call us heathens, coolies, slanty-eyed celestials. Do you know what those words mean, Jacob? Did you know that our eyes are enough reason for them to hate us?

Your eyes, my mother used to tell me, are the same ones I had as a child.

William is incensed now, bolstered by food and drink. The whites call themselves the superior race, he says. Before, they were at least secretive about their hatred. They burned and pillaged and killed, but they were not always so public about it. Now that the Exclusion Law has passed, they believe it is their God-given right to drive us out.

Surely, Nelson placates, surely this was not intended by those who wrote the laws.

William laughs again, although it is more like a bark now. I blame the people who wrote the laws most, my friend! They may not be the ones out there setting Chinatowns on fire, but they condone this violence through the laws they have passed. A tacit agreement, I would call it. What are we supposed to think? That they want to protect us?

They would not want violence, Nelson says firmly. Perhaps they did not imagine—

You are always assuming goodness in people, William says. I hear the pity in his voice. You always have. Sometimes I wonder if teaching those white students of yours, going into their white homes, has made you softer than I remember. Pass a law banning Chinese. Prevent our women from coming over legally so that there is only one woman for a hundred men. Did you know that in California, Chinese are not allowed to testify at our own trials? Trials where we have been the victims of looting, or our houses burned, our queues cut! With every piece of legislation, they are saying that we have no rights, we do not deserve safety, or love, or comfort. We do not deserve a life. They have already done it with the Negroes and Indians. They are saying, none of us deserve humanity.

Nelson is quiet. We had stopped eating long ago, our once-glorious spread of food now cold. William's anger, I think, confuses me. He speaks as if it is the end of the world, but as I watch him breathing like an enraged bull, I feel like it will all be for nothing.

But as the saying goes, William repeats, *Every action has an equal and opposite reaction.* And let me tell you two a little secret. I have been thinking of the perfect equal and opposite reaction.

On the other side of the room, a golden-haired boy smashes his hand into a plate of peas. There is a vicious certainty in the way his arm falls through the air. His mother attempts to restrain him while the father cleans up the mess. The boy's face falls at the interruption, then swells to red. It is not long before he is wailing and thrashing in his chair.

I have friends in San Francisco, William says, mainly speaking to Nelson now. They tell me of an organization there called the Chinese Six Companies. They have been around for decades, but only recently consolidated into one. San Francisco is especially bad right now, did you know that? The Six Companies are doing all they can to oppose violence against our people. They do good work, even returning brothel girls kidnapped by the tongs back to their homes in China. Sometimes, they will even return corpses.

Lin Daiyu grasps my arm, but she does not need to. I am paying attention.

William notices the shift. They are strong, he says, addressing us both now. But they need more money and people. They need resources. That is what I am telling you, Nelson. I am going to San Francisco to join them, join the fight. And I want you to come with me.

Nelson takes a moment. He supports William on this journey, he says, but he is not quite ready to leave Pierce yet. He has some important things to which he must attend. William asks, What in the hell is more important than this. I am wondering, too.

That is my business, Nelson says, not unkindly. He is done with this conversation.

William shakes his head. He is disappointed but not surprised. This is not the first time Nelson has said no to him.

He turns to me. How about it, Jacob, he says. We could leave in September.

Nelson places a hand on my shoulder. In his hand, my body feels like a part of him and I want to keep it that way, the two of us slowly fusing into each other. He is touching me as a warning, I know, but I am only noticing how warm his palm is, the way his fingers fan against my flesh.

Leave him be, William, he says. Jacob has enough to worry about without you taking him away to San Francisco. The best thing you can do for the both of us is to find out what happened to that couple. Just like he asked.

Nelson stands then, his hand leaving my shoulder. Without it, my body feels cold, like it is missing something vital. I am going to the washroom, he says. Leave Jacob be.

We watch him walk off, his confident gait carrying him easily through the cluster of tables.

Nelson is wonderful, William says, sighing. But he can be frustrating.

I want to go with you, I say.

Ah, he says, smiling. What a surprise indeed.

The look on his face is smug, as if he has triumphed over Nelson in some way. I ignore it, focusing instead on the slow happiness spreading through my chest. For so long, I had wondered how I would find my way home. The ideas were there—save enough money, journey to Washington Territory, sneak on a ship—but if I really thought about it, it was nearly impossible. The journey alone could kill me. With William's offer, the plan, once so flimsy, solidifies. I will travel with him—comfortably, judging by the quality of his clothes. He will protect us both with his money. And when I reach San Francisco, when I finally meet the great Six Companies, I will reveal my story. They will help me return to my home. They will help me find my grandmother. It is everything I have ever wanted, an answer so simple and easy that I can hardly believe it is true.

Take it, Lin Daiyu begs. Take it and take us home.

We leave in September? I ask.

The twelfth, William says. Come down and meet me here. Then we head west.

I extend my hand. He shakes it, the smugness returning to his face. Not going to tell Nelson?

I would rather not, I say. It makes the leaving easier. You understand.

I do, William says. You are a lot more than you give yourself credit for, Jacob Li.

I do not know what he means, but I say nothing. He believes that I am going to serve my people, that I have the same mind toward justice as he. I will let him keep believing that. Even from our brief time together, I can tell that he thinks himself righteous, filled with some great wisdom. He may love Nelson, but he also thinks himself above him. Above us all.

When Nelson returns, I keep my face blank.

We say our goodbyes out on the street. A few white people skirt past us, turning around to glare. I watch them walk away, reminded of the golden-haired boy with his peas.

It was nice meeting you, William tells me, shaking my hand again. He passes me an oddly shaped package wrapped in brown paper. I take it, surprised at its weight. I want you to keep this at the store and use it if you have trouble, he says. Nelson can teach you how.

I thank him. I do not know if I really like him or not.

⚫

The rest of the day is pleasant. With the new hope of returning to China and Nelson at my side, the memories of my first time in Boise begin to lighten. We walk through downtown, laughing at all the

things we cannot afford, and turn onto Idaho Street, Nelson leading the way. I sense a shift. The buildings here are unspectacular and
brown, but the air around them rattles with a familiar energy. Everyone
walking by looks like us, I realize.

Already knowing the answer, I ask Nelson, Where are we?

Chinatown, he says.

What Chinatown is: a block, or two, of buildings. We pass a general store selling merchandise, another advertising herbs and remedies.
Here, an office for a Chinese medicine doctor. There, a gambling house.
Across the street, a laundry's wash water streams out into the walkway.
There are dwellings, too, inside of which I imagine heads with hair
as black as mine. I feel a pang for my old home and sadness for this
current one—Chinatown ends when we reach Eighth Street, and the
space between is so small, so subdued compared to the country it calls
itself after. For many of its residents, this may be the only piece of
China they have left.

Nelson is watching me. Remind you of home?

You have never been to China, have you?

I am thinking of the mossy mountains and the thrust of the ocean. I
want to show Nelson the fishing village, to draw him out into the river
and cut through the water, pant legs to our knees and hands full of fish.
We would eat for days. We would become so full that all there would
be left to do was fall asleep. And maybe then I would show him Daiyu.

I will go with you one day, he promises. I know he means it.

⸺

Later, on our way to the theater, a patrolman stops us and demands to
see our papers. He squints at my picture, then at my face. This does not
look like you, he says.

That is him, Nelson says, stepping in front of me. If you have a
problem, we will happily wait for your superiors to get here.

It is late, and the patrolman has dinner waiting for him at home. He
hands my paper back, tells me to get a better picture, before walking
away.

I try to stuff it back in my breast pocket, but Nelson stops me. Let me see, he says, the paper already in his hand. I feel my heart beating very fast now. To a white eye, any Chinese could look like every Chinese. But Nelson is one of us. Nelson will know.

He does not say anything for what feels like a very long time. Then he hands the paper back to me. He is right, you know, he says, walking again. You should get a better picture.

—

Outside the theater, there is a commotion, another mob. I hear the words that have become very familiar to me now, words like *moon-eyed heathens*, *slanty-eyed bastards*, *tawny beasts*, *dusky throats*.

Closer to the theater entrance, we see that the mob is not here for the theater but a Chinese-owned laundry across the street. The owner, a short, sturdy man with flared nostrils, stands in front of the door. He is shouting back at them, defiance holding his body upright. Nelson tells me to lower my cap, hide my face with my scarf. He grabs my arm and I do not resist. We duck behind a white man in a hay-colored coat and his slender-calved wife, then swerve into the alley next to the theater.

I am sorry, Nelson, I say. The evening is ruined.

He shakes his head, as if this will somehow hide the disappointment on his face. I wanted you to hear what a real violinist sounds like, he tells me.

I can hear a real violinist anytime, I say. He is standing right in front of me.

Nelson looks down, but I can see a small smile. We begin walking down the alley, the mob's shouts growing fainter with each step. He still has not let go of my arm.

Your friend William was not lying about the mobs, I say.

He rarely does, Nelson says.

Then why not go to California with him?

In the aftermath of the mob, I am bold. As if to say, we have just survived potential death, so you will tell me the truth.

Ah, Nelson says. Our steps slow, each one heavy with anticipation. I wish I had a more interesting answer. The truth is that Pierce has always been my home. There are things there that are dear to me. I do not know if I am ready to leave.

Things like your violin students? I ask. Things like your friendships?

Yes, he says. Some things like that.

I am not bold enough to ask if he would count me in those things.

He turns to me then, both of us stopping at the same time. The lunch with William, the afternoon walking around Boise, even the encounter with the mob, it all seems to be leading us to this moment where we are standing so close we could fall into each other. His breath is indistinguishable from mine. I no longer feel my body, but instead a great melding, as if I have been a single drop of water in an ocean and am now finally letting myself be consumed by it. There is something lovely, heroic even, about letting another person look at you. In Nelson's eyes, I could save entire lives.

What about you? Nelson asks, his voice soft and bare. What is your real reason for not going?

And I remember then: He does not know the truth. He does not know that I am leaving.

Whatever magic holds us together dissipates. September is so far, I think. I will lie to him now, and I will continue lying to him until the day I leave. I take a step back, and it feels like I have traversed mountains and valleys and vast plains, landing on an earth he cannot reach. He sees the shift on my face, the old guard back up again. He steps back as well, arm dropping to his side.

We both look away. I let out a strained laugh. William is your good friend, I say. And I am grateful for his help. But this retaliation he talks about, this *fighting back with an equal and opposite reaction*—it is all foolish.

So you think it is better to do nothing at all?

That is not what I mean, I say. To me, William's talk is boastful. There are so few of us, so many of them. What can change, really?

Nelson begins walking again, but he is no longer looking at me. You know, Jacob, he says, I was thinking about Nam and Lum and even you. The mob almost killed you and Nam, and ever since then, they have been terrorizing you all. William is not wrong about it happening all over the country. Even if we do not go to California, we should not rule out doing *something*. You do not believe that is worthwhile?

I came here against my will, Nelson, I say. This is not my country. These are not my people. This is not my problem.

I see, Nelson says. I think we can get back to the inn from here.

I know I have disappointed him, but I also feel indignant. Why ask me to participate in something that I never asked to be a part of?

We emerge from the alley and turn onto an empty street, one that looks familiar but does not feel friendly. Nelson has not noticed it, instead walking with an easier step now that we are far from the theater. I do not match him. Something about this street feels very wrong.

And then I understand why. Halfway down the street, tucked between the pharmacy and an abandoned building, awaits the inn-temple where I stayed my first night in Boise.

Let us walk faster, I say, running to catch up to Nelson. I am eager to leave this place behind and never return to it again. As we walk past, I look down, ignoring the comfortable candlelight against the windows and the murmurs from the Chinese inside. A place like this should feel welcome, like home, I think bitterly.

A beggar sits at the front steps, watching us pass. He begins shouting in Chinese—a poem by the sound of it. I realize that he is drunk, the words crashing and rolling into each other. I try to hear what he is reciting—it is not a poem I recognize. And then, again, I understand.

Wait, I say to Nelson. I turn back toward the beggar.

I know this voice, heard it every night for an entire summer. From my pocket, I take out a match and light it, holding it close to the beggar's face.

Ungh, he cries, shying back. He tries to swat my hand away. Wassamatter wi' you?

His hair is long and matted, a few patches of black peppering his chin and jaw. Even under the grime and dirt and vomit, I recognize those eyes, as helpless as those of a cow.

Samuel?

Huh? He turns to me and the rank stench of stale alcohol hits my face. The match flickers.

Samuel, what are you doing here?

Nelson waits behind me. Do you know this man? he asks.

I ignore him. I cannot tell Nelson about Samuel, this boy who cried in my room all the way back in San Francisco, wanting so badly to be a man.

You have money? Samuel slurs at us. They kicked me out. He holds out his hands, cupping them together. When I look at them, I have to stop myself from retching.

One hand is there, palm facing us, outstretched. The other is not a hand, but just flesh, something without shape, the skin purple and mangled. The texture of sludgy porridge. His hand, I realize, has been excised of its bones. And then I smell it—the rot of flesh, of dried pus and rusted blood. I cover my mouth with my free hand.

My god, Nelson cries.

Samuel lowers his hands in disappointment. No good, he mutters, slumping. And he goes back to reciting his incomprehensible poem.

How do you know him? Nelson asks. Again, I ignore him.

Your hand, I say to Samuel. What happened to your hand?

Eh? Samuel shouts. This? He holds up the hand that is not a hand again, thrusting it in my face. This is my payment for all the things I have done.

What have you done? Nelson asks him, trying to sound kind.

Took something I should not have, Samuel says. How should I have known?

What are you talking about? Nelson says. What did you take?

Huh—huh—her, Samuel breathes. But she came at a price. He saw to that, he did.

I stare at the pulp of his hand. It is a hand I remember well. I watched it, resting there on his knee, all those times we sat on my bed in the brothel.

And then it starts to make sense, what he is saying.

Is *he*? I say, my voice faltering, unable to say his name. Is he the one who did this to your hand?

Eh, Samuel says, squinting hard at me. Him? Yes, *him, all of them*! He found me, had my half brothers with him. Told them nothing of her, though! At least there is one thing I am still good for!

Nelson nudges me in the back. I think we should go, he says. We cannot help this man.

Before me is Samuel, the boy of my past, and next to me is Nelson, a man of my present. He is right. There is nothing I can do now. I must keep moving forward.

But as I make to leave, Samuel grabs at my arm with his good hand. His grip is surprisingly strong, fingers hard as claws, clutching the part of my arm just beneath the elbow. Nelson jumps forward to pry his hand off me, but he does not have to—Samuel lets go before Nelson can reach, slumping back down and laughing.

Do I know you? Samuel says. I know someone who looks like you.

We should leave, Jacob, Nelson says to me again. He is drunk be-yond reason.

This time, I listen. We leave Samuel on the steps, his laughs haunt-ing us even after we arrive back at our inn.

What will happen to him?

Nelson looks down. You saw his hand, he says. He will not survive much longer without shelter. To be honest, I do not know how he has made it this long. The alcohol must be numbing everything. For now.

Upstairs, Nelson tells me to wash the part of my arm where Samuel touched. We agree to return to Pierce in the morning.

It is not until I close the door to my room, when I am sure that there is something separating myself from the world outside, that I allow myself to sob into my fist.

Samuel, the naïve fool, the eager boy who talked so often about his dreams of coming to Boise and achieving manhood. He must have let it slip to his half brothers at least once. It would not be hard for someone who was really looking, then, to find the half brothers and convince them to follow Samuel and punish him for his transgressions. That someone, in turn, could use Samuel to find me.

I have no doubt who the *he* in Samuel's story is. Jasper is here. And when I let his name materialize before me, so does the rest of him, until I am nothing but a small child in a room and he is bigger than the sky.

Now will you listen to me? Lin Daiyu urges, tugging at my hands. We must go. We are not safe here.

The Daiyu who was trapped in that coal bucket would. She would run fast and far. But that is not who I am anymore, I remind myself. This Daiyu has friends who are good, a bed that only needs her for sleep, and a safe way home. And this Daiyu knows things that Jasper does not yet know. Like my new name. Like my new face.

What about the gray-haired man? Lin Daiyu presses. He knows you are not a boy.

And I remember, once again, that night. Samuel crying on the floor and the gray-haired man leering at the door. If Jasper came across the gray-haired man, he would know everything about Jacob Li. The gray-haired man would not protect me as Samuel did.

So let us go, Lin Daiyu says. Run off as we did before. Keep running until we are home.

We could do it, I think. Leave in the night and make for the west now. Not even a note to Nelson. Nelson. The thought of him knocking on my door in the morning, only to keep knocking forever, fills me with sadness. And what would Nam and Lum say when I did not return? It was all so soon. I was not prepared to start the journey like this.

We do not have enough money to make it all the way west, I tell Lin Daiyu, hoping she will not see the other reasons brewing in my heart. Not without William's help.

She shakes her head back and forth, her silver-black hair whipping in protest. I am trying to protect you.

Remember, I tell Lin Daiyu, two years separate me from them.

This I do believe. Two years, and everything can change. The blood that flows from between my legs brings out new parts of my once egglike face. Blades for cheekbones, a wider nose. Still with the same sullen expression, but now it has a purpose.

Two years, and no longer a child.

Look, I say, stepping back to show Lin Daiyu my body. I am longer here, broader here. And you must agree that I am taller.

I agree, she says, inspecting me.

With Nelson next to me, it would be nearly impossible to distinguish me from any other Chinese man. I am far from that hungry little girl-boy at the Zhifu fish market. Far from the helpless crying girl-boy on a bed at an inn.

What was it that Master Wang taught me? I must be thick and strong, just like the black mark on the page. *A good line communicates inner strength. It belongs fully to itself, leaving no room for weakness or disarray of spirit.*

Thick and strong, thick and strong, I repeat to myself. Take in thickness and breathe out strength. I open my eyes and Lin Daiyu is standing, too, mirroring me, breathing in and out. Watching her calms me.

Jasper may be here, but he does not know the person I have become. Still, he is getting closer, and he will find me eventually, I am sure of it. The music of our day disappears, the warm feelings that stirred at the thought of Nelson's face seem laughable now. How could you grow so comfortable, Daiyu? And all this time, Jasper was moving in, getting closer. Look how close he has gotten after all.

Remember that this is not your home, I tell myself that night. You will have to find your way home before he finds you.

September feels very far away.

                    —

Pearl is crying, and Swan will not stop screeching about her frayed hems. Iris is giggling, her fingers covering her mouth like the bars outside our windows. Jade is there, too, her feet dirty and bare. We are lined up and waiting for Madam Lee to enter like she always does, go down the line, pick us apart. It is night, and the customers will be here soon.

Except it is not Madam Lee who enters. It is a woman with a mouth that looks more like a beak, orange-red and knife-sharp. The woman spreads her arms, but they are not arms—what I thought were the sleeves of her silk dress are actually wings. She stands before us and she opens her mouth, and inside all I can see is a gray tongue rooting around in the darkness.

When I wake, I write a letter to William asking if he will look into one more thing for me. A small favor. I would appreciate if he did not say anything to Nelson about it. *Personal matters, you understand.* I take it to the post office before the sun rises, fearing that daylight will make me more vulnerable, then run back to meet Nelson at the inn, the image of Swallow's hard gray tongue pressing against my skull.

14

June comes, and the earth is a swath of color. There are buttercups, orange poppies, and white clover, plants with buds like drops of water, gumweed, dog rose, flowers shaped like upside-down vases. Even more arresting are the pines that border the town, which have become erect and full in summer's pleasant thrum. Nelson tells me that there is no better place in the world for summer than Idaho, and when the flowers begin to bloom, dappling the paths that lead to the hills that lead to the mountains, like paint from a wayward brush, I believe him.

The summer is beautiful, but I am distracted and suspicious. Jasper may have just arrived in Boise, but once he realized that I was no longer there, he would upend every town in Idaho, asking about a girl who looks like a boy who looks like me. Pierce is a big town, but there are bigger, busier ones he would stop at first—Idaho City, Warren, Richmond, the Salmon River region. I remember the voice I heard that day on the docks of San Francisco, the faint sound of someone singing goodbye. He would keep searching, as summer blew into fall, riding along the same paths I did and eventually making his way here. He could not reach Pierce before September, I reason. And by the time he arrives, I will already be gone.

Now that it is warm again, Nam and Lum work even harder to bring more customers into the store. When the weather is nice, Nam declares, people want to spend money. He and Nam have a plan for increasing profits even more over the summer. We would not go the way of the Chinese laundry or Cheng's barbershop. Lum has calculated it, determined that jam will be the thing that people want the most of in a summer as good as this one. By mid-June, shipments of jam begin showing up at the store. Black currant. Boysenberry. Apple butter. Cantaloupe. Boxes crammed with jars overtake the back room, stacked until they graze the ceiling. Soon, there is no place to sit. Lum and I take turns coming in and out of the room for inventory, the faint smell of nectarine preserves and plum blueberry following us wherever we go.

None of us are surprised when Lum's predictions come true. It only takes one: a cheerful white woman, a churchgoing woman, who buys a jar of lemon curd. The next morning, there is a line of five people waiting before the store even opens. We are not the only store in Pierce selling jam, but we are the only place selling delicious, thick jam. No one has ever heard of our brand before. Nam tells me that it is special, from a farm in Washington Territory. I did not know about jam before I came to America, he tells me gleefully. It is a Friday, and the shelves are bare—our third Friday in a row. On days like these, days when sales are this good, Nam becomes a heightened version of himself, large, ebullient, his energy uncontainable. Would you believe me if I told you all the best jam is made by Chinese? he says to me. Would our customers believe me?

The owner of Foster's Goods no longer comes to stand outside the store. Lum thinks this is a triumph, a sign of Foster finally admitting his own defeat. Nam vows to bring Foster jam free of charge. A peace offering, he calls it. He sends me out with a sampling of our best flavors. I leave the basket outside Foster's front door and when I look for it the next day, I see broken glass, the jam glistening like blood in the sun. I do not tell Nam about it.

Pierce Big Store is not the only prospering business in town. The summer brings a new crop of violin students for Nelson, who becomes so busy that weeks can pass without any of us seeing or hearing from him. This is good, I tell myself. It is easier to lie to him this way—by not saying anything at all.

—

Your complexion is no good, Nam tells me one Sunday morning. You spend too much time indoors.

For once, Lum agrees. It is good to face the sun, he says. Good for getting rid of bacteria and disease. It will not hurt you to go outside, Jacob. That is how you kill the bad things inside.

In a rucksack, I carry bread and a jar of raspberry jam. Some garlic cucumber salad from the night before. The day is marvelous and I want to surprise Nelson with it, having not seen him in many days. For once, I forget about Jasper. Just let me have this one day, I think. A day where I do not have to look behind me.

But when I arrive at the Twinflower Inn and knock on Nelson's door, he does not come to answer. I press my cheek against the dark wood of the door, imagining all the times he has passed through it. The air here could be sacred. On the other side, the room is quiet and still. He does not have lessons on Sundays but must be out for lunch or running errands, I reason.

Outside, it is hard to ignore the reassurance of the afternoon sun. I remember what Lum said about the sun killing all the bad things within a body, and wonder if I stand there long enough, could it kill the demons that follow me? I close my eyes and turn in a circle, extending my arms out as if I could catch the light. It is a luxury just to feel warmth.

Dirty chink, someone mutters behind me. Wish you would hang.

I hear it a second too late; whoever said it is gone by the time I turn around. I retrace my path to the store, remembering William's speech that day, the outrage in his voice as he talked about all the atrocities against people who look like us. If I were him, I would be angry, too.

Good thing we will be home soon, Lin Daiyu says.

I agree.

The sun leans against my back, a buoyant, firm pressure that makes me at once full and weightless. Halfway to the store, I decide that it would not be bad to stay outside a little longer. The food in my rucksack knocks against the small of my back, a gentle reminder. I remember the afternoon when Nelson and I lay in the secret clearing behind the schoolhouse, a memory doused in the same halcyon light as the ones from my childhood. The trees in the clearing must be alive with green in every shade by now. I turn and walk toward the schoolhouse. Nam and Lum could wait a bit longer. This day would be mine.

At the schoolhouse, I follow the path Nelson once showed me, then barely visible, now flattened and worn. He must be coming often. I smile at the thought of him ducking in and out of the branches. Through the thickets, around the turtle pond. Four desiccated turtles sunbathe on a fallen log, their backs mottled brown, nearly smoking in the sun. I think of my grandmother, what the weather must be like in our village at this very moment. During the summertime, the heat melded with the wetness from the sea, making the village nearly unlivable—just one step outside and your entire body would stick to itself. But at least the plants there thrived, our vegetables and fruits and herbs. They loved the soil and the wetness, and so we thanked it for allowing us to survive within it and giving us continued life.

My grandmother told me that we would speak only when it rains. In Idaho, it is dry all the time, but I am no longer sad for it. We will be able to speak to each other soon.

The clearing is ahead, opening itself to me as I near. But I am not the only one here. Nelson is already there, standing at the center as if holding an audience with the surrounding trees. His back is to me, straight and wide, the healthy black of his hair shocking amid all the greens and blues. An intense happiness wells up inside me. I cannot wait to call out his name, to see his face when he turns and finds me standing there.

But Nelson is not alone. Someone else is there. Through the cluster of trees, a girl walks out, her skin alabaster and untouched. Her hair, a fine yellow thread, falls down to her shoulders. It could be something from my mother's loom. The girl is exquisite—everything from her fine clothes to the bonnet in her pale hand tells me that she is someone who is lovely, who is wanted. And I know when I see her that I will not call out Nelson's name, that I must stay where I am behind the thicket of haw bushes.

Nelson turns to the girl, beckoning her forward, and she obliges, her hands outstretched to meet him. Her face is long, the jaw wide, but her features are delicate—a flower bud nose, bow-tied lips, eyes iridescent and hazy, as if she has always just woken from a dream. When Nelson turns to her, her lips open across her face and her eyes reach for him. In the sunlight, her teeth gleam opal.

I watch as they embrace, the girl's head in the same place where Nelson rests his violin. Around them, the trees dance with the day's breeze, their leaves sweeping against the sky. Everything here is perfect for Nelson and this girl—the day perfect, the sun high, the wind gentle. Everything is where it is supposed to be except for me.

And suddenly, I am ashamed. I am nothing but a girl trapped inside a boy, a woman pretending to be a man. Love 愛, a giving up of self for another. But to do that, you must have a heart that is free to give itself away. I have nothing to give to Nelson, because nothing I have is true.

Nelson strokes the girl's head with his hand, the same hand that I believe is good and kind. I do not want to watch anymore. I am the spot that blemishes their otherwise sublime canvas. As softly as I can, I turn and plod my way back through the bushes and the trees. Only when I am sure that they cannot hear me do I run, my hands turned into fists, punching away the memory of what I saw. I do not look back.

I have felt many things, given them many names. This one I do not want to name. It is as if someone has tied a large stone to my heart, tied it so tight that the veins are full and swelling, and dropped the stone in the deepest part of the ocean.

I want to fight, but I know it is pointless. I am not sinking because of the stone but because I am the stone.

—

What did you expect? Lin Daiyu asks me later. For him to love you? He does not even know you. Ha! You do not even know yourself.

Shut up, I tell her. Shut up shut up shut up.

You are a girl pretending to be a man, carrying around a ghost. He would never love someone like you.

I know, I say. I want to blow her away. I never asked him to love me.

Then why are you crying?

15

Summer moves like a song coming to a close, circling its reprise. Every night, I count the sack of money hidden under my pillow. All those jobs and all that saving. I did everything I could do, I tell myself. The rest will be up to William.

I do not seek Nelson out anymore, and he no longer comes by the store. I assume he is busy with his students and the golden-haired girl. It is hard to believe that she could exist outside a place as magical and untouched as the clearing, but I believe that she must. Otherwise why would I feel the way that I do?

Ni Er Sen. His name is a forest of trees. Maybe that is where he has gone: a forest so dense I cannot follow.

One night when I am the only one awake, I sneak to the waste bin in the back alley. I am looking for a jar of jam, already spoiled upon arrival and tossed out. An embarrassment, Nam exclaimed. He was worried that one bad jar could ruin the entire business. We hid it at the bottom of the waste bin, under stained cartons and hardened pellets of rice. When I find the jar, I unscrew the top. The jam inside has turned furry white. There could be whole universes in there. Little by little, I scoop out the contents of the jar and fling them to the ground, until the jar is emptied, looking very much like the way I feel inside. Inside the jar, I whisper Nelson's name. I whisper his impeccable hands, the sure tenderness of him, that minted glow of a violin against a roaring fireplace. These are all good memories. These are all pained memories. And I whisper the golden-haired goddess, too. At least they will have each other. Around me, crickets screech into the night, and I take it to mean their approval. When I am finished, I screw the top onto the jar. Then I place it back at the bottom of the bin. This will do for now, I tell myself. If I can leave all this here, just let them be, then I can find a way to be happy.

You said you would kill anyone who hurts me again, I say to Lin Daiyu later in bed. It is not an accusation but a reminder. At least that is what I tell myself.

She says nothing. She knows that what I am asking of her is not real. No matter what I say, she knows that I do not have the strength to wish Nelson harm.

—

William writes me twice, but neither letter includes the information I am waiting for. Instead, he tells me about the progress of the Chinese Six Companies, how we will help them with his money and my fighting spirit. His words.

The plan: I would meet him in Boise first. From there, the two of us would take the train to San Francisco. Upon arrival, we would meet with one of the organizers of the Six Companies, a friend of William's who was waiting to receive us.

My plan: At some point, when the time was right, I would reveal my true identity to the Six Companies leaders. They would know what to do.

Can they be trusted? I ask William in a letter.

That should be the least of your worries, he writes back. He writes using bold strokes and a heavy hand, as if this is the only way for each character to be seen and understood. *They are the oldest, most powerful Chinese organization in America. If you cannot trust them, who can you trust?*

I remember the coal bucket, the filthy room that held all the girls

from the ship, the cries in the brothel at night. And then I see the Six
Companies, and for some reason all of them have faces like my father.
They are kind, benevolent, heroic even. There has to be some good in
this world after all, this I want to believe.

It is something. It is hope.

In my heart, there is little room for sadness at leaving Nam and
Lum, but still I feel it. They were some of the few men I encountered
in America with no evil agenda, who simply welcomed me and allowed me to live among them without judgment. When I watch Nam
coaxing customers or Lum frowning into his spectacles, I think of the
blood that runs through them. It is the same blood that runs through
me, a blood heated under the same side of the sun. We come from
the same land, speak languages that touch each other. For all of these
things, I think, I could love them. Still, I keep my departure a secret.
Like with Nelson, telling them the truth will make the leaving harder.

Do not, Lin Daiyu warns me, even think about it.

But I do think about it. I think about the jar at the bottom of that
waste bin, how the glass could break from all the things it is holding.
One day, in a moment of weakness and childish sorrow, I search for
it, my hands wading through rotted fruit and the damp drag of old
newspapers, knowing that the jar is long gone.

It is for the best, Lin Daiyu tells me. Now you can properly heal.

16

In the end, the decision is not mine to make. Nelson comes to me first
on the last weekend in August. It has been weeks since I have seen
him. I am repainting the store's name in fat letters, the heat from the
summer having cooked the paint to a crisp.

Hello, he says. Why have you been avoiding me?

I have not, I say. I have just been busy.

With the store? he asks. There have not been more protests, have
there?

If there had, would you care?

A pause, the sharp inhale of surprise. He says, What does that
mean? Are you upset with me?

No, I say. I say, Why did you keep it from me?

Keep what?

You know what. The brush is limp in my hand, yellow paint bleeding onto the dirt.

Ah, he says. So it was you.

I say nothing.

Caroline swore she heard something that day, he continues. There
is something there in the trees, she kept saying to me. I did not believe
her. Now I know that it was you. Right, Jacob? It was you in the trees
that day?

I feel embarrassed, as if I have missed something that everyone else already learned. I nod, wishing he would look away.

You are upset that I kept it from you. His tone is soft, pliant even. He says, You would be right to. We are friends and this is not what friends do. Will you accept my apology? I will tell you everything, if you want to hear it.

He is not angry, nor does he accuse me of spying. I turn to face him for the first time. His gaze makes my skin peel back, exposing all the raw things underneath.

Come on, he says, reaching out a hand. I take it.

—

The girl's name is Caroline, the older sister of one of Nelson's students. She sat with them for every lesson, watching as Nelson taught Bach sonatas and Vivaldi arrangements. He had not thought much of it— perhaps she was simply invested in her brother's improvement. And then one day, when the child was not looking, Caroline tucked a note into Nelson's violin case.

How sweet, Lin Daiyu says, gagging.

Back at the Twinflower Inn, in the privacy of Nelson's room, he tells me about her. Bright, he calls her. A good soul. Caroline has lived in Pierce all her life and dreams of becoming a teacher at the school-house. She is very good with children.

Does her family know? I ask. To which Nelson does not answer.

Do you expect to marry her?

I do not expect anything, he says. Least of all to marry, not while it is still illegal for us. No, I expect to try and be happy for as long as I can.

I imagine Nelson instructing the little brother in their home as Caroline watched. The secret glances and locked smiles he would ex-change with her, knowing that later, when they were alone in Nelson's room or in the clearing, they would come together in a unified heat separate from the outside world. Nelson's hands on her fine neck, a soft shimmer turned to song.

What a perfect scene, I think. I cannot hide the ugliness from my face, nor the deep want tugging in my belly.

Do not make ugly faces, my mother would tell me. Your face will get stuck and then you will have that ugly face for the rest of your life. Nelson does not notice. Nelson can only smile. It is a different smile, not one I have seen him give Nam or Lum or even me before. Light, effortless, something he fell asleep wearing the night before. It is as if Nelson's face has become stuck, too, only his has turned beatific.

What happens if you get caught? I ask. I remember a story Lum found in the paper about a Chinese man who was thrown in jail for fifty days for embracing a white woman in the street.

Nobody knows, Nelson says. Except, now, you.

I think of Madam Lee's brothel. None of the white men who entered and flung themselves on the women there, Chinese girls acting like women, were ever thrown in jail. They came and went openly. Whoever they were, they were always proud to be exactly that.

Do you think me stupid? Nelson asks, watching me.

I tell him no. I tell him that he is simply in love.

Have you ever been in love, Jacob?

I think of all the people in my life who might fall under that word, and I tell him yes and leave it at that.

At the door, Nelson puts his hand on my arm, and this time the weight of it is almost cruel. Nam and Lum will ask me how Nelson has been, why he has not been in to see them, whether or not I have finished recording the sacks of flour that sit in the back room. Going back to a life where I did not know this information feels strange, like it should not belong to me anymore.

Will you help me keep this secret, Jacob?

He trusts me so much. I look at him and say yes, thinking I will do anything to make sure he only ever knows the feeling of happiness.

17

When September comes, there is a marked shift in the air—the nights turn purple with a new kind of cold, one that promises a hard fall and a vengeful winter. In the early mornings, when I press my hand against the glass window of the store, I feel it pulsate with a coolness that runs from my arm up through my neck. In five days, I will leave for Boise to meet William. Home is so close I could slip inside and wear it.

But in a vast land to the east crowned with mountains and encircled by endless wind, a horrible thing happens.

Nelson is the one who brings us the news. Massacre, he calls it. I am eating lunch with Nam and Lum when he bursts in, the word sounding more like a broken dish than anything I have heard from the English language before.

Nam and Lum are confused. They do not know what the word means. I am not so sure, either.

Look who finally comes to visit old Nam and Lum, Nam says, faking indignation. Lum rises to grab another chair. But I am looking at Nelson's face, which is white. He is using this word for a reason. He is telling us something that will change everything.

Lum comes back out with a chair and places it at the table. Lunch is dried fish and steamed rice, the fish spines now eaten clean and stacked in our bowls. Nelson walks over to the chair, but he does not sit. He looks through us.

Nam claps his hands at Nelson's face. Hey! Are you sick? Do you want tea? Jacob, go get the ginger tea.

There has been a massacre, Nelson says before I can move. Twenty-eight were killed, fifteen more were injured. All were Chinese.

This time, everyone is listening. The light in the room changes to a sickly gray. The fish spines decay before our eyes, the comfort of our meal forgotten, now only reminders of bones and death.

Nam breaks the silence first. This cannot be true, he says. Where did you hear that?

It is all over town, Nelson says. It will likely be in the paper soon. Rock Springs, Wyoming. The white miners brought guns to Chinatown and opened fire. Some say there were buildings burning with bodies still inside.

Without meaning to, the character for fire 火 flashes before my eyes, orange and angry and licking. You cannot write fire without also including the character for person 人. Fire is a person trapped between two flames.

No, Nam says. We all know the word is meaningless, because what Nelson says must be true. We turn to look at the front of the shop, as if expecting the mob to be there now, this time holding rifles and shotguns instead of signs.

Nelson collapses into the chair. I do not know what to say. None of us knows. All we can do is imagine the Chinese, who must have screamed and fled. But their cries were pointless. They raised their arms in surrender, begging into the eye of a gun. All pointless. All for nothing, as blood burst from their bodies and they burned. I turn my hands over, staring at the dark blue veins in my wrist. The same blood that was heated under the same sun.

This is the way we sit, until we hear the door opening, the bell ringing. Somewhere, a customer needs something. This is how we remember that we are still alive.

18

Two days pass before we see anything about it in the paper. I should be making my final preparations for departure, but news of the massacre sticks in me, turning my movements sluggish, my head full of air. William had spoken of injustices against Chinese, but I never imagined something like this. Had the massacre been preceded by mobs, too? I think of Nam and Lum and pellets raining down on the store.

The money under my pillow stays hidden, uncounted. This annoys Lin Daiyu, who cannot stop talking about the journey. Why is this news any different from what you already know? she keeps asking. We already know this is what America is like. This is why we must go home.

I do not have a good answer for her. She is right. But the burning bodies make me sick inside. I dream of skies that rain blood, and when I wake, my hands frantically search under my nightshirt for my heart, to make sure it is still beating, that my blood is still my own.

⁓

When it does come out, it appears on the second page of the *Pierce City Miner*. The title is small, just below an advertisement for a new shoeshine formula:

ROCK SPRINGS RIOT: MINERS SPRING TO ACTION

The title does not use the word for what happened. *Massacre.* It does not mention the twenty-eight who died, the fifteen who were injured, the bodies that burned. I move on to the article and scan every word. *Miners in Rock Springs*, it says, *disgruntled from the unfair hiring practices that displaced them in favor of the Chinese, took matters into their own hands by rioting in Chinatown. While the outcome of the riot was less than ideal, one cannot ignore that there were extenuating circumstances surrounding the violence.*

I repeat the last sentence. I am searching for the meaning of *less than ideal*. Was the death of twenty-eight the thing that was less than ideal? The fact that they were trapped in their own town, a place they created for themselves? That their bodies lay out in the streets, blood mixing with dirt, staining the ground?

I take the newspaper with me to the Twinflower Inn. The white faces I pass stay trained on me, paint marks streaking across my field of vision. I feel, for the first time, a great contempt for them, as if they were directly responsible for what happened.

Have you seen this? In Nelson's room, I throw the paper down on the table in front of the fireplace.

Nelson is wiping down his violin with a yellow cloth. The strings groan and crunch as he rubs them clean. I saw it this morning, he says, sounding tired. I am not surprised. Are you?

His calmness, something I have always admired about him, infuriates me, another first that I am feeling just today. What does *extenuating circumstances* mean? I ask. Why do they not call this a massacre? Murder?

They are not the only ones, he says. His eyes meet mine slowly, as if the mere act of raising them is taking all the energy he has left. There have been several newspapers in Wyoming voicing support for the white miners. Many think they were justified.

How can they say that? This was murder, everyone knows it!

Sit, Jacob, he says. I know you are angry. I have been angry, too.

I sit.

I have been thinking about what William said, Nelson tells me. I was quick to decline his invitation, but I do not think he is wrong to want to help. Massacres like these will keep happening unless we do something.

I ask if this means he will join William in San Francisco.

No, he says. But William told me that in places like Boise Basin, California, and Oregon, people have tried to sue the city for atrocities that took place against the Chinese. I think my efforts should be here, doing something similar.

So you will sue Rock Springs? I ask.

I will try, he says. But hopefully, not alone.

Before his gaze, I shrink. He trusts in the goodwill of others. For Nelson, wrongs will right themselves, because this is the justice of the world. He thinks of me as someone who can be part of that goodwill and justice, but I am not, cannot. I am a child born of the world where evil has so far prevailed. How else do you think I ended up here, in front of you? I want to ask him.

I tell him no. I tell him I cannot.

That, he says, is a disappointment.

This is not my country, I remind him.

Do you think it is any of ours? he says. The people who live here now did not always. This land was stolen, and that stealing has become a sport. The people who took over this land have no one in mind but themselves, their own survival.

I am sorry, I tell him. I believe in what you want to do. Only I cannot help you do it.

Because you do not care?

In that moment, I need for Nelson to look at me with anything other than what is on his face, which is pity, which is disappointment, which is a rewriting of the good, courageous person he believed me to be. Because I am going with William to California, I hear myself saying. I am going to find the Chinese Six Companies and ask them to send me home.

His face does not change. We could have been in this room for years, and all we would know was each other, the thing dying between us.

When do you leave? he asks. It is not interest in his voice.

Three days' time, I tell him.

I see.

You think me stupid? Now I am the one asking him.

No, he says. I think you selfish.

Funny, how even after all the things I have experienced, this should be the thing that hurts most. I know that my face is crumpling before him. Now I am nothing more than a weed. Now I am useless. I should not say it. I know I should not say it. But his words, his quick judgment of my character, have taken something from me. Another first: the need to reclaim myself.

How can you call me selfish? I ask, knowing my words will take us somewhere we may never come back from. When you have been seeing *her* this entire time? She is one of them. How do you know she does not feel the same? If you are found out, do you really think she will go down with you? No, she will say you forced yourself on her. She will call you a heathen Chinee, just another coolie who unleashed his beastly desires on yet another innocent white woman!

The silence that follows could sink me. Nelson stands and walks to the door.

Please leave, Jacob.

I do not move. Can he not see it? If the world were so easily divided into those who were white and those who were not, then no one was exempt from that. There would always be those in power and those who had none.

Leave, he shouts this time, and it is the last first in this day of firsts, the first time I have seen him like this and know that he, too, is capable of anger and wretchedness and violence. I stand, trying to hold myself steady, but as his hard eyes bore into mine, I can feel myself collapsing.

There is no going back after this. When I am outside, Nelson slams the door. I hear the lock click on the other side.

—

By the time I return to the shop, it is dark and I have missed dinner. Nam and Lum are already asleep, but they left out bowls of rice, now lukewarm, and pickled vegetables. My heart squeezes when I see the bowls, a sign of someone caring about me, a reminder that once I was a child and a daughter, and that people loved me enough to always make sure I was fed and full. Tonight, I am not hungry. I set the bowls outside for whatever cat will be lucky enough to find them.

I should not have said what I said to Nelson. And perhaps I had been wrong about Caroline. But I could not let myself leave Pierce without knowing that I tried to protect him. If he hates me now, let it at least be for that. Knowing this, I can be at peace with everything that has happened here. Knowing this, my life in Pierce and my friendship with Nelson will not feel like a waste of time.

I do not ask him to love me. All I need is for him to be well. If he must hate me in order to be happy, I will allow it.

Remember, Lin Daiyu says, this is not your home. This is not your problem. Let them deal with their own sordid country. You have to return to China.

This sorrow will not last forever, I tell myself.

———

A line can only be called strong when it has the conviction to stay on paper. Strong lines are important, but how does one make a strong line with a soft brush? Answer: resilience.

A resilient brush is one that, after depositing ink on paper, can spring back up in preparation for the next stroke. But resilience is not achieved by pressing harder. No, the artist must master the art of releasing the brush, giving it the space and freedom to find itself again.

Resilience is simple, really. Know when to push and when to let go.

19

Two nights before my departure for Boise, a storm rolls through. Lightning splits the sky into pieces and I think, this is what I look like inside, not a whole, but a many, separated by something I cannot control.

In the morning, Lum drops a letter in my hands. Stopped by the post office and they gave me this, he says. Said it arrived days ago but had been misplaced in the storm.

In the top-left corner, a water stain. William's name is a black cater-pillar, engorged by the moisture. The weight of the envelope is heavier than usual, and when I pick it up, I feel a great rush of possibility. This is the one I have been waiting for.

Lum is curious. He asks me who my friend is. Nam overhears, and then they are both crowding at my door. They have noticed the letters I received, they say. The two of them decide that they will make a game out of guessing who William is to me. I listen to their jokes and laugh but do not tell them anything else. The letter remains in my chest pocket throughout the day, its weight a talisman. By the time dinner comes, Nam and Lum have decided that William is an unrequited lover.

When, later, their snores vibrate through the store, I slide out the letter and edge it open. My breaths come quickly. The letter itself has not suffered water damage. Relieved, I unfold the pages to see William's bold script, only this time the writing is slanted, perhaps even rushed. With one glance, Master Wang would call it preoccupied.

I light a match and hold it close to the first page.

Jacob, it begins.

Apologies that it has taken so long to get this information to you. It turns out the couple you asked about was more difficult to find than I initially thought. But we did find them in the end. Rather, we found out what happened to them.

Lu Yijian and Liu Yunxiang were tapestry merchants in Zhifu, likely before you met them. They moved to a small village not too far from the city years ago, where they had a daughter. From there, they continued their tapestry business. This must be where you also came to meet them.

Here is what you may not know: Lu Yijian and Liu Yunxiang were also aiding the Heaven and Earth Society, a secret society that offered protection for the lower classes. The details of their aid are murky, but I can guess that they were involved in helping Ming loyalists hide from the Qing court, likely by disguising them as Buddhist monks. The court had its suspicions about their involvement, but they could never prove anything; Lu Yijian and Liu Yunxiang were clever—they did not send letters, but instead wove all communications as artwork into their tapestries. To a naked observer, a phoenix was only ever a phoenix, a lotus a lotus. To those who knew how to read the tapestries, there were dates, times, instructions.

From what my contact can tell me, they were eventually ratted out by a Qing official posing as a society member. Whatever it was that prompted them to help this imposter, we may never know. Let us just call it the goodness of their hearts. Once found, they were thrown in jail and sentenced to death. Well, Lu Yijian was killed first. They made Liu Yunxiang watch. Then they executed her as well.

They left behind the daughter and Lu Yijian's mother, although I could not find out what happened to them.

On the topic of your second question, this was slightly easier for me to track down. The brothel in question is the one owned by the Hip Yee tong, run by a woman named Madam Lee. I should say formerly run, because it appears that the old madam was removed from her position by the tong. The new madam is called Madam Pearl, and she has a keen eye for business, according to my friend. The girl you asked about, Swallow, no longer works at the brothel. Nor can I find any record of her. That man you asked about, Jasper Eng? He was killed by the Hip Yee tong after one of the girls he sold them escaped.

I hope this letter brings you what you are looking for. Give Nelson my best. I will see you soon in Boise. San Francisco awaits us.

Fondly,
William

20

Many years ago, while playing in a ditch near our home, I found a grasshopper, fat and green, all of its legs arranged like the legs of an intricate chair. I had never seen one so big before. I picked it up by its back leg and ran all the way home, eager to show my parents. We could keep it as a pet, feed it until it grew to the size of a small cat. I burst into our house with one arm outstretched.

But when my parents came to see and I held up my hand, there was nothing. I was not holding the grasshopper anymore, just its one back leg. In my hurry to show my parents the grasshopper, I had run too fast, ripping the leg from its body. It could have been the wind, it could have been my arms jerking as I ran. Or perhaps the grasshopper had decided mid-journey that a life without one leg was better than whatever fate awaited, and so, ejecting its body, it left behind a leg no thicker than an eyelash, which at one point held all the power in the world. Now, nothing.

After it happened, my mother plucked the grasshopper's leg from my fingers and set it down on a window ledge, where it shriveled and curled in the sun. I stared at it for the rest of the day, wondering if it could come back to life just by my looking hard enough. After an unbearable dinner, my father asked me what I had learned that day. I began to cry. I am not a murderer or a bad person, I insisted. I needed them to believe me. I said, I just wanted to show you something great.

My mother was gentle. Your intentions were good, she said, but your actions betrayed you. From now on, Daiyu, you must learn that the two cannot ever be separate. No matter what your intentions may be, you also must think of your actions and act from a place of truth. Relying on just one does not make you a good person. Do you understand?

How could you have saved that grasshopper? my father asked. If you truly thought it was as magnificent as you said?

I thought about it. I was filled with regret. I could have carried it with two hands, I told them, cupping my own together. I could have run a little slower or simply walked. I could have come home and led you back to the ditch to see it.

Or, my mother said, you could have continued on with your life without touching it at all.

Her suggestion stunned me. How would anyone else know about the grasshopper if I did not have proof? But I did not ask them to clarify. The leg on the window ledge had browned and hardened by then, and I was tired of talking about the grasshopper, spent with mourning for its demise. The leg would eventually disappear from the ledge and be swept up and dumped out with the rest of the dead things in our house.

Staring down at William's letter, I think I am beginning to understand the answer. It would not matter if I had no proof of the grasshopper. If my intentions and my actions always matched, I would never need proof. My parents were trying to teach me that in a world such as this one, there is only me and my word.

It hits me then, an overwhelming sadness for all the things I have lost. My parents were never simply my parents. They were also people who worked for the things they believed in. They believed in me, so they worked to raise me well. They believed in family, so they made a loving home for all of us. And they believed in the decency of human beings, so much so that it cost them their lives. Their intentions and their actions were always one. That was what made them good, and that was what they tried to teach me.

Get out of there, Lin Daiyu's voice says from a place I think I remember. Move, we have to move!

Her voice is a rope that ties around my waist. I let it pull me, back through time and land and ocean, until I am back on the cot, in my closet, at the store.

My parents are dead. I will never see them again in this lifetime. My parents are dead.

It starts in the belly, a deep longing that travels through my entire body. It is a rock that cannot be moved, a sun that sets for the last time, a wind that will never stop howling. I miss them. I love them. I did not have enough time with them. I try to close my eyes, forget the images of their final moments and instead imagine them next to me, their heat, the measured pacing of their breaths. I would do anything to have them back with me. To hear my mother say my name again and know that no matter what happened, her saying my name would protect me from whatever came.

In the dark, I curl into myself, clutching the letter to my chest. I let myself cry. Lin Daiyu cries with me, her sobs like gasps for air. We both know this feeling. We both feel it the same way.

——

You look pale today, Nam tells me later that morning. Are you getting sick?

I tell him, No, I just had a bad night of sleep. He lets me take the day off. Eat some cantaloupe to cool the body down, he says while pressing the back of his hand against my burning forehead. After, I watch him tidy the iodine tinctures on the shelf behind the counter. I feel a welling of fondness for him. Here is a man who is simply trying to do the best he can. We are all just trying to do the best we can.

21

Why are you not studying the map? Lin Daiyu asks. Why have you not packed for our journey? We are still leaving for Boise tomorrow, right? Right?

I do not know how to answer her.

You promised, Lin Daiyu begs.

Yes, I tell her, wishing she would shut up.

⸺

There was a time when, bent inside the coal bucket and soaked in my own urine, I imagined revenge against Jasper. I was young then, so the word did not have a name. But in between those moments of nightmare and waking, when my forehead listed against the side of the bucket and I was able to close my eyes, I imagined a future where Jasper and I met again. I would be stronger, mightier, more sure of myself. I would be the exact vision of the most truthful and strong piece of calligraphy there ever was. Not even the wind could knock me down. And Jasper would be small, a shriveled thing. I would wreak my vengeance upon him. I would fill his body with dead, rotting fish. I would stuff him in a bucket and roll him down a hill and into the ocean.

In this fantasy, I am always the victor. But I suppose that is why it is dangerous to live in fantasies. Because all this time, I did not prepare for the truth: that actually, Jasper and I will never meet again.

He is dead and I am not. He is dead and I am not. He is dead. And I am not.

It should be relief, it should be freedom. It should be the triumphant pleasure of knowing that Jasper suffered the same end he sent so many girls to. I wait for it, ready for the great breath, unrestricted, that I have sought to breathe after all these years. But it is none of those things. Instead, it is just news of another death, another life extinguished in the wake of me. I do not mourn for him. I mourn for the self I was to have encountered him.

What do I have to fear, now that the threat of Jasper is gone? Who is Daiyu without her villain? Who will I be now that I can be anything?

———

The last answer in William's letter, another one I did not expect to hear: Madam Lee no longer works at the brothel. Pearl has taken her place.

Pearl. That tiny girl crying in the buggy the day we were both taken from the barracoon. She never seemed to be able to stop crying. This is the girl—the woman—who now runs the brothel?

And the news of Swallow, banished. All this time, I believed she was Madam Lee's loyal girl, the next one to take over. I remember her voice, something she said from our last conversation. *But at least inside, as the madam, I can do so much more. I can do more for these girls in here than out there.* I had been furious with her. I did not hear this sentence, at least not in the way I do now with the things I know. From inside, as the madam, she could do so much more. What had she been planning?

You know, Lin Daiyu says. You have always known. You were just too hurt to see. I do not blame you. I have felt the same way.

Yes, I did know. Swallow, who always tried to protect us from the worst of men, who took their bodies inside her own so that we would not have to. She would want to stay, to be given the power of madam.

To destroy the brothel from the inside out. Rather than running away from her fate as I did, she chose to meet it.

But she did not become madam, Lin Daiyu reminds me. Why did she not become madam?

She was right. Something happened to make Madam Lee turn away from Swallow. What had changed?

A bird holds a flower in its beak, Lin Daiyu recites. *Never again will the bird speak.*

My freedom must have cost Swallow hers. By escaping that night, I was also admitting Swallow's guilt—that she had indeed known about my plans. All those days confiding in her during our laundry work, all those small smiles and fond glances—how could Madam Lee not have noticed our friendship in a place where friendship could not survive? Swallow, who spoke few words to anyone else. She had given herself to me, and I handed her directly to Madam Lee. My intentions and my actions were worlds apart. I will always be the girl tearing the grasshopper into pieces.

I remember, now, writing Swallow's name twice before, thinking I had written it correctly each time. But each time, it was wrong. No matter how I wrote it, I failed to understand her. More importantly, I failed to see my own weaknesses.

Could I ever be whole like this? Could I ever call myself unified? I have not written a perfect character in months. Perhaps I do not deserve to.

In the list of things that I have lost, I add myself.

22

You promised, Lin Daiyu reminds me again. And a promise is a promise.

A promise is a promise indeed. But is it any different from the promise my parents made to me, that they would always be there for me? Or is a promise the one they made to themselves, that they would do everything in their power to help those without power? Both were promises. Both were important. My parents were good people. They loved me. But they had a higher calling.

Master Wang taught me about a beauty on the outside that matches the inside. He taught me about a heart that already knows the art, a hand that simply obeys. Calligraphy and a life of goodness, beauty, truth—they are all the same, I am beginning to realize. For so long, I have been grabbing at the little pieces of wisdom Master Wang gave me, using them to light my life in moments of darkness. But I never really knew how to use them, only ever tracing characters on the page. My parents, Swallow, even Nelson, these were people who held the brush firmly and let truth and passion and integrity funnel through. These were people who followed their hearts.

This is the intention. This is the idea.

I wondered once if I could forgive my parents for leaving me all alone. I wondered the same of Swallow. Now I realize that the only person I have to forgive is myself.

And I hope you will forgive me, too, I tell Lin Daiyu. She narrows her eyes, grips my arms with her sharp fingers.

Do not do it, she says. I have never seen her look so angry before. If you do it, there is no going back.

We can always leave next summer, I tell Lin Daiyu. But right now, people need help. And I know I can help.

This is not even your home, she snarls, standing up. Her feet are bare, her fists are clenched. She is furious, steaming. This is not your town, this is not your country, this is not your language. Have you forgotten who you are? Your home is China. Your family is China. Everything you know is China. You came here against your will. Why would you choose to stay with these people?

Our people, I say. Chinese people are dying. Chinese people have died. Who would I be if I did not help?

You never used to care, she cries. I am not afraid of anyone hearing her. No one ever hears her. Why now? Why! Is it because of him?

She means Nelson. I tell her, no, it is not because of Nelson. In fact, he has very little to do with this decision.

What do I do? she begs, and she is sobbing now, her head in her knees. She wants so badly to go home. I look at her, and all I can see is that little girl, orphaned, confused, lost in a big city.

For all her tragic beauty, her sympathetic past, Lin Daiyu the idol was not perfect. She used the sadness of her childhood and the horror of her death to ingrain herself in history as the faultless, motherless, loverless girl. Poor Lin Daiyu, people would say, shaking their heads. Just one tragedy after another. A child can only take so much.

But in the actual words of the story, Lin Daiyu was no angel. She could be petty and cruel. She could whine and scream and cry, and she could be ruthless and inconsiderate. The other characters in the story were blinded by her tragedy and so, too, was everyone in the real world.

I can see through it now. Lin Daiyu was no heroine; she could be the villain for all her sensitivities, her sickly proclivities, her immovable desire for the boy who would later marry someone else. The only reason she was a heroine was because she died too early in the story. I wonder who she would have become if she had not spat up blood in her bed and collapsed into that pool of crimson. It does not matter, though. Her story ended there. Mine has not.

Come back, I croon to her. Come back inside and you will understand.

I have never been able to touch Lin Daiyu before, but I reach out my hand anyway, put it on the thing that looks like her hand. I do not feel flesh under my fingers. It is strange to think that once I hated and feared her. Now I feel something different. She feels it, too. She stops crying and looks up at me, her eyes the shape of small crescent moons.

I took such good care of you, she tells me. Her cough returns, rippling through her body in delicate waves. You and I must never be apart.

I know, I say. Come back inside and let me take care of you now.

We sit like that for a long time, Lin Daiyu and I, and with each breath, I feel myself growing more certain of my decision, less afraid. As the sun begins its slow crawl over the horizon and light seeps through the windows, underneath doors, lighting up the corners of my closet, Lin Daiyu moves again.

I open my mouth for her. She raises her foot and slides it down my throat.

I am very tired, she says, childlike, her voice hoarse from coughing. Then she disappears down my throat, and I feel her settle deep within me. I close my mouth, hoping the beating of my heart will be enough to lull her to sleep.

———

Lin Daiyu was right: Once, I did not care. This was not my home. In the large world of things, all I ever wanted was to go home to my grandmother and find my parents again.

Selfish. That was what Nelson called me.

What would my parents tell me now? *Your intentions and your actions must always match, Daiyu.* I want to be thick and strong and straight, my lines as black as ink, my corners sharp and neat. I want to be someone I can be proud of. Not someone ruled by fate, but someone who can be certain that her life is a result of the choices she has made. This is the kind of person I want to be: the perfect line.

I am Daiyu, I want to shout to the world, and I am the daughter of two heroes. For the last three years, I have been putting on identities the way one does a coat—Feng, Peony, Jacob Li—when what I was looking for was the one who was in me first, the name my parents gave me.

Swallow knew. From the beginning, she knew who she was, knew how to protect others. I think of her name again, how the other characters sat on top of fire, and for the third time, I reconsider what her name means. Fire, as in the thing that burns brighter than anything else, that can only grow and grow, lighting the way for others, burning away disease, turning the dark into gold. That was who Swallow was.

I begin tracing two characters on my thigh. It is not until I have finished that I realize I have never tried to write them together before.

Daiyu 黛玉. The dai is black, the yu is jade. I had written the character for black before, imprisoned in that room back in Zhifu. Back then, I never thought about how the character for black is also a part of my name. The same mouth and soil sit on top of the same fire. The same fire that can be found in Swallow's name. Then the yu. An emperor with a dash inside. My name is made out of fire, of earth, of emperors. I am a precious piece of jade, a dark swath of greatness. The characters of my name burn themselves into my thigh. I ask myself if I can live up to my name. Not Lin Daiyu's name but my name.

The answer is very simple.

PART IV

—

Pierce, Idaho

Fall 1885

1

When Nelson opens the door, all he can say is, Oh.

Hello, I say.

It is early, the sun having just crowned over the horizon. A yawn hangs over us, waiting to break.

You are still here, he says. There is a question there.

Can I come in?

He should shut the door in my face after our last conversation, leave me in the hallway to wait forever, but he does not, because he is Nelson and Nelson is good. He opens the door wider and I slip through, noting the scant distance between his chest and my shoulder. On every surface, newspapers, law books as wide as my thigh, sheets of Nelson's scribbles, lie stacked in neat piles. He has not given up on his mission of suing Rock Springs.

I thought you would be gone by now, he says.

I imagine, with a dull prod of sadness, William on the train to San Francisco and the empty seat next to him.

I decided to stay.

Does William know?

I wrote him this morning, I say. But he will know when I do not meet him in Boise.

In the fireplace, flames flick and swat like tiger tails. Nelson's eyes are rimmed in red. It occurs to me that he may not have slept in days. I want to reach inside him and light whatever has gone out, breathe warmth into his body again. This fire alone is not enough.

You were right, I croak.

About what?

I was being selfish.

I should not have said that, he says, looking away.

Yes, you should have, I say. You were just telling the truth. I *was* being selfish.

What about your home?

Home can wait, I tell him. I want to help you fight. You cannot do this alone.

At this, he turns to me. I am surprised to see sorrow in his face. But it is not for him, nor for the miners of Rock Springs. It is for me and what he knows I have had to give up in order to be here now. I cannot meet his gaze, its frankness making my decision to stay all the more final.

What we need is a lawyer, Nelson says when the moment has passed. I have written to all the ones I could find here and in Wyoming. None of them will take our case. It may be dead before it even begins.

What about the Six Companies, I say. We can write and ask for their help. We will write it in Chinese, make them really listen.

Nelson looks down in shame. I do not know how, he says.

I can do it, I say without thinking. Another truth that took years to conceal, revealed in a matter of seconds. But being truthful does not scare me anymore. My writing is beautiful, I tell him. I learned from a calligraphy master.

At this, he laughs.

What? I say, feeling defensive. Do you not believe me?

How could I not, he says. Did you forget, Jacob? Before I even knew you, I told you that you have the hands of an artist.

We begin at once, there in Nelson's room. Nelson stands while I sit at the table, now cleared of its books and papers. In my hand, a pen. Not the same weight as a brush, not at all the same as kneeling before the endless expanse of a scroll, but still I feel an elation that can only come with the body mending itself.

The city promises to protect its residents, which means all of its residents, not just some, Nelson recites. In our time apart, he scoured newspapers and state archives looking for records of mining towns in Idaho, Oregon, and Wyoming with sizable Chinese communities. He found occurrences of anti-Chinese violence going back twenty years, some of which resulted in lawsuits against the perpetrators.

Negligence action . . . a violent purge . . . property destroyed, damaged, or lost . . . brutal mob violence . . . precedent, precedent, precedent . . .

I write. Water. Horse. Mountain. Tooth. Characters that have been pushed aside, shoved onto shelves long out of reach, come back to me now. Wood. Eye. Grass. Bird. The characters crowd at my pen point, impatient to be written. Some of the words I do not know how to write in Chinese, and for the simple ones, I think of the characters that could combine to create them, letting my heart lead the way, just as Master Wang told me. The others, Nelson helps me spell out in English. My arm moves quickly, the old muscles firing without hesitation. I envision the goddess Nuwa from Lin Daiyu's story. Every stroke I make is a celestial repair of myself.

The mind can forget all it wants, but the body remembers. And so I spend the afternoon there with Nelson, remembering. It is, I think, the most intimate thing I have ever done with another person.

Your writing *is* beautiful, Nelson says later, holding out the finished letter. Three pages, front and back. When he holds it up to the window, light pierces through and I can see all the black characters at once, like small bones in the paper's flesh. It looks strong.

I tell him thank you. I have never written calligraphy in the presence of anyone but Master Wang, and this feeling is new. For a moment, I expect to hear my old teacher pointing out all the flaws and inconsistencies of the script. You were holding too tightly here, he might say. The heart was not fully attuned there. But Nelson does not care about these things. Instead, he falls silent, admiring the characters he cannot read.

You should be proud, he says finally.

I tell him I am.

2

A week later, on the eve of the Mid-Autumn Festival, Nam and Lum close the store early to celebrate. We draw the blinds, lock the doors, hang up red lanterns, and burn incense to the deities for good fortune. Nam makes mooncakes filled with lotus bean, and they remind me of the ones my grandmother made out of syrup and lye water, their crusts soft and glossy. Back then, my parents and I would gather around the kitchen table and wait for her to cut the mooncake into four pieces, giving one to each of us. Nam does not rely too much on tradition and ceremony, instead laying them out and urging us to eat quickly. I bite into mine, and the lotus bean sticks to my gums. The flavor is sweet, but the taste is that of home.

Outside the store, we place oranges, pears, melons, wine. An offering to Chang'e, the goddess of the moon. The story is this: Chang'e was the wife of the archer Houyi. One year, ten suns rose in the sky and their collective heat crippled the earth. Houyi, with his great skill, shot down nine of those suns. Impressed with his work, the Queen of Heaven sent him the elixir of immortality, which would transport the drinker to heaven and turn him into a god. Not wanting to leave his beloved Chang'e behind, Houyi gave her the elixir for safekeeping.

But they were not safe, of course they were not safe. That is how these stories go. An apprentice of Houyi's, named Pengmeng, overheard the plan. One afternoon, while Houyi was out hunting, Pengmeng broke in and forced Chang'e to hand over the elixir. She refused, instead swallowing it and flying to the moon, the place in heaven closest to the earth. She wanted to be near her husband, you see. On the day of the full moon, Houyi displayed Chang'e's favorite fruits and cakes, hoping she could be well and full, hoping she could see how much he loved and missed her, even from the moon.

When I was little, we put out these offerings, too, so that the full moon could shine down on our fruits and cakes. I imagined Chang'e, the lonely goddess, sitting on the moon, her stomach bursting from all the food that was laid out. Deep down, I knew she could never really be full, not without the one person she loved most.

Inside the store, the home we have made for ourselves, the smell of food engulfs us. Lum has stewed a whole fish in garlic and green onions. There is rice, sweet sausage, steamed chicken with ginger, and Nam's lao huo tang, which simmered for hours. When the moon comes out, we will worship it and ward off evil by setting off firecrackers in the street. Nam and Lum are in good spirits, drunk from plum wine and flushed all over.

Nelson is here, too.

Nam uncorks another bottle of plum wine, splashes it into our cups. Without you two, he says, face so red it looks hot to the touch, I do not know how Lum and I would have done it. We are glad you two are here.

Yes, Lum announces, raising his cup. The wine has made him excited and affectionate, not at all the stern man who walks around with his face hidden in a ledger. To a thousand more years! Prosperity and fortune in Idaho!

Nelson and I laugh, raising our glasses, too. I think of how this feels like the closest thing to a family I have. For a moment, I consider waking Lin Daiyu, showing her what a family could look like. She would want to know.

But before I can, Nam pushes his chair back from the table and stands. Look, he exclaims, pointing to the window. The moon is out.

We ride on a wave of plum wine, bursting outside and falling into the hushed street. It is nearly midnight. The black windows of Foster's Goods glare at us in disapproval. Nam lights the first cracker and sets it down.

Five, four, Lum counts.

We funnel back inside the store, whispering loudly like children hoping to get caught. Three, Lum says. Nelson pinches my arm and I hit him back in jest. Two, Lum says with his whole body. Nam hops on his feet, his hands clasped under his chin.

One.

A burst, then a clap. The firecrackers snap and blaze, then explode into deafening pops. Each one is a tiny star cracking open, shooting off to join Chang'e on the moon. Nam whoops, then darts out to light another firecracker, then another, until the entire street, the entire world could be filled with the *puh–puh–puh* of the firecrackers. I wonder if we will wake anyone. I do not care.

I glance at Nelson. He is smiling the way one does when they think no one is looking, when the smile is untethered and weightless. His eyelids sit comfortable, heavy with wine. You can relax, Jacob, he says when he sees me looking at him, and I realize that even in this moment of extreme happiness, even knowing that Jasper is dead, I am still tense, because this is what I have learned to be since being sent off to Zhifu in a cart. But Nelson does not know any of that. Nelson only knows the man he sees now. He leaves my side to run at the firecrackers, hopping alongside them and yelling, his arms flapping out wildly as if he might catch the wind and fly away. Lum, so rarely moved by theatrics, joins him, his face pointed to the sky. Nam continues dropping firecrackers and lighting them up. I watch the three of them from inside the store, and then I am smiling the way Nelson did.

Come on, Jacob, Lum yells. Against the light of the firecrackers, he could be dipped in orange paint. I walk outside to join them. Nelson grabs my hand and shakes my arm. I let him, grinning. Our letter will soon find its way to the Six Companies, so tonight, we allow ourselves to feel invincible. He cocks his head back to the sky and howls, and I do the same, closing my eyes and throwing my voice somewhere far from me, wanting to release everything inside, every moment when I have been afraid, small, or beaten, perhaps even release Lin Daiyu. I let it all go, hoping that something different will take its place.

When we go to sleep that night—Nam brings out a pad for Nelson, who has drunk too much and cannot walk home—our stomachs are fuller than they have been for months. Nam and Lum stumble to their room, not bothering to soak their feet first. Nelson lies down beside the dried persimmons while I watch from the hallway. Even in the dark, he can feel my eyes on him.

I am glad you came here, Jacob, he says. And I am glad you are still here.

There are so many things I want to tell him, but I do not. Instead I wait for him to settle under his blanket before walking back to my own bed. The firecrackers do not stop dancing, even when I close my eyes.

3

I hear the banging first.

For a moment, I think I have overslept. The store must already be open for the day. But then I hear Nam and Lum speaking frantically from their room, and I know that they have just woken, same as me.

I pull on my pants, struggle to get inside my shirt. Check to make sure my chest is still bound and flat. By the time I get into the hallway, Nam and Lum are already ahead of me.

The banging continues, now louder.

Nam asks Nelson what it is. Nelson responds from the floor, his voice sluggish with sleep. Then I hear the front door being unlocked. A deeper, different voice joins the fray. I have heard this voice before. Nam and Lum fall silent, then immediately start shouting. I listen for Nelson's voice, but I do not hear it. I step out of the hallway, into the morning light.

Nelson, Nam, and Lum are all gathered around the door. The deep voice belongs to Sheriff Bates, who I have not seen since his first visit to the store after the protests. He looks like he has been awake for hours.

I try to get closer, stumbling and righting myself against a shelf. The noise startles Sheriff Bates, and his hand quickly moves to his side. He pulls out a shiny black object that I recognize as a gun. I hear a click, hear Nelson inhale sharply.

On the ground! the sheriff yells. He points the gun at me.

Nam and Lum are silent now, their hands raised to the ceiling. Nelson goes to the ground first, laying his chest flat against the floor. Nam and Lum follow. I do not go to the ground. I do not understand what is happening or why Sheriff Bates is pointing a gun at me.

I said *on the fucking ground*!

Jacob, Nelson says.

There is no time to understand. I do as the others did and lower myself. The wooden floor is cold. Last night, drunk and exhausted, we all forgot to tend to the furnace.

The door creaks, then Sheriff Bates shouts to someone outside. I am afraid to lift my head to see. I hear the door open again, then the sound of many heavy boots entering the store. Something clinks. Nam and Lum groan. Nelson remains silent. Then I hear the boots next to my ear.

Move and I will shoot, someone growls.

I think of the brown parcel William gave me that day in Boise, a small pistol, how I hid it in a sack of millet at the back of the storage room. How far away it is now. I feel my arms being jerked back, then two shackles slamming against my wrists, bruising the bones. Someone lifts me to standing.

You are under arrest for the murder of Daniel M. Foster, Sheriff Bates barks at us from somewhere I cannot see. You will be taken to the Pierce County Jail, where you will await trial.

My body flashes cold. That glowering man who stood so ominously at our storefront was dead? *A specter*, Lum had called him.

Nam reacts first, echoing my thoughts. Murdered? he cries. Foster?

How? Lum demands into the floor. When? Why?

Nelson is the last to speak, his panic rushing the words out. Does his family know?

Do not talk back to me, boy, Sheriff Bates says. Now walk out nice and easy with us and make no fuss.

We leave the store one by one, to a buggy waiting at the front of the store. The street is already crowded with an audience gathering around Foster's Goods. Some of the women are crying; others have their hands on their mouths. The men's faces are grim.

Nelson, I whisper as we climb inside the buggy. What is happening? What are they talking about?

Nelson does not respond. I am not sure he hears me.

We are not alone in the buggy—there is already someone else inside. He looks like us, I think. The young man does not acknowledge us when we enter. One of his eyes has begun turning purple.

The buggy moves forward. Our bodies lurch together. My hands are curled behind me, my arms numb. I try to write something, anything with my index finger, but the characters will not come.

4

A rot follows us through the jail. The walk to our cell is not long—
Pierce County Jail is a simple gray two-story block with ten cells and
no windows. Home of petty thieves and interlopers and now us. The
air inside the building is cold and stale. Here, we could be in a cavern
buried at the darkest corner of the earth. This is a place for forgotten
things.

One guard leads in the front, another behind us. We walk in a
row: Nam first, then Lum, Nelson, me, and the fifth man, who still
has not spoken. In front of me, Nelson's head is steady and centered,
the neck still so strong. Watching him makes me feel rooted in the
earth. Do not trip, boy, the guard at the rear warns, his words nipping
at our heels. I want to talk to Nelson, to ask the guards questions and
demand answers, but the dulled echo of our steps tells me that this is
not the time to be free with my words. Nam, Lum, and Nelson keep
quiet, too. We all know, without being told, that saying nothing is the
best defense we have.

Finally got those coolie bastards, a voice growls from a cell. Another spits at our feet as we walk by. Out of one cell, wretched howling.
I cannot bring myself to look at whatever is making that sound. The
guards are indifferent. I wonder if by now they have grown used to

such noises. If they no longer see those inside the cells as human, only flesh in a room.

Ours is the empty cell at the end of the hallway on the second floor. It is small; if we all lie down next to one another, we would barely fit inside. Another dark room from which there is no escape. Another cage.

We enter, the smell of days-old piss from a bucket in the corner overwhelming. The guard at the front, who now shuts the door, is gleeful. You chinks are finally gonna get it, he sings. He inserts the key into the padlock and turns it. A devastating click sounds throughout the building. Then he and the second guard walk away.

There must be a mistake, I say, turning to Nelson. How can they think we murdered that man?

I do not believe that he is really dead, Lum barks. I want to see the body. Where is the proof?

He cannot be dead, Nam says, timid. Who would want to kill a man like that?

What do you think? Nelson says, and it takes us a moment to realize that he is not speaking to any of us but to the fifth man.

The light is bad, but we turn to him. His hair is ragged, lips chapped and white. His face, I realize, is filled with bruises that have not yet burst. Were the men who captured us capable of doing a thing like this?

Nam is the first to step closer to the man. Yes, he says, encouraging and kind. Who are you?

The man is not used to this kind of attention. Perhaps he does not want it. He backs away, eyes wide. He shakes his head.

You can talk to us, Nelson says gently. Who are you? Why did they bring you here?

The man gestures again, pointing at his mouth. I watch his fingers circling around and around, and then I understand why he will not speak.

He is mute, I tell them. I address the man. You could not speak if you wanted to, right?

The man looks at us mournfully. Then he opens his mouth. In place of a tongue is a wriggling worm of mottled flesh. Headless. Nam steps back, clutching Lum. I turn into my shoulder to stop from retching.

Only Nelson does not seem to mind. He puts a hand on the man's shoulder.

Did those men do this to you?

The man shakes his head, wringing his hands. He points at his mouth, then shakes his head again. Then he points to his purpling eye and points to the place where the guards stood.

It must have been someone else, I say, swallowing my bile. But the bruises. They are fresh.

The man nods. He holds up a finger and begins tracing something in the air.

He is trying to write, Nam says.

I cannot read it, Lum says.

I walk to the man and grasp his hand. He looks at me as if I have pierced him. Here, I say, holding out my palm. Write on this.

He hesitates, then extends a finger, the nail sharp and pointed. On my palm, he traces out a character that does not take me long to understand.

Everyone, I say. This is Zhou. And I try not to pity the character for his name 周, which includes a wide mouth.

The victory is small but important. We take turns grasping his hands, and when Nam has gathered his courage again, he even looks inside Zhou's mouth, listing off herbs that we carry at the store, as if anything could regrow a severed tongue. The joy of discovery is fleeting, however. It is not long before each one of us finds our own space in the cell for standing, for sitting, for clutching our legs to our chests and weeping into our knees.

5

After learning of my parents' fate, I could not stop myself from imagining their final days. Pictured the dark of their prison, tried to conjure the fear in their bellies. If I could place myself there, I thought, it was the closest thing to reuniting us. There, at the end of their lives, at least I could be with them, too.

Now I do not have to wonder as much. Their dark is my dark, their fear sits solidly in my chest, finally a fear that I can call my own. This is the reunion that I yearned for all along, but it is not sweet. What is wrong, Daiyu? I ask myself. You have been in many bad situations before. You were not as afraid as you are now.

But now is different, I argue back. You have been through too much for this to be the end. Now it is more important than ever that you survive.

I am not afraid of death. I am afraid of no longer living.

My voice floats through the dark, aimless. We need a plan, it says.

The hearing, we learn from the guards, will take place the following morning. I ask Nelson what a hearing means. Will we be able to plead our case, defend ourselves? Will our regular customers be able to attest to our good standing? A hearing means that someone will be listening—who? Will they decide our fate?

It is good to prepare, Nelson tells me. But I would not get too hopeful. Remember what William said? In California, they would not even allow Chinese to testify at their own trials.

But a hearing is not a trial, I urge. And I remind him of what I know to be true, that we must practice and prepare, no matter what. When you have nothing else left in this world, at least you have that.

Together, we run through the day. Nam and Lum had closed the store early for the Mid-Autumn Festival. Did we see anything funny from Foster's Goods that day? The store, with the mysterious now-dead store owner inside, had had its usual set of customers. None of them looked suspicious.

We did not leave the store the entire day, Lum points out. How could we have murdered him? There have to be witnesses for this sort of thing.

Except me, Nelson says. I arrived in the evening, after my lessons.

But you are a good man, Nam says. No one would dare accuse you!

The four of us look at Zhou, the man without a tongue. We are all wondering the same thing.

I hold out my palm to him. Here, I say. Tell us where you were.

His finger is hard, the skin dry and calloused. I close my eyes and invite the sensation of his finger to materialize before me, running from the nerves in my palm through my body and onto an unseen floating tapestry. His strokes are slow. He wants to make sure I do not misread them.

He arrived in Pierce last night from Elk City, I tell the rest of the group. He had a drink at the saloon, then went to his lodging at the cabins down by the bank. The landlord there can vouch for him, he says.

Well then, Nam says. We are all innocent.

But Lum is not satisfied. They will twist this, he says. Everyone knows Pierce Big Store is in direct competition with Foster's. That gives us motive.

But we were doing better than his store, Nam protests. He was the one standing outside our store all those days. He had motive to kill us.

It is true—long before the protests, the first threat came from Foster's silent post outside the store. I remember his ominous face, then picture it rotting in death. The thought makes me shudder.

Who would do something like this? I say. And why accuse all of us of doing it?

It is obvious, Lum says. This is the best way to get us all out of Pierce. Our business is too good. They never wanted us there in the first place, but if they say we murdered him, they can get rid of us for good.

Nam looks like he will cry. The thought of leaving behind his store and the life we have built is painful to him. That does not account for you, Nelson, he says. Why they would lump you in with all this?

I wonder, Nelson says, but he does not finish his sentence.

Nam and Lum break into a pair and switch to their own language. Zhou sits back against the wall and closes his eyes, letting out a long exhalation. The conversation has exhausted him. I am exhausted, too, but I look at Nelson for comfort. There is something he wants to say, some truth that he is holding just out of our reach. I want to ask him, but the cell is too small. Instead, I sit back against the wall and close my eyes like Zhou. I feel Lin Daiyu breathe against my stomach, her snores rippling through my blood, but even with this new danger, she does not wake. Our last encounter must have weakened her. At some point, I think, the body will stop fighting and simply accept that what will happen, will happen. Then I am ashamed at the thought. How could you not fight, I urge myself. I look at Nelson one more time. He is staring at the floor, face blank, eyes vacant. Seeing him look this way scares me.

———

Hours later, our cell door opens and an unfamiliar man falls in. A sour smell fills the room. The door slams shut.

The man crawls to a wall and slumps against it, immediately falling asleep. His black hair is long, divided into two braids that rest against his bare chest. He wears buckskin leggings with a small cloth to cover the place where his legs meet. A large portion of his face is painted the color of wood. Nelson told me the very first Chinese miners in Idaho would have died if not for the Indians, who sold them crops and directed them to rich placer gold beds in the southern part of the state. I feel a sudden compassion for the man before us.

He must have drunk a lot, Nam says, prodding the man with his finger.

Should we wake him? I ask.

Let him sleep, Lum says. Being asleep is better than being in here.

We do not speak much for the rest of the day, occasional sprints of conversation quickly dying out. They take the drunken man in the evening, replacing him with some hard bread for us. He wakes and stumbles out, dribble coming out of his mouth. We watch him leave with envy.

What is the right step for this? I want to ask Master Wang. I file through the lessons he has taught me, the characters that could apply. There is no rule for dealing with injustice, for true danger. There is no rule for the uncertainty of being. Everything he taught me was about art, and I had applied that to my entire life. But there was no lesson for where I am now.

What good was any of it, I ask him, if it would always lead me here? Why carry around all these characters if I cannot do anything with them?

6

In the morning, the guards shove us into the buggy waiting below. We exit as we entered—hands bound, single-file, solemn. The sun is not welcoming this morning, but intrusive. I close my eyes against it, waiting for the glass clinking in my head to go away. Inside the buggy, our bodies knock against each other. It has been long since any of us have had a hot meal. Our cheeks all hold the same kind of hollow.

Outside the courthouse, a crowd has already gathered. I recognize one of the faces immediately: the white man who led the mob at the store, the one with the bared teeth. He is shouting something, but he is not alone—they are all shouting. Nelson bumps into me gently, meaningfully, and I am distracted enough to turn to him. His eyes tell me to keep looking at him, not at the crowd.

But they are angry, angrier than I have ever seen them. The guards have to yell for them to back up, and even then they are seething, a furious beast on the verge of eating us all. I want to break from my guard's grip and run away, through the crowd, into the mountains, all the way to San Francisco, and onto a ship that will take me across the ocean and to my grandmother again. But it is not so.

The guards form a loose circle around us, and we are carried, whether it is by them or the wind, toward the courthouse as one. I let my guard pull me up, my feet leaving the ground. I am so light that it is easy for him. Onward, onward, until I see the open door and Nam, Lum, Nelson, and Zhou funneled through it by the guards. I turn to look behind. The man with the bared teeth has his eyes locked on me—a promise he makes that he will find me wherever I go. I follow my friends through the door into the building. Then I watch as the door closes. It is the only thing separating us from them, and even then it does not seem like it will be enough.

We do not have time to recover before another door opens, the one to the hearing room. An unseen force is sucking us in, one by one. I feel my guard lifting me again, lifting me forward. I breathe until the empty panic in my chest fills. Then I let it suck me in, too.

7

I have never seen Judge Haskin, but I have heard the tales. Here is a man whose honor and righteousness have earned him fame across several counties. He put away a drunkard who killed his own daughter out of neglect, shamed burglars who forced themselves upon unlucky wives, indicted a transient who spent a night at the inn and attempted to leave before paying. The locals call him fair and just. But when he enters the hearing room and walks to his seat, a large thronelike chair with a high wooden back, I can only think of an emperor, one as pale and furious as the rabid crowd outside.

The hearing room is already full, rows of creaky benches filled with Pierce residents. They turn to us as we enter, faces displaying what I had feared: the unshakable belief of our guilt. No evidence needed. The ones I recognize as patrons of the store refuse to meet my gaze. Others I have seen passing by our window. Some were members of the mob. All of them are ready to see us gone.

Coolie bastards, someone snarls as we pass. Heathens, someone yells after him. Dusky throats! They call us pagans and satanics. They call us creatures.

Order, Judge Haskin shouts. I demand order!

The crowd settles. We are led to five chairs that face the judge. The chairs look flimsy, like an errant thought could splinter the wood.

You five are here, Judge Haskin calls when we are seated, for the alleged murder of Daniel M. Foster, the owner of Foster's Goods. Please state your names for the court.

One by one, we say our names: Lee Kee Nam. Leslie Lum. Nelson Wong. Jacob Li. The familiar syllables sound unwelcome in this cold room filled with strangers.

And this is Zhou, I say. He cannot speak.

Someone in the audience lets out a mocking laugh. The judge claps for silence.

This hearing is not to decide your fate, the judge says. It is to determine whether or not there is enough evidence for your trial to move forward. If so, you will be transported to the neighboring county of Murray, where you will await trial.

A flash of hope. There is a process, which means that there is also a chance that our case could get struck down. Please, I repeat in my head, let them find no evidence. How could they, when there is no evidence to begin with?

I would like to call the first witness for her testimony, the judge barks. Miss Harmony Brown.

A door opens behind where the judge sits and a woman I have never seen before enters the hearing room. She walks to a small stand next to the judge. I can see, from the hands that hold her hat to her ribs, that she is shaking.

Miss Brown, the judge calls out, you were the one who found poor Mister Foster's body?

I was, the woman says. Already, she sounds like she will cry.

Can you describe what you found? You may take your time—I know the scene was upsetting.

The woman's eyes widen—she looks as if she would rather do anything but. She gazes out into the crowd for support. Someone coughs encouragingly behind me.

I went to Foster's Goods for some items, she finally begins. But when I arrived, I saw that the door to the store had been broken.

The judge guides her. What happened next?

Miss Harmony Brown lets out a pitiful sob, then continues. The moment I walked inside, she says, I noticed a foul smell. A smell that turned my stomach over.

Can you describe that smell?

She shudders. Like meat that had been left out in the heat for too long. For far too long.

What next? asks the judge.

I was horrified, Harmony Brown continues. I had half a mind to walk out right then and there. But before I could, I saw a hand, all alone, with no arm attached to it. There were already maggots at the fingers. I walked a little farther, and I saw—

She falters here, brings up a hand to mask her sobs.

Saw what? the judge encourages.

There he was, she says, her body vibrating with the memory. Mister Foster, on the floor, chopped into pieces.

Was there anyone in the store, Miss Brown? Anything that looked out of the ordinary?

No, she says, except for Mister Foster on the floor. I took one look at him and ran out of the store, straight to Sheriff Bates.

The testimony over, her body crumples. A guard rushes out to catch her before she falls. The audience cries out in sympathy. Judge Haskin claps his hands.

Miss Brown, he says, you have been very brave. We thank you for your testimony today.

The guard helps her out of the room.

I turn to look at Nelson, who sits at my right. Miss Harmony Brown did not actually see anything happen. If this was the evidence, then I was beginning to feel hopeful. Nelson does not return my gaze, however. His eyes are trained ahead, his brow tense.

Judge Haskin's voice returns to the room, and the whispers cease. I would like to call the next witness in for his testimony, he says. Mister Lon Sears.

The door behind the judge opens. I recognize this Lon Sears, the drunken prisoner who was thrown in our cell in the middle of the night. Only this time he looks completely alert, as if he has never touched a drop of alcohol in his life. His long black hair is tied back neatly and the paint on his face is gone. In the daylight, his skin gleams pink and creamy. Next to me, I feel Nelson straighten.

Can you state your name for the court, sir? asks the judge.

Sears, the man says. Lon Sears.

Out of the corner of my eye, I see Nam and Lum looking around the court like nervous birds. I wish they would stop moving—the light catches easily against their black hair, drawing attention to their discomfort. I wonder if others in the hearing room are watching, if they will regard this as a sign of guilt.

Can you tell us everything you know, Mister Sears?

The man glances over at us and grins, as if we should be in on the joke. I still do not understand.

I got a telegram the other day from Sheriff Bates, he says. Asked if I could come down to Pierce for a little project. Said he had five suspected murderers, said he needed me to do some translation. You see, Judge, I learned Chinese in the mining camps of Warren. You had to, with all those coolies quacking about. Sheriff Bates had me dress up as a drunk Injun. Plan was for me to just sit there and listen to them confess.

I rush through the sequence of events. This Lon Sears had been with us for a few hours. What had we talked about? I struggle to remember, my time in the cell blurring and folding. None of us would have said anything, because none of us had anything incriminating to say. I stare at Lon Sears, whom I now hate, willing him to come up with nothing.

So you did, Judge Haskin says, as if he is praising the man. And what did you learn?

It was a little hard to hear, Sears says, but they talked about setting off fireworks.

Fireworks?

Yes, Sears says. And that got me thinking. What if the Chinamen set off fireworks to cover up the sounds of the murder? What if it was just a distraction, so no one could know what was going on?

Interesting, the judge says.

I clench my fists. That is not what happened, I want to yell. We were all there, we all danced around the fireworks until early in the morning! You are lying!

But this is not the time for me to say anything, and nothing I say will matter. I am beginning to realize that now.

Anything else, Mister Sears? asks the judge.

Just one thing, Sears says. All I know is that they are planning to come up with some sort of rebuttal. Heard them talking about it together at some point. Do not let yourselves be fooled by these sneaky bastards. They did it and they will do it again, whether it is to you or someone you know. I worked in the mines, I have seen them replacing the hardworking men who deserve to be there.

He turns to the crowd now, arms spread out wide. When they first came here, we let them, because they were not supposed to stay for long. They have opened up stores and edged out good, hardworking men and women. And now look what has happened. One of us has gotten murdered. By who? Who do you think? It is these chinks that done it. Guilty, guilty, the lot of them!

Sears's impassioned speech has incensed the audience. A hearing does not need witnesses after all, I realize. All it needs is to speak to the fear in people's hearts.

Quiet, the judge shouts. I will have order in my house!

The room is hot and flushed with anger. I do not think I can stand to be in it much longer. I wish this could all be done.

After Sears leaves, the judge declares that there is one more testimony. But this is a special case, he says. The witness is very brave to come forward, as her testimony poses a great threat to her reputation and well-being.

He calls out the witness's name. The doors behind him open, and this time, it is not just the five of us who are surprised. The entire courtroom falls silent, staring as the final witness walks out to the stand.

Judge Haskin uses a gentler voice than he did with the others. Can you, he says, state your name for the court?

Caroline, the witness says. Caroline Foster.

The girl from the clearing. I struggle to piece it all together. The girl who had been in the clearing was related to Foster? I nearly grab Nelson then and there, as if to say, Look, it is her! But he knows. He has always known. Next to me, his body goes rigid, the reassuring rhythm of his breaths suddenly gone.

Can you tell us what you know, Miss Foster? Judge Haskin asks in that same gentle voice.

Caroline closes her eyes and nods. Her yellow hair is pinned back today, her face unmade and muted. It is not hard to see that she has been crying.

I was involved with one of the men accused, she says. Her voice is deeper than I expected. He sits just there.

She opens her eyes and points to Nelson. At this, the audience loses itself. Foul, foul, foul, they chant. Disgusting beast! a woman cries. I want to stand and shield Nelson from the abuse, but all I can do is sit. Nam and Lum are staring at Nelson in shock. Even Zhou looks terrified at this new information.

This time, Judge Haskin does not call immediately for order. He lets the audience do its work, staring down at Nelson with an ugly expression. When, finally, the clamor subsides, he leans forward to address Caroline again.

Would you mind telling us how this . . . involvement . . . came to be?

Her story is not so different from the one Nelson told me. Her little brother started taking lessons with Nelson at the beginning of summer. Caroline had always been interested in music, possessing no talent for it herself, and was eager to observe and learn from Nelson.

Judge Haskin fills in the rest. He seduced you? What should have been an innocuous relationship turned into something more sinister?

Caroline shakes her head tearfully. It was nothing like that, she says. I did fall in love with him, sir. But I was young. I was naïve. I was simply in love with the music. I see that now.

So you do, Judge Haskin says sympathetically. Miss Foster, can you tell us what you know about Nelson Wong's plans for retribution?

At this, I look to Nelson, who is staring at Caroline with intense concentration. Everything the witnesses have said so far has made us sound powerful and conniving. If only they knew, if only they could understand that everything we have done has been out of survival.

Father never liked the Chinese, Caroline says, now looking directly at Nam and Lum. He believed they were spying on him, stealing all his customers.

And was Mister Wong aware of this?

I mentioned it once or twice, Caroline says. I knew he was good friends with the store owners, but I did not think anything of it.

Did Mister Wong talk to you about your father?

Scantly, Caroline says. I wanted to keep our affair a secret, but he wanted to go to Father together and reveal our relationship. It terrified me. I could not bear the idea, so I told him we could not see each other anymore.

A good girl, Judge Haskin says. The crowd murmurs its agreement.

After that, he came by a few times when Father was not home, Caroline continues. He told me he was working on something big. Something that could change everything, perhaps even allow us to be together one day. And then all of a sudden, he stopped coming by. And a few days later, Father was . . .

Her body, which had been straight until this point, relents, shoulders heaving with every sob. The audience is full of encouragement for this pretty, chaste girl who simply got caught up with a perverted Chinaman.

I think I can surmise the rest, Judge Haskin says, addressing the audience. Miss Foster, am I right to say that you believe Nelson Wong and these four others were involved in your father's murder? Because he knew your father would come between you, he had your father dealt with in the most brutal fashion?

We cannot hear Caroline's response in between her sobs, but this is enough for Judge Haskin and the audience. I am afraid to look anywhere but forward—not at Nelson, and certainly not at the rabid animals behind us. It is over, I think. There is no coming back from this.

They guide Caroline out with her face buried in her hands. When the door opens for her, I see the rest of her family—the mother with an unforgiving face, the little brother who will never pick up a violin again—before the door snaps closed. And then it is just the five of us against Judge Haskin and the furious audience demanding blood and punishment.

Judge Haskin's voice overpowers the din. After hearing all three testimonies today, he calls out, I have no choice but to order that this trial move forward in Murray. These witnesses brought forth indisputable evidence that something was afoot that dreadful night, and perhaps even long before it.

These words are wrong, so utterly wrong. I want to protest until my voice shatters the windows. As if he can read my mind, Nelson nudges me with his foot, a warning.

The trial will take place in two days' time, the judge continues. You will set out for Murray in the morning. May God have mercy on your souls.

The hearing is over. I watch the judge step off his seat, motioning for the guards to take us. The audience begins to cheer.

8

Back in the jail cell, Nam will not stop rubbing his forehead with his palms, a nervous habit he developed after the protests at the store began. He asks Nelson if it is true.

All eyes shift to Nelson, my friend who, I am realizing, has just as many secrets as me. His back falls in an unfamiliar slump, arms hanging at his sides. He cannot look any of us in the eye.

It is true, he says finally.

Nam sinks down to the ground. Lum, however, steps forward, his sharp face furious.

What were you thinking? he hisses. You are going to get all of us killed!

Gone are the days when Nam and Lum praised Nelson as the upstanding young man who saved Nam's life from the mob. Born is the reality: that Nelson is just a boy.

I did not mean for it to happen, he tells us. She was just an infatuated girl, I knew that. But I thought—I thought if we could bring our relationship to Foster, if he could see how much his own flesh and blood loved a man who looks like me, it would change his mind. He was just one man. I wanted to believe that I could change just one man's mind.

William's comment about Nelson comes to me now, snide and pompous. *You are always assuming goodness in people. You always have.*

Nelson looks down at his hands. Without a violin and a bow, they look lost. I did not tell you because I did not want to trouble you, he says to Nam and Lum. I really thought I could do something meaningful, enact some small change. I was wrong.

Nelson, Nam says, shaking his head. Oh, my boy.

And the retribution? Lum demands. The *great plans* the girl said you were working on?

Now it is my turn to speak. I tell them about writing to the Chinese Six Companies and our plans to sue Rock Springs. It had nothing to do with Foster, I assure them. We just wanted to stand up for what was right.

It does not matter now, Nelson says. The harm has been done. Everyone thinks I had reason to kill Foster and that you all helped me do it.

At this, the cell falls silent. Zhou, who has been watching the entire exchange, stands up and clasps Nelson's hands, as if to say that it is all right. But when he returns to his spot on the floor, I see his face fall into a new kind of despair, one that knows all the doors have begun to close.

———

The next few hours pass slowly. Our lives stutter around Foster's murder and now all that is left to do is wait. Nam has his hands over his chest, chin resting on top. Lum remains against the wall, his back obstinate in its straightness. I have to admire him for this. Zhou drifts in and out of sleep, and every once in a while, his leg kicks out or a moan will escape. I wonder what horrors he has been through. I wonder what horrors await us.

I look at Nelson, only to see that he is watching me.

What are you thinking about? he asks.

They would not even let us speak, I say. At our own hearing. Just like California.

Nelson breathes in deeply. Not long ago, he says, some justice in

California decided that all *Asiatics* migrated to America across the Bering Strait. He said we descended into Indians. And because Indians have little to no rights in this country, neither should the Chinese. What happened today is not shocking to me.

William, I say. I cannot believe the solution has taken me this long. We will write to him. He must be with the Six Companies by now. He will know what to do. Ask to write a letter before we leave, Nelson. They have to allow us that much.

Nelson looks down and sighs. I do not think he will be able to help us where we are now, Jacob.

This is not the answer I want to hear. This is not the Nelson I know. What has happened to your hope? I cry. Lum startles awake but does not say anything, instead watching in careful silence. We are not dead yet, we are not even convicted! And yet you act like we are.

He folds and unfolds his hands. He does not look at me.

So we wait, I say. We wait and accept whatever happens. We might as well have our tongues cut off, too.

Look at him, Nelson snaps, pointing at Zhou. Do you really think we are any different from him? We may have our tongues, but in the eyes of the court, of these people, we are the same. Our speech makes no difference. Even though the words that come out of our mouths are in English, the court still sees the mouth that speaks those words. To them, we will always be foreigners.

There has to be a way, I say. The words are meaningless and silly, but still I want to believe. Nelson turns away from me.

Lum speaks up for the first time. Perhaps it is good to rest now, Jacob, he says.

Zhou is the only one who hears her silent arrival, who smells her perfume through the rot. She does not ask the guards to call us awake, nor does she rap on the door. She stands with a deadly calm until Zhou begins rousing us one by one, and when I open my eyes, I see a familiar figure, an enviable figure, waiting just outside.

Caroline?

Nelson rises from beside me, walking to the cell door in three short strides. The girl steps back.

What are you doing here? he whispers. Nam and Lum are awake now, too, taking in this girl who changed everything.

Caroline raises her head. Her lips come into view first. Then her rosebud nose, and finally her eyes, which are bright and wet. She has not stopped crying, I realize. But there is something else in her eyes, a storm on the verge of breaking.

I have come to see for myself, she says.

Caroline, Nelson says, steady with reason. You cannot believe that I would harm your father. Please let me explain.

Father is dead, Caroline says. They say it was you.

Nelson takes a step back. You cannot believe what others are saying. You have to remember me. Remember us.

There could be a pause there, an uncertainty in her eyes that wants to believe him. There could be a memory of happier days in her father's home, her little brother bouncing on his feet, Nelson laughing, and her, completely intoxicated by the handsome young man with so much knowledge. But then she takes in the scene in front of her, the five dirty Chinese in this cell, the door that separates her from us, and Nelson, who no longer holds a violin, who has nothing more to teach her about music. Her face changes, the uncertainty gone. I know then that her mind is made up forever.

How dumb you are, she says. Not even the law would allow us to be together.

Laws can be changed, Nelson says.

Is that what you told him before you killed him, she says, bristling. I cannot believe I let you touch me, dirty Ch—

But she is stopped by another voice, strange and strong.

I think you should leave, it says.

It takes me a moment to realize that the voice is my own.

She looks at me for the first time. I am struck by her beauty, terrible in its anger, the haughtiness blazing from her face as it takes in my small stature, my solemn eyes. I do not look away, just as I did not look away from the fish woman in the market that day. Caroline looks at me, but she does not see me.

May you hang, she says.

Leave, I say again, and my voice only grows louder, bigger, until it feels like it could break through the door. Go!

She turns. This time we hear the clicks of her heels on the stone. After she is gone, the only thing that remains is the scent of her perfume, like magnolias.

9

It would seem, by the way the guards greet us in the morning, that they will accompany us to a grand celebration.

Nelson asks if they will let him write a letter.

Sure you can write a letter, they say.

They hand him a pen and paper. Nelson scribbles something on it, then passes it back through. The guard who takes it glances at it, then crumples the note in his front coat pocket.

Will you send it today? Nelson asks.

Sure we will send it today, the guard says. He looks at the other guards and grins.

Downstairs, Sheriff Bates waits with another buggy. Sheriff, Nam pleads. But the sheriff will not look at him, and Nam falls silent. He knows that the sheriff will never look him in the face again.

This is ridiculous, Lum says in Nam's stead. He, too, is ignored.

They load us into the buggy one by one. The bindings on my feet are tight, and I stumble over the footrest as I climb into the cart, landing at Nelson's feet.

Come on, Jacob, he says, lifting me up with his own bound hands. Sit up straight.

I think, I have been a poor excuse for a man these last few days.

Do you believe she will change her mind? I ask him, knowing the answer. It is the first time we have spoken to each other since Caroline's appearance the night before.

Nelson bows his head. I wanted to believe the best in people, he says. I was wrong. It is hard to hear him through his shame.

I remember the things I said to him in his room, how his face crumpled when I told him that Caroline would betray him in the end. A man like William would bring those things up to Nelson now, wave them in his face and rejoice in his righteousness. I am not that kind of man.

Are you all right? I say instead.

Nelson knows what I mean. Do not speak to me about it yet, he says. Then a pained smile as he lifts his head to look at me. I am sorry if I sound harsh. My heart is only bruised.

She never deserved you, I blurt out. I am aware that this sounds odd and childish coming from Jacob Li's mouth, yet I do not stop myself. I need Nelson to know that he is so much more.

Murray is an entire day and a half away. We will travel through the night. The winds are fervent as they beat against the tarp that covers the back of the buggy, creating a disjointed dirge. The little I know of Murray does not make it sound promising. A mining town, which means that its people will be hostile toward any Chinese they believe stole their jobs. Judge Haskin never gave us a chance after all.

I am thinking so hard that I do not notice when the buggy comes to a stop.

Once again, Zhou senses it first. He grabs on to Lum's sleeve, tugging at it with both hands. Lum opens his eyes, pauses, then pulls at Nam. Nam listens for a moment, then calls to us. Nelson, Jacob, he says. Something is happening.

The voices outside are new, not the ones that have accompanied us from the jail. These voices are wilder. One of them says something to Sheriff Bates, who speaks back calmly. It is hard to hear over the sound of the wind. Then a hand slides through the flap of the cart and a face wearing a white cloth mask appears.

Do as I tell you, it says. Get out here now!

Nam and Lum jump out, followed by Zhou.

Are we resting here? I ask Nelson. He shakes his head, both hands against my chest, holding me back.

Think yourself a hero, doncha boy? the stranger says. His hand disappears through the flap and returns. I recognize the black metal shine of a gun. He points it at Nelson's head. Let us see if you are so tough now.

All right, Nelson says, and he puts his hands out in front of him. Jacob, I will go first.

He jumps out. The man watches him closely, then brandishes the gun at me. I know that I am to follow. And I do, making my way slowly, closer and closer to his masked face. The wind clatters against the sides of the buggy, its guttural howl full of warning. If you leave here, it says, you will never come back.

I jump out.

The first thing I see when I straighten up is not the confused sheriff and his men, not my friends with their sunken faces, not the new group of masked men who have arrived with more guns, but the white man with the bared teeth who led the mob at our store. He has fulfilled his promise after all: He found me, no matter where I was.

I forget that I am a man. I forget that I am Jacob Li. I lift one foot to crawl back into the buggy, but I have also forgotten about the bindings around my ankles. When I fall, my nose slams against the footrest.

A crack, then a burning. Tears fill my eyes.

The man starts laughing. I know it is him. Get him up, I hear him say. Get him up with the rest of them.

Someone grabs me, drags me away from the buggy. I cannot open my eyes. The pain is an enormous log pinning me down, and I am useless under its weight.

Sheriff, please, I hear Nam say.

There is nothing I can do, the sheriff says. Teddy and the boys have our weapons. Right, Teddy?

Sheriff is right, the man named Teddy says. He sounds gleeful, like a child who has discovered a new way of wrongdoing, one free from punishment. Bates cannot save you now. You five belong to us. The seekers of justice, the ones doing the Lord's work! We will show you the true meaning of justice for the monstrous deeds you have committed. For too long have you poisoned our town. But that is over now.

Please, I hear Lum saying. We are just owners of a store, just a small store. We sell jam and good food. We want nothing to do with this. Let us get to our trial.

Teddy ignores him. Leave the prisoners with us, Sheriff, he says. Take your men and go back to town. When they ask what happened to the Chinee, say you lost them on the way.

Sheriff, Nelson says for the first time.

It is out of my hands now, the sheriff says, emotionless.

A whistle, then a flurry of movement. I hear horses turning around in the grass, the buggy's wheels grinding against rocks. One group leaves, one group stays. We are staying. Why are we staying?

No! I yell out. Do not leave us!

Something comes down on me, slamming against the center of my face. I hear another crack as my nose breaks, and this time there is no log holding me down, no great weight that could be called pain. There is only white, and this white has no name.

Dumb chink, whoever hit me growls. You will learn to listen to me.

It is too much for me. I close my mouth, trying to swallow the burning. I think I am crying, too, the tears mixing with snot and blood, warm and slow as they pool at my chin.

Teddy's voice returns. The rest of you, it says. Move. Now.

10

They arrange us in a row with Nam and Lum in front, tied together by their queues, the stupendous braids now limp and frayed. The masked men flank us, their guns pointed at our temples. Zhou brings up the rear. The men in the back kick his feet with every other step, laughing when he finally falls face-first into the dirt. They pull him up, then kick him back down again.

We walk in silence. We are past the time for trying to plead.

I look at the trees and bushes we pass, trying to find something familiar. We have been walking toward the mountains for a while, the wind accelerating with each step. Pierce is a whole life away, and I no longer believe that Murray is still the destination. My broken nose burns, the blood having finally slowed into a red crust on my lips. I remember nights in Madam Lee's brothel when my lips did not look much different.

On and on we go, up a hill that seems to have no end. Overhead, the sun pulsates, elongating the shadows behind us. We are the ones who walk upright and we are the ones who slant along the earth. I stare at my shadow, willing it to break free from me and run the other way. It remains, faithful.

Teddy reaches the top first. He leaps off his horse and stands at the peak, sunlight flooding his body and casing it in a fever. We lunch here, he calls to the men still trailing on the hill. The rest of the group moves forward, renewed by the promise of food. A few men stay behind, holding on to us.

Tie them up, Teddy tells them.

They drag us back down the hill to a cluster of pine trees. Nelson, Zhou, and I are tied to our own trees. Nam and Lum are taken not far from us, the men yanking them by their grotesque queue bond, and tied together. Their scalps must be burning. Still, neither one cries out, and for that, I am proud of them.

The rope is as thick as my wrist. The masked men wrap it around and around, binding my arms and torso to the tree trunk, until I am the tree and the tree is me. When they are finished, I could carry the entire tree on my back.

It is still difficult to breathe. My broken nose throbs.

Satisfied with their work, the men leave us and begin the climb back up the hill to join the rest of the group. They are not worried. Their work was good. We will not escape.

Nelson is tied to a tree on my right. I turn my head, the only thing that can turn, and call out to him. What do we do?

There is nothing we can do, he says. They have guns, Jacob.

No, I say. I thrash, jerking my body against the rope. If I move with enough force, I can slacken the rope and slip out. I remember: I am small. Good for tight spaces. Someone told me that once and they were right. Be small, I chant. I throw myself against the rope. Be smaller than you have ever been. The smallest you will ever be.

It works. The rope begins to give. I pull my arms out from under the rope and air fills me up, delicious and wide. I use my hands to push the rope away from me, inching my body up and up, until my torso is free and I topple over onto my hands and knees. Then the only thing left to do is kick my feet out from the rope.

I look up the hill. Teddy and his men are busy with lunch, ripping jerky with their teeth. To my left, Nam and Lum celebrate my escape silently, their heads waving from side to side. I run to Nelson first. He could help me free the others.

But Caroline's betrayal has dimmed him. No, Jacob, he says. Even if we escape now, they will find us. They always do.

More laughter from Teddy and his men. Lunch will finish soon, and when it does, we will have no more chances. I feel as if I am still carrying the tree on my back. Trees remember for years and years. Long after we are all gone, they will remain, imprinted with memories of everything that has ever happened to them.

Nelson, I say to him. There is something I never told you. I share my name, my Chinese name, with a character from a story. Since I was young, I have hated my name. I wondered if my name tied me to some sort of destiny—the same tragic destiny that took this character's life. I have spent my life fighting against it, but somehow, I still seem to end up in bad situations.

Then you were right all along, he says, looking even more despondent. This could be part of your destiny.

Maybe, I say. But I discovered something along the way, as we were sitting in that prison cell. Everything could be leading me to the same tragic demise. Or it could not at all. Or I have been silly and romantic and suspicious this entire time, and the only thing leading my life is me.

I do not understand, he says, still not looking at me.

No, you do not, I press on. But I am telling you that I have to try. Even if there is a tragic destiny written for me, I do not care. I refuse to believe that this is it, now. It cannot be. I am telling you that *I* have to try.

He looks at me, and for a moment I think it has worked. But then I know why—I have forgotten to sound like Jacob Li, the smooth lyric of Daiyu slipping through instead. Nelson catches it, his eyes widening, but I do not look away. I want to tell him. I want him to know. But before I can, another bolt of laughter shoots down the hill from Teddy and his men, shocking me back to our present danger. Now is not the moment to tell him, because there will be many moments in the future. I promise myself and I promise Nelson.

I am sorry about Caroline, I say, my voice returning to gruffness. But you cannot let this be the end. You cannot let this be our end.

It is enough for him. His eyes refocus, the sharp touch of mahogany clear and purposeful. For you, he says. For you, I will try. And then his body starts moving, too.

I keep my eyes on Teddy and his men. Their teeth gleam like knives in the sun, cutting through the feathered green of the hill. We have gone unnoticed until now, but not for much longer.

Nelson leans against the rope, pushing with his chest. His neck turns red from the effort. I dig my feet into the earth and pull. Do not give up, I urge him. I think I can see more give in the rope. But Nelson is not small like me. He stops long before I do, panting, and his head falls back on the tree.

Jacob, he says to me. I do not hear him. I pull and claw at the rope. Jacob, he says again.

I fall back into the grass. I do not know when I started crying.

Go, Nelson says. He is smiling again for the first time, a genuine one. You should go home.

But I am not listening to him. I am looking up at the hill, where, just a few feet away from the men, guns lie in the grass, scattered and free. I remember the fish woman in the market and all her silver fish. Back then, I did not have enough time to run away. This time, I will not make the mistake of hesitating.

What are you— Nelson begins, but I am already running away from him, away from Nam and Lum and Zhou, running up the hill, toward Teddy and his men. The tree is no longer on my back, replaced instead by wings that could be as big as an ocean. I have heard tales of immortals who descend from the sky, of dragons that turn into wardens who turn into human forms. Of those who protect people like me, like all of us. This is who I will myself to be.

How many breaths—one hundred, two hundred? None of them see me coming. No one sees me until I have my hands on a gun, its burnished handle glinting in the grass. Waiting just for me. This gun is heavy and long, not at all like the small pistol William gave me that day in Boise, but I swing it off the grass, powered by the same thing that allowed me to fly up the distance of the hill. I nestle the gun against my collarbone the way I saw the masked men do. It is not so different from cradling a violin under one's chin.

I find Teddy and point the snout of the gun at him.

Now the masked men see me. Now they yell, dodging with hands over their heads. They are sluggish from their lunch.

Stop, I tell them. Stop or I will shoot him.

They look at me, then look to Teddy. He holds my gaze for a moment, a sneer spreading across his lips. Then he nods.

The men still.

A knife, I yell. Who has a knife?

No one answers. I move the snout of the gun to the right of Teddy's head and squeeze the trigger the way Nelson taught me to. The gun slams against my chest and a clap explodes, almost sending me back down the hill. The masked men curse, ducking. Teddy looks unbothered.

I will shoot again, I warn.

I have one, a masked man near me says. Just here.

Toss it to me, I say. At my feet. Toss it slowly.

He reaches into the grass and withdraws a hunting knife the size of my forearm. I keep the gun trained on Teddy's head. I will kill him if you try anything funny, I say.

The knife lands at my feet. I put one foot on the handle. I have the knife and I still have the gun. But even with these two things, the distance between me and my friends could be infinite. I wish I had thought this far ahead.

It is a losing battle, a sad voice inside me says.

I push it down. I have to try.

Stay where you are, I tell the masked men, bending down to pick up the knife. If anyone even thinks of moving, I will shoot.

I step back. This is my first mistake. The masked men loosen as soon as my right foot touches the grass, no longer bound by the spell of the gun. I can see their chests moving up and down now. There is no time to wait. I lift my left foot and place it behind me. Again, the scene mutates. The men grow taller, more solid. I can see their eyes flitting back and forth. They are looking at each other, planning their next move.

There are fifteen, maybe twenty of them. I would have to outrun them all and get down to the others before they could reach me. Could I kill two or three as I ran? Could I kill anyone at all? The gun is suddenly heavy in my hand, its weight dragging me to the earth. I wonder if it would be better to throw it aside and run unhindered.

Below, Nelson calls my name, breaking my trance. I take another step back. Then another, until I am stumbling down the hill. With each step backward, the men shrink, but they also grow bigger, chests puffing with anticipation for the chase ahead. I wonder who will be the first to act, them or me. It will not be much longer now.

In the end, it is them. The first man moves when I am nearly at the base of the hill. A small movement, barely noticeable, but I see how the wind bends around him, how the fabric of his shirt flutters against his elbow. He moves, and I know that I will have to run. Because the others are moving, too. They take a step forward, then two. They are cracking their knuckles now. They are looking for their guns. Behind them, Teddy stands with his hands at his sides, amused.

I raise the gun, my hands numb. There is no time to find a target— there is only time to point at a white mask and pull the trigger. But they are too far now and my aim is bad. The shot disappears into the wind. I fire another, hoping the sound will keep them back.

On the fourth shot, they begin to run. They are faster than I imagined—or just as fast as I feared. How many shots do I have left? I raise the gun again, but I am shaking now, and even as I fire the final shot, I know that it has done nothing.

Nelson yells my name again. It is enough. I turn to run.

My journey down the hill was not for nothing—my friends are closer than I anticipated. But even as I hurtle toward them, I feel a great hopelessness. Zhou has managed to escape his bonds, but Nam and Lum and Nelson are still tied. There is no time for a new plan now. Behind us, the men holler and yip, loose wolves darting down the hill. It will not take them long to reach us at this tempo.

I rush to Nam and Lum first, knife outstretched. *Together*, I gasp, and then I am sawing as they strain against the rope with all their might, the three of us working furiously until the rope unzips, each thread bursting apart, and they topple onto the grass gulping for air.

I run to Nelson next, looking behind me one more time. One of the men has nearly reached the base of the hill. He will be upon us soon. In the wind, his white mask blows back against his face. I can almost make out his features, the man he is underneath the mask. Before the mask. Whose father are you? I would ask him. Whose brother?

My hands are not strong. They shake, leaves on the lip of winter. I have no business holding a knife, no business trying to cut this rope, no business in still pretending to be this person who is capable and fierce and strong. I am nothing but a girl without her parents. This is no place for me.

I hear Nelson say my name. Listen to me. Are you listening? You have to cut me free. It must be now.

His voice is urgent but muffled, hidden behind a wall. I could be far away from all this, I think. It has been so hard to keep on running, to keep on fighting. I could let them take me and I would not have to suffer anymore.

Cut the rope, Jacob, Nam says from somewhere beside me.

What is wrong with him? Lum's voice now.

It would be so easy, I think, to give up. Like finally putting your head to a pillow after a long day, or sitting down after running for hours, nights, days. There would be pain, yes. But there would also be relief. Not even Lin Daiyu wants to come save me now. She knows that there is peace in sleep.

We are done for, Lum moans. Jacob is gone.

But Nelson's voice, although soft and far away, is still there. And it is calling to me. Listen to me, it says. You have to cut the rope so we can run. If you do not cut it, they will kill us.

Do we not deserve to live? Nam wails into the wind.

Nelson says my name again. Then it is all he is saying. And something else, too. But all I hear is my name.

My name.

I open my eyes.

I see the knife in my hand. And I see Nelson, still tied to the tree. From the corners of my eyes, I can see Nam and Lum and Zhou hovering. Yes, it would be much easier for my journey to end here. But that would end their journeys, too.

I lift my hand, my heavy, tired hand, and begin cutting.

Yes! Lum shouts. He turns to the group of men now pooling at the base of the hill. They have slowed for some reason. You still have time, he tells me. You can do this.

Run as fast as you can, Nelson says to the group. Run for the trees and run hard. Trust that we are all going to the same place, because we are. Do not run in a straight line—that makes it easier for them to shoot us.

I am halfway through the rope. The men have stopped running now, but their sounds are louder than ever, jeers and hollers that fuse to the blood now speeding through my body. My body, my very alive body. Nelson begins straining against the ropes again. Nam, Lum, and Zhou jump in to help, their hands prying at the rope. Just a little more, I think.

The first bullet flies past my ear and lands on the tree, marking it with a sharp crack. I nearly drop the knife, but my hand is stronger than I remember. Another bullet lands above Nelson's head. The men shriek with delight. They are not aiming to kill us, I realize. They are hunting us like game.

When the third bullet flies through the air, the knife makes its final slice against the rope. And then Nelson is free. We know what to do. Let this not be the last time we see each other, I beg them. And then we scatter for the trees. I think about the tree that Nelson was tied to, now marked with bullet holes, and how it will remember Nelson's body and bleed from those bullets for the rest of its long life.

Nelson runs straight back. Nam and Lum veer to the right. Zhou goes to the left, and I am somewhere in between all of them. Through the pines, over the forest floor, we run, dodging roots and dead branches and rabbit holes, the five of us spurred by our despair and, yes, our hope, holding on to nothing or to everything, holding on to each other and willing that we, together, will make it.

Run, boy! my pursuers shout, beginning their chase once more. They were waiting for this moment, I realize. There was never a world where they would let us run free. They fire off two more shots, neither of which come close to hitting me. But the sound is enough to distract me, make me trip and fall. I scramble up again and dart off, fresh blood pluming on my palm. Behind me, the masked men cheer.

Another shot sounds, this time somewhere to my left. Then a different noise joins the fray, a howling that travels over the treetops, netting us all in its pain.

Zhou.

I could keep running. I could run and run until my legs gave out, until I somehow reached the edge of the ocean. I could do it. But Zhou's choked screams tighten around my chest, pulling me back. My body wants to keep moving forward. My heart will not let it.

I turn and run back to the source of the noise. The masked men pursuing me are nowhere to be seen—perhaps they have lost me or perhaps they have captured someone else. I can reach Zhou and carry him off, I think. If he can be quiet, we can survive.

When I find him, he is splayed in the grass, fists pounding the earth. Blood snakes out of his left calf. Zhou, I say. He sees me and moans. His face is white.

The blood comes quicker now, hot with release. I rip the sleeve of my shirt and wrap it around his wound the way I have seen my mother do for my father. Zhou jerks. The shirt floods with scarlet.

We have to keep going, I tell him. I kneel and wrap one of his arms around my neck. He is bigger than me, but he is light. I can carry us both, I think. I have to carry us both.

He leans against me. Just one step, I tell him. One step, and we move. My head is full of his breathing, of the whispers in the trees and the blood that is everywhere, washing against my temples. My head is full of everything but the one thing that I should be listening for, and when I do hear it, it is already too late.

Click.

Click.

Click.

One by one, the masked men emerge from the trees, their guns pointed at us. Two of them are dragging Nam and Lum by their queues. Their bodies are ragged in the grass. I look around for Nelson; I do not see him. At least one of us escaped, I think.

I am wrong. Of course I am wrong. Because it is Teddy who steps out last, and he has something that looks like Nelson in his hands. Looking for him? he asks. The blond hairs above his lip are wet and matted with anticipation. He shoves Nelson in front of him. Nelson stumbles, then falls to the ground on his knees. His eyes are closed, as if he cannot bear to look.

The five of us, together indeed.

11

The price to pay for our attempted escape is Nam and Lum, who they hang from an old oak. Not to kill them, but to show us that they can. Nam ascends into the sky first, his face turning from white to red to violet, his eyes bulging and swollen. He reaches up to clutch the rope around his neck. A horrible croak leaves his body. Then, just as he looks like he will draw his last breath, the rope loosens and he drops to the grass. It takes a moment. I fear that the fall alone has killed him. But he comes back, sputtering and gasping.

Then it is Lum's turn. Unlike Nam, he does not make much noise. Stoic, bored, he floats into the sky and fixes his eyes on Teddy, who watches him with a humorless smile. When they drop Lum to the ground just before his lips blanch, he lands on all fours and straightens back up as if he had done something as mundane as retrieving his ledger from the bookcase.

They grab Nam once more, dragging him to the rope. As they wrap it around his neck and pull the rope up, he begins to cry. This game will never end, I realize. They will play and play with us until something— someone—breaks.

As if he has read my thoughts, Teddy speaks. Gents, he says, I can do this forever. All I want is for someone to own up to killing that poor Foster fellow. Whose idea was it? Tell me, and I will end this.

We protest, our voices clamoring for room. We did not do this! We are innocent! Teddy nods to his masked men, who bring Lum back to the rope. They draw him up and off the ground, a grotesque ornament that dangles overhead. When he drops, I can see purple welts on his neck.

One after the other, Nam and Lum go up into the sky, and each time, it seems that they hang for longer, the bruises around their necks turning into black collars, their foreheads growing so red with blood that I fear they will explode. One after the other, our eyes follow them through the air, the retreating sun at their backs, the only thing holding them steady in the sky.

How many rounds? How many breaths remain? How many bones must be cracked for a man to die? Even Lum, the invincible, disdainful Lum, looks like he cannot take much more.

Teddy nods again, and the masked men bring Nam back for his turn. When I look at him this time, I know that this hanging will be the one that kills him. Nam, the jolly store owner who I have come to care for, the man who was indestructible as long as he was armed with good cheer and steamed man tou, who always faced the world with kindness and generosity.

But Teddy does not care. Teddy says, Draw him up, because Teddy only sees yet another Chinese who needs to know his place.

The masked men move without hesitation. They, too, know that Nam will die from this one, and they are eager for it. They have eaten their fill, but a different hunger roils through them now. One of them picks up the rope. Another shoves Nam toward it.

But a voice slides through, soft and sure, holding the space between Nam's neck and the noose. No, the voice says. It was me. I killed the man.

My first fear is that the voice belongs to Nelson. I whip around to look for him, but his head is still bowed.

You? Teddy says. He is speaking to Lum.

Me, Lum says.

No!

I do not know who shouts it—perhaps it is Nelson, or me, or maybe even Zhou. Perhaps it is all of us at once. At Lum's confession we revive, the gravity of what he has done now devastatingly clear for all of us.

Teddy gleams. That was not so hard, was it, gents? He strolls up to Lum and spits on his face. So you planned it. And you had these other pigtails help you?

No, Lum says. It was just me. They had nothing to do with it.

No!

The chorus of our voices, again. But it does not matter anymore. Lum's confession has already set whatever will happen into its final act.

Not him, Nam rasps from beside the rope. Me. I killed the man.

I look again to Nelson. How do we stop this? Both of them are lying. Both of them are trying to save the other. The defeat in his still-bowed head tells me that he does not know, either.

You did it? Teddy demands. The two of you together?

No, Nam says, clearer this time. Just me.

He is lying, Lum says. It was just me. You can let them go.

Teddy regards them both. Then he turns to assess the rest of us—me, eyes frantic and wide, Nelson, shoulders sloping, Zhou, who prays to the sky—and his lip curls.

It does not matter, he says. Come morning, you will all answer for what you have done.

12

The desire to scream. Scream as loud as I can until my insides become outsides and I can bury myself in my own blood. I want to tear through my bindings, fell the tree upon which I am strapped, raze the forest. I want to gouge out the eyes of everyone who has caused me pain. It feels good to rage, even better to hate. I could get lost here and I want to, badly, sitting in the pain until I absorb it and it becomes all I am.

Swallow's question returns to me, as tender and open as it was the night I was to take my first customer at the brothel: *Do you have somewhere else you can go?*

There is only one place left to go. I follow Swallow's question until I am flying again, as ecstatic and delirious as when I crossed the ocean in a coal bucket, until I stand at the dusty steps in front of a red building with a peanut-colored roof.

But the school is empty. Instead, there is only Master Wang, who waits at the front of the classroom as if this is any other night and he has just finished lecturing. The sight of his benign face makes me fall to my knees. There are more lines than I remember.

I have been wondering when you would come home, he says.

I tried, I say. I tried so hard.

Master Wang watches me deflate. There is no judgment on his face. One day, he finds a street urchin on his steps. One look tells him that this is a motherless child, perhaps even a fatherless child. It has a sullen face and hollow cheeks, and a body that says it will do anything in its power to be safe and wanted and full. For him, it is so easy to say yes to that. It is so easy to give your heart to another human being.

You are angry with me, he says. Perhaps you have always been.

Yes, I say. It is the first time I allow myself to speak it fully. This man who taught me so much, and yet, I wonder if he has taught me anything at all. I wish that I could be Feng again, the boy of the wind. Strip the world away and I would just be a student, with a brush for a hand and ink in the veins. Feng's could have been a peaceful life. Feng's could have been a happy life.

Why did you not come look for me? Did you even care that I was gone?

I cared, he says. You were my best student.

It stings to hear him say this, another reminder of what I have lost. Then why was it so easy to let me go?

Do you think it was easy, Master Wang says. It was not easy. I wondered if I had done something to upset you, if I indeed fed you too little, if a relative found you, if you simply changed your mind about calligraphy. I wondered if I had been a bad teacher. It was not until months later that I wondered if you had been taken against your will. But it did not matter. Remember what I taught you? In calligraphy, as in life, we do not retouch strokes. We must accept that what is done is done.

I shake my head, hating how easy it is for him to say these words. You let me go, I say. You sacrificed me for the sake of your beliefs about art.

Master Wang turns his back to me and walks to the podium. The podium, which I remember being as stately as Master Wang, now unremarkable and dulled from disuse. There was never a sacrifice, he says. A calligrapher serves what the paper demands. In this life, I will only ever be the brush. You, though? You are not the brush. No, you are the inkstone and you always have been.

Speak words! I scream. You do not make sense! I did everything you taught me. And look where I am! I am nowhere near unified. I am tired of trying.

Then you have not been listening, Master Wang says calmly. I have taught you the characters, the technique, the strokes. I have taught you the way a calligrapher should be in the world. But until you learn to write on your own, without my hand, then you will never become unified.

It is safe in the classroom, but I cannot stay here forever. I gaze one last time at all the tapestries on the walls around us. Poems and characters and victorious wisdoms, the embodiment of calligraphers like Master Wang. The school could crumble and fade, but these characters would still look as magnificent to me as the first day I stepped foot inside.

You have the hands of an artist, Nelson once told me. I was suspicious of him then, believing he was only speaking lies to lure me in. But what I was really suspicious of was myself. The hands said I was an artist. The heart, not so much. All that practice and all those characters. In the end, what becomes of them is up to me.

———

The last of the Four Treasures of the Study, the inkstone, is most important because it allows the calligraphy to begin—in order for the ink to become ink, it must first be ground against the inkstone.

The inkstone is considered a treasure and should be treated as such. There is a saying, *An artist loves his tool just as much as a mother loves her son.* It is good to know that a stone is never just a stone, but something vital, powerful even. The inkstone asks for destruction before creation—you must first destroy yourself, grind yourself into a paste, before becoming a work of art.

13

They wake us in the early morning, just as the sun crowns the treetops. On any other day, the swath of pink in the sky would be considered beautiful. On a day like today, all I see is the promise of blood in the horizon.

They tie our hands, leash us with rope. Nelson is behind me, to my right. I turn to look at him, but he is just beyond my line of vision, and all I can hear is the sound of his feet dragging across the grass.

A worm stirs in my stomach, curling against the thin soup they fed us before night fell. If I vomit now, what can they do to me? Chop off my tongue? Kick me in the face, breaking my already broken nose? The man leading me yanks his rope, pulling me forward, but I cannot hold it in any longer. I open my mouth, wait for the bile to come.

But the bile does not come. Instead, it is Lin Daiyu.

I am, I should say, happy to see her. It has been so long. During her time in my body, she has grown peaceful and even more beautiful than I remember. Her skin and hair glow with health and good rest. Her eyes are tinted with sleep but still dear. She is happy to see me, too, but then her eyes shift to the man holding the rope.

What is this? she asks me. For the first time, she looks scared. She huddles close to me, running her hands up and down my arms. What is going on?

You slept for a while, I manage to say. I did not want to wake you.

But you should have, she says. You did this on purpose.

I promise I did not, I tell her, even though I am not so sure anymore.

She leaves me then to circle the entire party. She dips in and down to inspect Nam, Lum, Nelson, and even Zhou before jetting back next to me.

What is going on? she says. What has happened?

I will tell you, I say. It will not take very long.

———

Tell them, she says. Reveal your true identity. They would never hang a woman.

Would they not? I ask her. Look at what they did to my mother.

That was different, she says. That was back in China. America is different. You will see.

When I do not respond, she quiets down and rides on my back, nervous and alert. Her suggestion lingers in me. Yes, I could reveal my true identity now, but then what? They may let me go, but not my friends. Or they would pass me around, until I was nothing more than a vessel for the ugly things in between their legs. I know enough about men like these.

Or. Or I stay silent. I go wherever the rest of them go.

Let this not be where our story ends, Lin Daiyu whimpers.

I think our story ended a long time ago, I tell her. I am not trying to be mean. I am just telling her the truth.

14

The clearing they take us to is not so different from the one in which Nelson and I laid that day in Pierce. By now, the sun has risen high, and the morning is beautiful and warm. I am reminded of the summers of my childhood, chasing rabbits through the tall grass, later soaking myself in ocean water. The water always left a brine that caked my arms and legs. No matter how hard my mother scrubbed, I do not think the salt ever truly came off. There may still be some left in the crooks of my elbows and knees now. Be careful with me, I want to tell the man who has dragged me to the end of the line where Nam, Lum, Zhou, and Nelson kneel. I am carrying an ocean.

They take Nam first, because he is the easiest. Weakened by the journey and by the hanging of the previous day, his body bends without question, and when they pull him to his feet, I can see how loose the clothes have become on his frame. Between two black pine trees, they sling a pole and drape a rope over it with a hole just big enough for a head at one end. This time, it is no game.

They wrap the noose around Nam's neck. His jaw is bigger than the opening of the loop, so they have to tug it down his face. Nam is talking as they do this, pleading to each man to let him go. You have the wrong Chinese, he keeps saying. I know we look the same to you, gents, I know! But you have the wrong one. Why would we kill Foster? He was just friendly competition to us!

And as it has always been, they ignore him. Instead, Teddy steps forward and speaks.

You have been brought here to answer for the horrific crime you committed, he says. By the court before you, you have been found guilty. Today, you will hang.

Please, Nam interjects, looking around. None of the masked men move.

Do you have any last words? Teddy calls out.

Nam opens his mouth. He looks at each of us. When his eyes reach mine, I know that this is the last time I will see them open.

Let us have a drink, he says, when we meet again.

It takes three men to pull the rope. Three men, then the rope begins sliding across the pole on which it rests. Three men, and Nam's feet begin rising up off the ground. They kick this way and that. They could be dancing. I remember the night of the Mid-Autumn Festival, how he danced in front of the firecrackers and offered his body to the sky. Now there is no earth beneath him that can hold them.

Three men, and Nam's face grows redder and redder. Three men, and Nam's face turns to a dull shade of violet.

The final gasp, then a crack. Three men, and Lum has his face in the grass.

Nam falls down.

You bastards, Lum cries over and over again. What have you done?

There is no time for him to say much. Because he is next. They grab him easily, tall and slender Lum. Lum, whose spine now looks like spikes through his shirt, whose pants now hang at his thighs, the widest part of him anymore. They make us watch as they remove the rope from Nam's head. I cannot look at his body, so I look at Nelson. Nelson is not looking, either.

Will you say nothing? Lin Daiyu asks me.

They have no trouble looping Lum's head through the hole. A face as sharp as a bird's, a neck that shows every tendon and muscle. Teddy repeats the decree. Lum is furious. He will not let Teddy speak without a roar of his own voice after every word. The masked men get nervous, fingering their guns. I know that Lum cannot do anything, but I am glad to know that he makes these men a little fearful, even now.

Do you have any last words? Teddy finally calls out.

May you suffer, Lum bellows. Every one of you.

And then he closes his eyes. His feet leave the earth. He stays erect and straight, letting the rope do its work.

Next, Teddy says.

It is Zhou. They make quick work of it. Teddy asks again, Do you have any last words? The men watching laugh, aroused for what is to come. Zhou opens his mouth in a gasp, blunt tongue wiggling from molar to molar.

Nelson, I say to the man next to me. I am thinking of the moment he saved my life from the mob at the store that day, how afterward, I was so suspicious of him when really, all I have ever wanted is for him to know me, really know me, in the way I have come to know myself. It is all I have left to give to him, and I want to, badly. I say, I have something to tell you.

It is all right, he says. It is all right.

Zhou hangs. It is fast. 'Cause the boy has no tongue, the man guarding me says to no one in particular. Less meat for the rope to cut through. I turn to snarl at him, but he just shoves my head back with the heel of his palm.

Next, Teddy calls. The violin boy.

Nelson, I say. They are lifting him to his feet now. Nelson, I say again. His eyes do not leave mine, brown and steady. The bodies of Nam, Lum, and Zhou lie off to the side, three small mountains that the earth will one day swallow. Nelson, I call to him one last time. His head bows to one side, an apology. No, I tell him. You were perfect.

Even with a noose around his neck, he looks handsome. He stands as straight as he can, back erect, legs locked. The hands I have so admired, folded neatly in front of him. Even now, I think, I love him more than ever.

You have been brought here to answer for the horrific crime you committed, Teddy says. The words are familiar by now, no longer terrifying but dulled. Not just for your involvement in the murder of Daniel M. Foster but also for your violation of the most scared law: lying with a woman not of your race.

Disgusting chink, the man who is my guard spits.

Slit-eyed cur, adds another.

Bet she begged for a good white cock, shouts a third. The masked men holler in approval at this, until the wood around us is filled with it.

By the court before you, Teddy concludes, you have been found guilty. And today, you will hang.

Nelson looks ahead, his vision already flying beyond where we are now. He does not seem scared. Do you want me to go to him? Lin Daiyu asks me. So he is not so alone?

She does not wait for my answer. She knows me well. When Teddy asks Nelson if he has any final words, Lin Daiyu glides effortlessly to Nelson's side. She stands as straight as he does. I never noticed how tall she could be.

I will say only this, Nelson says. His eyes slide to mine. When your wives and daughters and granddaughters ask you who killed who, I hope you will remember that it was you.

Hang! the masked men shout.

Nelson, I say.

I am here, Lin Daiyu says.

When he hangs, I cannot help thinking that he looks beautiful. He does not kick, does not protest against it. Instead, his body sways in the air, much in the way that a brush does just before it touches the paper, when it is still in the calligrapher's hand, sacred and warm, a beloved instrument, something to be trusted and cherished and held. And I could swear, even if it is just a wish in my own head, that he calls out my name before everything goes quiet.

Let us have the last one, then, Teddy says.

The man hovering above me lifts me to my feet. I am surprised at how quickly I am able to steady myself. All those years of walking along the ocean must have come in handy. Later, running. Always running. At some point, my feet have learned how to carry more than just my own weight.

Do something, Lin Daiyu pleads. She is next to me again, her hands like sails in my face. Let me do something.

The choice wavers in front of me: Say nothing and hang, or reveal myself as a woman and stay alive, but horribly so. Neither seems like a good choice. My friends are dead.

All my life, I have felt shunted along by circumstance. I was only in Zhifu because my grandmother sent me there; I only found Master Wang because a noodle shop owner told me to; I am only in America because of Jasper; I am only here because of a murder someone else committed. And throughout it all, the nagging question: Is my life my own? Or have I always been destined for tragedy because of my name?

My name. The characters that have haunted and plagued me since the beginning appear before me again, precious with their weight and familiarity. This thing that I have hidden, that I have changed and added to, this thing I have yearned for all along. I am the constellation of all the names within me, of every name I have ever inhabited. And this is the truth I see for the first time: I have only been able to survive because of my name.

I ask myself again, Will I be the one holding the brush or will I be the one who is written?

The answer is simple. I know how to write well. Take the brush in your hand, Daiyu. See, really see the blank space before you. It is so much space. Dip the brush into the well of the world, let your heart sing through your arm. Move how you want. Not how you have been told, not how the scholars say is best, not even how Master Wang has made you believe. Make of your art what you will. It is yours, after all. It belongs to no one else. That is the beauty. That is the intent.

That is unification.

Lin Daiyu understands what this means. Perhaps she understood all along. Do you know I love you, she says.

I love you, too, I tell her. We have been together long since before I was born.

And it is true. I do love her. But as herself, not as a part of me.

One a girl, one a ghost. Still I know not which I loved the most.

———

A masked man slips the noose around my neck. I look to the sky. The clouds above list to the right, and soon they will be far from where we are now, in another land, floating above an ocean, and who knows where they will end up or if they will end up at all. I never thought about it before, but every cloud I have ever seen must have been on its way to somewhere. Those who witness clouds only ever see a moment of their journey. In this way, I could call myself a cloud.

You have been brought here, Teddy begins, but I am no longer listening. Lin Daiyu tugs at the noose around my neck. I want to cut you free, she begs one last time, but I cannot. I do not have anything sharp on me.

It is all right, I tell her. Tears roll down her face, glassy, swollen droplets enough to flood this entire forest. Are you not tired?

Yes, she says, almost guiltily.

I know, I say. Perhaps it will be good to rest.

Teddy's voice returns now. He wants to know if I have any last words. I lower my gaze and stare out at the white masks before me. I could be looking into a field of ghosts.

I know who you are, I say, my voice as straight and thick as the boldest of strokes. But you do not know me. Let me tell you. My name is Daiyu.

Even as the words leave me, I marvel at my name, this name my parents gave me, mine, all mine, especially now, the final thing that none of them, not Teddy, not the masked men, can take away from me. Names exist before the people they belong to, the oldest part of us. My name has existed long before I was born and so, I think, I have lived for a long time.

Their eyes are fixed on me, this time not out of contempt. This time, there is fear. They do not know whether or not to believe me, but even as they try to unhear my words, they begin to see it. The man before them does not look like a Jacob Li after all. The man they see is turning into something else, a woman perhaps, her eyes alight with the sun, her body on fire with heat that does not come from this autumn day. The rope around her neck is just a formality. She could break free if she wanted to. Indeed, she could fly away.

You will never forget me, I say to them all.

The rope squeezes my neck. My feet leave the ground and I am lifted into the sky. A different kind of flight. Below, one of the masked men rolls Nelson's body next to Nam and Lum and Zhou. Lin Daiyu returns to my side, though she is no longer crying.

In calligraphy, there is an advanced technique called split brush. The calligrapher will twist the brush so that the bristles split, transforming the one brush into many smaller brushes. A feat of brushwork, Master Wang used to call it. To any observer looking at the finished work, it would seem that the calligrapher must have drawn many strokes, but this is simply a sleight of hand. There was one stroke all along.

When I was a child, no one ever asked me what my name meant, because they always assumed I was named after Lin Daiyu. For that, I hated my name. But if you ask me now to write my name, the one I was born with, I would do so carefully, with great attention. I would write it with love. And if you, like so many others before you, ask me what it feels like to be a girl named after another girl, a woman following in the footsteps of another woman, a life already set upon someone else's fate, I will say that it is nothing, really. Or it is everything. My life was written for me from the moment the name was given to me. Or it was not. That is the true beauty. That is the intent. We can practice all we want, telling and retelling the same story, but the story that comes out of your mouth, from your brush, is one that only you can tell. So let it be. Let your story be yours, and my story be mine.

EPILOGUE

Zhifu, China
Spring 1896

Today, the tide is strong. The ship that docks has been traveling for a while, all the way from the coast of California. But it will not rest for long; soon, it will be readied for another journey across the Pacific. For now, though, its crew members are allowed to disembark, glad to set foot on land again.

The crew unloads along the dock. They are carrying crates, packages, barrels, buckets. All goods they have brought from California and beyond. They carry heavy things, personal things, things to be traded and sold and resold. Sometimes, they even carry dead things.

In one crate, there are such things: five long wooden boxes. This is not the only crate—there are stacks of them.

Some of these do not have addresses, a crew member tells his mate.

Aye, the mate says. Boss says to toss it in the ocean if no one comes to claim it.

What is in them, anyway?

Do you not know, the mate says. They are the bones of all the Chinese who have died abroad.

The crew member recoils from the crate as if it will come alive. They went through all the trouble of mailing their dead back here?

I hear it is a religious thing, the mate grunts. They dig the bones up, wash them, and send them back here. Kind of nice, though. Gives them the chance at a proper burial.

Must be lonely to die over there, the crew member says. So far from home and all.

⟶

Not too far from the shore, an old woman wanders the streets of Zhifu's Beach Road. No one has ever seen her before, and they are sure she has just arrived, for her white hair is dirty and her shoes are caked with mud. Her mouth is open and she is calling out a name. No one there has ever heard of a person with this name, although they wonder if the old woman has confused this name with a name from a famous story. They ask the old woman if she is all right. They ask if there is someone at home who can take care of her. Where are your children? they ask her. Where is your husband?

The old woman does not answer them. She continues to call out the name. She passes a red building with a peanut-colored roof, dilapidated and crumbling, that looks like it has been closed for several years. She wonders if the person she is looking for could be in there. Maybe she will go ask the owner of the building, she thinks. She decides against it, returning instead to the ocean.

But is she alone? Somewhere along the shoreline, a figure—once a girl, then a woman, now something else entirely—watches the old woman call out this name. And then the figure's cries join the old woman's, until both are calling out the name long after the world has gone to sleep and nothing remains but the storm clouds brewing on the horizon, echoing their wails to the place where the moon meets everything else.

In the morning, spring rain.

AUTHOR'S NOTE

In 2014, my father returned from a work trip through the north-western region of the United States with an interesting anecdote: He was driving through Pierce, Idaho, when he saw a marker refer-encing a "Chinese Hanging." The marker described the story of how five Chinese men were hanged by vigilantes for the alleged murder of a local white store owner. My father asked, in all seriousness, if I could write the story out for him in order to solve the mystery of what happened.

Five years later, I returned to the request in the last semester of my MFA program at the University of Wyoming. Upon doing some initial research, I was surprised to find that there were very few help-ful resources online that documented exactly what happened—three search results on Google, in fact. The only sure vestige of the event lay with the historical marker in Pierce, Idaho, but even then, I read that the sign had been frequently vandalized and stolen. Even more alarming was my discovery that this event was not isolated—a slew of anti-Chinese violence occurred across the country during the mid- to late nineteenth century, including the Rock Springs Massacre in Rock Springs, Wyoming, the Snake River Massacre in Wallowa County, Or-egon, and countless others (Jean Pfaelzer's *Driven Out: The Forgotten War Against Chinese Americans* documents hundreds of instances).

It is important for me to mention that while this history of anti-Chinese violence has not been "forgotten" by scholars and historians, it is largely unknown by the majority of Americans. Even as a Chinese American immigrant, I did not learn about the Chinese Exclusion Act until I took an Asian American intro course in my senior year of college. I experienced passing shouts of "Go back to where you came from!" growing up but had no idea that this was a call descended from decades of racist initiatives toward Chinese immigrants by the United States. The Chinese helped build the railroads, that I knew, but what about everything else? What about the part where we were not wanted here, where we were killed for being here?

I finished the first draft of this book in the spring of 2020, just as COVID-19 was making its way across the country and the former president was calling it harmful, racist names, like "Kung Flu" and "Chinese Virus." I read articles about elderly Chinese people who were spit on, physically and verbally attacked, and dehumanized. I thought about my own parents, both in their late fifties, and feared that the same things would happen to them. So little, I thought as I imagined Daiyu and Nelson and their friends, had changed. In the era of Trump, then later in a post-Trump world, it became even more vital for me to remind people—not historians and scholars but my friends, my coworkers, my hairdresser—of what the United States was and still is capable of.

The town of Pierce is a fictionalized version of the real Pierce, Idaho. Additionally, the story and its circumstances are imagined. Larger portions—the murder of the store owner, the involvement of the vigilantes, and the hanging—are all true, but I have changed the names of some of those involved. Also true are the countless atrocities, acts of violence, and microaggressions experienced by the characters. If historical markers are one of the few things documenting these acute instances of anti-Chinese violence for the general public, and those markers are at risk of being rewritten or destroyed, what will we have left to remember? I wanted to tell the story, not just of the five Chinese who were hanged, but of *everything*—the laws, tactics, and complicity that enabled this event and so many others. My hope is that this book brings the United States' history of anti-Chinese violence out of scholarship and research and into our collective memory.

—

This book could not have happened without research, and for that, I am grateful to the historians and scholars whose work guided me. What follows is my best attempt to document and thank the scholarship that has most informed this book:

The story of Nuwa and Lin Daiyu comes from the David Hawkes translation of Cao Xueqin's *Dream of the Red Chamber*.

The Four Treasures of the Study, a name that refers to the brush, ink stick, paper, and inkstone (文房四宝), is an expression that comes from the Southern and Northern Dynasties (420–589 AD).

In developing the calligraphy portions of this book, I quoted from and consulted several sources, which I will do my best to cite here. Dr. Peimin Ni's research was instrumental in crafting Master Wang's philosophy about calligraphy, and many of Master Wang's statements about calligraphy are adapted from Dr. Ni's article "Moral and Philosophical Implications of Chinese Calligraphy." Similarly crucial was Xiongbo Shi's article "The Aesthetic Concept of Yi 意 in Chinese Calligraphic Creation."

"Practice will . . . make your energy full and your spirit complete" is derived from a quote by Wu Yuru.

The Dao as "the heavenly nature in humans" comes from Xu Fuguan.

The idea of calligraphy as a cultivation of one's character comes from Shodo, as documented in *Dictionary of Chinese Calligraphy* by Liang Piyun.

The quote about inkstones on page 307 comes from *Chinese Brushwork in Calligraphy and Painting* by Kwo Da-Wei. The descriptions of the Four Treasures of the Study and the split-brush technique are also adapted from this same book.

Finally, I also referenced *Chinese Calligraphy (The Culture & Civilization of China)* by Zhongshi Ouyang and Wen C. Fong.

I relied on Lucie Cheng's scholarship to understand how Chinese girls and women were smuggled into America, namely her article "Free, Indentured, Enslaved: Chinese Prostitutes in Nineteenth-Century America."

There is not much known about the inner workings of Chinese brothels in San Francisco, and even less about their physical interiors. Scholarship and work by Lucie Cheng, Jingwoan Chang, Gary Kamiya, Sucheng Chan, and Lynne Yuan, and Judy Yung's book *Unbound Voices: A Documentary History of Chinese Women in San Francisco* helped shape my interpretation of what life may have been like for women in these brothels.

Madam Lee's origin is based on Ah Toy, purportedly the first Chinese prostitute in San Francisco.

The description from Daiyu's grandmother about the first railroad built in China on page 131 comes from an article by Yong Wang, found on Sina Online.

Depictions of Chinese in Idaho and the West are based on John R. Wunder's *Gold Mountain Turned to Dust: Essays on the Legal History of the Chinese in the Nineteenth-Century American West*, Gordon H. Chang's *Ghosts of Gold Mountain: The Epic Story of the Chinese Who Built the Transcontinental Railroad*, M. Alfreda Elsensohn's *Idaho Chinese Lore*, the Idaho State Historical Society archives, and scholarship by Ellen Baumler, Randall E. Rohe, Liping Zhu, Priscilla Wegars, and Sarah Christine Heffner, among countless others.

The Chinese temples Samuel describes were known as "joss houses."

Jean Pfaelzer's book *Driven Out: The Forgotten War Against Chinese Americans* and Beth Lew-Williams's *The Chinese Must Go: Violence, Exclusion, and the Making of the Alien in America* were instrumental in understanding the countless atrocities committed against Chinese in the nineteenth century, many of which are reflected in this book.

I consulted scholarship by Lawrence Douglas Taylor Hansen for information about the Chinese Six Companies, and Kevin J. Mullen's *Chinatown Squad* for information about the tongs. My descriptions of the Heaven and Earth Society are a result of scholarship and writing by Cai Shaoqing, Helen Wang, Tai Hsuan-Chih, Ronald Suleski, and Austin Ramzy.

Little has been written or documented about the murder and hanging by which the last portion of this book was inspired. However, I did have luck consulting newspapers of the time as well as The No Place Project and markers in the real Pierce, Idaho. The historical marker for the hanging can be found along State Highway 11 at Mile Point 27.5, just south of Pierce. It is categorized as Idaho State Historical Site #307.

For information about burial proceedings, I consulted scholarship by Terry Abraham and Priscilla Wegars.

As with any work of fiction, there are places where I have taken creative license, such as Jasper's tendency to wink at Daiyu. I do not believe winking was common in nineteenth-century China, but it is understood as a lewd and suggestive gesture in Chinese culture. Additionally, what we know today as the Chinese Exclusion Act of 1882 was actually referred to as the Chinese Restriction Act during its time.

Finally, I would like to address an anachronism in the writing of this book—the text uses Hanyu Pinyin to romanize Chinese characters. However, the version of Pinyin that appears in this book was not standardized until 1950. My idealistic self likes to believe that Daiyu would have been able to come up with a similar romanization system on her own, based on what she knows about English and Mandarin.

ACKNOWLEDGMENTS

They say that writing is a solitary task, but I have found that while the physical act of writing is something you do alone, the emotional and spiritual act of writing and being a writer is something you share with a community. As such, I must thank my community—although thanks will never be enough:

To the whole team at Flatiron and Macmillan, for believing in my book, especially Megan Lynch, Bob Miller, and Malati Chavali, for being such vital, early advocates.

To my editor, Caroline Bleeke, who championed this book and ushered it through, and who somehow made the daunting task of publishing my first book the most smooth and pleasant thing ever. I didn't know it could be like this, but I'm glad it is, and I'm glad it's with you.

To my agent, Stephanie Delman, who must be something out of a dream. Thank you for believing in me. Thank you for believing in Daiyu. This book could not have become what it is now without you, and I am grateful for this fact every day.

To my UK editor Jillian Taylor, for your ardor, the lovely notes, and understanding the book and my vision from the beginning, and to everyone at Penguin Michael Joseph for the same.

To Stefanie Diaz, Sydney Jeon, Katherine Turro, Claire McLaughlin, Keith Hayes, Kelly Gatesman, Erin Gordon, Eva Diaz, Molly Bloom, Donna Noetzel, Kathleen Cook, Muriel Jorgensen, Steve

Wagner, Emily Dyer, Drew Kilman, Vi-An Nguyen, and Iwalani Kim for your exceptional work on the book's behalf.

To spaces like the Kenyon Review Young Writers Program, VONA, and the Tin House Writing Workshop, for giving me a place to write and connect with other writers. Most importantly, for letting me come back to myself. To Catapult, and especially to my editor Matt Ortile, who encouraged me to pitch the column that started it all.

To my English and writing teachers throughout the years: Mrs. Kriese, Mrs. Dupre, Reyna Grande, Oscar Cásares, Brad Watson, Alyson Hagy, Andy Fitch, Rattawut Lapcharoensap, Danielle Evans, Courtney Maum, and T Kira Madden. Thank you for breathing life into me time and time again.

To the University of Wyoming MFA program, but especially to Alyson and Brad. Alyson, who nurtured this book into being. Brad, with whom I wish I could share a whiskey right now. To my friends and classmates, we'll always have the Ruffed-Up Duck. And to my cohort: Tayo Basquiat, Francesca King, and Lindsay Lynch, for making our time in Laramie magical and weird.

To those who read the first few drafts of this book and gave me their valuable time and feedback: Garrett Biggs, Laura Chow Reeve, Lindsay Lynch, Rachel Zarrow, Sue Chen, and Cuihua Zhang. This would be a lesser book if not for you.

To all my friends for their love and support. To Jennifer Choi and Mala Kumar, my stud gang and smooth baes. To Sue, who can always give it to me straight and makes sure I'm warm enough. To Bangtan, for providing the laughs and, crucially, the soundtrack.

To Joe Van, my adventure partner, for the dance and the karaoke and the soup dumplings. And to Maebe, the best and most wiggly butt.

To my family in China. 我想你们. To Ye Ye and Nai Nai, for allowing me to grow.

To Lao Ye, who wrote the most beautiful calligraphy and kept the most beautiful garden.

To Zhang Cuihua and Zhang Yang, my mom and dad, who are tireless and selfless and admirable, and whom I love more than anything in this world.

ABOUT THE AUTHOR

Jenny Tinghui Zhang is a Chinese American writer. Her fiction and nonfiction have appeared in *Apogee, Ninth Letter, Passages North, The Rumpus, HuffPost, The Cut, Catapult,* and elsewhere. She holds an MFA from the University of Wyoming and has received support from Kundiman, Tin House, and VONA/Voices. She was born in Changchun, China, and grew up in Austin, Texas, where she currently lives.